RUNNING FROM THE GODS

BOOK ONE OF
THE SEVENTH SHAMAN

D.T. Read

Theogony Books
Coinjock, NC

Chris Kennedy/Theogony Books
1097 Waterlily Rd.
Coinjock, NC 27923
https://chriskennedypublishing.com/

Publisher's Note: This is a work of fiction. Names, characters, places, and incidents are a product of the author's imagination. Locales and public names are sometimes used for atmospheric purposes. Any resemblance to actual people, living or dead, or to businesses, companies, events, institutions, or locales is completely coincidental.

Cover Design by Shezaad Sudar.

Ordering Information:
Quantity sales. Special discounts are available on quantity purchases by corporations, associations, and others. For details, contact the "Special Sales Department" at the address above.

Running from the Gods/D.T. Read -- 1st ed.
ISBN: 978-1648555343

For David Wolverton-Farland,
my longtime mentor
and my friend,
who believed in me
even when I didn't.

Chapter One

Two mouthfuls of stew remained in the cooking pot when I came in from mucking out the shegrul barn. My spoon rasped on painted clay, stirring up a burned smell as I scraped overcooked meat from the pot's bottom. My five step- and half-siblings watched me tensely while they continued to eat.

My stepmother watched, too, like a carrion hawk. Same beady eyes, though with fleshy pouches sagging beneath them. Same hooked nose and hunching shoulders.

I met her glower. Held it. Read resentment in her eyes as I dumped my scant spoonful into a gourd bowl. I thrust my chin at her. *Go ahead. Hit me now and get it over with.*

She dropped her gaze, but not before I glimpsed a sliver of fear. "Stinking boy," she muttered, words laden with loathing. "You eat like a shegrul."

"At least I work for my food," I said.

I sat at the end of the half circle, next to my eight-year-old half-sister Kimama. She leaned to peer into my bowl. "You can have some of mine, Ku," she said and started to tip her bowl.

"No, Kimama." My stepmother lunged across the circle to slap her, hard enough to knock her backward. Her bowl clattered and rolled, spewing its contents, and her head smacked the adobe floor. When I leaned up to shield her from a second blow, the fat hand with its heavy stone rings struck my mouth.

5

Silence fell like an ax, chopping off all sounds of eating. The others froze on their woven rugs, staring from their mother to me, their eyes wide. My half-sister Taima gasped, but our older stepsister Kotori scarcely blinked.

My years of combatives training, necessary in the Awénasa Territory because of exiled criminals, had emphasized restraint as much as disabling and killing. I loosened fists that had reflexively knotted and glared at my stepmother.

Tears welled in Kimama's eyes. I scooped her from the floor and gathered her to my chest. She reached for the bump on the back of her head and whimpered. Purple already smeared her cheekbone.

When I glanced up, my stepmother appeared stunned at what she'd done. Shock paled her face and widened her eyes, and her mouth hung slack.

I ducked past her to the food chiller, snatched a couple frozen pouches, and carried Kimama through the darkness of the adjoining sleeping room. Dim light from the square hole in the ceiling guided me to the log ladder. I bundled Kimama up it onto the roof.

Rain clattered on the nironnium dome enclosing the whole enclave, the warm but heavy rains of late spring.

I set Kimama on my blanket bed, between one of her mother's container gardens and the solar-heated cistern, then pressed one food package to her cheek, and the other to the knot rising on the back of her head under her tousled hair.

She shivered. "That hurts."

"It'll feel better in a minute. Sit still." Ebbing anger hardened my tone.

Kimama tipped her head to stare up at me. "You didn't get a pouch for you. There's blood on your chin."

I touched my smarting lip. Already swelling. Wet heat oozed from it. "It'll stop."

She sniffled for a few minutes while I held the improvised cold packs to her bruises. "Sing the pain chant for me, Ku," she said.

I blinked. "What?"

"I know you can," she said. "I saw you do it for Tok when he fell down the stairs."

My half-brother Tohoka. Two years older than Kimama, he ran headlong everywhere he went and seldom watched where he was going. His fall had happened more than a year ago. I was amazed Kimama remembered.

"I haven't done it since then, and I don't have any oil-paste," I told her.

The sacred oil-paste for anointing came from bulbs that grew in clusters under the fleshy limbs of python trees. I guessed even the enclave's chanters had a limited supply of oil right now. It had been two or three years since the last harvest ceremony.

Kimama's tear-damp lashes blinked. "Mama has some oil-paste in a little thing up on her shelf." She shaped a cup with both hands. "You still know how, Ku. Please?"

During my apprenticeship with my father, the enclave's chief chanter, I'd been granted power to perform two healing chants; one to relieve pain, the other to induce sleep. I'd used the one for pain many times for one family member or another.

Don't know if I still have the power to do it, even if I had oil-paste.

"Please," she said again, her small face upturned to me.

I sighed. "All right, Butterfly, I'll go look for it. Sit still and keep those cold packs on your head."

Sliding down the ladder bypassed the log rung that always creaked. I landed soundlessly at the bottom and paused to listen. Even with the door-blanket between the sleeping and gathering rooms, I could hear the others' voices, low mutters of indistinguishable words.

In the darkness, I had to use touch more than sight. I ran my hand along the stone wall as I picked my way through the room to find my stepmother's shelf, a broad slab of polished knotty pine imbedded in the wall at the level of my shoulders.

Its contents lay in a jumble, some items teetering at the edge. I searched with cautious fingers, breath caught in fear of knocking something off to smash on the floor or roll into a corner or under a floorbed.

My probing fingers found more bulky rings set with semiprecious stones, the marriage earrings from my father that she'd stopped wearing after his death, a few rel coins, and a ball of mending thread, made from her own hair, with a needle stuck through it. All dusty.

I discovered the needle by running my finger into it. I stifled a yelp, shook my hand briefly, and sucked the iron-tasting bead of crimson off my fingertip before reaching in again, more warily.

It took several seconds to locate the oil cup, smaller than a hen's egg and with a tight lid, tucked in a gap between stones behind the ball of thread. Holding my breath, I pried the cup out with two fingers and slipped it into my pocket.

Something hit the floor with a distinct *clunk* as I twisted away. I didn't wait to see if anyone in the gathering room had heard, but dashed for the ladder and scrambled to its top.

"You found it!" Kimama beamed when I drew the cup from my pocket and dropped to a squat before her. By the dome's bluish lighting, I discerned patterns painted on the tiny container.

I eased the top off and dipped out a russet blob the size of a maize kernel with one finger, then smeared the glyph for pain on her forehead.

Python-tree oil smelled faintly of rotting meat, a scent not lessened by blending it with flour-fine soil to make a stiff paste. We wrinkled our noses as I spread my right hand on her head and began the Chant to Relieve Pain of the Body. "O, Ancient One who made us, blood and flesh and bone, drive away the spirits of suffering. Drive away the spirits of pain and bring peace to your child."

She stopped sniffling before I finished the prayer-song a second time.

"Better?" I asked.

She nodded and handed me the food pouches. "I don't need these on my head anymore."

I chuckled, and tossed their thawing weight from hand to hand.

"Mama hit us because her soul is hurting again, isn't it?" Kimama asked.

I hesitated. "Ya."

"We did something wrong and made it worse, didn't we?"

"Not you, Kimmie." My gut twisted. *My fault.* I should've stayed away from supper.

When Kimama nestled into my blankets, I moved around the cistern to give her privacy. Latent heat radiated through the tank's green-painted metal, warming my back, and I stretched my legs out toward another container garden.

Chili plants sprouted, verdant and sturdy, from gardening soil imported from Solienne, or one of its commonwealth worlds. The local soil didn't grow food plants hearty enough to produce. The box creaked when I pressed my soles to its lumber frame, but my stomach's rumble seemed louder. I hefted one of the silvery food pouches.

"Yi, Ku!" Kimama called from behind me. "See what I found in your blankets? It's you and the man we miss."

Even at eight, she knew to speak obliquely of the dead.

I leaned around the cistern, and she held out my image plate. Like all other advanced technology on our homeworld, Tempest, it had been imported from another Commonwealth world. Even our livestock was imported. Except for shegruls.

Exuberant drumming issued from a miniature speaker, and a video rippled in the plate's display.

"When was this?" she asked.

"Gratitude for Harvest Ceremony." I crawled back to join her. "I was in my eleventh summer. You were just learning to walk."

Our father had died that winter.

I watched Kimama absorb the video, her eyes bright with wonder. In it, my father and I danced side-by-side with other fathers and sons, the farmers of the enclave. Miniature bone rattles on our ankles chattered with each stamping step, and our faces and muscular chests gleamed with sweat and celebratory symbols painted in earthy pigments.

My father's hair, gray streaks stark among the blue-black, fell loose from his high forehead to his waist. Thick brows shaded his brown-black eyes, and below his broad nose spread a warm smile of even teeth. His smile deepened the creases about his eyes, emphasized the cleft in his chin, and cast a sharp contrast with his desert-brown skin.

"Your smile is like his," Kimama said, "and your eyes and hair. Except you have dimples when you smile."

"Got those from the woman who gave me life," I said, and switched the plate to an image of both my real parents.

Kimama regarded me seriously for a few seconds. "You look more like him, except with no wrinkles and no gray hair."

I grinned. "I better not have wrinkles or gray hair."

Her next words prompted a deeper ache for her than I bore for myself. "You're the only one who's kind to me like he was."

Once she settled in, I returned to the other side of the cistern. There I sat, listening to the rain's cadence on the smoke-colored dome, with its network of solar-collection cells and dim lights. The rain's intensity had lessened since the previous night, but it still fell noisily enough to mask approaching footfalls.

If her mother follows us up here…

My hand closed hard enough on one soggy bag to pop it. Maize kernels and bits of green chilies burst across my lap. Their sharp aroma roused more growls from my empty stomach.

I ate everything in the pouch, relishing the chilies' mild heat, then hunted scattered kernels by the dull lights in the dome. I devoured the squash chunks in the other pouch as well.

Kimama stirred and sighed somewhere behind me, but I resisted sleep. I had decisions and plans to make.

I had toyed with leaving before, to escape my stepmother, but until I'd earned my pilot's license, I hadn't seriously considered it. Weather, wildlife, and deported criminals made surface travel too dangerous.

Then the war began. As it escalated during the next three summers, I knew I'd be conscripted when I reached my twentieth. My stepbrother Bimisi, a moon older than me, was exempt from conscription as the eldest son of a widow, to be her provider. My younger half-siblings had no escape from her increasingly volatile temperament, so I waited it out for their sakes. This was the first time she'd struck Kimama, but I knew it wouldn't be the last.

Sometime after midnight, when my tailbone began to ache from sitting on the adobe bricks, I curled onto my side and pressed my back to the warm cistern.

An indistinct grunt startled me awake. *My stepmother?*

I jerked upright, one arm raised to fend off a blow, and froze.

A spectral shape drifted before me. A bucket-like dancer's mask, with a mouth full of pointed teeth and a mane of swishing rags, wafted pale as vapor between me and the container box.

My blood iced in my veins. I seized my knife from my belt—as if I could use it against a ghost.

I swallowed when I recognized the eyes that laughed at me, mocking me through the mask's eyeholes. *My eyes.*

"The Chant to Relieve Pain of the Body?" the apparition mocked.

My voice. I gulped at my heart's wild pounding.

"A feeble pain chant." Its tone dropped, seductive. "We have greater power than that. Our purpose is to inflict pain, not heal it. We are Machitew, the Death Bringer."

The ghostly mask swooped at my face, jaws gaping. Teeth five thumb-widths long, like pale, curved daggers, filled my vision, and a breath of winter wind swept off the desert chilled my cheek. I stiffened, my back pressed to the cistern, and squeezed my eyes shut against the impending strike.

Another mask seemed to encase my head, limiting my vision to what I could see through carved eyeholes. As if watching a vid, I saw myself crouched in some shadowed corner of the enclave plaza below with my knife glinting in my hand.

The phantom loomed at my shoulder. "She's in our power. It's our right to seek revenge for her abuse."

Clearly as if I moved beside her, I watched my stepmother limp down the stone steps from her third-level dwelling. Through the eyeholes, I discerned every crease that puckered her lips, every droplet of sweat on her lined forehead. She puffed with each step, and I grimaced at the unhealthy stink of her breath.

She held the cord handles of two buckets in one fat hand and extended the other to balance herself when she swayed on a crooked step. She grunted as she gained the cobbled plaza and waddled across it, her back to me.

Through the ghostly mask I observed myself shifting on my haunches, gathering myself to spring.

"Now," the apparition ordered.

I saw myself leap from cover, dash across the plaza, and seize her shoulder from behind. She swore when she realized it was me.

"Revenge from Death Bringer," my other self said through tight teeth. I watched my hand slash my blade across her throat, sending hot crimson pulsing over my fingers.

I recoiled out of the vision. My head bashed the cistern with a deep *thunk*. My heart hammered my ribs, and the sweat of nausea swelled about my nose and mouth. I flung my knife from clammy fingers, only faintly hearing its clatter on the adobe.

Machitew's spectral mask dissipated before me like mist in a breeze, but the rain pounding the dome didn't diminish his victorious roar.

* * * * *

Chapter Two

I t took some time for my racing heart to settle to its normal pace and sweat to stop beading on my forehead. As some semblance of calm returned, one thought throbbed in my mind.

If I don't leave now, someone else in my family will die.

Among my people, the Chalca, an enclave's chief chanter performed a prayer-song called a Birth Chant on every newborn baby. The child was not to learn its contents until the Coming-of-Age Ceremony when he or she reached twenty, but others were free to discuss it outside his or her hearing.

Usually the child's whole clan witnessed the chant, but only three people had heard mine. One had been my father, who'd pronounced it. The other two were my maternal grandmother and the woman who'd become my stepmother.

She must have told the whole enclave about mine after my father's death. Only that could explain why voices fell silent and eyes shifted away whenever I joined a gathering, and why I'd often glimpsed sadness in my father's eyes while he taught me the chants.

I dragged in a breath, as if around a knife in my chest.

Kimama still slept in my faded blankets when I rose from behind the cistern, which had grown chilly during the night.

I'll take her to Gram. Then I'll go… where? That slowed me for only a second. I'll decide later. Right now, we need to get out of here.

My link buzzed in my trouser pocket, and I drew it out. A flat gray rectangle, it fit comfortably in my palm. Its display glowed white, bright enough in the fading darkness to make me blink, and it pipped with each touch as I contacted Dome Control to file a flight plan to Awénasa City.

Gray light filtering through the dome warned of a drizzly dawn, but muffled creaking and shuffling from the rooms below increased my urgency. *The rest of the family's already up. We won't be able to leave unseen.* I gently shook Kimama's shoulder to wake her.

The bruise still marred her cheek, visible in the partial light. I grimaced.

"We're going to Gram's," I said. "Put everything you can in your backpack. We need to hurry."

"Yi!" she said through a yawn and beamed.

We found the sleeping room vacant on descending the ladder. Long, windowless, cool as a cave, and dark both day and night, with floor bricks uneven enough to catch toes, it smelled of the warm bodies who'd occupied it through the night.

I touched the nearest solar-battery lamp on, in its niche in the curved wall. Solar-powered lights had replaced the amber radiance of oil-burning lamps with the installation of the dome a few years earlier, but the scent of oil remained, along with soot smudges in the niches.

I replaced the oil-paste cup before turning to my own shelf. Half a dozen shelves and a couple rows of stout pegs held our clothes and personal belongings. I dropped our backpacks on the floor with a soft *thump* and stuffed my image plate, shirts, socks, shorts, and trousers into mine. I made sure Kimama put clothes in hers, along with her yarn-animal dolls.

Tales of Machitew the Death Bringer haunted me while I loaded my pack.

The Machitew dancer in the annual ceremonies wore a cloak of black rags and an ash-stained mask fitted with teeth from a hatchling askuk, the massive snakes that twisted across the Awénasa desert.

Machitew would be born to torment the Chalca people, the sacred tales said, and the ceremonies portrayed his deeds. He would inflict death and destruction until Wanikiya, the seventh shaman and last of the Ancient Ones, came to save our people from Machitew's terrors.

I already have a history of death and destruction.

My mother had died of internal bleeding soon after giving birth to me.

In my twelfth winter, I'd witnessed my father's death, in blinding lightning and ground-quaking thunder, while he performed a storm-stilling chant on the sacred mesa.

A few moons ago, while flying sentry for my fifteen-year-old half-brother, I'd watched with my heart clenched in my chest as the ice of ebbing winter split a stone column from the nearby wash's eroded bank. My brother and half my stepmother's pod of shegruls had vanished under crashing sandstone slabs and sheets of crusted snow.

My guts knotted in remembered horror. My throat ached, remembering my shouted warnings as he charged toward the rim. "Shirik, stop! Let them go!"

I shuddered at the memory as I shouldered my pack.

Machitew's right. I'm him. I'm Death Bringer.

Kimama and I found our other siblings already seated around the dome-shaped stone oven when I flung aside the door-blanket between the sleeping and gathering rooms. They peeked cautiously over the rims of their bowls and slid wary glances at their mother.

The aroma of maize porridge with honey teased my nostrils until I could taste it. I ignored the eager rumbles from my midsection.

"Where are you two going?" my stepmother demanded.

"To buy your supplies," I said.

"Liar. Why are you taking Kimmie?"

"I want to go see Gram." Kimama's tone held defiance.

Ten-year-old Tohoka sniggered. "Your lip looks like a shegrul pulling itself in two, Ku."

I didn't waste breath on a response, just fixed a hard glower on him.

The fire in the oven caught my eye. The flames' lively motion taunted me like waggling tongues, and anger snaked through my soul. I began to murmur the Chant to Extinguish Fires under my breath as I crossed the room.

My father's cautioning words whispered across my memory. "This chant must never be used lightly, son. Like the Chant to Ignite Fires, it's for teaching, to build an apprentice's skill. Fire spirits can be dangerous and vengeful, and must be treated with respect."

I squelched a guilty pang, nudged Kimama ahead of me, and peered around my shoulder.

The flames still writhed, spirit dancers in bright plumage in the oven's firebox.

I wasn't surprised by it, but I swallowed a lonely sense of abandonment. The Ancients and their spirits don't even care enough to punish me when I violate a chant.

My knock on the wooden door to the outside came only from habit. As we stepped through and I hauled it closed behind us, I considered the irony of rapping on its logs to scare off evil spirits lurking outside. *They got in a long time ago.*

Kimama hopped down the stairs, *scuff, scuff, scuff* on dusty stone to the circular plaza, but I lingered on the step to survey the enclosure that had been my home.

As children, my friends and I had raced across the quarter-range plaza, and up and down the gritty steps from cobblestones to flat rooftops. Our shouts had echoed off the walls and the original log-and-soil dome, mingling with babies' cries and sentry dogs' barks.

I'd felt safe in the enclave as a child. That had ended the day of my father's death.

I blew out a breath and followed Kimama.

On the second level, below the dwelling, I ducked into the storage room to gather dried cactus fruit, pouches of shegrul jerky, hard honey-candy, and canned drinking water. Food for our flight.

Scents of squashes, melons, dried herbs, and maize in large bags tickled my nose. I paused to inhale their sweetness and watch dust motes swirl in the lantern beams—until I spotted the kosa trap tucked in a cobwebbed corner. A rodent's desiccated, black-bristled tail and hind foot protruded from beneath the deadfall weight.

That'll be me if I stay.

On the ground level, despite the previous day's labors, odors of shegrul manure and trampled maize-husk bedding drifted from the barn into the adjoining hangar. Their stench, combined with the bitterness of aircraft lubricants, watered my eyes.

Behind the barn door, the shegruls crunched about in the husks. "I won't miss any of you," I muttered under my breath. "Kotori will have to deal with you now." Still, I tugged the door open to peer in on them.

A dull lamp in the log ceiling clarified thigh-high shadows into eight leathery creatures, like enormous, gray caterpillars. Shegruls lacked eyes and ears. They relied on sensory whiskers and olfactory probes instead.

Two new shegruls, recently divided from one, still had only three body segments. I squinted through the dimness, searching among developing four- and five-segmented shegruls until I spotted the last six-segmented one against the far wall. Old Dibe.

I waded in among them, prodding them with my knees until they wheezed in protest through the paired respiratory ducts along their lumpy backs and lumbered out of my way. Pushing clear of the milling pod, I approached Dibe.

In the last phase, it had stopped eating. The crease between its middle two segments had tightened like a drawstring bag, preparing to pinch them apart, and whiskers and a proboscis had emerged above its stumpy rear legs. It would partition, or tug itself in two, in a few more days.

Imagining my older stepsister handling the partition, I said, "I hope Kotori won't be cruel to you," and rested a hand briefly on its wrinkled back before I left the barn.

My father's aircraft waited next door. His climbing bear totem painted on the pilot's door appeared faded and forlorn in the dust and semi-darkness. I flipped the hangar's door opener, and the rising panel's clacking alarmed the chickens pecking about the landing skids. Kimama chased the plump birds out onto the plaza, laughing at their squawking and flapping.

I tied down our backpacks in the hold and inspected the Darter quickly but carefully, the way my father had taught me.

"Come on, Kimmie." I waved her to the aircraft and boosted her into the copilot's seat. She insisted on fastening the harness herself. I watched to be sure she cinched it tight enough before I swung into the cockpit and switched on the engines, one after another.

Through their awakening grumbles I remembered how I'd asked my father if I could fly the Darter to Yuma's Knife mesa for the storm-stilling ceremony.

"You have the mental quickness for flying in a storm, son," he'd said, "but it takes physical strength as well. Let's see how the winds are."

He'd let me take the steering yoke part of the way out, though I could barely see over the instrument panel.

That evening, with the blizzard unabated, I'd flown the Darter home, my older cousin, Hanuk, in his aircraft at my wing, and my father's blanket-wrapped body secured in my hold.

My throat tightened at the memory.

Checklist completed, I strapped in and tied back my waist-length hair before I donned the comms headset. White noise hissed through its earphones.

Lumbering movement at my periphery caught my eye. My step-mother had followed us down to the hangar. When I shifted to face her, she shouted something about kidnapping her daughter and stealing her airplane.

I didn't reply. I gave her a tight smile as I pushed the throttles from idle to full power. The engines' roar in the hangar's confined space instantly muted her rant. She stood there mouthing words and jabbing a thick finger at me.

When I switched to Dome Control's frequency, the white noise subsided like bees settling in their hive. "Dome Control, come in," I called.

"Dome Control, here," a familiar female voice answered. *"Your callsign today is Red Wash Six-Two. You're flying to the city in this rainstorm, Akuleh?"*

"Ya, Chepi," I said. "Requesting clearance to enter the plaza." *Are you relieved Death Bringer is leaving?*

A rumble outside our hangar drew my gaze, reverberations felt more than heard as the nironnium dome's flight panels smoothly retracted.

Rain drove through the opening, pelting the cobbles. Roiling thunderheads darkened the widening gap as I taxied to the launch position at the plaza's center. Drops as hard as pebbles beat a rapid tattoo on my cockpit canopy.

Dome Control said, *"You are cleared for launch."*

"Six-Two launching," I answered. The blast of my vertical thrusters obliterated all other sounds as I rocketed the Darter into the torrent.

A glance at the open dome below drew ice along my spine like a chilly finger. Machitew's baleful eye seemed to follow me, watching me through a hole in the desert floor.

* * * * *

Chapter Three

The imagined eye seemed to track me as we climbed, and I shivered at an unexpected reality.

I can't run far enough to escape Machitew.

Rain blurred the cockpit canopy. The old rain-scrapers, squeaking with every back-and-forth swipe, cleared brief, streaky semi-circles across my view.

Like all aircraft on Tempest, my Darter had four massive, vertical-takeoff-and-landing engines, and broad wings for stability in the planet's violent air currents. It also had four seats—two in front, two behind—and landing gear equipped with skids. Though pitted and scraped, the skids remained rugged enough to land on sand and gravel in summer, and the usual two or three hundred spans of snow in winter.

Red Wash Enclave lay the time of two sun positions from Awénasa City, but we had a headwind. Contrary gusts caught us, making the aircraft bounce and slewing it sideways. Fighting to keep it straight and level, I considered what lay ahead.

Where can I go? Can't stay anywhere near family members. I don't want to kill anybody, not even my stepmother.

Kimama spent most of the flight with her forehead pressed to her rain-spattered window. "Look, Ku!" she said once. "I can see an askuk swimming. I think it's a hundred foot-lengths! I can see the saws on its back."

I peered out and whistled at the snake's size. "No, it's more like a hundred arm-lengths."

Only the serpent's twining movements, stirring orange ripples in its wake as it sought high ground, made it visible against the temporary sea of snowmelt flooding the russet desert. The fetid smells of a marsh whooshed into the cockpit through the air vents.

Another time Kimama said, "The python trees are starting to uncurl their limbs. Don't fly too close to them!"

We flew at an altitude of three thousand Commonwealth Standard spans. "I won't go anywhere near the python trees, Kimmie," I assured her with a smile.

I couldn't blame Kimama for being anxious. During our six moons of winter darkness, the carnivorous trees shriveled to scaly trunks with five or six fleshy limbs coiled at their tops. In spring, the limbs relaxed and dangled like octopus tentacles pretending to be willows, long enough to wrap around and crush any creature unwary enough to touch them.

That must be why the oil smells like rotting meat when we crush the bulbs to release it.

The rain subsided, the clouds thinned, and the turbulence eased. Kimama opened the bag I'd filled in the storeroom. We chewed seedy cactus fruit and peppered shegrul jerky, and sucked on honey candy.

The overcast sky cleared as we approached the city. The sun burned it to a blue as bright as the stones in local artisans' jewelry, as if to warn us of the six moons of searing daylight to come.

We had to climb to five thousand spans to clear the Ghost Cat Mountains, which stood like a wall hemming in the desert. Soaring over the crest, I blinked at the gleam off the languid expanse of Blessing River to the south. Beyond the river, the nironnium domes of Awénasa City swelled, a cluster of smoke-colored blisters on the ochre high desert.

When I toggled my comms to the general aviation frequency to contact the city airfield's control tower, my stepmother's voice burst through my headset, prompting a cringe. "If you don't bring my child and my Darter home right now, I'll drag you out of the enclave and cut off your hair myself!"

Has she been yelling through the radio all this time?

Even Kimama heard her. She startled and stared at me.

I snorted. "You'll have to drag me back from Awénasa City yourself first, and the Darter was left to *me*, not you." I switched frequencies before she could respond.

Something golden, a blur of solidified sunlight, flashed past my left eye at that moment, an instant before something hit the craft with a sharp thunk. It jolted.

Kimama's eyes widened. "What was that, Ku?"

I didn't answer. The aircraft's nose had dropped left, setting off a grating buzz that pulsed in synch with a red symbol blinking on the instrument panel. Smoke wisped past the cockpit, bitter with the stench of burning feathers and flesh.

My lower port engine's dead.

I brought the nose up, my hands sweat-slicked on the yoke's cracked cover, and reached across to give Kimama's seat harness a swift yank.

She yelped. "Yi, that hurt!"

"Sorry, Kimmie." I tugged my own harness. "Tighter is safer. Hold on."

I scanned my instruments. I had begun my descent. We flew at forty-three hundred spans. A lee wind off the mountains butted at my damaged craft.

I knew I could maintain altitude with three engines in Tempest's one-and-a-half standard gravities, but with one port engine gone, the small aircraft yawed left. Its frame groaned with the stress. I shoved the right rudder pedal to return it to the correct heading and switched the radio to my destination's frequency.

"Awénasa Control." Putting all my weight on the rudder pedal brought my words out in gasps and I had to shout through the persistent damage buzzer. "This is Red Wash Six-Two. I think I hit a large bird. My port engine's dead. Do you copy?"

"*Six-Two, Control,*" a male voice said through faint static, "*we copy. Can you make the airfield?*"

My attention dropped to my fluctuating instruments. "I'm thirty ranges out and losing power, and I've got my little sister with me." I don't know why it seemed so important to tell Control about Kimama.

"*We're clearing the field,*" Control said. "*Report status changes.*"

"Roger that."

Kimama stared at me. "Are we going to crash?"

I met her anxious gaze. "No." My mouth had gone as dry as the wind-carved peaks behind us, but I could taste the pungent smoke filtering into the cockpit. "We'll sing the Pilots' Chant. We'll be protected. Sing it with me, as much of it as you know."

Her high voice didn't waver as we began the prayer of all Chalca pilots. I emphasized the last line. "O, Ancient One who formed the winds, who gave the Mother Worlds breath, lift me on the shoulders of air spirits. Let me ride upon them to bear me safely to my destination."

Sweat dampened my armpits by the time we finished.

"Keep chanting," I told Kimama. "Don't stop."

I checked the compass. *The hardest part will be maintaining a straight course.* My right leg burned from holding the rudder pedal down.

"*Six-Two,*" the controller's voice rattled, "*you are cleared for landing pad four-two-four.*"

"Roger, Control."

By the time I spotted the landing pad, already covered with crash foam, my right leg was shaking violently. Sweat rolled in itchy rivulets down my chest and back and stuck my loose shirt to my skin. "Control, Six-Two, rotating engines for landing," I said, and added, "Keep chanting, Kimmie."

I reduced power to the lower starboard engine to counter the damaged one's lack of thrust when I rotated all four. Their noise swelled from a steady growl to a protesting whine, but if I didn't reduce power, the Darter would flip.

At the same time, I increased power to both upper engines to keep the Darter from plowing into the ground. A double roar smothered their whine. The aircraft's vibrations grew more violent.

"Ku?" Kimama's voice quavered.

"Keep chanting," I said.

I rubbed one damp palm, then the other on my trouser legs before I spread one hand across the throttle switches and nudged them forward.

The engines' roar rose and faltered. The Darter wobbled as its engines pivoted, tilting the horizon outside its canopy.

My heart rate accelerated. I held my breath. The stink of my own sweat reached my nose.

Kimama continued to murmur the Pilots' Chant. I slipped a glance at her. Tension—but not fear—filled her round face, and I gave her a shaky smile. "Keep chanting. We'll be safe."

Emergency vehicles ringed landing pad four-two-four. The pad farthest from the rest of the airfield, of course, in case we exploded on impact. Billows of gray crash-foam practically concealed its approach guidance beacons.

Good for smothering flames, but it wouldn't provide any padding if we came down hard. And it was slippery.

I glimpsed crash trucks with fire suppressant nozzles the size of energy cannons, and ambulances with flashing red and yellow lights. The thin wail of a distant siren threaded through the driving buzz from my instrument panel.

Miniature people in silvery firefighting suits scooted with apparent urgency among the vehicles. I could see their helmets tipping to stare at us.

Like carrion eaters waiting for a wounded animal to die.

Annoyance rose from my tension. "Thanks for the show of confidence, Control."

As I continued my descent, another warning light began to flash on the engines diagram. The upper port engine had begun to lose power, too.

The aircraft rocked, then tilted left.

Fresh sweat rose on my scalp. It dampened my hair and tickled its way down my jaw. I yanked at my seat harness once more and joined Kimama in singing the Pilots' Chant. "O, Ancient One who formed the winds…"

My vision flicked from altimeter to artificial horizon and back again. "Keep it on the line, keep the nose up," I coached myself through gritted teeth.

I fought the controls as I watched the altimeter spin down too swiftly. Fought to keep my failing aircraft centered and level above the landing pad.

"Lift me on the shoulders of air spirits," Kimama sang from the copilot's seat.

I eyed the altimeter, counting.

Four hundred spans, three hundred spans, two hundred…

* * * * *

Chapter Four

The surface rushed up as if to devour us. Bracing myself in my seat, I chanted aloud, "...bear me safely to my destination," but in my mind I pleaded, *Let us die instant-ly.*

A burst of wind thrust upward from beneath us. I understood ground effect, but that alone wouldn't have so noticeably slowed the altimeter's blurred spin in the last few seconds. I didn't have time to wonder about it. The gust into the cockpit choked us on the smoke of charred engine components.

The Darter struck the crash foam with all the grace of a rock splatting into mud. I must have set it down at a slight angle, because it fishtailed as if I'd hit ice.

The shock slammed us against our harnesses with enough force to wind us. I gulped for breath, and Kimama gasped.

Gray slop splashed the cockpit canopy, thick as mud, and noisy as hail. It obliterated my view of flashing lights and the figures running toward us, but not the howl of a siren and several shouting voices.

As soon as the Darter stopped sliding, a man in a silvery fire-fighter's suit yanked open the pilot's hatch. His eyes widened behind his faceplate on seeing me, and a chuckle issued from his voice grid. "Text-vid emergency landing, boy. I was expecting a combat veteran in here."

"Not for a few more years," I said, and watched him slash my harness. "Get my sister out."

"Can't reach her. Got to get you first." He hustled me from the cockpit as if he thought it might explode, handed me off to another firefighter, and clambered inside for Kimama.

The second man steered me clear of the crash foam. My boots slipped in it, and he pulled my arm across his shoulder. Ashen foam swished around our feet and spattered everywhere. It tasted of bitter chemicals when a blob of it struck my mouth.

I paused to spit, winced at the smart in my split lip, and twisted in the fireman's support to search for Kimama. His crewmate followed us closely, carrying her in his arms above the stifling foam.

An ambulance crew in green uniforms surrounded us. They instantly spotted my swollen lip and the bruise marring Kimama's cheek.

"Bidd, they need cold-packs," a white woman with anxious eyes said to someone behind us in Commonwealth Standard. She asked us, in fair Chalca, "Did you bump your faces in your flyer?"

"No," Kimama said. "Mama—"

I squeezed her hand to stop her. *Last thing we need is an interrogation about her mother. Some off-worlders actually give battered children back to abusive parents, and if her mother accuses me of kidnapping Kimmie, I could end up in jail.*

"Dual steering yokes," I said in Standard. "Thought I tightened our seat harnesses enough, but…" I shrugged.

Somebody brought cold packs. The woman wanted us to lay on pads they'd unrolled on the steaming tarmac, but Kimama crawled into my lap. Heedless of the gray muck coating me, she buried her face in my shirtfront. "Don't let them take me away, Ku."

Despite the foam, Kimama smelled faintly of the homemade herb soap her mother used to wash her hair. She had her mother's flat face, but our father's eyes, warm and friendly, and his ready smile. Her grin, with a couple baby teeth missing, dimpled her cheeks. She wore her hair loose, so it covered half her back, but she'd lost her toddler chubbiness to the sturdiness that came from living on a high-gravity world.

"We're *fine*," I told the medics, hoping the irritation in my voice masked my embarrassment.

"What's your clan?" a Chalca medic asked, crouching beside us. "How old are you, and where are you from?"

"Clan Masou," I said and indicated Kimama. "She's my half-sister, clan Etena. I'm almost twenty, and she's eight. We're from Red Wash Enclave, out there." I pointed with my chin to indicate the desert beyond the enclosing Ghost Cat Mountains.

With quick fingers, the medic entered notes in Standard characters into her link and left. Kimama relaxed against my chest.

A cry rose from the direction of my Darter. I jerked around in time to see the small crowd examining it leap clear as if from an electric shock.

"Call a chanter!" someone shouted, his voice distraught.

Two firemen separated from the group and crossed toward us, their silvery suits glaring in the sun. They dropped to a squat in front of me, their faces grim.

"Do you know what you hit, boy?" one asked, his black eyes fierce with accusation.

"No," I said. I swallowed dryness. "I didn't see it. I only saw sort of a…"

My words trailed off. In my gut, I knew, even before the other reverently held out on both open palms a single tattered pinion feather. A tan pinion with the first golden band along its edge. A juvenile sun eagle's wing pinion.

Sun eagles weren't native to Tempest. Along with chickens, goats, cats, and dogs, my ancestors had brought seven pairs of eagles on their Crossing from Solienne. Like our people, the birds had thrived here. We Chalca named them a protected species, not because they were rare, but because they were sacred, spirits of the air granted flesh, the messengers between mortals and the Ancients.

My stomach clenched. *I am* Death Bringer. *I must be, to kill a sun eagle.*

InterClan law officers formed a silent cordon around my aircraft to keep everyone away until the chanter came. One man posted himself at my shoulder as if to keep me from leaving. The green-clad medics, having decided we were all right, handed us water bottles along with the cold packs and left us alone.

We waited a whole sun position for the chanter to arrive from Awénasa City. I tracked its climb, evaporating rain puddles on the tarmac. I watched vapor rise in misty shimmers like wavering ghosts while the crash foam hardened on my shirt. I sneezed when its chemical odor intensified.

The pads left by the medics, barely a thumb's width thick and covered with off-white canvas, seemed to grow thinner and harder the longer we waited. My tailbone felt bruised, and shifting about on it didn't help. At least the pads put a layer between us and the hot surface.

Kimama stomped around the pads, pausing every minute or so to tug at my hand. "Come on, Ku. I want to go to Gram's house."

"We can't go until the chanter comes," I told her.

I ached to leave as well, to escape the curious gazes of white So-liennese military personnel and the disgusted glowers of every Chalca who passed. I felt like somebody had seized my soul with clawed hands and begun to wring it. *Death Bringer, Death Bringer*, throbbed in my head with my pulse.

The law officers in the cordon certainly appeared to think so. They stood well back from my Darter as if expecting a demon to erupt out of it.

Machitew. Death Bringer.

It had been whispered behind my back ever since my father's death, and more frequently after the loss of my brother. Especially by my stepmother.

The chanter's arrival drew me from my ruminations. I lifted my gaze from the pad's coarse surface to study him.

A stooped and wizened man, he approached my aircraft with the slow shuffle of reverent dance, singing a mournful song I didn't rec-ognize. I'd given up my chanter apprenticeship after losing my fa-ther, so I'd never learned all the prayer-songs.

I couldn't see what ceremony he performed from where I sat. My throat closed in a convulsive swallow, and I ducked my head away when he reached into the damaged engine, his hands draped with pale cloth.

I didn't lift my gaze until a pair of leather boots, scuffed and stained with wear, stepped into the downcast circle of my sight. I cringed when I met the old chanter's eyes, like bits of flint set among leathery crags as deep as junnikar bark. Those eyes held no condem-nation. He only asked in his wheezy voice, "Are either of you in-jured?"

"No, Chanter," I said, and Kimama shook her head.

"I'll perform the Warding Chant for you." He reached for the worn pouch at his belt.

As he withdrew a lidded cup carved from bone, I glimpsed a blood smear on his veiny hand. *The sun eagle's blood.* My innards wrenched, and I swallowed, a tightness in my throat.

He spread oil-paste on our foreheads first, shaping the shield glyph. A wisp of restless air carried the oil's putrid scent to me through the headache-inducing odor of the caked crash foam.

"You must perform a purification ceremony as soon as you can, young man," the old man said.

"Ya, Chanter." I choked on the words.

Demon hands twisted at my heart and lungs as he began the Warding Chant. *It won't do any good!* my mind screamed. *I'm Death Bringer.* I gritted my teeth to keep the scream inside.

By the time he finished the blessing song and departed, two men wearing grease-stained coveralls printed with the logo of a repair depot had clamped my aircraft under a hovering lifter with flaking red paint.

Only then did I fully see the shredded lower engine, still ribboned with the eagle's blood, and the splayed blades in the upper one. The stench of seared feathers and flesh, like some profane sacrifice, triggered a gag. Kimama clamped her hands to her nose.

Machitew. Death Bringer, echoed in my head. *You even killed your Darter.*

"You two can ride with us," one repairman said. "We have a jump seat up front. Do you have payment reserves? We'll need to access the information."

"It's in the flight computer," I said. "It'll come up when you run the diagnostics."

I had no trouble imagining my stepmother's livid face. *She's going to have a screaming fit when they contact her.* Didn't matter. Not even Machitew could drag me back there.

* * * * *

Chapter Five

A repair pit yawned beneath us, a cavernous mouth cluttered with heavy equipment like grungy teeth. Seated on my lap, Kimama pressed her back against my chest as if resisting our descent into the mechanical gullet.

Minutes later, we stood on the shop's oil-stained floor. Kimama stared around us, clinging to my hand while I talked to the owner. We had to shout across the clangs and clatter.

"Your reserve payment provides a loaner," the owner said, "for as long as your Darter is here, but we won't have one available until tomorrow."

"Doesn't matter," I said. "We're not in a hurry." *I don't know where I'm going from here, anyway.*

The man's gaze rested on my swollen mouth. "Looks like you two took some damage as well. Do you have somewhere to stay and a way to get there?"

"We're going to our gram in the city," Kimama said.

"I have a straddlejet," I said, "if somebody can take us to our family's hangar bay."

The owner beckoned at the lifter pilot. "These two need a ride." To me, he said, "I'll contact you when we finish the repairs."

I retrieved our backpacks from the Darter's hold, and the lifter pilot drove us to the hangar my stepmother shared with a local uncle.

The hauler lurched and bucked its way along rain-sodden lanes, and Kimama giggled at the rough ride.

Clattering tracks kicked up rust-colored mud that speckled the windshield, and the old motor radiated the odor of burning oil. The hauler's rumbles echoed through the canyon of bowl-shaped hangar bays like the growls of an irritated ghost cat.

I nodded thanks to our driver as I hefted Kimama from the cab outside our hangar. When I tapped the bay's lock code, its sand-pitted door grated slowly open. *Really needs a lube job.*

Built of adobe bricks and stone, the hangar bay retained the musty chilliness of a cave.

"Lights," I said, and they flickered on, a pale ring around the top of the wall that glinted on the spiral launch hatch. I found the dimness comfortable after the sun's steamy heat. Some insect followed us inside and buzzed noisily along the light ring.

We crossed to the straddlejets propped in parking stands against the curved wall. Like skimmers and rocket-bikes on other worlds, straddlejets lacked wheels. Due to Tempest's high grav and rugged terrain, ours traveled on repulsors more powerful than the ones used elsewhere.

I owned the newest one in the hangar. A sleek machine with chrome handlebars and a swept-back windscreen, it had eight in-line repulsors, and auto-compensation thrusters for mountain riding. It had taken me three years of hard work, butchering shegruls, to earn enough rels to pay for it.

Momentary wistfulness swept me. My cousin Hanuk and I and our friends had raced across the sun-cracked floodplain on our straddlejets, roaring after tavos and kosas, screaming around brush and boulders, flying off the ragged banks of Red Wash. Preferring our own transportation around Awénasa City, with better chances of meeting girls, we'd brought our straddlejets here a year or so before Hanuk's departure.

What are you up to now, Huk?

I sighed and ran my hand along my ride's polished frame before I removed my helmet and gloves from the compartment behind its single seat and stuffed our backpacks in their place.

Kimama fetched her helmet from its low hook on the wall and put it on. Pink with blue butterflies. She poked loose strands of hair inside, and I fastened the faceplate for her.

My faded poncho hung near her helmet. Thinking of the mud along the hangar lanes, I took it down. The heavy cloth made a ripping sound as I cut a slit in the front with my pocketknife. "Now we can both wear it."

Kimama crowed. "We'll be a two-headed monster!"

I grinned. "Ya, that pink helmet is pretty terrifying."

She stuck her tongue out at me.

Some of my hair had pulled loose from its leather binding, and it stuck damply to my head. I combed it with my hands and retied it in a horsetail at my nape before tugging my helmet on.

"All right, let's go, Kimmie." I hefted her in front of me on the straddlejet's seat, where I could steady her with my arms and legs, and she pushed her head through the poncho's new hole.

No weather dome covered the nine-range route between the airfield and the city. The sun stood at its zenith, blinding after the rain, as I maneuvered the straddlejet among the hangar bays to the main route.

"Maximum sunscreen," I said, and my helmet's full-face visor darkened to smoky amber.

My straddlejet's repulsors sounded like a purr after the thumping tow-lifter and grinding hauler. The repulsors provided a smoother ride, too.

The route to the city began at the airfield and passed the interstellar vortex terminal and lavish Aponivi Hotel, both enclosed in a smaller version of the city's nironnium domes. An illuminated notice, rippling across the dome's surface near its entrance, caught my eye as we approached. I decelerated enough to read it.

All Eligible for Conscription
This Quarter: Last Day to Report
For Induction is 12/30/238 CSY

I puckered my forehead. *That's only a few days from now.*

I'd seen the same notice three moons ago when I'd come with Hanuk's family to see him off.

Four more moons until I get my own conscription notice. I blew out a breath of frustration. *Won't come soon enough. That'd solve my problem of where to go.*

I accelerated with a thrum of engines.

In the distance, the city's domes loomed like a mound of grimy eggs, but on either side of us, fleeting spring plants thrust green starts from the flame-colored soil.

We got muddy, even wearing the poncho. The repulsors spouted water from every puddle on the road, and the poncho flapped as rapidly behind us as a bat eating buzz-seeds. We got chilly, too. Kimama shivered against my chest, and my teeth chattered so noisily, I could hear them inside my helmet.

A separate small dome protected the old section of the city. I took the exit into it, reducing my speed as I entered its arch, and said, "Sunscreen off." My visor's tint dissipated.

Old Trade Center had begun as Awénasa Enclave, the first Chalca settlement on Tempest. It had expanded for decades, each new generation building another concentric ring of dwellings and shops outside the previous one.

Like Red Wash, Old Trade Center's plaza stretched a quarter range across. Its original three-level structures of dwellings, storage rooms, and barns, tiered like seats in a sports arena, had been built against the fortress wall like buttresses. Back then a single gate had opened to the east, toward the sunrise.

Merchants and craftsmen occupied the ground levels now. The community well-house had been removed with the installation of plumbing and pumps in each dwelling, and subterranean ceremonial lodges had been filled and cobbled over when the annual events moved to the new city center. Instead of one gate, three lanes now ran like the spokes of a wheel from the plaza to other city sectors, and to the outside.

Our grandmother's herbal apothecary stood on the southeast side of the plaza. My real mother, Gram's eldest daughter, had grown up there. *Hope Gram's home. I didn't think to call her first.*

Kimama darted ahead while I locked the straddlejet into a parking stand. Its bar fell into place with a heavy *clunk*. Gram must have heard or seen us through her open doorway, because she stepped outside, beaming.

A stout centenarian with her silvery hair bound in a traditional bob at the nape of her neck, Gram had deep-set eyes and an abundance of laugh-lines around her mouth. Aromas of herbs and baking drifted about her like a welcoming aura.

She spotted the bruise on Kimama's face at once, and my split lip in another heartbeat. "Names of the Ancients!" she exclaimed, and hustled us inside. There, she retrieved a small pot labeled Sample from a low shelf.

The salve it contained, python-tree oil blended with local honey and crushed pads from the ground-hugging raincup cactus, accelerated healing of minor injuries. Kimmie crinkled her nose at the raincup's astringent scent but stood still while Gram spread the thick mixture on her cheek with gentle fingers.

"I'm fine," I said when Gram straightened and reached up to me, but she dabbed salve on my mouth anyway. The raincup pulp thankfully overwhelmed the python oil's rotten odor. It tasted as sharp as it smelled despite the honey mixed into it, but I managed not to wince at the burning sensation.

Gram leveled a stern eye on me while she applied it. "What happened, Akuleh?"

"Mama hit us," Kimama said before I could speak. "She was mean to Ku for scraping the pot, but there was hardly anything left. When I told him he could have some of mine, she hit me. Then she hit him, too."

Gram's ire revealed itself only in how she pursed her lips and drew her thinning brows together.

Shame shifted my gaze from hers and dropped it to the stone floor. "It was my fault, Gram. I spent all day mucking out the shegrul barn, and I was starving, so I took all that was left."

"No." Her scowl softened into sadness. "It *wasn't* your fault, either of you." She met Kimama's anxious eyes and stroked her disheveled head. "Your mama wasn't always this way, but you can stay here with me if you choose to."

Gram returned her attention to me. "When the brother of the man you miss married her many years ago, she was a hard-working, pleasant woman. Losing one husband after the other, and then a child, has crushed her soul, I think. There's a great weight on her shoulders and deep pain in her heart."

So she spreads the pain around. Memories of bruises and welts from her beatings shot phantom pain across my back.

"I've got to leave," I said. "She hit Kimmie just for trying to share her food. I don't know what I'd do if she hurt Kimmie again." I held Gram's gaze. *You recorded my Birth Chant. You know what I am.*

Gram regarded me briefly. "Take some time to calm down, Aku-leh." She patted my elbow. "You two must be hungry. Come wash up, and I'll make you something to eat."

Kimama and I followed her up the rear stairs to her home above the shop. Her long skirts, colors faded but gathered and full, swished with every step.

I pumped water for Kimama to wash her face and hands, then shooed her from the washroom so I could strip to scrub off the grime. I reveled in the tickle of cool well-water on my skin.

Gram had smoked shegrul, maize bread with honey, and fresh pimiberries waiting when I came out. She handed me a shirt that had been my grandfather's. It fit fairly well, except for being a little too snug across my broadening shoulders.

Halfway through the meal, Kimama set down her bowl and yawned. "I'm too sleepy to eat anymore, Gram."

"Go take a nap, Kimama." Gram pointed her to the dark sleeping room. "Akuleh, I can use your help in the shop this afternoon."

I never left a meal hungry when I stayed with Gram. Only out of habit did I finish Kimama's abandoned shegrul meat before I followed Gram downstairs to the shop.

"I need you to stock these things for me." She pointed at a large box. "I can't reach the high shelves so well anymore."

Scents of native herbs and imported spices teased my nose. I had barely noticed them when we'd arrived earlier, but they released comfortable memories of the time I'd spent with Gram after Grandfather died. I'd been younger than Kimama, not yet old enough to begin my chanter apprenticeship.

Having spent as much time as I could with Gram ever since, helping in the shop and learning her herb lore, I could've found any of her goods in the dark. Herbal salves and cactus blossom honey in painted pots, medicinal teas in carved boxes, spices and seasonings in narrow jars with bright labels, packets of dried plants for poultices.

Customers came and went through the afternoon. I recognized most of them, and they greeted me in turn.

Elder Chavat, the hardware dealer, leaned heavily on Gram's front counter. "Need something for my aching back," he said with a groan. "Both my workers got conscripted this quarter."

I retrieved a clay pot of salve for sore muscles. I hadn't known his workers well, but I said, "My cousin got conscripted last time. What have you heard about the war?"

"Man named Osaga Safa from Kanek," Chavat said. "Way down the galactic arm. Religious crazy. Calls himself the Supreme Leader. Trying to make everybody convert. They captured Gimel last phase. Killed most of the colonists." He shook his head, and his thinning horsetail twitched on his back. "They'll probably attack Ardonar next."

"Ardonar?" I stared at him. "That's halfway up the galactic arm from Kanek. Halfway to us."

"Too close for me," Chavat said.

Elder Macawi came later. She bustled inside, a short woman about Gram's age and build, one of Gram's longtime friends. While I gathered a variety of herbal teas for her, she added details to Chavat's report.

"The Supremacy is taking slaves," she said, "and using the factories on the worlds they capture to build their own weapons. My grandson in the Ground Forces told me. This Osaga Safa sounds as terrible as Machitew."

I suppressed a shudder.

"My grandson says they need more combat pilots," Macawi went on. "The Solis are desperate for pilots."

"My cousin Hanuk got a pilot's billet," I said. "I'm going to try for one myself when it's my turn. He said you just have to show them your pilot's license."

Gram kept me busy until she closed to go make supper, but I lay awake for some time that night, thinking about where I could spend the next few moons.

I scanned the sleeping room and noticed Kimama cuddled close to Gram on their floorbed. *Can't stay here, thanks to Machitew. Sooner or later I'll put them in danger.*

The recruiters' sign glowing across Aponivi Hotel's dome surfaced in my mind. *Burn! Wish I was closer to twenty.*

Elder Macawi said they're desperate for fighter pilots. Wonder if I could sneak in now instead of waiting? It's only four moons.

The thought kicked my brain to full throttle. My eyes fixed on the smoke-smudged ceiling beams. I'd have to get my birth record and pilot license altered, but there were plenty of crims here who could do it. One of Huk's friends had done it to get into adult nightclubs.

The hard part will be coming up with enough rels. I think it cost Huk's friend about three moons' pay. Maybe Gram will pay me to work for her. Maybe Elder Chavat will hire me, since his workers are gone.

I yawned and rolled over. *I'll worry about it when I find a crim who can do the job.*

* * * * *

Chapter Six

Sometime near midnight, I woke at a grunt near my head. A grunt I'd last heard on the roof of my stepmother's dwelling. I scrambled to sit up, my breath stopping in my chest.

Machitew's spectral mask loomed before me, barely an arm's length away and a little higher than my head. "You can't refuse our combined power forever." His voice rattled like a gusty breeze in Gram's reed window coverings. "It's our duty."

As before, my sight abruptly closed to a view through a mask's eyeholes. I watched myself, knife in hand, splash a nondescript scene with the blood of people I didn't know until gorge burned my throat.

When I lunged for the washroom, and Gram called anxiously after me, the apparition vanished.

Morning found me still unsettled.

"Are you all right, Akuleh?" Gram asked when I came out to breakfast. "You had a restless night."

"Lot on my mind," I said. My stomach lay uneasy under my ribs, but I devoured everything Gram offered. Afterward I told her, "I'm going to ride around for a while and think."

Outdoors, I took my knife from my backpack and slid it into my boot within easy reach before I put on helmet and gloves. I didn't meander. I remembered Hanuk's friend pointing into one of the

47

outer rings that had been added to the enclave. "If you ever need anything official-looking done, the crim down there can do it."

I glided warily up the main lane from Old Trade Center on short repulsor bursts. They whipped grit into stinging spirals, and their brief roars echoed from the close stone walls as I maneuvered carefully among pedestrians and laden float-carts.

The shop stood in a curved alley that stank of urine and rotting garbage, even through my helmet visor's filter. Trash tumbled across the cobbles, scattered by the straddlejet's repulsors.

Goreflies as big as my thumb ricocheted between the rundown structures like rounds from a projectile weapon. Unprotected eyes, mouths, and open wounds attracted goreflies. I'd seen stray animals blinded and cankered by them.

I located the shop by a hand-scrawled sign across its façade that read "Document Services" in Commonwealth Standard.

Dismounting, I surveyed the alley as far as I could, until its curve obstructed my view. Stillness settled like an ambush waiting to happen once I shut off the straddlejet. I glimpsed movement behind a cracked window across the alley. *Somebody watching me.*

Shadowed dimness loomed beyond the shop's open door. I hesitated, holding an internal debate as I tugged off my gloves.

Not sure this is wise, Ku.

How else am I going to pass as conscription eligible?

Drawing a breath of resolve, I popped out my straddlejet's ignition core and activated its shock-shield. No core, no start, and the shock-shield packed enough voltage to hurl a would-be thief across the alley.

I didn't take my helmet off as I approached the murky doorway. The back of my neck prickled.

Goreflies swarmed on a dark smear up the doorpost. The flies reminded me of newborn kosas, the quill-coated rodents, larger than most worlds' street rats, that pilfered family food supplies. The goreflies launched a buzzing whirlwind about my head, smacking into my visor as I drew near. Resisting the urge to fan them away, I said, "Night vision."

I flattened myself to one doorpost to slip inside, both to admit as much light as possible, and to avoid becoming an easy target from the light silhouetting me in the doorway. I also searched the ceiling. People died, my combatives instructor had often told us, because they didn't check overhead when they entered closed spaces.

"Hmph," sounded through the gloom as a tall man, body heat glowing in my night visor, stepped to his counter from a back room. I took off my helmet only when a sweep of the place proved he had no buddies hidden in the corners.

His face appeared sickly pale compared to my own skin, and he slouched as if his bony shoulders couldn't bear the weight of Tempest's gravity. Graying whiskers matted his face, and his lank hair hung as long as mine. "Help you?" he asked in pidgin Chalca.

I advanced cautiously to his counter, thankful for the knife pressing my leg inside my boot. "I want to join the Soliennese Defense Forces," I said in Standard.

The man's extremely bushy eyebrows rose like outstretched wings above his eyes before his gaze fixed on my cut mouth. "Do I look like a recruiter to you?" he asked with such a drawl I could barely understand him.

"No. I need you to fix my records."

He smiled, a mirthless expression that chilled me. "Your birth record?"

"And my pilot's license." I set down my helmet and fished my link from my pocket. It held two fingernail-size drives, snugged in their ports. I saved my documents to one drive, ejected it, and placed it on the counter. "I need to turn twenty tomorrow, and I need them in three days."

"Three days?" He stared as if I'd asked him to wrestle a python tree, but he scraped my drive off the countertop with his dirty nails. "Two docs in three days. That'll cost you your straddlejet." He inclined his head toward the door.

I suppressed surprise. His opening bid. Fine.

"I want them digital, not made of nironnium," I said. "Five hundred rels."

His wild eyebrows lifted as if to take flight, then lowered. "I don't do your haggling thing, boy. Quick-turn work costs extra. I want the straddlejet."

"It's worth more than six documents done overnight."

"How bad do you want them, soldier boy?"

"I can get them done somewhere else." I stuck out my hand.

Eyebrows dropped the drive into my palm and smirked. "Good luck."

I rode to a better part of Old Trade Center, with tidy shops and a lot of pedestrians, before I parked the straddlejet on idle and ran a swift search on my link. Two prominent businesses popped up, both in the main city.

They wouldn't do what I need. They'd probably call law enforcement. The people who'd do it wouldn't be listed.

Cruising through a few more sleazy sectors, I searched for another documents shop. *Eyebrows can't be the only forger sentenced to this rock.*

I even asked a couple men squatting in front of a rundown boarding house and clutching dark bottles. One pointed in the direction from which I'd originally come. "You want Bodeker."

Only echoes of my stepmother calling me Death Bringer spurred me back into the fly-blown alley to that dark shop. I locked my glower on the criminal's smug face as I handed him my drive and snarled, "Get snipped."

He chuckled, his broken teeth bared. "You can't take the straddlejet with you anyway, soldier boy."

Seething, I scooped up my helmet and strode out of the shop. I surveyed the alley while I deactivated the shock-shield, tugged on my helmet and gloves, and pressed the straddlejet's ignition core into its socket. I gunned its repulsors, long and loud, to voice my anger.

I roared up the alley at full throttle, much too fast for the narrow space, and glared behind my visor. *My straddlejet! Reeking kosa.*

The float-cart drifting along the intersecting main lane didn't become visible until it slid across my path. I caught one glimpse of flat shipping cases stacked higher than my head. I just had time to release the throttles and wrench the handlebars hard left. My leg reflexively thrust out to brace the straddlejet from a fall.

It flipped, skidding two or three arm lengths, its steel nosecone shrieking on stone. I clenched my teeth against a yell when its weight rolled onto my leg.

* * * * *

Chapter Seven

With a *crash*, my overturned straddlejet rammed the float-cart. It lurched and rocked. Pinned by my machine, I watched several flat cases fly off the stack to clatter on the cobbles behind me. One narrowly missed my head.

A sharp cry seized my attention. I twisted toward the sound, shoving at the straddlejet. *Rot, I've hurt somebody.*

My left palm throbbed, and my leg burned from hip to calf, but I scrambled out from under my 'jet. Teeth still tight, I levered myself off the stones, tested my weight on my left leg, and winced. Tawny grit coated my whole left side.

People in the main lane squeezed around the float-cart, staring at me with more annoyance than concern about whether I'd been injured.

Two women rushed from behind the cart. Slender off-worlder women, like wildflowers in their fluttery blouses and loose-fitting tan trousers. One appeared a couple years older than me, her brow puckered and lips firm with displeasure. The other I guessed to be in her early forties.

I peeled off my helmet. "I-I'm sorry," I said in Standard. "Are you all right? I heard someone cry out."

The younger woman studied me narrowly over the straddlejet through eyes as dark gray as a rising storm. Her irritation abated, replaced by stern concern. "Are yew quite sure *yew* are a' righ'?"

She spoke Standard with a lilt I knew didn't come from anywhere on Solienne, and her fragrance reinforced my first impression of wildflowers. Her auburn hair had been cut so short, it appeared feathery about her face, and freckles sprinkled her small nose like grains of russet desert sand scattered across pale clay.

"I'm fine," I answered and tried to inconspicuously flex and extend my bruised hand.

She saw it. "Le's see yer hand, then. Glove off."

I worked it loose. It hadn't torn, but embedded gravel studded its leather palm. I held out my hand, blotched with red where the grit had dug in. Seeing it intensified its ache.

She leaned forward to examine it, planting her fists on willowy hips, and I noticed a black brace about her own left wrist and hand. *She's got some injury herself, and she's worried about me?*

Lips pursed once more, but with less exasperation now, it appeared, she eyed my leg, where my shegrul-hide trousers had been scoured white on the cobbles. "Yew'll have a beastly great bruise." Her voice grew as serious as her expression. "Even yer mouth's bruised. Pity I've no healant to put on i'."

Ya, that is *a pity.* My face heated.

At my periphery, passersby muttered together and shook their heads as I dropped to my heels to check the float-cart. I tugged off my other glove to probe the cases the straddlejet had struck. My fingers found dents, but no cracks or breaks.

"I'll pay for whatever I damaged," I said, though my mouth was dry. *Ya, with what, Ku?*

"I should think so, young man." The older woman strode forward, brushing ocher dust from her clothes with slim hands, and scrutinized me. "The least yew can do is poin' us to Amber Cliffs Gallery. I'm to host an exhibition of my paintings, opening tomorrow, but we've met with one trouble after another from the momen' we arrived on yer world, and everyone demands an exorbitant fee to help."

"Were they Chalca?" I asked. "My people?"

The woman's fine eyebrows lowered, intensifying a hawk-like study of me. "I don' believe so. They all looked to be Soli or Sathi to me."

"Ma'am," I said, "you're really lucky you're both safe. Tempest is the Commonwealth's penitentiary. This is where they send the violent criminals."

The older woman paled. The younger one's lips set in a firm line. Her eyes narrowed, and she thumbed the wrist brace where it extended to her forefinger.

"Bu' yew keep the criminals in the deserts, don' yew?" the older woman asked.

"Soli authorities vortex them there, but they don't stay." Eyebrows' glower prickled at the nape of my neck, and I glanced into the alley behind me. "You've got to be really careful."

They stared at me in silence, seeming to melt a little in the gravity and the day's heat.

"You're going the right direction," I said, trying to sound encouraging, and pointed with my chin. "This lane leads to Old Trade Center. The gallery's in a tall, yellow building there. I can tow your floater to it with my straddlejet if you want."

"And how much will yew be wanting to do tha'?" the older woman asked with obvious suspicion.

Indignation stiffened my spine. "Nothing. I'm Chalca, not a crim."

The women exchanged dubious glances. Grimness tightened the younger woman's face. Distrust glinted like sparks of lightning in her storm-cloud eyes.

I collected the fallen cases and hefted them, all at once, onto their float-cart. Trying not to cringe at a twinge through my left shoulder, I righted the straddlejet.

The sight of its raked nosecone prompted a grimace. *Good thing I'm not selling it. I'd be lucky to get a thousand rels for it now. Hope Eyebrows doesn't ask for something else.* I brushed grit from the gouged paint as gently as if from raw wounds before I attached the float-cart to its hitch.

"I'm sorry it doesn't have another seat so one of you can ride," I said. "I'll go slowly so you can keep up. It's only a couple ranges away."

"Ranges?" the older woman questioned, cocking an eyebrow.

"Measure of distance," I said, "like miles and kilometers and leagues on the Commonwealth worlds."

The petal-like sleeves of her pastel blouse seemed to wilt, but the younger woman leveled a warning glare on me that said as plainly as words, *If yew sa much as contemplate making off with those paintings…*

I held the straddlejet to little more than an idle, so it thrummed like a ghost cat's purr, and glanced back often to keep from getting too far ahead of them. When we entered Old Trade Center, I pointed out the yolk-colored building towering like a cliff between the flanking three-level dwellings. The young woman nodded.

They drew up as I parked the straddlejet. The float-cart's repulsors released a tired *whoosh* and a spray of sand when I lowered it before the gallery's double doors.

I stayed to help them unload, trying to conceal a limp as I carried stacked shipping cases into an air-conditioned workroom. They both kept wary eyes on me, as if fearing I might take off with the cases, but the young woman offered a stiff "Thank yew" every time I placed a stack on the curator's table.

Watching them unpack and inspect each painting, I couldn't help fidgeting. The older woman visibly relaxed on finding no damage from the crash, and I allowed myself a breath of relief.

I'd never seen pictures like them before, bright pigments applied to rectangles of cloth pulled tightly over wooden frames. Most of the gallery's displays consisted of sculptures in stone, wood, or bone, decorative pottery of various shapes and sizes, and a few imported holograms with moving digital designs.

Many of this woman's paintings were landscapes. Grassy plains rolling to the feet of rugged mountains, chalk-white cliffs plummeting to gray-green waves, brilliant sunsets casting pink and gold blades of light across palm-treed beaches. Very different from anything I'd seen on Tempest.

I noticed portraits, too, of rosy-faced children with blue or green eyes, pale hair, and colorful clothing.

The gallery staff carried the paintings into the exhibit hall one by one. When the mother followed them, I suppressed a wince and dropped to my heels, facing the daughter across the next case. I helped her lift out the picture it contained. "Let me get it so you don't have to put weight on your wrist."

Mild amusement quirked one corner of her mouth.

"I didn't know people still actually painted," I said. My vision rested on the dusting of freckles across her nose. Chalca girls with their brown complexions didn't have freckles. When I realized I was staring I added, "Most people call me Ku."

"Thank yew, Kew." She seemed a little more at ease, but she said only, "Mother learn' to use oils on canvas because it's a dying medium."

"Where were they painted?" I asked.

"On several worlds along the Lesser Arm." She motioned at a few pieces still leaning against a wall. "Painted on Obolli, tha' one was, and these on Nichi. This was done on Solienne, and those las' on Ardonar."

"Which one's your homeworld?" I asked.

She studied me briefly, as if wondering why I wanted to know, until I feared that asking about someone's homeworld must be taboo among her people. At last she murmured, "Ardonar."

I immediately remembered what Elder Chavat had said about the Supremacy's advance. "Has the war come there?"

Her vision snapped to mine again, laden with a different angst than before. "No' yet, bu' it's coming. Too soon, I fear."

I hesitated, then said, "I'm leaving in a few days to join the Soli Defense Forces and fight the Supremacy. I'm going to be a combat pilot."

A small but genuine smile curved her lips, the first I'd seen from her. "Saints' blessings on yew, Kew."

I had no idea what 'saints' were, but I said, "Thanks."

She returned to her silence, but I longed to hear more of her melodic speech. It danced in my soul like butterflies on desert blossoms, as if to spite her cautious demeanor. *I could listen to her talk forever.* So I asked, "Is your mother going to paint any scenery while you're on Tempest?"

"Per'aps," she said, "if we can find a trustworthy guide to take us into the desert."

"Most of the Territory is flooded right now," I said, "but there are mesas, and the cacti will bloom soon. They're really colorful. I'd offer to take you out in my Darter, but I took a bird strike flying in yesterday. Completely destroyed one engine and damaged another. It'll take a couple phases to repair."

Her eyes widened slightly. "*Yew're* the one we heard tell of. Yew were all the talk at the vortex terminal."

Dismay raised my eyebrows. *Couldn't have been anything good.* I groaned. "About the idiot who—?"

"Oh, no! Everyone said i' was a brillian' landing."

The expression in her eyes assured me she wasn't mocking. I gaped at her while surprise wrestled down pride. "Comes with lots of practice," I said at last, struggling to keep my tone humble. I shrugged. Still, I couldn't help thrusting my chest out a little.

When a tickle at my nape prompted me to glance around, I found her mother watching us. Watching *me*, to be specific. I shifted where I squatted. "Ask about guides at the lodge where you're staying. They'll know the best ones." I pushed myself to my feet.

The daughter's vision followed me. Something about her eyes prompted me to add, "I'll fight for your world, too."

She chuckled. "Thank yew, Kew."

I resisted limping as I started toward the outer doors. As I crossed the foyer, I nodded to her mother, working at a table draped in black cloth as fuzzy as a baby tavo's pelt. She'd been fussing with a multitude of small objects spread on it for the last while. She beckoned.

The table displayed miniature paintings on porcelain, pendants meant to be worn as necklaces on ribbons or chains. Most were of intricate flowers or birds, but I spotted a few portraits among them. One of her daughter caught my eye.

"Please, do choose one," she said, "as paymen' for yer assistance."

"I don't need payment," I said. "It was the right thing to do, especially after I crashed into you."

"To thank yew, then." She motioned insistently.

I took some time to study all of them. I knew which one I really wanted, but I pointed at a pendant of bright flowers. "My grandmother would like this."

The woman scrutinized me long and hard, making my innards squirm at wondering what she might be thinking. She wrapped the oval in crisp paper of rich blue and slipped it into a miniature box.

When she gave me a formal smile as she placed the box in my hand, I knew I'd been dismissed.

* * * * *

Chapter Eight

My vision settled on my straddlejet's clawed finish as I exited the art gallery. Circular gouges described how the machine had pivoted on the cobbles with my knee as its fulcrum.

Eyebrows isn't going to like this. I shuddered at recalling his menacing glower.

I slipped the small box into my trouser pocket, unhitched the float-cart, and thrummed around the plaza's perimeter to Gram's apothecary. The heat had begun to ease for the day, and the noise and dust stirred by people moving about had begun to settle. I locked the straddlejet into its stand near the door before I strode inside.

"So, Akuleh," Gram said on seeing me, "did you get all your thinking done?"

"Ya." I sighed. *What'll she say when I tell her I'm entering the military early?*

Quick pats of small feet across the stone floor drew my attention. Kimama raced up the aisle, her hands outstretched. "Ku!" She flung her arms around my legs. "Where've you been?"

I flinched when she squeezed the bruised one.

"Akuleh," Gram said, "how did you injure your leg?"

She'd started calling me Akuleh, Chalca for Looks Up, when she'd found me gazing skyward with rapt attention the day after my birth. My father had called me Only Son and Long-Awaited, but Looks Up had stuck. Gram never called me Ku.

I should've known I couldn't hide my limp from her, but I tried to make a joke of it. "Two off-worlder women took out my straddlejet with an out-of-control float-cart." I told her about the incident, described the paintings and how I'd stayed to help, and fished the small box from my pocket. "This is for you, Gram."

She opened the box and lifted it to the sunlight to study the pendant inside. "Those are rosellas from Solienne. The petals are used for a tea to soothe strong emotions. Thank you, Akuleh." She tucked the box carefully into her skirt pocket, then pressed her little pot of python-oil salve into my hand. "Use this on your bruised leg."

Kimama returned to her yarn dolls in the back corner, and I began setting out narrow bottles of spices on a top shelf. I didn't lead up to my announcement, just said straight out, "I'm going to enter the military now, Gram."

She peered at me. "You're not twenty summers yet."

"Only by four moons. They'll waive that." I said it with more hope than certainty. "Yesterday Elder Macawi said they're desperate for fighter pilots."

Gram faced me directly. "The Ancient Ones have set a Path for you, Akuleh. It's best to walk the Path you're given."

Ya, Machitew the Death Bringer. I squelched a shudder. "I'm not ready for that."

"No, you're not," she agreed. "Not yet. It will require a great deal of preparation."

To become Machitew? I doubt it. I scrunched my brows.

After a pause, she said, "There's not enough time to hold a Going-to-War Ceremony for you."

I remembered the ceremony for Hanuk and the others from Red Wash before they left, dancing by firelight with ancient shields and spears, and blessings pronounced by the chanters.

"I'll be fine without it," I said.

"It petitions the Ancients to bless you with courage and protection."

I grunted. The Ancients wouldn't give a bean for me.

With the spices shelved, I unpacked a wooden box containing jars of golden honey from local cactus blossoms.

Gram closed shop for the day when I finished. I didn't talk while we ate supper. Unless Gram or Kimama spoke to me, I kept busy scooping in black-bean soup, maize bread sticky with some of the local honey, and tangy red fruit from a container with a Sathi label.

After supper and washing, I climbed to Gram's roof and drew my link from my pocket. *Haven't had a vid from Huk for a while. Even a scrip. Need to let him know I'm coming.*

A vid of Hanuk's grinning face appeared when I tapped his call code. "Things are really intense right now," he said in his message. "Leave a message, and I'll call you when I graduate."

"Ai, Huk! I'm on my way," I said into my link's voice pickup. "Maybe we'll see each other before then."

* * *

The echoing ring of mallets driving tent stakes woke me the next morning, along with cheerful voices calling across the plaza. I visualized the traders' hide tents rising like bulky animals clambering to their feet.

Market days. Haven't been here for that in a long time.

Anticipation awakened me fully, along with a dim idea. One of the out-of-town traders might know a reputable guide for the artist and her daughter. Maybe I could ask around for them. Then I could introduce them.

I stifled a snort. As if they'd want me showing up again, the sheg-brain who'd slammed their float-cart.

Still, I saved them from steering their cart through crim-infested alleys. Crims usually leave off-worlders alone when they have Chalca escorts. Maybe that counts for something.

Maybe.

I felt surprised at how much I wanted to see those storm-gray eyes again. And those freckles.

I don't even know her name.

Maybe I can show her around the market here on the plaza and we can try some of the food venders. No big deal.

Then what? My mind went blank, and my stomach flip-flopped under my ribs. *This is new territory. Completely new.*

In the washroom, I pumped chilly water into Gram's metal trough of a bathtub. I scrubbed thoroughly in spite of the bruises and pulled on my spare trousers. Shuffling out to the gathering room with a fresh shirt slung over my shoulder, I tried not to think about the artist's daughter.

The roasted-grain scent of strong kasse, mingled with aromas of smoked shegrul bacon and eggs scrambled with chilies, brought moisture to my mouth.

Gram peeked around from scrambling the eggs and paused in her traditional grateful cooking song. "How is your leg this morning, Akuleh?"

"Better." I shrugged into my shirt and raked my fingers through my damp hair before binding it. "The salve helped."

Gram took a pottery bowl from the shelf near her head and scooped a slab of bacon and a mound of scrambled eggs into it. "There are more pimiberries, too."

I eased myself to the nearest sitting rug. Under her stern eye, I rattled through a brief gratitude chant before wolfing all the food she offered me.

A short time later, I strolled onto the plaza. Parked beyond the booths and awning-shaded displays stood a heavy hauler with tracks that appeared rugged enough to take on the open desert. Stacked bundles of small logs filled its shell. Firewood for people like Gram, mostly elders who wanted to maintain the old ways as much as they could in the modernizing world.

I had tried once to talk her into changing. "Firewood is so expensive, Gram. The woodcutters have to travel long distances into mountains and crim-infested areas to find dead trees to harvest. You have better power here in the city than we do at Red Wash."

Gram had smiled and patted my arm. "I can afford the wood, Akuleh. I use solar power from the dome to heat water and light my shop, but I don't like how food cooks in those modern stoves, and a fire on the hearth invites the peaceful spirits who guard the home."

Gram didn't need firewood today. I shook my head, smiling dimly at the memory, and approached Amber Cliffs Gallery. Its marquee, set above the double doors and filled with illuminated Standard characters, snagged my attention.

AN EXHIBITION OF TRADITIONAL OIL PAINTINGS BY

MADAM FENELE GRAEBEL, ARTIST LAUREATE OF ARDONAR

One name problem solved. Would've been awkward to just ask for the artist and her daughter. I puffed a relieved breath as I pressed the bell beside the door.

Committed, my nerves caught up with me. I bounced on the balls of my feet until a surprised employee partially opened one door.

"The gallery doesn't open for another sun position," he informed me.

"Is Madam Graebel here yet?" I asked. "You can tell her it's Ku."

He raised an eyebrow, but ushered me into the foyer and disappeared into the exhibit hall. I studied a display of local pottery while I waited.

Sharp footfalls on the smoothed stone alerted me to Madam Graebel striding briskly across the foyer. Her glower radiated an unmistakable warning.

I swallowed. *Did they find damaged paintings after I left?*

Before I could speak, she demanded, "Wha' do yew mean by calling on my Derry so early in the morning, young man?"

Her name's Derry. I locked it in my mind as I stepped back. "It's market time on the plaza, ma'am. I thought your daughter might like to see it." I added, "Maybe we can find a guide, if you want to paint desert scenes."

Madam Graebel's stare burned into mine as if assessing me once more, her lips not pursed, but as firm as her daughter's had been the day before.

"I'm not a crim," I reminded her.

"No, but yew're a boy," she said. "Trouble enough, tha' is, when yew've an attractive daughter."

Derry emerged from the exhibit hall and stopped abruptly at the threshold into the foyer. "Mum?"

I offered her the kindest smile I could manage and waited.

Madam Graebel spoke without shifting her fierce gaze from me. "The young man's come to ask if yew've a mind to see the market with him today."

Derry eyed me as long and deeply as her mother before she crossed the foyer, radiating her floral fragrance. An emotion darker than shyness shadowed her eyes.

"Is something wrong?" I asked.

"Yer dratted gravity," she said, still watching me. "It's verra wearing."

"We won't leave the plaza," I said. "We can take it easy and rest, and come back when you want to."

"Stay in the plaza?" She considered for a moment. "A' righ' then." She glanced at her mother and stroked her brace with her thumb as she'd done the day before. "It'll be fine, Mum."

Nervous habit, or does her wrist ache? I wondered.

Some of the traders had barely finished raising their hide awnings and laying out their wares on tables and display racks when we stepped from the gallery.

Derry kept an arm's length from me as we strolled, well outside normal personal space for my people, but one glimpse of her set expression kept me from sliding into hers. I noticed her alertness, how her vision darted about the market. *Wonder if she's had combatives training, too?*

Interest lit her eyes when she spotted a stall draped with bright blankets. The weaver, busy threading a loom of small logs worn with grooves from years of use, beckoned to us. "Take the blankets down and handle them. The heavy ones are rugs."

Derry stroked the nearest ones and deftly fingered their tight weave. "Is this wool?"

"Cotton," I said. "My ancestors found it growing wild when they came to Tempest. Some people grow it near their enclaves, where there's enough level ground. During winter, when it's dark and there's too much snow to go outside, they spin it into thread and yarn and dye it."

"By hand?" She appeared incredulous.

"With hand-held spindles."

She unfolded one blanket to study its pattern of reds and oranges and yellows, like a sunset mirrored in a lake. "How do they ge' such brillian' colors?"

"They make dyes from roots and berries and stuff. I don't know which ones, but my grandmother would."

"Does yer family grow cotton?"

"No, we raise shegruls. They're our main source of meat and leather." I craned around for a minute, searching the nearest market stalls, and pointed with my chin. "Leather goods are over there."

The luxurious scent of skillfully tanned leather greeted us as we approached a nearby booth. Its tables displayed shoes, boots, belts, and pouches, including some made of askuk skin that still bore ridged scales. The pouches and belts had been dyed various colors and decorated with intricate tooling. Only the rugged work trousers remained the murky gray of natural shegrul hide.

"Live shegruls don't smell good," I said. I described their size and shape and galumphing stride, providing animation with my hands. Derry appeared cautiously amused.

That prompted a desire to make her laugh. I gave her a sheepish expression. "My cousin Hanuk and I tried to ride them when we were little."

"Tried?" Derry arched an eyebrow. "Yew didn' succeed?"

"We kept sliding off their rumps."

A hesitant smile touched her lips, and I explained, "Their skins ripple when they move, and they sort of rolled us off."

Derry studied me for several seconds, as if imagining me at the age of six sliding off a shegrul's backside. At last she chuckled, and some of the tautness left her frame.

I felt giddy.

"Ponies don' do tha'," she said, "bu' sometimes they scrape their riders off under low tree branches."

"What are ponies?" I asked.

"Small riding animals for children," she said. "Yew don' have horses or ponies or kaluçes here?"

"No. I've heard of horses and some riding animals from other worlds, but not ponies."

"Small horses, they are," Derry said, and held a hand at waist height. "Mine was dapple gray with a black mane and tail. We bought him on Satha, and I roamed our mountains on him in summer."

We resumed venturing through the traders' tents, with me conscientiously maintaining her preferred distance.

Studying the increasing crowds milling around us, Derry asked, "D'yew live here in the city, then?"

"No, I'm from the Territory." Keeping my own eyes on the bustle as well, I described the russet rock and sand, the stone-and-adobe enclave, the withering, endless daylight and heat of summer, the darkness and enclave-burying snowdrifts of winter.

"Yew'll miss i' when you leave," she said.

I hesitated. To my surprise, I realized I would. "Yes, but I won't miss mucking out the shegrul barn." I grinned. "Do you miss Ardonar?"

"Of course." Her stormy gaze never stopped sweeping the market. "I miss the smell of the sea, and the pines growing on the rocky crags, and the grea', sloping moors. Bu' it's good to travel with Mum sometimes, and have a peek a' other worlds and other people's lives."

A display of items carved from stone and arranged on rugs caught Derry's eye, and she knelt to examine several pieces. I stood back to scan the plaza while I waited for her, listening to the rise and fall of voices haggling around me.

A whiff of wood smoke told me there'd soon be food to buy, as well. I squinted skyward and glimpsed tendrils curling like thin ghosts toward the dome's fanned vents.

"Kew?"

I pivoted to find Derry pointing at a deep vessel about the size of a head. The lamp had been shaped and polished from semi-translucent milkstone into a fanciful version of the razor-petaled desert raincup. With a candle or oil-wick lit inside, it would radiate a glow like a full moon.

"Lovely, i' is," she said, enchantment lighting her face. "How do yew say i' in Chalca, and how much does he want for i'?"

Another opportunity to impress her. I grinned. "Would you like me to do the haggling for you?"

Her eyes widened in apparent gratitude, and I noticed her long lashes. "Yes, please. Tha' isn' how we do i' a' home."

I motioned to the trader and indicated the lamp. "I'll give you thirty rels for that." I spoke in Standard for Derry's benefit. Normally I did my trading in Chalca.

The merchant spoke Standard, too. "Thirty? That's an insult to my craftsmanship. You won't find another lamp this beautiful anywhere in the market. Ninety-five rels."

"It's pretty to look at," I said, "but it'll probably crack the first time she lights a candle in it." I indicated Derry. "Thirty-five."

The trader shook his gray-streaked head. "I can't even get a raw chunk of milkstone this size for thirty-five. Then there's all the days of labor I put into it. Ninety rels or leave it."

"Fine. We'll go somewhere else." I turned my back as if to leave.

"All right, all right," the merchant called from behind me and waved his hands. "Eighty rels."

We took nine or ten minutes to settle on sixty-two rels. We shouted and gestured vehemently along the way, and got nose-to-nose at one point.

"Done," the trader said at last, "and I'll add a jar of oil to burn in it." He placed the jar in the lamp's hollow.

I slid a triumphant smile at Derry.

It dissolved when I met her wide eyes. Her expression revealed embarrassment for my supposed obnoxiousness. I'd seen the same reaction from other off-worlders in the market.

Should've expected that. We sound like a kosa fight when we really get going.

The stoneworker must have seen Derry's shock as well because he chuckled. "You just saw two experts at work, young woman. It's like a competition, except we both win. I made a nice profit, and he got a very good deal." He nodded to me. "Come and barter with me any time, Akuleh."

I returned his grin. "Thanks, Elder."

Derry let out a breath and counted rel coins into the man's hand. She regarded me closely, though, when we resumed our stroll, and she slightly widened the personal space that had begun to gradually decrease between us.

Minutes later, a different movement caught my eye. I spotted one-eyed Demothi wending through the maze of tents, shuffling steadily toward us.

He had always seemed a couple centuries old to me, like a storm-blasted tree. Or maybe a scarecrow, with hair as grizzled as a bird's nest, and waving skinny limbs draped in an overlong shirt. No one knew how he'd lost his right eye, but a dozen tales drifted around the city.

"The time of greatest danger is coming!" he wailed in Chalca. His reedy voice cut through the market noise, and Derry's attention fixed on him. She fingered her wrist brace.

People edged away, repugnance etched on their faces, as he made his uncertain way among the merchants' stalls. He seemed complete-ly unaware of them.

"It will come from among our people," he shrilled, "when one brother makes war against another. It will consume our world, and Wanikiya will battle Machitew for the souls of the people."

His rant never changed. He'd been in the market, shouting about the time of greatest danger and the war between Machitew and Wanikiya, the first time my father had brought me to stay with Gram when I was five.

Demothi abruptly broke off and stopped waving his arms when his protuberant eye found me. He hobbled directly toward me, exuding his unwashed odor, and poked me in the chest with his withered twig of a finger. I drew myself up, trying to project defiance, but he kept scrutinizing me. He dropped his voice to a rasp, still in Chalca. "I know who you are. I know what you will become."

Everybody near enough to hear him stared at me, including Derry. My heart seemed to freeze. I smirked to make a joke of it, for my own sake as much as for the onlookers. "What will I become?"

"The Ancient Ones have set a hard Path for you," he said.

"What Path?" I demanded. *Come on, tell me to my face. Tell everybody in the market I'm Machitew.*

He didn't answer. Instead, he swung about to study Derry. His mouth cinched like a drawstring bag for endless seconds before he said in a hoarse whisper, "The white bird."

The white bird?

Derry had stiffened, her jaw set, eyes narrowed in warning, her left hand positioned as if in a combat stance with her thumb pressed to her brace. Her right hand clutched the stone lamp like a shield.

Not sure what's going on here, but I think we should leave.

"Come on, Derry," I said, and slipped an arm about her shoulders to steer her clear.

She wrenched free and whirled to face me. "Ge' off me!" she hissed through her teeth. Lightning flashed in her stormy eyes. A short blade glinted in her left hand.

I sprang backward under the stares of a dozen startled traders, my hands raised and open in a non-threatening manner. "I'm sorry,

I'm sorry! I was just trying to get you away from him." I glared at Demothi over her shoulder.

After an eternal minute, the flame in Derry's eyes subsided, though the heat remained, banked coals prepared to flare again if fanned. She lowered her blade, but didn't sheath it. "I know," she said, jaw taut. Her breaths still came too forcefully. She slipped a wary glance behind her. "Bu' when yew…"

Her words trailed off. More seconds crept past before she retracted her blade into its wrist sheath with a *snick*.

"Are you all right?" I asked. I stayed a couple arm lengths clear of her.

She gave a stiff nod. "Le's ge' away from here."

Resuming my place at one arm's length from her, I pointed the way out of the crowd.

With the busiest area behind us, Derry asked, "Who is tha' smelly old man? Whatever was tha' abou'?"

"Crazy hermit who wandered in from the desert. He's been around since I was little." I forced bravery into my voice and tried to smile, though Demothi's taunt echoed in my ears. "My cousin Hanuk calls him the Voice of Perpetual Doom."

Some of the tension left Derry's frame.

"Would you like to go back to the gallery now?" I asked.

She didn't reply at once. She stood stroking her wrist sheath with her thumb while she drew several steadying breaths. At last she said with surprising firmness, "I'm a' righ'."

"You're sure?"

"Aye, I am."

"Want to get something to eat?"

"A' righ', then."

I guided her to a spacious tent full of baked goods. Warm aromas of honey and spices and cooking maize bread enveloped us when we entered.

My gaze fell on a tray of pinion pastries. "These," I said, "are my favorite. They're stuffed with honey and dried fruit and pinion nuts from the desert. We call them awanatas, the Chalca name for the reptiles you call tortoises, because of the maize shell around the filling."

I chose some awanatas from the tray, and the rotund woman behind the table slid them onto sheets of brown paper. I paid with a transfer from my link, and we found an unoccupied sitting rug inside the tent on which to eat, a rug woven with vivid figures of desert animals.

We sat facing each other, the papers laden with awanatas spread between us. Derry kept her gaze downcast, her features grave as she nibbled an awanata.

"Are you sure you're all right?" I asked.

Her eyes flicked to meet mine. "I though' I was," she said, "bu' some things…" I watched her try to suppress a shiver despite the early summer heat.

"What do you mean?"

Her vision locked on me. She studied me for a full minute before she dropped her gaze and said with bitter but determined firmness, "If yew mus' know, Kew, when I was fifteen and verra naïve, a schoolmate took a fancy to me. He was two years ahead of me, and quite handsome, the boy every girl in school dreamed abou'. We'd go ou' walking, and he'd pu' his arm 'round my shoulders."

Grimness in her tone warned me what was coming. I listened in rising horror, aching to tell her she could stop, but I couldn't unclench my teeth.

She lifted her face, and her jaw hardened once more. Furious sparks returned to her eyes when she leveled them on me. "Then one nigh' he raped me, in the forest on the school grounds."

Though I'd already guessed it, something slammed into my solar plexus like a heavy fist. I recoiled, stared. Some beast, some inner ghost cat, or maybe an askuk, reared to her defense in my soul, fangs bared.

Derry doubtless witnessed my shock, but she pressed on, as if she'd set something in motion that couldn't be stopped until she finished. Her accent became more pronounced. "When I fough' him and called out for help, he tried to strangle me. I survived only because I passed ou' and he though' he'd finished the job.

"I gave birth to his child a' the age of sixteen. Mum adopted him. She's bringing him up as my little brother Donnol."

Derry's gaze returned to her lap, her expression heavy with obvious shame. Her voice grew grim when she spoke again. "Mum and Da go' me help straightaway and stood with me through the trial. I' was the most humiliating thing I've ever endured, bu' the attacker's rotting in prison now." Her features remained hard. "I though' I'd deal' with it, bu' when yew put yer arm..." She visibly shuddered. "Some things still cause flashbacks."

"I'm sorry." I croaked the words and grimaced at how hollow they sounded. "I won't do it again."

She shrugged. "Yew didn' know."

Silence drifted between us for a couple minutes. Finally I said, "If you didn't already have your own knife, I'd give you mine." I indicated my boot. I hesitated before I asked, "Can I have another look at yours?"

Angling her arm to avoid slicing either of us, she flicked the tiny lever on her wrist brace to catapult the grip of a blade three thumb lengths long into her palm.

I couldn't prevent an appreciative, "That's killer!"

Derry extended her hand, and I leaned closer. She released and retracted the blade a couple times, let me test its edge with my thumb, and try its grip.

"Too small for my hand," I said, "but perfect for yours. Show me how you hold it."

She demonstrated a few grips, for thrusting, for slashing.

"Does the brace impede your wrist movement?" I asked. "You need to have full flexibility for your wrist."

"No, it's sof', this par'." She flexed, extended, and rotated her hand.

"Good. Very important." I smiled. "I'd offer to spar with you, give you some practice, but—" I stopped. *Too much, Ku.*

She returned a tight smile. "Yew bes' believe I know how to use i'. Da made sure of tha' when he go' i' for me."

"Good," I repeated and squelched mild disappointment.

A couple heartbeats later, she surprised me with, "Tomorrow, per'aps? Yer gravity's taking a toll today."

Only then did I notice the fatigue in her eyes. She wrapped the rest of her awanatas in the paper, and I escorted her to the art gallery.

"Tomorrow?" I asked from the threshold.

Once more she regarded me for several seconds through those stormy eyes. Her expression remained cautious, but no longer so distrustful. "Aye," she said. "Tomorrow."

* * * * *

Chapter Nine

*O*ne more day until I have to leave. The thought made me pause in my poking through the storage room behind Gram's shop. My stomach tightened around my breakfast. Anticipation mingled with nervousness, and I huffed out a breath. *I'll get conscripted next quarter for sure, even if I don't go now.*

I resumed my search. *Know I left some practice blades in here somewhere.*

At last I found the tarp bag, coated with dust and hanging from a peg in a dim corner behind strings of various drying herbs. It contained several wooden daggers, half a span long with blunt points, but thoroughly nicked from use.

Carrying the bag and a couple bulging waterskins, I sauntered toward the marketplace. I scoured it for Demothi. His staring eye, pointing finger, and raspy declaration haunted me.

How does he know I'm Machitew, and what did he mean about Derry being a white bird? Her white skin?

Demothi hadn't returned, but I spotted a man who could've been Eyebrow's brother lurking in the shadow of a knifemaker's tent. I kept an eye on him while I strolled among the booths. *If he's here because of me and the straddlejet, I'm not leading him to Derry. He doesn't need to know about her. Reeking kosa.*

I didn't go anywhere near Amber Cliffs Gallery until the crim left the plaza.

"Good morning to yew, Kew," Derry greeted me when I came into the foyer. Both she and her mother seemed more at ease than the day before, if not openly cheerful on her mother's part.

"Ready for some sparring?" I asked.

An impish light touched her eyes. "Are yew sure yew're ready?"

We found a group of young people performing combatives drills in an open area beyond the market tents. Most practiced grappling rather than working with blades.

Derry eyed them briefly. "Yer people take i' seriously, their defense training."

"Have to on a penitentiary planet," I said.

As we assumed combat stances, wooden blades in hand, I realized aloud, "I've never done this with a lefty before."

Derry grinned. "Maybe I'll be teaching yew a few things, then. It'll be good practice for facing a left-handed enemy."

"So c'mon." I beckoned—and narrowly blocked a swift slash meant for my eyebrow that came from the wrong direction. *Yi!*

With my next heartbeat, I thought, *Good. Blinding your assailant with his own blood usually stops him long enough for you to escape.* I recalled the first rule of combatives. Never use more force than necessary.

Derry deftly slid her blade off mine and thrust at my midsection. I parried and countered with a slice at her throat. She shunted it neatly aside. She never succumbed to my attempts to distract her, but kept her eye on my knife hand, and she moved more easily than I'd expected for an off-worlder.

Half a sun position later, I tossed a waterskin to her. Sweat stuck damp hair to our faces, and we both panted, though Derry's breathing came with more effort than mine.

"Your father taught you all that?" I asked between gulps from my waterskin. "Is he a soldier?"

She took a swallow from her own, then chuckled. "No, he's at Banch'ry University. Professor Garnan Kerk." Her smile grew sly. "He teaches Ancien' Warfare and Weapons in the College of History."

"With a practical application?" I teased. *I could spar with her all day.*

She smiled, tipped her head back for another drink, and my heart clenched when I spotted a long, pale scar running beneath her jaw.

From that demon's attempt to strangle her? What did he use to wound her like that? My grin died, and my hand tightened on my wooden dagger.

Later, with the gravity wearing at her again, we settled on a rug in another food vendor's tent. Between eating circles of flat maize bread folded around smoked shegrul, homemade goat cheese, and seasoned black beans, we drifted into an exchange of language lessons.

"What's your birth language?" I asked after I'd told her the names of a dozen nearby objects in Chalca.

"Caerdish," she said. "It's one of the mos' ancien' languages on Ardonar."

"Why are you called Derry?" I teased, "Do you milk your family's cows?"

"No, silly!" She laughed, a sound as musical as freshets of snowmelt splashing through Red Wash in early spring. "Tha's 'dairy.' My name is 'Derry.'" She pronounced it with a rolling burr my tongue couldn't master even after several tries.

"Does it have a meaning?" I asked and told her how I'd come to be called Akuleh.

"No." She rolled her eyes. "My eccentric mother named me for a village she made a painting of, a landscape, yew know, afore I was born. The village's proper name is Donnolderry. My... 'little brother' got the Donnol par'."

She scrunched her brow. "I believe she brough' the painting for the exhibition. Would yew like to see i'?"

"Sure." *I'd like to see anything that has to do with you.*

We gathered the remnants of our meal and made our way to the gallery.

Minutes later, standing before a framed landscape of a thatched village seen from a green hillside, Derry said, "Mum says i' was the mos' charming hamlet she'd ever seen."

With my next breath I heard myself say, "You're the most charming girl I've ever seen."

Derry eyed me for a space, her expression questioning. "Yew find a girl who wields a knife charming?"

"Yes." My face felt as if I'd stuck it in Gram's oven, but I answered firmly, and sent my mind scrambling for my next words. "All Chalca girls can use knives, but you made sparring look like a spring feast dance."

She continued to study me, head cocked, probably wondering if I was making fun of her, before her features softened. "Tha's verra kind of you, Kew."

The heat in my face promptly intensified.

* * *

After supper, dreading what I had to do, I played tickle-tag with Kimama. At last her squeals left her breathless, and I snugged her in my lap, my arms tight about her. "I have to tell you something, Butterfly."

She twisted to peer at me, clearly startled by my abruptly serious mood. "What, Ku?"

"I have to go away in the morning."

"Go away?" Her eyes grew round. "Why? To where?"

"So you'll be safe," I said. "You can stay here with Gram."

InterClan law gave abused children some choice in their guardians, if the potential guardian agreed, and had the means to provide for them.

I concluded, "I'm going to Solienne to become a fighter pilot like Huk."

Her face clouded, and she wrapped her arms about my neck. "Huk hasn't come back. Will you?"

I hesitated. "When I can." I drew my image plate from my pocket, touched on the video she'd found, and forced a smile as I put the plate in her hands. "Now you won't forget what I look like while I'm gone."

Sometime in the night I woke to find her gripping my fingers in her sleep, her arm stretched across from Gram's floorbed, as if to keep me from leaving.

I lay awake for a while after that. *I'll have to say good-bye to Derry tomorrow, too. Burn.* I imagined taking her in my arms, stroking her hair, pressing my mouth to hers. *I've never seriously kissed a girl before. Is it too soon to think about kissing her?*

My dreams, when I slept once more, didn't include Derry. I faced Eyebrows across his scarred counter. He waved my document drive in my face, and seven or eight thugs materialized out of rancid air, white and shrunken mummies with whiskered visages.

My heart rate accelerated. I gauged their locations and distances and shifted my knife in my damp hand. I assumed a combat stance, my feet wide apart, my left arm positioned to block.

The thugs surrounded me, their blades bared.

I woke sitting rigid in my tangled blankets. *How does it end? I didn't see how it ends.*

I never slept again before dawn, but I got up well after Gram and Kimama. My hands still quivered as if from receding adrenaline.

They had already eaten breakfast by the time I entered the gathering room. I forced myself to eat. Gram eyed me closely while I downed a couple bowls of maize porridge and half a slab of shegrul bacon.

After breakfast, I rolled up my clothes, dirty and clean, and stuffed them into my backpack. Gram and Kimama went downstairs to open the shop, and I followed a few minutes later, shouldering my pack.

I paused by her front counter. "I have to report to the recruiters today, but if it's the same as when Huk went, we won't leave for Solienne until tomorrow." My stomach tightened a little at the thought.

Gram nodded. "Tell me what time, and we'll come to the terminal to see you."

"Thanks, Gram." I gave her a strong hug, then swung Kimama up off her feet. "You'd better come to the terminal, too."

She clung to my neck and whimpered. "I don't want you to go, Ku."

"I have to, Butterfly. I'm sorry. I'll vid you as often as I can."

"Why do you have to go *now?*" she asked.

I sighed. Considered. Finally, I settled for, "Because of what your mother thinks about me. It wouldn't be good for you if I stayed."

I knew by her puzzled face that she didn't understand, but I couldn't say anything else. She watched, pouting, as I released the straddlejet from its stand. Keeping my eyes averted from her and the straddlejet's scraped finish, I skirted the closed market tents on the way to Amber Cliffs Gallery at a near idle.

The same staffer as before admitted me when I rang the bell, and I stood fidgeting in the foyer.

Derry stepped out of the office, a genuine smile lighting her face. "Hello, Kew."

My mouth dried out. Dust dry. "I have to go now," I said, "to report to the recruiters." I took a breath, and the words I'd put together in my mind spilled unchecked. "We'll probably never see each other again, but I meant what I said yesterday. About you being charming, I mean. I forgot to say how beautiful you are."

I shut up and opened my arms, feeling completely awkward.

"Yew're so sweet, Kew," Derry said. Her eyes and voice carried concern. "Please, do be safe."

She reached into a trouser pocket before she drew closer, though not into my embrace, and took my hands. She placed a tiny box in my palm, like the one in which her mother had wrapped the pendant for Gram, and gazed into my face. Her floral fragrance wafted about us like a springtime meadow. "Go on and open i', then."

I fumbled the lid off and pushed the crisp paper aside. My eyes widened when I recognized the oval among the blue folds, the portrait of Derry I'd noticed the first day.

"Something to remember me by," she said, and her face grew rosy. "Mum painted i' for my birthday a few months ago, when I reached twenty."

"This will always be a treasure to me," I said when I found my voice.

She paused briefly, her face betraying conflict, before she leaned in to press a quick kiss to my cheek, very close to my mouth. She blushed again, offered another shy smile, and squeezed my hand. "Blessings be upon yew."

I nodded, unable to find appropriate words, and keenly aware I couldn't have spoken them if I had. My fingers maintained their touch with hers as long as they could when I turned away.

The warmth where her lips had met my cheek lingered when I left the gallery. My boots seemed not to touch the cobblestones as I pushed the tiny box deep into my front pocket and crossed to my straddlejet.

Demothi stood waving and ranting, a demented stickman planted on the far side of the plaza. I circled a group of women and children, putting them between him and me as I steered the straddlejet into the high-walled lane and thrummed my way carefully through it.

By the time I reached the trash-strewn alley, I'd cleared my mind of everything but the coming encounter with Eyebrows. I scrunched my nose at the sour odors rising on the heat-shivered air as I surveyed the empty passage with its shadowy structures. Alert to any movement in the area, I parked the straddlejet and popped its ignition core.

I shrugged my pack off and slung it loose on one shoulder. *If this ends in a fight…*

The knife in my boot lay reassuringly cool against my calf as I strode to the dark door. Recalling my dream, I scanned the brick walls and ceiling for thermal glows before removing my helmet.

Eyebrows stood behind his dusty counter. "So, soldier boy," he said. He fumbled under the warped board and slapped my document drive onto it. "Here you go. Where's the straddlejet core?"

"Not until I look at this." I snatched the drive before he could stop me and plugged it into my link. Tapped my ID code and opened one document, then the other on my link's display.

Keeping half my attention on my surroundings, I scrutinized both documents in detail. Eyebrows had done a meticulous job of slipping new dates into the originals.

He'd created a third document as well, a bill of sale. My straddlejet to him in exchange for services rendered. I scowled as I read it, but at last I said, "Fine," pocketed my link, and set the ignition core on the counter.

"And the helmet." Eyebrows waggled his fingers in a summoning motion.

"That wasn't in the deal," I said.

His stare hardened. "Neither was you ripping up the nose of *my* machine."

I froze, questioning him through narrowed eyes. I knew the answer before the other crim appeared through the doorway behind Eyebrows and joined him at the counter. The man I'd seen at the knife dealer's stall in the market.

I'd have no use for the helmet without the straddlejet. I grudgingly set it on the counter. "Satisfied?"

Eyebrows smirked. "Nice doing business with you."

Shooting a glower at him, I wheeled toward the door.

Outside, I swiped at a dozen goreflies that closed in on my face while I paused to survey the curved passage.

The main lane lay half a range away. It seemed a much longer distance on foot than it had on the straddlejet.

Half the ramshackle buildings along the alley stood vacant, their doors hanging open or completely gone. Ideal concealment from which to track unwary intruders.

My combatives training kicked in. *What do I do if I get jumped? What if I'm jumped by more than one of them?*

* * * * *

Chapter Ten

In combatives instruction, we'd trained for every possible scenario. A lot. *That was training. Now comes the test.*

I allowed myself one last appreciative study of the straddlejet's streamlined contours as I strode past it up the alley. I didn't glance back.

Setting an easy, confident pace, I constantly scanned my surroundings and listened for telltale sounds behind me. When the first crim swaggered out from under a sagging porch at my left, his boot scuffing on grit, he didn't take me by surprise.

In the next second five, six, seven more shapes appeared from decrepit buildings on both sides of the alley. Sinewy, pale thugs brandishing knives. They surrounded me as if to block my escape.

Like my dream.

I sized them up. Every one of them stood a head taller than me. Most off-worlders did, but my muscular build gave me the weight advantage. Born into Tempest's high gravity, I moved easily. I immediately picked out the newest arrivals among them because they slogged as if dragging chains.

The first man, scabby faced and slow on his feet, planted himself in front of me. "Looks like Bodeker got that nice straddlejet," he drawled, "so an'thing else you still gots in the backpack."

"Pretty much," I said. "Spare shirt, worn underwear…" To my relief, my voice sounded casual, relaxed. I noted the others' positions through the corners of my eyes and added, "But you'll have to come and take it."

The scabby crim charged, his knife flashing in his hand.

Letting my pack slide from my left shoulder to my hand, I dropped to one knee and thrust the pack upward to deflect the blade. It swished over my head.

I whipped my knife from my boot and lunged to my feet in one motion. My blade caught Scabby's forearm on his backslash, and he yelled and stumbled. I drove my knee into the nerve inside his thigh, and he dropped like a bag of maize, raising a dust cloud.

The others all closed at once, the two least adapted ones showing reluctance with their tightened jaws.

I swung my backpack like a bulky club, swiping three or four faces with enough force to make their owners stagger, before I slammed the pack into the last one's chest. Clearly a recent addition to the gang, his center of gravity threw him. He toppled backward, clutching at my pack to save himself, and struck the dirt with an "Oof!"

Two thugs more acclimated to Tempest remained between me and the open alley. I drove my fist into the solar plexus of the one at my right. Something grazed my arm as I drove my knee up into the other one's groin, hard enough to lift him off his feet. He crumpled face down at my feet, puking. I trod on his back as I lunged for the passage's mouth.

In another second, shouts rang behind me.

Are they going to start shooting? I didn't wait to find out. Ducking and dodging and sweating in the heat, I sprinted half a range to the intersecting lane.

A few arm lengths from where I'd met Derry.

A public transit stop with a restroom hunkered across the lane from the alley. Two shabby men and a woman, their faces gray with exhaustion, eyed me with alarm, and I realized I still gripped my knife in my hand.

"Sorry," I panted. I wiped it on my trouser leg and slid it into my boot.

The outside of my right forearm burned. I pushed up my loose sleeve and found it stained with a fine line of fresh crimson. A superficial cut ran halfway up my forearm, and blood oozed to my elbow. I knew it'd stop in a minute, but I couldn't show up at the recruiting office as filthy as the street thugs. I had enough against me already.

I scrutinized the restroom. Like everything else in the vicinity, it displayed the attitudes of the local inhabitants. Vulgarities, dug into adobe with knives or painted on, riddled its walls. I drew my knife again as I approached its door.

The odor assaulted me before I ventured inside, and I recoiled. Feces mingled with old urine in an ammonia stench so strong it watered my eyes. I grimaced and held my breath.

No maintenance crew had been inside for years. One ceiling light flickered spasmodically in the dimness. The other two had been shattered.

Both urinals bore stained cracks. Squatties clogged with malodorous sludge lay behind stall doors sagging on broken hinges. The harsh buzzing of flies around the lone wavering light didn't overpower the repetitive high-pitched squeaks of the ceiling fan.

Sidestepping puddles slick with green algae, I crossed to the trough-like wash station.

At least there's water. No soap dispensers, though.

Somebody had tried to tear them off the wall. Their metal cases hung open, and their tubing bulged like plastic entrails.

I positioned myself where I could keep an eye on the door and my back to a wall.

Rust from ancient pipes had streaked the wash trough so darkly, it might have been old blood. I put my boot to the trough's pump, operated by a foot pedal, and had to stomp it several times before sun-heated water gushed out. It sprayed in every direction around a clog in the spout, splashing my face and soaking my shirt. Rust tainted the water a dull orange and gave it an iron taste.

I placed my knife on the trough's edge, where I could grab it quickly if I had to, before I peeled off my shirt and slung it into the trough. I scoured and squeezed the blood from its sleeve until only a faint stain remained, then scrubbed the shirt's underarms as well.

Don't want to smell like a thug, either.

The ooze of blood from my arm had stopped by then. I washed the cut gingerly so it wouldn't start bleeding again.

Finished, I wrung out my shirt and struggled into its damp bulk. I wouldn't have bothered to dry it even if the dented hot-air blowers still worked because the heat outside would do it in minutes. I'd relish the cool from its dampness as long as it lasted.

I cleaned my knife before, starving for a breath of clean air, I exited the restroom. The three people who'd been facing each other across the graffitied bench were gone. *I missed the transport. Sket!*

Putting my back to the restroom wall, I dug into my trouser pocket for my link.

My fingers brushed the oval pendant beneath it. Derry's gift of her portrait. I briefly curled my fingers around it and felt renewal, imagined or real, rush through me.

A sequence of strokes on my link's display produced city transit routes and schedules.

A whole sun position until the next ride out of the city.

I paced about the transit stop, keeping an eye trained on the alley for any sign of approaching crims.

No one else arrived before the next transport grumbled to a halt at its stop. I paid with a transfer from my link, sank beside the window into one of the few empty seats, and leaned my arm against its frame.

Smarting prompted me to push my sleeve up. A little fresh blood had stuck the pale cloth to my skin, which meant I'd have to wash the sleeve again before I faced the recruiters. I spent the ride out of the city gripping my arm to keep it from staining my sleeve any worse.

I straightened in the seat when the bright sign rolling across Aponivi Hotel's dome came into view. I stiffened and swallowed hard. The conscription announcement that had held my hopes for the last few days had vanished.

* * * * *

Chapter Eleven

My heart slammed to full throttle with fresh anxiety as the transport entered the dome's muted daylight. I sprang from my seat and shoved the vehicle's stubborn door open before it lurched to a complete stop. As I strode through the hotel's shushing automatic doors into its expansive atrium, chilled air hit my face forcefully enough to make me blink.

Transparent lifts in the atrium's center drew my gaze up thirty levels. At the ceiling's peak, light flashed in a kaleidoscope of rainbows through the crystal facets of a false skylight.

I had come to Aponivi Hotel with Hanuk and his family when he got conscripted. I remembered hologram signs shaped like pulsing arrows set about the atrium, pointing conscripts to the second level.

The holosigns were missing.

My bootfalls echoed in the lobby's vastness as I crossed it. I spotted only one sign, casting a garish, green reflection on the gleaming floor.

Have the recruiters shut down already? It's barely midday.

The lone hologram arrow, flashing electric-green, stood near the door to the emergency stairs. They'd be faster than waiting for a lift, all of which I could see in their glassy tubes hovering at various floors near the building's top.

I took the stairs three at a time, my boots ringing on steel steps in the narrow pourstone shaft. I entered a corridor with blue-gray carpeting so dense, my running feet made no sound. There, another holosign pointed to an open doorway.

Bursting through, I found temporary workstations on long tables in various stages of being packed away by uniformed men.

A Chalca conscript stood in front of the last operating workstation. I fell in behind him as if in line and observed him while I waited.

He stood a head taller than me, unusual for Chalca. Like mine, his hair hung all the way down his back, but it held a brown hue rather than being pure black, and I didn't recognize the enclave totem on his hair binding.

His clothing fit like the Solis' military uniforms, cut from some kind of smooth cloth instead of native cotton or shegrul hide, and he spoke with the local crispness.

He's from here in the city.

Waiting gave my mind time to hatch a dozen new fears.

How good is Eyebrows at forging? What if they find a mistake in my documents? What if they reject me? What if they arrest me for falsification?

My pulse increased a few beats.

The tall conscript accepted a brown packet from the man behind the table, wheeled around, and his eyes met mine. He grinned. "Ai! I'm not the last one after all."

Something about his open cheeriness reminded me of Hanuk. "Ya." I grinned back.

"Next," said the man at the console. "I need to see your conscription notice." He held out a pudgy hand for it.

"I didn't get one." I met his gaze directly and kept my voice firm. "My birthday was only two days ago." I popped the drive from my link and handed it to him.

I held my breath as he plugged it into his unit. He studied its display in silence for a minute, his pale eyebrows drawn together, before he swiveled in his chair. "Sikkes, come check on this one."

My heartbeat accelerated to a sharp staccato under my ribs. I wiped damp palms on my trouser legs as an older man with shorn gray hair, a white scar on his cheek, and seven stripes on his sleeves moved to stand behind the other's shoulder. He flicked a glance at me before scowling at the display.

"What do you think?" the younger man asked. "Another UA?"

What's a yoo-ay? I wondered.

"Probably." His senior scrutinized me as if trying to remember something. "Do your parents know you're here, son?"

"My parents are dead, sir."

"Do you have a legal guardian?"

"A stepmother. She doesn't want me." *Why is he asking me these questions?*

"This says you're from Red Wash Enclave. Where is that?"

"Two sun positions west of here by air, sir."

"Sun positions?" The elder furrowed his brow. "Is that a measurement of time or direction, son?"

"Time, sir."

"What we call hours?"

I hesitated. "I think so, sir."

He arched an eyebrow. "The Territory. At what age did you learn to fly?"

"Ten, sir." My tongue seemed coated with dust. "The man in my family taught me."

"So you've flown through storms?"

"Yes, sir. You have to learn how to get your license."

He nodded, and his scowl abruptly lifted. "And you've made at least one emergency landing." He smiled. "I knew I'd seen you before. I was at the airfield the other day when you landed your bush craft on two engines. Well done, son."

I blinked. "Thank you, sir."

He addressed his subordinate. "Go ahead and sign him in." He continued to study me as the clerk drew a brown packet stamped "Pilot Candidate" from the shorter of two stacks on his table.

"There's a room key in here," the clerk said, "and a card for meals and incidentals. You'll share the room with another conscript. Wake up is 0400, and departure is at 1000 tomorrow."

"Yes, sir." I reached for the packet. "Thank you."

"Just a minute, son." The senior spacer pointed. "Is that blood on your sleeve?"

I stared at it. A crimson smear glared back at me. In my urgency to arrive in time, I'd completely forgotten about it. I froze, mortified.

"Have you been fighting?" the old spacer asked. His tone grew stern, and his scowl returned.

Is he going to change his mind about accepting me? I stiffened. "I didn't start it, sir."

"I trust you finished it."

"Yes, sir."

"Is your adversary in worse shape than you?"

"Two or three of them are."

The man guffawed. "Well done again. But save it for the lumpies, son. Fighting in the ranks is a punishable offense."

What are lumpies? I wondered.

As I left the room, I overheard him telling the clerk, "We'll take every desert pilot we can get. The conditions those boys grow up flying in make them natural combat pilots. Pity we're not allowed to clone them."

In the corridor I searched my packet for the room key, a plastic card printed with "512." I rode the lift to the fifth level and followed the key card's blinking LED arrow to the correct door.

When it slid open, I spotted the tall Chalca conscript I'd seen earlier sitting on one of two platform-like off-worlder beds, his link in his hand. He smiled. "Ai! You're just in time to order lunch."

"Good," I said, "but I need to go wash." *Blood off my arm, and crim stink off the rest of me.*

"Come order first," the other said. "It'll take them a while to deliver, and I've got the menu up."

My new roommate flicked through several choices. Pictures of food appeared in succession on a display that filled most of one wall.

"This looks good." I pointed with my chin at one picture.

"Slow-smoked ribs of equatorial wild boar," he read the Standard-character description. "Good choice. I think I'll get ribs, too. Where's your meal card?" As I drew it from my packet, he added, "I'm Apenimon clan, North Gate Enclave. They call me Kota."

"Masou clan," I said, handing him my card, "from Red Wash Enclave. I'm called Ku." Kota tapped in our orders, returned my card, and I said, "Yell when the food comes."

The entire bathroom seemed to have been chiseled from one huge chunk of black-ribboned marble, and smoothed to such a high gloss, I didn't need a mirror. Towels as fat and fluffy as bales of new cotton perched on a shelf, and the huge bathtub had massage jets.

I started the water, sighing with anticipation as vapor coiled from the tap, and reached to tug off my backpack.

No straps hugged my shoulders. No backpack.

I slammed it into the thug. Burn. I groaned in annoyance.

"What did you do, scald yourself?" Kota called from the bedroom.

"No." I peered from the doorway. "Reeking crims got my last pairs of clean underwear."

Kota burst out laughing. "There's a tale I've got to hear." He slid off his bed to squat by a large pack dumped at its foot and began to dig through it. "My ma must've got me a dozen new pairs. I think you're close enough in size. Here." He hooked a pair of shorts with his forefinger, stretched the waistband, and let fly.

"Thanks." I snagged them out of the air and joked, "These had better be clean."

"Never been worn—" Kota grinned "—but I sure don't want them back."

While the tub filled, I mentally inventoried the contents of my lost backpack. Socks, shorts, shirts, hygiene kit. Nothing I couldn't replace, but I'd be handwashing every night until uniform issue.

Sighing, I slid into water to my neck. Its heat soaked through my skin, easing my muscles. I examined the cut on my arm more thoroughly than I had in the public restroom and found it to be a shallow scratch, barely deep enough to smart and bleed.

At least it's stopped.

I hauled my shirt and shorts into the tub and washed them, as well, since I'd have to wear them the next day. It took some effort to remove the new bloodstain from the shirtsleeve.

Something chirped about the time I exited the bathroom, combing my damp hair with my fingers.

Kota hefted a stack of containers out of the vacuwaiter tube in the corner. They emanated mouthwatering aromas on puffs of steam. "Chow's up."

We talked between devouring a mound of seasoned tubers and meat so tender it fell off the bones, smothered in a spicy sauce that smeared our chins and made our tongues tingle.

"Pa's from Satha," Kota said. "He's a gourmet merchant."

Mouth full, I only nodded. Kota's Sathi parentage explained his unusual height and brownish hair.

"I was his apprentice until I got conscripted," he added between chewing. "I've gone to Solienne and Satha with him a few times, and to Obolli once. How about you?"

"Never been off Tempest," I said. "The man who gave me life was our enclave's chief chanter. I was his apprentice, too."

Kota stopped eating to stare at me. "A chanter? You're tugging my braid! What can you do?"

I shook my head. "You make it sound like magic. It's mostly a lot of memorizing and practice, like apprenticing for anything else. Then the one who teaches you has to bestow power on you to use it."

"Can you summon spirits of the elements?"

I snorted. "All I have power to do is a couple healing chants, to relieve pain and induce sleep." I licked red sauce off my fingers before I told him about my father's death, and I didn't dampen my bitterness. "It ended my apprenticeship."

"That rots." Kota sounded disappointed. "Sorry." He started on another rib and stripped it clean before he said, "Healing is good. Have you done it much?"

While I peeled smoke-flavored meat off a rib with my teeth, I thought about performing the pain chant for Kimama, and how Machitew had haunted me afterward.

"Last time I did a chant to relieve pain," I said, "I had a nightmare." *Better to call it that, even though it wasn't.*

"What about?" Kota stopped eating again.

I hesitated. "Saw somebody I know getting murdered." I left it there. Kota didn't need to know I'd watched myself do the killing, especially in a vision.

He paused, a half-cleaned rib in one hand, and his brow furrowed. "Have you ever had a dream that actually happened?"

I started to say no, but remembered how similar the crim attack in the alley had been to what I'd dreamed the night before. An icy sensation skated under my skin. "Once," I said. "Sort of."

What if it's only the first one? What if my dreams do start really happening?

The icy feeling closed around my heart like a shell, making it pound as if trying to punch free. I dimly wondered if Kota could hear it.

My hunger rolled into a ball of nausea in my stomach. I must have paled, because Kota asked, "Are you all right?"

"Fine," I said, but I couldn't eat anything else. Desperate to shift Kota off the topic, I asked, "What kind of stuff does your pa bring from other worlds to trade on Tempest?"

Kota and I spent the afternoon exploring the hotel and met several other recruits doing the same. On returning to our room that night, I tried to contact Hanuk again. As before, I got only a vid recording, so I left him another message. "Where in the Dark are you, Huk? I'll be on Solienne by this time tomorrow."

* * *

A blast of brassy music ripped me from sleep. Across the room, Kota sat up with a gasp. Outside our huge window, predawn pink tinted the nironnium dome.

I groaned. "Why do we have to get up at oh-dark-stupid if our vortex isn't until 1000?"

Kota hurled a large pillow at me. "Because getting through vortex security takes time, and if you haven't noticed, sheg-brain, there are about three hundred of us."

"Shegruls don't have brains," I said through a yawn, "just a neural cluster in every segment."

"My point exactly." Kota grinned.

I winged the pillow back at him.

We scrambled to dress. My handwashed shirt and shorts had dried stiff and wrinkled, and dampness lingered under the shirt's arms, but at least it didn't smell of sweat. We collected our belongings and brown packets and joined the shuffling human river flowing toward the bank of lifts.

"Emergency stairs." I pointed the way with a jut of my jaw. "They'll be faster."

We clattered down the steel stairs, leaving them vibrating under our boots, and dashed into the atrium as the first wave of bleary-eyed conscripts spilled from the lifts.

"Everyone with 'pilot' on your packet, over here," somebody shouted. "Pilot candidates to me."

Kota and I eeled our way toward a recruiter wearing golden pilot wings on his chest. We weren't the only ones. A foursome in green crewshirts with a black aircraft image on their left shoulders eyed us through smug expressions.

The evident alpha, vid-drama handsome with his square jaw, drew himself up. "We are the Hevovitas Aerial Performance Team. My family calls me Huritt, but you better call me Hevo Lead.

"This is Hevo Two." He nodded at the youth on his right, whose head resembled a badly carved wooden block. "That's Hevo Three." He indicated the ax-faced companion on his left before waving at the wiry one left of Ax Face. "And Hevo Four. You've never seen our show?"

"Wasn't on my required viewing list," I said.

Square Jaw scanned me and snorted. "So you're hunting for your big brother? He'll be over there with the other dirt dogs." He jerked a thumb at the sleepily milling crowd of ground forces conscripts a few arm lengths away.

"Your mistake." I held up my packet with its distinct Pilot Candidate stamp.

"Ya?" He leaned in. "I think I can see three beard hairs."

Kota stroked his own chin. "Same as me."

I thought of Kimama comparing me to our father. Maybe a few gray hairs or wrinkles would've been good.

Square Jaw chuckled at his companions. "The Solis must be really desperate if they're taking shegrul herders from the desert." He addressed me again, sneering. "What do you fly, sheggy-boy? One of those crates with skids, glued together with shegrul slobber?"

"I fly a Darter 186 Quad," I said. "What does your team fly? Shiny little remote-controlled fighter models?"

Square Jaw appeared indignant. "We fly Hornet 98s with augmented performance engines."

I managed to mask impressed surprise without so much as a blink, but he continued, "You probably haven't heard of the Distinguished Graduate medal, either."

"No, I haven't," I admitted.

Square Jaw swelled like a sniper lizard preparing to spit. "It's presented to the top student of every Primary Piloting class. If you'd ever seen us perform, you'd know the only real competition will be between us." His circular gesture included his three friends. "So don't waste your time trying, Sheggy."

I yawned. It was completely involuntary, but I made the most of it by following up with a smug smile. "I'll remember that when they're pinning it on me."

The other's features darkened like a storm gathering on the Awénasa desert, and his prominent jaw hardened.

"Not wise, Ku," Kota muttered as Square Jaw and his pack strutted off. Kota's puckered brows and tight mouth conveyed concern as much as annoyance. "The Hevovitas clan is notorious for escalating grudges."

"Nobody messes with my reputation as a pilot," I said.

It's all I have.

* * * * *

Chapter Twelve

The recruiter wearing pilot's wings startled us with a sharp whistle. We whirled to face him.

When the other pilot candidates huddled in, about a dozen of us all surreptitiously sizing each other up, he did a head-count and jerked a thumb at a pile of rucksacks by the front doors. "Take one and form up outside."

The vortex terminal stood only a hundred or so arm lengths from Aponivi Hotel. We crunched single-file along the gravel track, a line of two-legged ants. A late spring wind hissed persistently across the enclosing dome as we leaned into our strides. The terminal's automatic doors whooshed apart to admit us when we approached.

"Pilot conscripts to the end station!" a voice rang across the check-in area. We paused to find the speaker, who jabbed a hand in the right direction, and moved to queue up.

When we reached the counter at last, the agent scanned our orders from our links and indicated our rucksacks. "Get your parkas out and put your personal belongings in. It's cold where you're going." As he handed us our passes, he said, "You're in Falcon Group. You'll leave through Portal Three in two hours." He pointed it out. "Listen for your group on the PA."

Hours, I thought. *What they call sun positions. Need to start thinking that way.*

Families were arriving by the time we entered the cavernous departure area. Every sound seemed louder there, from the hum of luggage-bearing float-carts sliding by to the muted rumble of several hundred voices.

I caught snatches of regional accents I couldn't place and spotted totems on hair-bindings that identified enclaves from one end of the continent to the other. I picked up scents of fish, machine oil, and hewn wood, and tried to guess peoples' home regions.

Kota craned around, searching for his family. I swept the concourse for Gram and Kimmie.

No sign of them.

I observed fathers with resolute expressions, mothers wearing anxious ones, and children gripping their conscripted siblings' hands or leaning on their shoulders.

My parents should've been here, too. Unexpected loneliness swallowed me. *Where are Gram and Kimmie?*

"There they are." Kota's relieved voice snapped me from my musings. "Come meet my family, Ku."

Sighing, I followed him.

I nodded respectful greetings as he presented me to his lanky Sathi father, who wore his graying, blond hair long in the Chalca manner, and his mother, a stout woman with a friendly face. She carried a large pouch on her shoulder.

Kota's younger sisters and brother shared his gangly build and dark-brown hair. One sister, maybe sixteen and nearly as tall as me, slipped me a shy smile.

"Is your family here, Ku?" Kota's mother asked.

"My grandmother and little sister are coming," I said, and scanned the area again. "They're all the family I have."

Kota's mother appeared apologetic. She didn't say anything, but she patted my arm.

We startled at a *bing-bong* from a hidden speaker overhead, and a strident voice declared, "Locking in vortex to Camp Boros, Solienne. All personnel in Doma Group taking Vortex 215-Alta to Camp Boros, report to Portal Two at this time."

The announcement echoed into silence across the open space, and Kota said with evident relief, "Not ours."

I watched families around us hug their sons and daughters one last time. The conscripts, most appearing apprehensive, shuffled in a loose crowd toward their portal.

Once the last of them had disappeared, I checked the large chronometer suspended high above the shifting crowd.

Where are you, Gram?

When the chrono showed 0945, I left the small knot of Kota and his family and started to pace back and forth by my piled rucksack and parka. I fingered the plastic portal tab in my trouser pocket and fought to swallow an embarrassing tightening in my throat. *She's not going to make it.*

About the time I'd given up, Gram's anxious voice asked, "Akuleh?"

I spun around.

Kimama seized me about my legs, and Gram enfolded me in her sturdy embrace. I had to bend to return their hugs.

Gram held me tightly. "It would've been better if you'd had a Going-to-War Ceremony, but this is a good choice, Akuleh." My surprise at her change of mind must have shown in my face, because she said, "This will prepare you for the Path the Ancient Ones have set for you. Keep your courage and be wise."

The Ancient Ones. I managed not to snort, said only, "I will," and hugged her long and close, the woman who'd been my mother more than anyone else. "Thank you, Gram." I ached to say more, but I couldn't think of the right words.

On a sudden thought, I dug into my pocket for the pendant and held it out on my hand. "Derry, the artist's daughter, gave me this when I went to tell her good-bye."

The tiny painting captured her long lashes and expressive eyes, haunted despite her slight smile, but her mother hadn't painted her freckles.

"Her hair's been cut off," Gram said, obviously appalled.

"Chalca women are the only ones who don't cut their hair, Gram," I replied.

Kimama studied the pendant intently when I passed it to her. "She's pretty, Ku. Are you going to marry her?"

I chuckled, abruptly self-conscious. "She's from Ardonar, Kimmie. That's halfway down the Lesser Arm. I'll probably never see her again."

Another *bing-bong* rang from the PA speaker, and the crisp voice stated, "Locking in vortex to Belsken Field, Solienne. All personnel in Falcon Group taking Vortex 223-Alta to Belsken Field, report to Portal Three at this time."

Gram released me to cup my face with her warm hand. She'd done that since I was younger than Kimama when she wanted my full attention. I glimpsed a thousand hopes and fears for me in her eyes. "Remember why I called you Akuleh," she urged. "Never stop looking up."

Puzzled, I paused before I said, "I won't, Gram."

Kimama hugged my legs again, her arms snug as the coils of a baby askuk. "Be sure to vid me, Ku."

I squeezed her, too, gently detached her, and ruffled her hair. "As often as I can, Butterfly."

Collecting my parka and rucksack, I searched the area for Kota. I spotted his mother stretching onto her toes to hang her pouch on his shoulder and grip his arm. As he started away, his somber eyes found mine. We crossed to the portal together. I resisted the urge for a backward glance.

"Parkas on, boys," said the woman at the operator's podium. She gave us a minute to shrug into their fur-lined weight and shoulder our rucksacks before she held out a hand for our portal passes. "Have you two done this before?"

"A few times," Kota said, and the operator waved us on.

"I haven't," I said as we approached the tunnel's shadowed mouth.

"Walk fast," he said. "Keep moving forward, and don't puke when you come out the other side."

I stared at him. "People actually do that?"

"Usually only the first time." He grinned and strode briskly into the tunnel.

Great way to start, humiliating myself in front of the whole piloting class. I clenched my teeth and jogged after Kota.

Around the tunnel's sharp bend, its gray tiles vanished in a halo of blue fire. Beyond the wavering ring, I could see only blackness. A few steps ahead of me, Kota peered around. He smiled as he stepped through the blue-lightning ring—and disappeared.

I swallowed and hesitated before I lunged through the fiery circle after him.

I slammed into an invisible barrier like a wall of ice. The impact took my breath. In the next instant, some intangible force shoved me from behind. Every molecule of my body seemed to flatten, crushed into the blackness like a bug on my cockpit canopy. I fleetingly wondered if Solienne was a two-dimensional world.

A heartbeat later, I burst out the other side into waning darkness and gulped for air, as if breaking the surface of an icebound lake.

With my first step, I thought I would spring off the ground.

Kota caught me by the shoulder. "I forgot about the gravity difference. I just about landed on my face." His words billowed through vapor on frigid air.

We'd landed in an open area the size of an enclave's plaza, but square rather than round. Buildings with steeply sloped roofs hemmed it, boxy and colorless under a thin layer of new snow and a few scattered lights on tall poles.

Beyond the buildings, a wall of mountains towered steep and pointed as askuk teeth, far higher than the Ghost Cat ridge. Their sheath of snow reinforced the impression of fangs.

A snaky vehicle, like five or six public transports from Awénasa City hitched together, and a shadowy man wearing a uniform coat with an upturned collar occupied the otherwise empty square.

"Onto the crawler," the man ordered. "Take the first empty seat and secure your rucksack on your lap."

Starting toward the vehicle, I seemed to bounce with every step. "Yi! How long will this last?"

"You'll adjust to the lower gravity in a day or two," Kota said. "Solienne is 93 percent of one standard gravity. Tempest is 1.6."

I swung aboard the crawler ahead of Kota. Hot air from a ceiling vent brushed my face, bitter with burned dust, and I stared into what resembled a snake's gullet. A dim light-tube ran along the ceiling where a spine would've been.

Conscripts from other worlds had arrived ahead of our group from Tempest. Seated along both sides, shoulder-to-shoulder like ribs against the crawler's shell, they watched with curiosity as we sidled to the remaining empty seats. Through the crawler's idling grumble I made out a few subdued voices.

Most conscripts were Soliennese, I guessed, from various continents and nations. I counted seventeen girls in our crawler car alone.

I'd never seen people with ebony-colored skin before. Some had tightly curled hair, and some had shaved heads, but they all appeared tall, even seated.

"Where are they from?" I asked Kota over my shoulder.

"Some may be Sathi or Soli," he answered, "but most are probably from Obolli. Pa says Obolli has a larger population of black people than brown and white combined, and they have the most exotic food goods in the whole Lesser Arm."

Like Kota's father, most conscripts had fair hair of one shade or another, and blue or hazel or light-green eyes. My vision locked on a girl with generous curves, blue eyes I could have drowned in, golden-blonde hair, and pink-painted lips. Every young man sitting near her leaned close to talk to her. I did a double-take, but oddly found myself wishing I'd spotted Derry instead. *She'd probably be good at this.*

One group of five conscripts, two of them also girls, I couldn't place at all. They had olive complexions, dark eyes with a slight upward slant at the outer corners, and brown-black hair like Kota's, except very wavy.

"Looks like the whole Commonwealth is here," Kota said at my shoulder, "plus some extras." He jutted his chin toward the group I'd just noticed. "They're from somewhere on Fuago Mono. Only a few of its countries entered the Resistance Pact. I bet they're Bird People."

I slid Kota a *You're tugging my braid* expression.

He chuckled. "That's their nationality. Pa says their real name is too long and hard for most people to pronounce correctly, so their country is just called the Bird Islands."

We sank into the first empty seats, Kota across from me, and hauled our rucksacks onto our laps as Huritt and his trio stumped aboard. "We can go now," Huritt shouted, throwing his chest out. "All the important people are here."

Through the window behind him, I watched the last Chalca conscripts appear from the blue lightning hoop, most stumbling as I had. Moments later, the vortex portal crackled, sparked, and dissipated into the predawn half-light.

Huritt's short friend dropped into the seat next to mine, his blocky face pale and streaming sweat.

"If you're going to hurl, Two," Huritt said from the seat next to Kota, "do it on Sheggy. He won't notice. He already smells like a shegrul." Huritt leered at me.

I glared back. "Better than your kosa stench."

When the last conscript dropped into a seat at the front, the officer in the long coat swung aboard. He flipped something in the cab that produced a whistle as shrill as a child playing with a chanter's flute. Everybody jumped and faced him.

Broad-shouldered and with skin as dark as strong kasse, he surveyed us through an imperious expression until the chatter ceased.

"I am Journeyman Officer Russom," he said. "The unlucky ones among you will see a great deal more of me than you will wish to during the coming six phases of the moon."

He glared, mouth briefly pursed between his meticulously trimmed mustache and goatee. "Teaching you young pimple-pinchers to march, salute, and wear your uniforms properly isn't my regular job. I was line-of-sight volunteered for this duty, and I'm not pleased about it." His eyes, black as coal, leveled on me. "If you're smart, you won't make me any unhappier."

* * * * *

Chapter Thirteen

Russom kept his scowl on me for so long, I knew he'd singled me out, but I returned his stare without blinking.

Hooking an arm around the safety pole by the front seat, he punched a button on the control console. The vehicle lurched and groaned into motion, and swung toward an open gate out of the square plaza. Russom stood firm in the crawler's movement.

Huritt leaned toward me and sneered, "Looks like you have an admirer, Sheggy. Or maybe he knows you're underage."

I glowered, about to respond, but Russom started speaking again.

"Our first stop is the clinic for your physicals." Speakers carried his voice through the crawler, over its low growl. "From there, you will go to the orderly room to check in, followed by Clothing Issue. Do all of you have rucksacks?"

Without waiting for a response, he continued, "Now that I have your complete attention, I will explain the demerit system. I will explain it only once. Since demerits will determine which of you continue to pilot training and which will be sent to the ground forces, I advise you to listen carefully."

Murmurs farther up the crawler abruptly ceased. Every face grew taut. Conscripts in cars to the rear gawked at ceiling monitors like baby birds waiting to be fed.

"There are two hundred forty cadets aboard this vehicle right now," Russom said. "We have only one hundred fifty pilot billets.

That means at least ninety of you will be culled, an average of seven trainees from each flight.

"All you have to do to be cut is receive one thousand demerits during the next six phases. That," he gave a menacing smile, "is a great deal easier to accomplish than it may seem."

A slim hand rose halfway down our car. One of the Bird girls from Fuago Mono. When Russom acknowledged her with a curt "Yes?" she said, "Cadet Ga'olani M'oke Keatii, sir. I wish to, um, *understand?* why people receive demerits." Her voice reminded me of a rafter dove's coo.

Russom's smile, however, reminded me of Eyebrows, devoid of humor, when he said, "An excellent question, Cadet Keatii." He paused to study her. "M'oke Keatii, as in the sword-making family of Makura Island?"

"Yes, sir." She blushed through her olive complexion and made a slight bow where she sat. "Eighty, um, generations, I think, of sword masters, sir."

He eyed her for a few more heartbeats before he said, "In answer to your question, Cadet, camp rules are posted in your barracks. Memorize and apply.

"In addition, each training officer may set his or her own rules for his or her flight and is at liberty to amend them as he or she sees fit. Ignorance of changes will not exempt one from the consequences."

Cadet Keatii appeared perplexed. Her hand rose once more and Russom asked, "What is it?"

"I wish to make a new question, sir. How will we, um, learn when rules are changed?"

"You may not know," he said, "until you break one."

Cadet Keatii's expression remained confused, but she didn't ask anything else.

"One more point," Russom said. "Twenty-six cadets on this crawler are on probation. There are three ways one acquires that undesirable status. The first is a criminal record, the second is not meeting physical standards, and third is being underage."

My throat closed as if in a noose, but I resisted the urge to swallow.

"The training officers and command staff know who all of you are," Russom said, "and *why* you are on probation. When the culling begins, probats are the first to go. That is because they begin with one hundred demerits."

Across the aisle, Huritt smirked at me. "Shegrul herders should get a hundred demerits for their smell."

"Stink for yourself, kosa," I hissed back.

* * *

At the trainees' clinic, the women were directed down one hallway, and the men into another. We underwent vision tests, hearing tests, equilibrium tests, and coordination tests. I passed all of them easily.

From there, they sent us to the lab for bloodwork. When a medtech pointed me to a chair and slapped a draw kit on its desk, all the blood drained from my face, and my hands grew clammy. *That needle's the size of my stepmother's leather awl. If she jabs me with that, I'll pass out for sure, right in front of the Hevos. That's all I need.*

I stared at a wall full of gleaming metal cabinets while the tech swabbed my arm with something cold and said, "Make a fist." The needle burned like a gorefly bite, and I set my teeth. *Don't pass out. Not with Huritt watching. Don't pass out, don't pass out, don't...*

"Done," she said.

I rose cautiously, pushing through a head-rush, and left the lab on unsteady legs.

Finally, we stripped to our shorts and waited in a slow-moving line in a chilly room for molecular body scans.

"These scanners," the technician informed us, "can detect an anomaly as small as a pimple on your face or a chip in your tooth."

One by one, we stood in the cylindrical booth, legs apart and arms above our heads, while a metallic ring whirred from our fingers to our feet. Radio waves, bounced across the ring and translated into digital code, produced full-color cross-sections of our bodies as life-size, three-dimensional displays.

In the locker room afterward, I found Kota shrugging his shirt on. He grinned. "Now you know what it's like to go through vortex security on Nichi."

I chuckled and reached for my trousers. "Remind me never to visit Nichi."

Gray daylight had come by the time we left the clinic. We tramped to the crawler under early sunshine. Within minutes, it began to coax vapor from the slushy tarmac, which rose in wisps like thin smoke.

The crawler delivered us to a long building with a bulky stone marker in front. Blocky Standard letters had been engraved across its smooth face.

HEADQUARTERS 33RD AEROSPACE TRAINING WING

A tall pole with a dark blue flag snapping at the top stood beside the marker. Random gusts tugged at the banner, briefly unfurling it to reveal a helmeted face printed in white, which seemed to stare as if assessing us.

"Their king?" I asked Kota.

"No, that's Thrüss, their god of warriors," he said. "You'll see him all over the base. You'll also see red flags above medical facilities, amber ones in the business district, and green ones in the restaurant sector, all with a different deity's face." He smiled. "Feel like you're being watched?"

"Ya," I said. *Better Thrüss than Machitew, though.*

The orderly room—the Wing's administration and records-keeping office—contained a mutter of business-crisp voices and clickety-clacking equipment. *Sounds like a human beehive.*

Personnel stood by to download our orders from our links and create digital folders in which to start the military record that would follow us through our careers.

After they entered our data, a printer ejected a paper copy of our orders and a checklist for in-processing. As my sheet shushed into the printer's tray, my vision locked on a single word printed boldly at an angle across it.

PROBATIONARY

I froze. I knew the reason, but my guts tightened. *I'm starting with a hundred demerits.*

Without reading the rest of it, I shoved the page into my rucksack to keep anybody else from seeing it. Especially the Hevos.

Leaving the orderly room, Kota asked, "What's your flight?"

Reluctantly, I fumbled the sheet out again, keeping the printed side away from his view. "Juno."

"Good. So am I." Kota studied his orders. "Barracks Ten, Training Officer… Ah, sket, we've got Russom."

"That rots," I said through my teeth. "Officer Don't-Make-Me-Any-Unhappier."

At Clothing Issue, a woman asked for our names and order numbers to access our medical records. "We determine your uniform sizes by your body-scans," she explained.

We sidled along a smooth counter that appeared to run the building's entire length, nudging our growing mounds of uniforms and gear with us. At the far end, we stuffed everything into our rucksacks as a clerk called out each item on our lists.

At last we traipsed outside to board the crawler.

It had left. Several trainees dropped their rucksacks onto the damp tarmac with squishy thuds and queued as if at a public transport stop.

When Russom showed up, wearing a tight smile that gleamed in his dark face, I knew we wouldn't see the crawler again. "Your barracks are two ranges down the track," he said, jerking a thumb over his shoulder.

The tarmac lane disappeared into green dimness under rows of towering conifers.

"You had better get moving," he said. "You have a lot to do before chow time."

I shrugged my rucksack on and paused in surprise. I had expected it to be a lot heavier. *Must be the lower gravity again.*

As everyone started away, dismay etched on several faces, I noticed the Bird girls. They were so petite they could've fit inside their rucksacks if they sat on their heels. I watched Cadet Keatii lift one rucksack from the tarmac, but struggle to boost it high enough, as if trying to place it on her squatting friend's head. Its bulky size appeared to be more of a problem than its weight.

Somebody chuckled behind me. "Toothpick women," Huritt said. "No use for swords here. They'll break in two days."

He and the other Hevos strode past, Blockhead at Huritt's right, Ax Face and Wiry trailing off his left as if flying in fingertip formation. Wiry kicked one of the girls' rucksacks as he passed.

"Reeking kosas," Kota muttered.

Trading glances, we dropped our own rucksacks and crossed to the Bird girls. They eyed us warily when we scooped their packs up.

"Brace your feet," I said, "and hold your arms out."

With a flicker of understanding, they planted their feet in what was clearly a familiar combat stance. Kota hoisted Cadet Keatii's pack high enough for her to slip slender arms through the straps and settle it on her shoulders, and I did the same for her friend.

"Are you all right with those?" Kota asked.

"It's common at our home to carry large bundles," Keatii's friend said, "but balance is better when we carry them on our heads."

Cadet Keatii said, "We pay you for, um, kindness…" Her pinched brows questioned us.

"Call me Ku," I said, "and him Kota, but you don't need to pay us anything."

"My, um, mother-given name is Ga'olani," Cadet Keatii said. "All of my names together mean, in your language, Heavenly Seagull Born of the Flames."

Kota and I blinked.

Cadet Keatii's friend introduced herself as well, speaking so quickly I caught only her family name.

Tagolwe. I think.

"My pa," Kota said, "told us you're called Bird People because you build your homes up in trees, like bird nests. Is that true?"

Cadet Keatii appeared mildly confused. "Slowly?" she said.

Kota repeated the question carefully, indicating the tall pines sheltering the track.

When Ga'olani cocked her head in a bird-like manner, eyes still scrunched in apparent puzzlement, Cadet Tagolwe spoke to her in a singsong tongue as intriguing as Derry's Caerdish lilt.

Cadet Keatii smiled. "Ah. Yes, we build houses in trees, away from, um, *floods?* I think," she glanced at her friend for confirmation, "and tides. I must say sorry. I learn your language only for, um, fifteen days."

I gaped. "You're doing a lot better than I would with your language after fifteen days." *I better keep both eyes on her.*

The Bird girls started up the track at a brisk pace while Kota and I retrieved our own rucksacks.

Watching them go, Kota said with a sly twinkle in his eye, "I don't think they'll be the ones who'll get broken if the Hevos harass them."

We didn't shoulder our packs right away. We bundled our parkas into them, and Kota dug his mother's pouch out of his. He removed a spice-scented loaf from the pouch before we took up our rucksacks once more. "Sun-squash bread," he said, and inhaled as he peeled off its paper wrapping. "Want some?"

"Thanks." I accepted a moist chunk of it, and we set off under the arch of pine boughs.

I'd seen images of conifers, but they never conveyed how tall they really were. Nor did the images carry the trees' spicy fragrance. I squinted through layer after layer of sweeping boughs to the pointed tops. *They must be a few hundred spans high.*

The tallest trees I'd seen in the Awénasa Territory were the pythons, which stood thirty spans at most.

"Don't strain your neck, Ku."

Kota's voice startled me. I felt mild embarrassment until I spotted other cadets ahead of us staring skyward as well.

"Have you seen trees this tall before?" I asked.

"Only on Satha and here on Solienne."

Movement among the branches, like ashen ribbons whisking and twining between them, caught my eye. I pointed with my chin. "What's up there?"

"Silvertails," Kota said. "I saw some when Pa and I came to So-lienne once. They're rodents like kosas, but they have such short legs, they look more like fur-covered eels. Don't leave any food in your room, or you'll have an invasion. They can squeeze through really small openings."

"Thanks for the warning," I said.

The light snow I'd seen coating buildings around the square where we'd exited the vortex hadn't sifted through the forest canopy to its floor. Layers of damp needles cushioned our feet and silenced our steps as thoroughly as the carpet in Aponivi Hotel.

After consuming the squash bread and licking its sticky sweetness from our fingers, we increased our pace to distance ourselves from stragglers.

"What do you know about the Hevos?" I asked after we'd put some distance between ourselves and everybody else.

Kota snorted. "More than I want to. We're from the same en-clave." He sucked spiciness off his thumb before he said, "Huritt's mother is second to the chief of the Great Council of All Clans."

"I've heard their name," I said, "but we don't get a lot of news out in the Territory."

"You know how the Council works, don't you?" Kota asked.

I nodded and skirted a muddy patch. "Every enclave on Tempest chooses somebody to be their Voice in the Council and sends the person to vote for their enclave."

At a sudden memory, I said, "We had to go to Awénasa City for supplies during the winter, and the whole place was lit up like Night of Light Ceremony. Elder Macawi, one of the traders, said it was for the Gathering of the Council. She said the Voices had all come to elect a new chief." I glanced at Kota. "They do it every five years, don't they?"

When he nodded, I remembered something else. "She said she'd like to see a chief from the coasts or the Territory for once, because the last few had all come from Awénasa City."

"Ya. It happened this time," Kota said. "Great Chief Mochni is from Leaning Palms Enclave on the southwest coast. He's really outspoken and direct, but he's a wise man. There was a wide margin between him and Huritt's mother, but she took the next highest vote count, which makes her the chief's second. The other city candidates came in close behind her."

Kota scooped up a pinecone and hurled it into the shadows, where it struck an unseen tree with a startling *pock*. His voice hardened when he spoke again. "The Hevos are trying to limit eligibility to clans that can prove an unbroken maternal line back to Chanter Yuma. They say it gives them a birthright to the chieftainship."

"What?" Surprise widened my eyes. "We've never chosen chiefs by ancestry."

"I know," Kota said, "but the only people the Hevovitases consider legitimate are themselves and the Dezba and Kesego clans." He gave me a direct stare. "Huritt started his airshow team to demonstrate what a great leader he is, in hopes of inheriting from his mother. The other three are his cousins."

"Do you think he'd be a good leader?" I asked.

"Only for shegruls."

I chuckled. "You can't *lead* shegruls, Kota. You have to prod them along." I considered. "Though they might follow if you smelled like food."

"What do shegruls eat?"

I grinned. "Mostly what every other animal in the desert leaves behind."

Kota's roar of laughter rang among the overarching trees, but he sobered quickly. "Remember when he said the only competition for the Distinguished Grad medal would be between himself and his cousins?"

"Ya."

"Don't fool yourself. He'll make sure even they don't come close." Kota's expression grew serious. "When he told you not to waste your time trying? That wasn't a challenge, Ku. It was a warning."

* * * * *

Chapter Fourteen

We caught up with Cadets Keatii and Tagolwe and passed most of the others long before we reached the isolated barracks. The sun eased above distant treetops, warming the shadowy chill with bright blades of mist-laden light.

The barracks stood in a clearing, a row of two-level structures with high-peaked roofs to shed snow, and crumbling plaster coating their timber walls. The few cadets who'd arrived ahead of us sat on their rucksacks on the drill pads in front of each building. Cadet Tagolwe left us at Barracks Seven, giving a small bow.

"Which flight are you in, Cadet Keatii?" I asked.

She crimped her forehead. "Um, Juno Flight. And you?"

"Same," I said, and surveyed the handful of trainees already waiting at Barracks Ten.

Huritt stood on the pourstone doorstep, joking with another youth, while Blockhead hunched stolidly at his shoulder. My eyes narrowed. Apparently feeling my stare, Huritt shifted his gaze in my direction. "No shegruls here," he called, and waved as if to shoo us on.

"I can see two shegrul piles right in front of the door," Kota muttered.

I strode across the drill pad, holding Huritt's vision with mine. "Your problem, Hevovitas."

More conscripts arrived in twos and threes during the next few minutes, many of them puffing and sweating under their rucksacks, and with faces red as ripe cactus fruit.

When Russom stepped out through the front door, Huritt and Blockhead cleared off its step, and the trainees who'd sat down popped to their feet like kosas from flooded burrows.

"Fall in," Russom ordered, indicating the drill pad. "I want four ranks with five of you in each."

Twenty of us scrambled, pushing and rolling lumpy rucksacks out of the way.

Kota and I stepped into the second rank alongside Cadet Keatii, but Huritt barged in at my right and Blockhead on my left. I didn't have to see Huritt's smirk to know they'd taken those spots on purpose.

"Fair." Russom paced before us, golden pilot wings glinting on his chest in the midday sunlight. "Pay attention to whoever is in front, behind, and to either side of you, because this will be your permanent place in formation. At least until some of you wash out." He fixed his vision on me. "Next time I say 'fall in,' I want you in place in fifteen seconds."

Russom strolled across the tarmac, assessing us like a hungry ghost cat. The overhead sun and evaporating snow produced damp heat that moistened my skin with sweat. I wasn't the only one. I watched a rivulet trickle into the collar of the female cadet in front of me.

"For the next six phases," Russom said, "you will undergo Basic Military Training. For those of you who strutted your way through some uniform-wearing institution that styled itself a military prep school," he leveled a meaningful stare on somebody behind me, "welcome to the real thing."

He strode clear of the drill pad. "Once I dismiss you, you will have half an hour to change into the uniform of the day, stow your gear, and prepare for uniform and room inspections. Room assignments are posted inside the door; women upstairs and men down. *Dis*-missed."

We broke ranks like a small explosion. Everyone tugged their parkas and rucksacks out of the careless pile on the sidelines and charged inside, briefly clogging the doorway.

I found my name paired on the roster with another Chalca, a youth called Nayati from Kosumi clan. *At least I'm not stuck with one of the Hevos.*

We hauled our rucksacks through an echoing hallway redolent of floor polish, scanning each door for our room number, and I asked Nayati, "Where are you from?" I indicated the fish carved from milkstone dangling from his hair binding. "Where's your enclave? I've never seen your totem before."

"Glacier Bay," Nayati said, "on the northeast coast. We run fishing boats on the ocean."

"I'd like to see the ocean," I said. "I've only seen vids of Tempest outside Awénasa Territory."

"Someday I'll show you the ocean, and you can show me the desert." Nayati smiled, revealing a chipped front tooth. We were about equal in height, but he had a rangy frame and a more prominent nose and cheekbones.

Our room, a nine-by-nine-span cubicle that smelled of mildew, contained only two lockers and two folding camp beds. Yellowed sheets and scratchy blankets had been stacked in stiff squares on their thin mattresses. The air tasted dusty, but the window wouldn't open when I tried it.

Opposite the window with its faded cover, a chronometer loomed on the wall above the door. Its red digits showed 1258.

Past high sun already? Explains why I'm so hungry.

We dumped our rucksacks on the beds and rummaged for boots and gray-green utility uniforms. Unlike my own, the issued boots had straps across their insteps and shins.

"You fasten them like this," Nayati said. "My brother got conscripted two years ago, and he showed me how."

The ankle straps didn't fit well. Depending on which notch I used, they were either too loose or too tight.

By the time I gave up trying to make them fit, Nayati had half his clothes in his locker. "Hurry up, Ku, it's almost time for inspection."

I slung my clothes onto metal objects he called hangers and practically tossed them into my locker.

"They go in a certain order," Nayati said, "and they have to be buttoned and zipped." He pointed at his.

His service blues hung at the rear, utility uniforms next, with his parka in front. His boots and shoes stood in a tidy row on the bottom, their heels against the rear wall.

"Why? That's stupid," I said.

"I know." Nayati rolled his eyes. "That's what my brother said, too."

I fastened my uniforms, spaced the hangers as carefully as I could on the pole, and lined up my footgear.

"Now the beds." Nayati shook out a sheet in a billow like a glider's wing, sending more dust swirling into the air. "I think I remember what he showed me."

I followed his lead, tugging and tucking in threadbare sheets and rough blankets, and hoping they wouldn't rip.

"When Russom comes in," Nayati said as we worked, "come to attention. Curl your hands at your trouser seams like this—" he demonstrated "—and stare straight ahead. It's easier if you find a spot on the wall or something to stare at. Just don't move your eyes. It's called caging them. And don't say anything unless he speaks to you. Then all you're supposed to say is, 'Sir, yes, sir,' or 'Sir, no, sir,' or 'No excuse, sir.'"

"Uh, ya," I said. "Thanks." *Hope I remember all that.*

We hadn't finished folding our physical training uniforms before Nayati glimpsed Russom at our door. Nayati gasped and leaped up, rigid as a log and balling his hands at his trouser seams. "Room, at-ten-*shun!*"

I scrambled to copy his posture and fixed my stare on a dent in my open locker's rear wall.

Russom stalked in at the edge of my vision, pilot wings gleaming on his uniform. "We don't tuck trousers into boots here, Kosumi," he said, circling my roommate, and added a few more comments.

Nayati answered, "Sir, yes, *sir!*"

At last Russom pivoted to address me, his expression calculating but also amused. "Akuleh of clan Masou."

"Sir, yes, sir!" *What's so funny?*

A corner of his mouth twitched. "You followed Kosumi's bad example of tucking your trousers into your boots. Pull them out."

"Sir, yes, sir." I crouched to obey.

"Five demerits, Mess-you."

I jerked upright and stared at him. *For what? And how did he just say my name?*

"Close your shirt at your collar," Russom said, "and get your hair cut before evening chow. It's out of regs."

I stiffened. Cutting off one's hair meant rejecting one's identity as Chalca. When Winéma's children separated from my ancestors and became Pahana, the Lost Ones, four hundred years before the Crossing to Tempest, they cut their hair before they began to ritually tattoo their faces.

When a Chalca criminal was condemned to death under Chalca law, the enclave elders cut off his hair before they shot him with the black arrows. Even Machitew's rag mane hung halfway to his waist.

Russom paused at my right, so close his breath brushed my ear, and I glimpsed his coal-black gaze through the corner of one caged eye. My pulse accelerated, and my curled hands knotted at my trouser seams. I swallowed but stood stiff. Jaw taut, I said, "Sir, *no,* sir!"

Russom smiled and arched an eyebrow. "Your choice. Fifty demerits, Mess-you."

Fifty more? On top of the hundred I started with?

He pivoted on his heel to inspect our lockers, leaving us standing at attention.

My stomach grumbled.

Russom apparently heard it and peered at me. "Hungry, Mess-you? You can go to chow as soon as you pass inspection."

He drew a gauge from his pocket and measured the spacing of our hangers. "Sloppy, Kosumi," he said. "Hangers must be placed exactly one thumb-length apart. Get yourself a gauge."

He dragged our physical training clothes from our drawers and shook them onto the floor. "Fold those into eight thumb-length by eight thumb-length squares and ground them against the side of the drawer."

He seized our bedcovers at the top and stripped them off the mattresses, leaving them in crumpled heaps. "Pathetic, Mess-you. These are the worst beds I've seen so far."

Finally he said, "You two have fifteen minutes to make this room passable. I will keep tearing it apart until you complete it correctly. Unlike you, I have no other duties for the rest of the day."

He scowled at the clicker in his hand. "You two wastes of oxygen have already set a new record for the most demerits on the first day." He didn't show us the count, but he shook his head. "Especially you, Mess-you. Not a promising start for a probationary. You seem determined to be the first one culled.

"We won't send you off to the ground forces right away, however." He favored me with a belittling smile. "*You* will go home to your mommy for a few months so you can try again when you reach legal age."

My gut twisted like an askuk in thick mud as he wheeled and left the room.

* * * * *

Chapter Fifteen

I t took us several heartbeats to relax after Russom left.

Nayati stared at me. "You're a probat?"

"Ya. What about it?" I gathered my blue dress shirts and greenish utility uniforms off the floor. Shaking dust out of them prompted a sneeze.

Nayati collected his clothing, too. "Why'd you sign up early?"

I glowered and let irritation shade my voice. "Not my choice. My stepmother kicked me out." *Close enough. I'm not saying I left because I'm Death Bringer.*

"Yi." Nayati appeared stunned. "Sorry I asked."

I shrugged and changed the subject. "Can they really make us cut our hair?"

"No," Nayati said. "It's part of the harassment. My brother checked on it. The regs allow us to wear our hair long because of religious significance, like the earlobe plugs some Obollans have, and the little god-figures Osfelgs wear on neck-chains. As long as you keep it tied back, you're safe."

"Good." Only partially relieved, I dragged my bedcovers off the gray tiles and shook them out as well. "Why did he give me the first five demerits?"

"You moved, broke attention."

"But he told me to pull—"

Nayati cut me off with a hand motion. "Always wait until he leaves the room to make corrections. When you're at attention, you don't move at all. My brother warned me about that, too." As if remembering he hadn't fixed his trouser legs yet, he abruptly knelt to do so.

I joined him. *How am I going to remember all this?*

* * *

Once every room had passed inspection, Russom ordered us to the drill pad with a bellowed, "Fall in!"

We scrambled into bulky field jackets and barreled outside into a light snowfall. The sky sagged like a blanket thrown over the treetops, muffling the sun in pale gray like raw cotton. We slipped and slid to our places in formation, and a couple cadets collided with each other in their hurry.

"Sound off," Russom said when everyone stood stiffly at attention.

The cute girl who stood directly in front of me, I learned, was named Lista Dois, from the Soliennese nation of Steenslund. Sturdier than Ga'olani, more like a Chalca, she had light-brown hair cut straight across her nape. Like Derry, she had freckles.

The last rank included two of the four Obollans in our flight and a giant of a young man from Ardonar. Rinn Stormun came from the nation of Golmolor, and his guttural accent didn't sound anything like Derry's Caerdish lilt. His crooked nose and the scar crossing his upper right cheek to the outer corner of his right eye appeared more menacing than his build.

"I have the miserable duty," Russom said, his words rising on a vapor trail, "of teaching you snot-noses how to march." He appeared impervious to the drifting snowflakes that tickled our ears and noses as he strode about. When some trainees raised hands to brush them off, Russom said, "Five demerits each."

I caged my eyes and fought the urge to twitch as a feather-sized snowflake slid from my cheekbone to my chin.

"You will go everywhere in formation during the next six phases, including to meals," Russom said, "so if you want dinner, you will learn quickly."

He began with basics like right face, left face, and about face. Step, pivot, feet together. Our boots stamped and rasped in unison on the gritty pavement, and our views of barracks, forest, and trainees drilling on neighboring pads switched every few heartbeats.

Shouted orders carried from the flights training on either side of us. A stealthy sideways peek revealed fellow conscripts maneuvering like pieces on a game board.

We spent a whole sun position on facing movements because Blockhead kept lurching in the wrong direction. Doing one about-face, he tripped on his feet and would've gone sprawling if Kota hadn't caught his arm.

"Ten demerits for wearing your boots on the wrong feet, Hevovitas," Russom shouted.

I clamped my teeth on my lip and fixed my vision on the back of Lista Dois' head to kill my grin. *At least he's not bellowing at me for once.*

With gray daylight deepening to blue dusk, we set out for the chow hall. Russom strode alongside, his breaths puffing misty clouds as he yelled at us all the way. "Out of step again, Zoreba, that's another five. Keep up, Sajjad, longer strides. What a pathetic batch of thumb-suckers."

Nearing the chow hall, whose radiant windows seemed to beckon, Russom said, "Left face. First rank, forward march. Second rank, fall in after them."

Facing left put Huritt behind me. As we started forward, something struck my heel.

Huritt's toe. Was it accidental or deliberate?

He kicked my foot harder on his next step, as if trying to make me slip on the ice.

I sidestepped his third kick. Huritt's slush-coated boot met only air, and his flailing arms entered my peripheral vision. Recovering himself, he growled, "If I'd fallen, Sheggy, you would've paid for it."

* * *

We couldn't talk in formation, so Kota and I rarely spoke to each other during the first several days. The threat of demerits didn't deter Huritt, though. Whenever Russom strode away, he'd make snide comments under his breath. "You know, a shower would kill that shegrul smell. Do you rabble from the Territory even *have* showers?" or "Started to grow a beard yet, Sheggy?"

Several times I had a retort poised on my tongue, but Russom paced within hearing distance. I fumed, hands fisted at my trouser seams, and watched Huritt and Blockhead shake with silent laughter on either side of me. Once Russom caught Blockhead sniggering and said, "Five demerits for giggling in formation, Hevovitas."

Blockhead's eyes rounded, and he scrunched his mouth shut, his cheeks bulging as if preparing to blow on a fire. Kota and I waited until Russom strolled off to yell at somebody else before we exchanged grins.

Between physical training in the frigid dark before dawn, polishing the barracks floors every night, and six or seven sun positions a day on the parade ground, meals became the only times we sat. Our tablemates consisted of those in our rank, which meant Kota, Ga'olani, and I had to eat with the Hevos. As if the food wasn't unappetizing enough.

Once at lunch, Huritt "accidentally" knocked over my mug. I leaped clear, saving my lap from the scalding he'd no doubt intended, but kasse splattered like murky rainwater in every direction when it spilled off the table and struck the seat of my chair.

I seized my handcloth and dropped to the floor, gritting my teeth. Kota and Ga'olani joined me at once, their faces taut with disgust.

Kota's head jerked up at the sound of footsteps behind me. He stared past my shoulder, eyes wide, and I braced for Russom's usual tirade.

"Ten demerits, you two," said a female voice, "for sitting there like warts on a toad instead of helping."

I wrenched about to see a woman training officer pointing at Huritt. "You, get a bucket and mop from the kitchen, and you," she motioned at Blockhead, "get some damp towels."

"They did not, um, accept that," Ga'olani said when they'd slouched away.

"Expect," Kota corrected her. He glanced at me and added, "He won't do that again."

Watching Huritt return across the chow hall armed with bucket, mop, and a scowl reminiscent of my stepmother, I said, "No, he'll be sneakier next time."

* * *

The day Blockhead mastered corners without coming to a complete halt first, Russom marched us to the parade ground.

"Today you will learn the Fifty-Command Drill," he said. "You will pass it off by the end of this phase. The first person to do so will earn fifty *merits*. Some of you—" his intense gaze passed over the flight and settled on me "—desperately need merits, so I suggest you pay attention."

To pass the drill, one had to march the flight through a string of commands in the correct order while keeping everyone inside a small, marked area.

Only the flight commander received a grade, but Russom gave demerits to anyone who got out of step, turned the wrong direction, or responded too slowly. Kota sometimes fell out of step when he got nervous, so I said, "Left, right, left" under my breath and kept an eye on Russom while everyone took turns leading the drill.

I missed "Eyes right" and didn't shout "To the rear, march" quickly enough on my first attempt. Like several others, I took the flight an arm length or two outside the white-painted boundary before resuming the sequence.

Blockhead got as flustered as a shegrul without its pod on his first try and marched us off the parade field into the pines before he remembered to yell, "Flight, halt!" Huritt roared with laughter, but relief enveloped me.

At least I didn't do that bad.

By the time Nayati and I went to bed—rolled in our field jackets on the tile floor, because no one touched their bunk once it passed inspection—I wondered if I'd dream about shouting orders on the drill pad all night.

My dreams began with marching, except my flight mates morphed into shegruls who galumphed into the woods. I chased them through green-black shadows, dodging pine boughs that raked me with their needles while I shouted, "Flight, halt!"

The shegruls scattered in all directions, leaving me in a clearing face-to-face with a tree whose ribbed bark resembled Russom's sneering face. "Five hundred thirty-nine demerits, Mess-you," the tree said in a raspy voice. "Fifty-three for each shegrul, and nine because you haven't cut your hair."

I woke sitting straight up and stared around the room. *I'll be the first one washed out of here. I know it.*

A mumble from my left made me squint through the dimness. Nayati lay sprawled on his back, talking in his sleep. "Right face, left face…"

Shivering in the room's chill, I reached into the drawer that held my PT clothes, to the corner designated for personal belongings. Two items lay there, my link and the pendant of Derry. I scooped out both in one swipe. I hadn't seen or touched either one since our first day.

How long ago was that? Feels like moons already. Now I know why I've never heard from Huk.

For a while, I simply held them in my hands, two solid connections to the life I'd left behind. At last I touched on my link. It chimed to life, and I used its display's pale light to study the miniature portrait of Derry.

Seeing her hesitant smile triggered the memory of her good wishes when she'd told me good-bye. I touched my cheek where she'd kissed me, so close to my mouth, and reflected on her demonstration of affection. *Why didn't I ask for her call code? Wish I could hear her voice again.*

Vids from Gram and Kimmie waited in my mail queue. I nudged the sound down, though it probably wouldn't have awakened Nayati even at full volume.

Gram's vidmail contained pretty much what I expected. She asked how I was doing in Basic. Was I getting enough to eat? She was proud of me, she had confidence in me, and she said the chants for me every day.

For what the chants are worth. I rolled my eyes, but her warm gaze held comfort.

Kimama, her eyes glittering with delight, showed me a baby tavo somebody had given her. A ball of russet fur with oversized ears and hind haunches, it squirmed in her small hands. "I don't know what to call him yet," she said.

I chuckled and touched the Call pad.

Only Gram's recorded vid message answered, so I swallowed my disappointment and left a message. "Ai, Gram and Kimmie! I can't talk long, it's night here, but I wanted to tell you I'm fine. Thanks for your encouragement. I really appreciate it."

I fell asleep with my face pressed to the cold floor and woke with my link still in my hand when *On Your Feet* sounded.

* * *

Cadet Keatii passed off the Fifty-Command Drill the next day on her first try, without a single mistake.

"Fifty merits to Cadet Keatii," Russom said, "though I'm not surprised." He swept the rest of us with his usual sardonic sneer. "Some of you would do well to follow her example."

Rinn Stormun, the burly cadet from Ardonar, passed it off next, as crisply and precisely as an automaton.

Huritt practically begged to do it after Rinn, and Kota and I swapped grins. A Hevovitas couldn't be shown up by a robot and a toothpick woman, after all.

He didn't take us outside the lines, but he avoided it only by adding a "Flight, halt" and "Left face" to the sequence.

"Five demerits for inattention to detail," Russom said.

Huritt returned to formation, grumbling like an incoming thunderhead.

I waited until a few others had made their attempts to try it myself. Everyone made mistakes that earned them at least five demerits. I knew I had the sequence down. I'd recited it under my breath and pictured it in my mind while everyone else did it. The trick lay in snapping out each new command as the flight executed the previous one, no more than two seconds apart.

Doing it proved harder than I'd expected. I had to watch constantly to gauge the leading rank's distance from the boundary. At the end I yelled "Flight, halt!" just in time to stop five gleaming boots from stepping across the line.

Perfect. I blew out my breath.

"Hmph," Russom said. I hadn't expected praise, but his eyes narrowed. "You haven't cut your hair yet, Mess-you."

I met his jeer. "Sir, no, sir!"

"Ten demerits for personal sloppiness."

I gaped. *He hasn't given demerits to Kota, the Hevos, or Nayati for their hair.*

Returning to my place in the flight, I matched Huritt's scowl, except Huritt's face had lit with a gloating leer.

* * *

"The girl who passed it off first today, Cadet Keat-ii," said a Soli youth with curly hair, "she must be really smart."

The rest of us, seated on a circle of wobbly chairs in the day-room, peered up from polishing our boots.

"Smarter than you for sure, Domonk," his roommate said with a smirk. "You never did it in the same order three times in a row."

"She only started learning Standard two phases before she got here," I said, and everyone stared.

"She's kind of good-looking, too," said Zoreba, an Obollan cadet.

"If you like toothpick women." Huritt flipped his polishing rag in Zoreba's direction. "Smart won't help her on the obstacle course, and I can't wait to see her trying to handle a rifle as big as she is." He snorted. "Sword masters. Who uses swords anymore?"

Kota and I smothered grins. Somebody's already feeling the competition.

"Cadet Sajjad has nice eyes," Nayati said, "and she smiles more than Keatii."

I rotated my boot in my polish-smeared hands to check its shine. "Cadet Dois is kind of pretty." *She reminds me of Derry.*

Huritt twisted toward me. "Too bad you're too young to do anything about it, Sheggy."

"What, are you underage or something, Masou?" Domonk asked. He had a permanent foggy expression as if he'd been unexpectedly awakened.

Kota and Nayati didn't speak, but Kota's jaw tightened, and his eyes narrowed on Huritt.

My innards tensed but I said, "Three and a half moons until I'm twenty. Who cares? The recruiters didn't. I've had my license since I was fourteen."

"To do what, hold hands?" Huritt scanned the group as if he expected them to laugh at his wit.

Everybody gawked at me, a couple blinking like burrowing owls routed at midday.

"Dois and Keatii might care," Huritt said. "You've never even kissed a girl, have you, Sheggy? Let alone gone all the way. Baby cheeks." He reached for my face.

I caught his arm and pulled. He cut a clean arc in mid-air, hit the floor on his back with a *thunk* and an "Oof," and lay there staring, mouth open in evident shock.

Kota, Nayati, and a Sathi cadet named Santiago uttered whistles and startled exclamations.

I backed off from Huritt's sprawled form with the first rule of combatives training ringing in my memory. "Never apply more force than necessary."

If Huritt's got any brains, he got the message.

Still, I kept one eye on him and my face impassive as I collected my brush and boot and returned to my creaky chair.

Noticing Blockhead's shocked expression, a new realization kicked in. *If this gets back to Russom…*

"Yo, Hevo." Ogundo, another Obollan, offered Huritt a hand. "So, we've resolved that little matter. I don't know about the rest of you, but I'm sure not gonna mess with the Ku-man." He gave me a broad smile, his white teeth flashing in his ebony face.

Impressed with his smooth closure of the situation, I returned a grateful nod.

Huritt accepted Ogundo's hand and plopped onto his chair, red-faced. He shot a murderous glare at me, but Domonk elbowed him in the ribs. "Looks to me like he's got a license to *kill*."

Everybody laughed. Huritt managed a strained smile.

Kota caught my eye. His grave features reminded me of a chanter who's performed every healing ceremony and knows there's nothing else he can do.

"Now," Ogundo drawled, "how about that Sathi girl in Golo Flight? There's one blazing lady." He mimed her curvaceous silhou-ette with his hands and slid an appreciative grin around our circle.

"Way out of your universe, Guns." Zoreba rolled his eyes.

"Not necessarily." Adrian Borbala's eyes held a sage glint. "I know from personal experience that she's adventurous and well-versed in the game. She will go with any man once," he gave a sly wink, "so long as he does not drool in his sleep."

We all hooted, but Rinn said straight-faced, "Sewati will not qual-ify, then."

Blockhead reddened.

I'd never heard what he was called except by Huritt, who always called him Two. I guessed Blockhead and Rinn must be roommates.

"Have you set a record for demerits yet, Two?" asked Zoreba.

"I have calculated it," Rinn said, in the precise manner of one practicing a new language. He placed his boot and polishing brush on the floor to tick off points on his polish-smudged fingers. "To receive one thousand demerits in six moon phases, one must receive a minimum of one hundred sixty-six point six demerits in every phase."

"I think he got that many just on the parade ground today," Do-monk said. "Have you added them up?"

While everybody else tallied Blockhead's demerits, I mentally counted my own.

"Two hundred eighty-nine in less than one phase!" Santiago shouted, and hilarity rang about the room.

I didn't join in. My innards clenched. My own count stood at two hundred eleven, including the hundred hits I'd started with as a pro-bat.

I'm going to wash out of here right along with Blockhead.

* * * * *

Chapter Sixteen

Our days began with physical training, including a two-range run in formation around a track. Shoes pounded a rhythm beneath towering pines, and banners of Thrüss snapped like gunshots in the wind. Even while running, those who fell out of step took demerits.

The buoyancy I'd experienced on first arriving had long passed, but I still ran more easily than I ever had on Tempest. I breathed the pine-crisp air in time with my strides and never broke a sweat.

Solienne's lower gravity made push-ups easier for us Chalca as well, despite the grit on the tarmac biting into our palms.

Once in our third phase, Kota caught my eye with his roguish grin and began doing push-ups one-handed, alternating between right and left. Nayati noticed and started doing them, too, grunting out the count like a hungry shegrul. Spotting Russom nearby, I slipped them a warning stare.

"Apenimon, Kosumi, Mess-you!"

What did I do? I glowered at Russom's continued mockery of my clan name.

We sprang to our feet and braced at attention, eyes caged. Around us, everyone continued doing push-ups to the PT leader's monotone call, but several faces shifted stealthily toward us.

"Can't resist showing off, can you?" Russom said. "What have you got to say for yourselves?"

152 | D.T. READ

"No excuse, *sir!*" we shouted together.

Russom paced across our line of sight, a head and a half taller than Nayati and me. With my eyes caged, my vision leveled on his neck. I watched a vein throbbing there when he yelled, "What was that?"

"No excuse, *sir!*" we shouted again.

"Ten demerits for all of you," Russom said. He stopped to scrutinize each of us. "And Mess-you, get your flea-infested hair cut."

"Sir, no, sir!" *Why does he only pick at me about my hair?*

"Fifty more demerits, then." He leaned in to give me his disparaging smile. "At this rate, you'll be packing out of here by the end of the phase."

That was 535 now!

Huritt, still pumping push-ups, gave a derisive snort.

"Think it's funny, Hevovitas? Take fifty yourself," Russom said without wasting a glance on him. "As you were," he told my friends and me and stalked off the exercise ground.

We dropped to our bellies so swiftly, I skinned a knee. I resumed push-ups with my knee smarting, my ears burning, and Huritt doing his usual impersonation of a storm cloud.

Kota peered sideways at me. "Sorry."

I couldn't shrug in the middle of push-ups.

Entering our barracks afterward, Nayati jutted his jaw at the notice board in the hall. "Obstacle course today! My brother said that's the best part of this. We can vid each other doing it." He shoved my shoulder cheerfully.

Changed into our utility uniforms, we marched to breakfast, a block of gray-green ants.

A whistling wind had risen to sway and rustle the pines by the time we returned to the barracks, and we ducked our faces away from its bite. I dreaded our trek to the obstacle course, despite our rugged field jackets.

Journeyman Russom ordered us onto the drill pad and shouted, "Pa-rade *rest.*"

The ice-dry wind tugged at us as it sighed through the conifers. My fingers grew numb inside my gloves. A swift scan of my fellow trainees revealed their faces reddened by its chill.

Is this some kind of endurance test?

At last a crawler with heavily fogged windows chugged into the clearing. It trundled to a halt before our barracks, issuing a burst of steam, and Russom ordered, "Fall out and get on."

"Fall out" meant we didn't have to march aboard by ranks. Even more surprising, Russom didn't board with us.

"There's an excuse for a feast." Kota grinned.

He, Ogundo, Nayati, and I chose seats near the middle of the snaky vehicle, under one of the heater vents. We removed our caps and leather gloves, poked them into our pockets, and pulled our horsetails out of our coat collars.

Next thing I knew, Lista Dois slid onto the hard bench beside me. Perching close enough that her tangy perfume masked the heater's scorched scent and her knee nudged my thigh, she said, "You cadets from Tempest have the most beautiful hair."

My pulse accelerated, but my face warmed under Kota's amused regard. I managed a chuckle. "Wish Russom thought so."

"Aw, he's jealous." She smiled. "I've never seen you with it loose. May I?"

I shrugged. "Go ahead."

Lista unwound my hair binding. Her light touches sent electric thrills through my spine. *Wish it was Derry doing it.*

She beckoned Kota and Nayati to do the same. "Come on, you two."

Nayati promptly untied his hair, shook it out like a dog shedding water, and beamed at her.

Lista drew my freed hair forward over my shoulders so it covered most of my chest. She ran her fingers through it as if it were black ribbons and studied me appraisingly. "Honestly, if my hair looked good this long, I'd never cut it, either."

"Thanks." In another heartbeat I impulsively said, "I think you'd be even prettier with long hair."

Other stares prodded me as I gathered my hair and retied the binding. Huritt and Blockhead sat near the rear of the crawler, jealousy darkening their faces.

I favored them with a smug smile. *Maybe Lista doesn't care if I'm underage after all.*

The crawler carried us to a corner of the base where brine overwhelmed the scent of wind-bent pines. A distant crashing roar reached us on the persistent gusts.

"The ocean," Nayati said, and inhaled hungrily.

Snow had fallen overnight, but somebody had come out to sweep it off the obstacles. The equipment appeared stark and rugged, black skeletal structures cast against the low sky.

"This is high-risk enough without snow and ice," said Master Spacer Kipoly when we'd exited the crawler. His vapored breath melded into the wispy fog. "Usually we do this for time, but we'll skip that today. We'll have spotters at every site for your safety."

"Can't wait to get going," Nayati said, stamping his feet in the cold.

"Ya there!" I agreed.

We scaled two pourstone walls, one higher than the other and devoid of finger and toeholds, so we had to use knotted ropes. We slithered under razor-wire in six thumb lengths of icy mud that soaked our field jackets and gloves and coated our faces like ceremony dancers wearing gritty paint.

We half-ran, half-jumped along a track of offset span-high rings and crossed a frozen stream by swinging from a horizontal log ladder ten spans high and fifty long. It had rungs spaced so far apart, we had to swing hard from one to reach the next.

The object of our greatest anticipation towered at the end of the course. We had to climb forty spans up a cargo net to a log three times thicker than our bodies, roll over the log, and slide down a rope on the other side.

"Perfect," Nayati said. "It's as high as the rigging on our fishing boat. I'll vid you if you'll vid me, Ku."

Ga'olani Keatii scampered up the net like a spider on a web while the other girls cheered. When she slid astride the log under the watchful eye of the spotter perched there, he handed her the fat rope and gave her a few instructions we couldn't hear from the ground.

Ga'olani nodded, her features concentrated beneath smears of black mud. She swung one leg around the rope for a fast-rappel and landed on the wet gravel with acrobatic lightness.

"Wonder if she'd like rock-climbing?" I asked Kota.

Huritt pushed forward next, and Kota and I traded *what-did-I-tell-you* smirks. His narrowed eyes and the set of his square jaw betrayed his desperation to outperform Ga'olani.

He clambered up the net so rapidly, the spotter called, "Slow it down, Cadet. This isn't for time."

Huritt seized the rough rope and copied Ga'olani's descent, then surveyed the rest of us as if expecting applause. When his stare slid past my shoulder, I peered around.

Lista stood there with her arms folded. "Show off."

Huritt chuckled, but I glimpsed in his eyes a yearning to impress her. "I'm naturally athletic."

I snorted. "C'mon, Lista, you can do better than him."

"Me?" Her blue eyes expanded, so they and her freckles prompted more memories of Derry. "I don't think so." She backed off. "I'm petrified of heights."

"What if I climb it with you?" I asked. "If you keep your eyes on the spotter, you'll be fine."

With my encouragement, she started up the net, her jaw firm with determination. Huritt's glare seared my back as I followed her.

I stayed close enough to reassure her, with a hand at her upper back, and to keep speaking encouragement. "You're doing fine, don't stop." At last the spotter grasped her wrist and helped her onto the battered log.

"Good job, Cadet." He grinned. "See, it wasn't so bad."

Lista returned a wan smile and peered down. "Getting off of here will be."

Straddling the log behind her, I could see her shaking through her heavy field jacket. "Do you want me to go first and hold the rope for you?" I asked.

"Would you, Ku?" She'd gone paler than the clouds.

Hanuk and I had done a lot of rock-climbing and rappelling before he left, but I paid attention to the spacer's advice for handling the rope anyway. I slid easily to the ground and steadied the line while Lista worked her way down.

Six spans from the bottom, she let go and reached for me. I caught her under her arms as if she were Kimama and set her on her feet.

"Rappelling from a cliff is actually easier," I told her, while the other girls hopped about us, yelling, "You did it, you did it!"

Huritt stood off, arms folded across his chest, his expression turbulent. I ignored him, though I didn't turn my back on him.

A few more cadets made the climb before Nayati handed me his link. "I want to send this to my brother."

I zoomed its viewfinder in close enough to see his grin, wide as a ghost cat's with a mouthful of shegrul. Nayati didn't need to show off. He seemed as at ease on the cargo net as in the rigging of his family's fishing boat.

Watching through his link, I unexpectedly *knew* something was about to happen. I shouted a warning.

As Nayati rolled off the log, and the rope took his weight, the bracket anchoring it inexplicably tore loose. A short yell cut the frost-fogged quiet. The spotter swiped for him, but missed. Nayati plummeted and struck the gravel like a full bag of maize.

I lunged for him and dropped to my heels beside him.

Nayati's dark eyes sought mine as he fought to recover his breath. Chalca or not, his face had lost all color, and sweat welled around his mouth and nose.

"Broke something," he gasped. His left hand, rigid as claws, clutched his right shoulder.

"Get a medic!" I shouted as the other cadets closed in. My heart slammed into high gear, and my voice shook. "Lie still, Nat. You're going into shock."

I shrugged off my mud-caked field jacket with quivery hands and pushed it under his head and torso. *Got to put something between him and this cold gravel.*

Nayati clenched his teeth at my efforts and dragged in raking breaths.

"Ku!" Kota crouched beside me, urgency tightening his face. "Use your healing chant."

My stomach wrenched. "I told you what happened when—"

Kota cut me off. "That was a nightmare, Ku, it wasn't real. He's in pain. This *is* real. Do the one for pain."

I faced Nayati. A plea filled his eyes.

My heart lurched. *What if my dreams are becoming real? Was what I just saw a dream?*

"Do it, Ku," Nayati begged through clenched teeth.

Burn you, Machitew.

I shoved shaking hands in the pockets of my sodden utility trousers. During my apprenticeship, my father had taught me to always carry...

No oil cup. I didn't have my oil cup.

Only reflex had made me reach for it. I hadn't carried an oil cup since I'd given up my apprenticeship.

"I don't have any oil-paste." I searched the Chalca faces in the circle of anxious cadets. "Do any of you have some?"

Several cadets, including non-Chalca, shook their heads.

"I've never done it without oil-paste," I told Nayati. "I don't know if it'll work."

"It's good, it's good, do it anyway," he said. He closed his eyes, as if blocking the dull daylight would block his pain.

Kota's gaze locked on mine, insistent. "At least try."

"All right." I shaped the pain glyph on Nayati's brow with a finger dipped in cold mud, then placed my right hand on his head, closed my eyes to shut out the others' curious stares, and began shakily in Chalca. "O, Ancient One who made us, blood and flesh and bone, drive away the spirits of suffering. Drive away the spirits of pain and bring peace to your child."

My voice steadied as I chanted. I drew myself up and started again when I finished. Kota joined me, solemn and earnest.

Two more voices began to fumble through the words. My eyes flicked open.

Huritt and Blockhead stood over me, their faces somber.

Surprised, I shut my eyes and kept chanting.

Halfway through the fourth repetition, Nayati relaxed under my hand, and his breathing steadied. When I glanced at him, he tried to smile. "Keep going, Ku. It's working."

"Coming through!" someone shouted behind me.

I didn't lift my hand from Nayati's disheveled head until a medic shoved me aside. Then I withdrew into the knot of anxious cadets and watched as one medic tore open Nayati's field jacket, while the other pelted him with questions.

One man immobilized Nayati's shoulder with a plastic brace and bands, while the other checked his blood pressure, pulse, and pupils. Finally one of them asked, "Do you think you can walk with assistance, Cadet?"

Nayati nodded, but he bit off a groan and paled when the medic helped him to his feet.

The other man thrust my field jacket at me as he started away. "Put that back on, Cadet, or we'll be treating you for hypothermia next."

Only then did I realize how hard I was shaking.

Boarding the crawler for the return trip, my fellow flight members eyed me when they passed my seat. Some of their faces revealed curiosity. Others kept as far away from me as they could in the narrow aisle, their eyes fearful.

What do they think I am, a demon?

Actually, if I'm Machitew, I am a demon.

Lista hesitated beside my bench. "May I sit here, Ku?" Her tone held a wariness it hadn't earlier, and her eyes bore a mix of awe and… apprehension?

"Sure you want to?" I returned. Exhaustion slumped me in my seat. My shaking had only begun to subside.

She didn't sit as close to me as she had the first time. She studied my profile for a while, as if gathering her nerve to ask, "What did you do for Nayati? Was it some kind of magic?"

I shook my head. "No, it's not. I don't have any powers. I just memorized some healing chants."

"But it worked," she insisted.

"It shouldn't have," I said. "You're supposed to put sacred oil-paste on the person's head first." My vision settled on the watery mud filling the rubbery flooring's ridges. "I don't know why it did. Maybe Nayati and Kota believe in it enough so the missing the oil didn't matter."

"You don't believe in it?"

I shrugged. *Not for myself.*

We rode in silence for a while before Lista slid closer and reached for my gloveless hand. Her bare fingers lay like soft icicles entwined with mine. "He'll be all right, Ku."

"Ya." Doubt roiled in my mind, but I didn't disengage my hand from hers.

When Huritt flung himself with a thump onto the bench opposite ours, I lifted my head. He stared at me for a full minute, his probing eyes shadowed with misgivings, but for a different reason than the other trainees.

I returned his stare, and he jeered, "Trying to be a chanter, Sheggy? Who'll chant for you if you have an accident?"

"Better not be you," I said in a snarl. Lista's hand tensed in mine, but I added, "You don't know the words."

Huritt snorted. "I don't need to. My father can hire real chanters who don't smell like shegruls." He smiled at Lista and puffed out his chest. "You've got better choices than Sheggy, Dois. He's only got a license to hold hands."

She blinked in obvious puzzlement, but he didn't explain. He simply smirked at me, shoved himself to his feet, and returned to the rear of the crawler.

* * *

Winter's early dark enveloped our barracks long before the crawler huffed to a halt before it. We tumbled out, and our boots clattered like hoofbeats in the barracks' tiled hall.

I stopped short in the doorway to our room. Nayati's gear had been cleared out already. I didn't need the coiling in my gut to tell me he wouldn't be back.

* * * * *

Chapter Seventeen

I jumped at a bootfall behind me and wrenched about. My fists reflexively knotted.

Russom stood there. In my weariness, I hadn't heard him approaching. He noted my clenched hands and sneered. "No, you do not get your own room, Mess-you. You are moving in with Silva and Borbala, though it seems a waste of effort. I don't expect you to remain much longer yourself."

I didn't answer, just glowered at him.

"You have until chow to pass room inspection," he said, "so you had better get busy."

"Yes, sir."

Entering the cavernous hallway, where his voice carried its full length, he added, "And write up fifty merits for rendering appropriate first aid to an injured flight mate."

I froze. Did he say fifty *merits?*

I shed my muddy gear before I tugged the sheets off my camp bed and hauled my clothes out of the locker. *Don't want to get everything else dirty.*

By the time I lugged my first armload into the next room, Silva and Borbala had finished showering. Both wore warm PT uniforms and deep scowls. They'd been expecting something. Silva's camp bed had been replaced by a wooden stackbed with bare mattresses, and a third locker had been jammed in behind the door.

Returning their frowns, I shoved my clothes onto the upper bunk. "Wasn't my idea."

I'd barely hung up my uniforms and dumped my underwear, socks, and shoes into the locker so I could make the upper bunk when Russom arrived.

We snapped to attention, but he didn't enter the room. He eyed it from the doorway instead, a malevolent god surveying his subjects. "Twenty demerits each."

Silva and Borbala stared, but Russom said, "The three of you should have this room in good order by now. Nobody goes to chow until it passes. Keeping everyone waiting will earn all of you another twenty demerits, not to mention the ire of your flight mates."

He left, and we glared at each other. Mostly, the other two glared at me. Blaming me.

"I'm not missing supper," I said. "Silva, you help with my top bunk, and I'll help you with the bottom one. Borbala, see what you can do with my locker." I pointed with my chin at the dented cabinet.

Russom returned fifteen minutes later. He started with the stack-bed and scowled at the underside of the upper bunk. Mouth pursed, he opened my locker to scrutinize my uniforms and footgear. Through the corner of one caged eye I noticed my roommates holding their breaths.

"Passable," Russom grunted, "but barely." He addressed me. "You are out of uniform, Mess-you. You have five minutes to remedy it."

"Yes, sir." I snatched my hygiene kit, towel, and a PT uniform and charged for the showers.

Seven minutes later, my damp horsetail froze on the march to the chow hall. I didn't care.

* * *

My new roommates slept on top of their beds, lying rigid as logs to avoid messing them up, but I flung my moth-eaten blanket on the floor at the foot of my locker. They'd have to go out of their way to kick or step on me there.

I pressed myself into the corner, my spine against the cold metal, the blanket providing no padding beneath me. I hoped the self-imposed discomforts would hold off sleep. I knew too well what would happen if I succumbed. My supper lay like a stone in my stomach.

Machitew's bodiless mask materialized, drifting a little above me, the moment both roommates' breathing slowed and deepened. The toothy mouth gaped open, hungry. The too-familiar eyes gleamed at me from their ragged holes.

"Another healing chant." The voice hissed this time, an icy breath in my face. "Why do you continue to deny the Path the Ancients set for us?"

My stomach knotted. So did my hands. "The Ancients haven't set any Path for me." I said it through gritted teeth, spitting defiance. "They don't care that I exist."

The vaporous shape uttered a humorless chuckle. "Then we will make them take notice."

When the stifling sensation of the ghostly mask enclosed my head, I raised both hands to cover the eyeholes, to block the horror I knew would come.

My hands found no mask. I shoved their heels to my eyes instead.

It did no good.

The rope's rusted attachment wrenched from the log with a metallic groan when Nayati gripped it. He yelled, and I watched him hurtle to the gravel, clutching the limp rope.

I saw myself lay my hand on his head to begin the healing chant, but it lolled on a broken neck. Sightless eyes fixed on me, glassy and blank. His mouth hung open.

The apparition swirled like smoke to hover at my left shoulder. Its frigid breath raked the nape of my neck and its voice, my voice, gloated. "We have claimed him for ourselves."

"No." I watched my other self cradle Nayati's pale head in my hands. "He's not dead."

"Death is more powerful and permanent than life," the ghost said. "Once we join, we'll be able to defeat the Ancient Ones. They know it, and they fear us."

I remembered the sense of abandonment when my Chant to Extinguish Fires had failed to smother my stepmother's cooking fire.

"Ya." Bitterness flavored the specter's tone. "They don't care about us. It's time to accept who we are, time to accept our power."

"No." I witnessed myself releasing Nayati's sprawled form to stare at my hands, slick with blood, though he had no external wounds. I shook my head inside the enclosing mask. "He didn't die, Machitew."

The apparition didn't seem to hear me. "We must accept our role together. We cannot avoid it. We only have to see things, the way we saw the members of our family and class, to exercise our power."

"No!" I repeated. Cold shrouded me like the mist on the obstacle course, and shivers gripped me again. "He didn't die."

A voice I didn't recognize for a second banished the wraith and released me from the ethereal mask. "Bogeys, Mess-you?"

Borbala.

I had to drag in a breath before I could speak. "Yes, it looked a lot like you."

With my next heartbeat, I flung my locker open with a shaky hand. In the echo of its *clang* I scooped out the oval portrait along with my link. I hesitated before curling my hand around it so tightly, its metal frame bit my palm.

Ya, that'll help, too.

The hallway with its gray tiles appeared angular and tilted in the minimal light. I padded toward the stairwell, set like an airlock between the ground floor and the outer doors. *Nobody will bother me there. Got to talk to Gram.*

Already thumbing my link with the hand holding both it and the pendant, I absently pressed the door's tarnished bar-latch with the other.

A blast sounded directly overhead.

The fire horn! I jumped, and the pendant slipped between my fingers. I scrambled and managed not to drop my link, but the pendant struck the gleaming floor with a sharp *clink* between the piercing honks. My breath stopped as I followed its skittering course up the hall, halfway to Russom's quarters.

Leaping after it, I plowed into two cadets, their eyes as round as owls' as they barreled from their room. A stampede followed, audible even through the repeating blasts, and I lost sight of the pendant.

Running footfalls upstairs echoed the floor-shaking thunder around me as everybody headed for the exits.

The fire horn shut off as suddenly as it began, and an unmistakable bellow cut the ringing silence. "Hall, atten-*shun!*"

We slammed to attention, our backs to the plastered walls.

Russom stood at the top of the hall. He wore only PT trousers and his dog tags, swinging on their chain around his neck, but his muscular chest and the fury flaring from his dark eyes made him appear far more menacing than in full uniform on the drill pad.

He scowled at something on the floor a span from his bare toes and swooped to pick it up.

My stomach dropped. I knew exactly what he'd found even before he began to search the hall for me.

"Masou, front and center," he said. He kept his tone dangerously quiet, but it carried from one end of the hall to the other. Something about him using my real clan name for once curdled my blood.

I stepped clear of the wall, pivoted at the center of the hall, and paced to six spans from him. I stiffened into a brace and kept my face expressionless, caging my eyes on the pulse in his neck.

Somewhere in that eternal march I realized my hair hung loose and unkempt about my shoulders. I had unbound it before retreating to my corner. *One more mark against me.*

"So." Russom kept his voice just loud enough to ensure everyone would hear him. "Decided you've had enough and tried to go AWOL, Masou? Maybe not. I can see your link in your hand."

My fingers tightened on it, curled at my trouser seam.

"Trying to call home to Mommy?" Sarcasm pickled his words.

I locked my vision on his jugular and stayed mute.

"Crying about how mean I am to her baby boy?"

The Hevovitases chortled behind me.

"You think it's funny?" Russom's tight stare flicked past my shoulder. "Both Hevovitases, Domonk, Zoreba, and Borbala, write up ten demerits each."

All sound snuffed out.

Russom returned his attention to me. "Or, Masou, were you calling your girlfriend?" He raised his hand. For an instant my gaze followed it, and I glimpsed the pale oval between his thumb and forefinger.

My innards tightened, and I clenched my teeth. *If he says something vulgar about Derry…*

"She is indeed a beauty, Masou," Russom said. "You have good taste in women, even if you have nothing else going for you. I think I'll keep this."

I stared in horror as, with a soft *swish*, he dropped the pendant into his trouser pocket.

"Whatever idiocy you were up to," he went on in his deadly quiet tone, "you seem to be ignorant of the fact that barracks doors are armed at night, so you woke me up."

I gaped, wondering how he could blame me for tripping the alarm, and he displayed a wolfish smile.

"Let this be a warning to all of you." He addressed the cadets crowded behind me. "The barracks have security vid-pickups at key locations, including the doors. The monitors are in my quarters." His narrowed vision returned to me. "I watched you hit the bar-latch, Masou, which is the only reason we're not having this conversation outdoors in the cold.

"Besides me, you woke your flight mates. You triggered a false alarm and induced panic in a crowded place. That's worth at least five hundred demerits, don't you think?"

Five hundred? My heart stopped, a cold stone in my chest.

"Don't you, Masou?"

"Sir, yes, sir," I said.

"Good." Russom's smile reminded me of Eyebrows in his lair. "Flight dismissed." He wheeled and withdrew to his quarters.

I pivoted toward my room, too.

The girls had packed into the doorway when they'd dashed downstairs at the fire alarm. Lista's eyes held mine for a second, bright with hurt.

My puzzlement at it, amid the jibes and shoves from male cadets, evaporated with one thought that left me weak.

Five hundred demerits. I'm done. It's over.

* * * * *

Chapter Eighteen

Borbala grunted as we slouched to our room. "Clever of you, Mess-you."

I glared a threat at him.

He didn't push it.

"Wise of you, Borbala," I said.

Wrapped once more in the rodent-scented blanket, I wedged myself into the corner by my locker to wait for my roommates to sleep once more. Moonlight sliced past the window cover, and the wind shushed across its panes. When their breathing grew even and rhythmic once more, I crept out to the hall, sat against the wall, and drew out my link.

I didn't dare speak aloud in the empty silence, so I thumbed a message to Gram on the keypad. "Machitew haunting me, wanting me to join him. Don't want this."

She already knows. What will she tell me?

Minutes passed as slowly as moon positions while I waited for a reply. The cold deepened, and I hugged myself for warmth. I tipped my head to the wall, eyes closed, and listened to the wind strengthening outside.

The soft chime signaling an incoming message rang like a gong in the hall. I sat motionless as a tavo in the shadow of a circling hawk, eyeing Russom's quarters door.

171

As my heart's panicked surge subsided, I switched off the link's sound and squinted at its display. Gram's precise text glowed out at me.

"My Akuleh, I've expected this. I'm sorry it's begun so soon. Keep your courage and be strong on the Path. Always say the Warding Chant before you sleep. I say the chants for you every day. I love you. Gram."

I stifled a groan. *How can I ward off myself?*

I slipped into my room and returned to my corner. There I sat, my back to the chilly locker, shivering and staring at the darkness until I could no longer keep my eyes open. Even after *On Your Feet* snapped me from fractured sleep, images of Nayati's lolling head and glassy eyes lingered.

What if something went wrong, and he died last night? I need to find out.

Bleary-eyed, I jammed my feet into my running shoes and charged into a tickly snowfall, feathers from molting clouds.

"You're still here, Mess-you?" Domonk asked as we formed up on the drill pad. "I thought you'd be gone by now."

I opened my mouth to retort, but Russom exited the barracks. "Ten demerits for talking in formation, Domonk," he snapped.

Beyond snide mutters from a few flight mates, I managed not to draw any unwanted attention during PT. Russom's sneer rekindled my anger about him taking my pendant of Derry, and concern for Nayati nagged me. I scowled through calisthenics.

As I entered the barracks afterward, Lista made a wide circle around me to the stairs, her nose scrunched as if I'd stepped in a shegrul pile. Her pursed lips and downcast eyes betrayed hurt and bitterness.

I touched her elbow. "What's wrong, Lista?"

She jerked away and glared at me, her jaw tight, her eyes smoldering. "You really don't know?"

Having no idea what she meant, I watched, wordless, as she whirled and charged up the stairs.

"What was that about?" I asked Kota.

He shrugged. "No idea. I don't have a lot of experience with girls."

Warmth and the aromas of food welcomed us into the chow hall later. *Hot kasse, kippered fish, and porridge. Always kippered fish. Sure do miss shegrul bacon.* My stomach growled, and I peered around to be sure Russom hadn't heard it.

Automaton servers, simple robotic arms that whined and whirred, dumped grayish mounds into ceramic bowls as we sidled through the food line.

"What's this?" Blockhead asked, eyeing the lumpy contents.

"Oats, I think." Kota sniffed his but appeared doubtful. "It smells like oats. Try putting a lot of honey in it."

I hoped that would help, but I requested a couple extra little fish and a sweet roll just in case.

The tables stood in precise rows the length of the chow hall. We carried our trays to the first empty one, centered our flight caps under our chairs, and sat at attention to eat. We had twenty minutes to get our food, shovel it in, and march out, alert for prowling training officers the whole time. We rarely spoke while eating, but Keatii always made amiable eye contact.

Not that day. She kept her eyes lowered as if embarrassed.

About sharing a table with me?

"Table, atten-*shun!*" Huritt barked and practically knocked his chair backward as he snapped to his feet.

The rest of us sprang up, too. A prickling at my nape, like a spider tiptoeing across my neck, warned me exactly where the officer stood outside my peripheral vision. I steeled myself for the usual derision.

"Mess-you," Russom purred, "were you not instructed to center your flight cap under your chair?"

"Sir, yes, sir."

"Why didn't you do it?"

I didn't miss both Hevos' eyes gleaming with restrained mirth, but I said, "No excuse, sir."

"Fix it," Russom said. "Five demerits for noncompliance with a directive." He strode off, and we dropped to our seats.

I leaned to adjust my cap's placement, and Blockhead and Huritt exchanged grins. My cap lay a span from where I'd put it. A muddy toe mark confirmed Blockhead had pushed it there.

"You must be in the demerit pit by now, Sheggy." Huritt snorted. "Five hundred demerits last night, and five more this morning."

I already knew it. *They'll announce my name first at Commander's Call.* My stomach rolled as I imagined the humiliation. My hunger curdled itself into nausea.

"Shut up, Hevo," Kota said.

Huritt appeared about to retort, but Blockhead blinked and cast a worried stare at the wall chrono. "It's time to go."

"Fine with me." I wiped mud off my flight cap and stood.

As we filed out, Kota cast a longing gaze at the unfinished food on his plate.

A crawler waited outside, its windows fogged as usual. We recognized Indigo Flight's training officer waving us aboard, into the blowing heat and normal burned-dust smell.

"Indigo and Juno Flights," he said, "you're going to the shooting range this morning."

My mood lifted. *Something I'm actually good at.*

In the next heartbeat, it plummeted. The shooting range. *There's a haunting from Machitew waiting to happen.*

The ghost's words coiled across my mind, an ethereal snake. "We must accept our role together. We can't avoid it. We only have to see things, the way we saw the members of our family and our class, to exercise our power."

I shuddered, recalling my split-second glimpse of the loose rope bracket. Too-fresh memories through the spectral mask made my skin crawl.

I'll take the last position on the firing line, where I can't see anybody. If I can't see them, Machitew can't make something happen.

Cadets from both flights filled the long seats, hunkered in their field jackets. Kota beckoned me down the aisle, and we found a couple empty seats next to Ogundo.

When Ogundo leaned away to talk to someone else, I nudged Kota. "Any word about Nayati?"

"I haven't heard anything." Kota furrowed his brow. "Why?"

I described the haunting as if it had been a nightmare.

"He walked away with the medics," Kota said. "You saw him. It was his shoulder he injured, not his neck."

"I know." I hesitated before telling him about my prescient glimpse of the loose rope bracket, wondering if he'd think I'd gone off a mental cliff. "It was like a split-second dream."

Kota's features grew serious. After a while he said, "I think they would've told us if he'd died."

The morning's overcast lowered on the base and darkened like a premonition. I didn't feel reassured.

* * * * *

Chapter Nineteen

My sense of impending threat deepened through the ride to the range. I locked my hands between my knees and forced away fears of accidents on the firing line.

The tension ebbed on entering a brightly lit classroom full of long tables, where we spent a couple hours familiarizing ourselves with the standard-issue combat energy rifle.

The M-29X appeared to be a militarized version of my hunting rifle back home, so I had no trouble taking it apart and reassembling it when we were instructed to do so. Clipping miniature parts together and threading them through one another came naturally to my fingers.

I shared a table with Sajjad. She'd been pleasant in the past, but now she studiously ignored me. *Like everybody else. Fine.*

Still, I stage whispered, "Red end points forward," when she inserted the cylindrical energy generator backward. Left uncorrected, it would've caused a powerful enough explosion to destroy the weapon when fired, which would've killed her.

She flipped the generator around without acknowledging me.

I didn't miss Machitew's grunt of displeasure at my ear.

Sajjad and I raised our heads in unison when a shadow abruptly fell across our table. Russom studied us for several heartbeats. He didn't say anything, merely quirked an eyebrow and moved on. Sajjad blew out a breath and resumed assembling her rifle.

We exited to the range in a wind that slapped and tugged at us and moaned like a premonitory ghost. Its wails sent shivers coursing along my spine. *Wonder who else locked their energy generator in backward?*

Stomach twisting, I strode deliberately to the firing line's last position, where I could face away from all the other shooters.

Kota followed, watching me through questioning eyes.

"It's better if I can't see anybody," I said.

He nodded, his expression grave.

We shot from standing, half-kneeling, and prone positions, with and without barriers, and at increasing distances until our targets were reduced to fingernail size.

Stretched out for prone-position shots, it felt as if I lay on an ice slab rather than pourstone. The cold penetrated my field jacket and heavy trousers, chilling my belly and thighs. Between the wind and the weapon's frigid steel, my hands ached in my fur-lined gloves.

I hadn't done much winter hunting, but I knew how to adjust for wind, though it affected projectile rounds more than energy bursts. I braced my legs wide apart to stabilize my body and lined up my shot in the sights.

A boot scuffed nearby. I didn't bother to check. I knew very well who stood there. *He'll wait until I start to squeeze the trigger, and then he'll kick my foot or something.*

Teeth tight, I anchored my boots and drew a breath.

"Commence firing," the range master ordered.

I focused on the first target. Released my breath as I steadily squeezed the trigger.

My first sizzling burst lit the length of the misty range, trailing a sharp carbon scent past my nostrils, and leaving a bitter taste in my mouth. Zips and hums sounded up the line behind me. Fearing a blast any second, I shifted the muzzle a hair to the right for the second target, up for the third, left for the fourth.

I lowered my rifle and clicked the safety on, and my innards unknotted. I released a breath. A gust swept the smoke off the targets, and I peered through my scope. I couldn't keep from smiling despite my anxiety. Each target bore a small sear-mark at dead center.

"Cease firing," the range master called.

"Nicely done, Cadet," someone said behind me.

Not Russom. I twisted around.

Indigo Flight's training officer, Journeyman Quinron, stood near my feet. "Those are the best shots I've seen today. Write up twenty merits."

Surprise dropped my mouth open. "Thank you, sir."

With our rifles cleaned and secured, we formed up to wait for the crawler. I scanned both flights with a sigh of relief. *No spooky glimpses, no accidents. Beat you this time, Machitew.*

A subtle nag persisted. *The day isn't finished yet.*

Boarding the crawler, Journeyman Quinron announced, "You'll return to your barracks now to clean up before lunch."

"Yes, sir!" we shouted in unison.

We never learned if the same thing had happened to Indigo Flight, but we found our barracks ransacked. Every bed had been stripped, locker contents strewn everywhere, and tiny paws had tracked mud through hallways, latrines, and sleeping rooms, upstairs and down.

"Silvertails!" somebody shouted. "Who was stupid enough to open a window?"

A firing squad of glowers locked on me.

"It wasn't Masou," Silva said. "Our window's sealed."

I nodded thanks. "I'll mop. I've had lots of practice. You two take care of our clothes."

Something occurred to me as I started for the janitor's closet. *First time I've even come close to thinking about my stepmother since I got here.*

I paused at another realization. *I'd rather mop here and get bellowed at by Russom than mop back home and get beaten by her.*

The closet contained two mops with splintery handles and two metal buckets. It would take far too long to scrub all the ground floor rooms if everybody waited for a turn, I knew, so I did some haggling. "I'll mop all your rooms if you'll help my roommates with our beds and clothes."

"What if our room doesn't pass?" asked Zoreba.

"If it doesn't," I said with more bravado than certainty, "it won't be because of the floors."

What if it is, though? What if everybody misses lunch because their floors aren't clean enough?

I squelched the thought. "Kota!" I yelled. He spun around, and I flung a mop to him, like a spear with a head of soggy cords. "You start at that end of the hall, and I'll start here."

While I ran steaming water into one bucket, I surveyed the impatient crowd outside the closet door. "Any of you good at making beds?"

Rinn's large hand shot up.

"Good." I pointed. "You make Kota's bed while he mops. Teamwork here."

I dumped greenish floor cleaner with a nose-biting scent into the rusty bucket and shoved it toward Kota. "Make sure you reach all the way under the beds and into the corners, and don't leave any streaks."

"Yes, *sir*!" Kota popped a comic salute and retreated down the hall, his bucket sloshing.

I seized the other one and froze. *Sket, I sounded just like my stepmother.*

Huritt planted himself in the doorway like a surly gate guard when I reached his room. "You're not coming in here, Sheggy."

"Fine, but you can't use my mop until I'm done." I dunked it in my bucket and swished it past his boots, "accidentally" splashing them.

"Mess-*you*!" Russom's roar from the head of the hall silenced chatter in mid-word. We froze at attention.

Yi, did he see me do that? I tucked the mop handle to my side like the flight's guidon staff. "Sir!" I shouted.

"Did I give you permission to take charge of this crew of losers, Mess-you?" Russom demanded.

Take charge? I didn't do that. Did I? Baffled, I said, "Sir, no, sir."

Russom eyed me for endless seconds, a threatening smile curving one corner of his mouth before he said, "Carry on," and returned to his office.

I resumed mopping, more bewildered than before. He didn't even give me demerits. I must be up to twelve hundred by now. He's got to be playing with me.

Anger clenched my teeth.

Domonk chuckled as he passed me, stepping awkwardly over a sudsy puddle. "You must be really excited about Commander's Call, Mess-you. I bet yours is the first name they'll call."

* * *

Officers in Charge used Commander's Calls to address their troops. Sometimes they announced changes to regulations, while other times they briefed things like safety issues. In active duty units, commanders held the gatherings to present medals or conduct promotions. In Basic Training, only washouts had their names read aloud.

We marched to the parade ground after breakfast at the end of our third phase. Skies as gray as unwashed cotton and a wind pushing at me like an executioner's prod reinforced my sense of doom.

"Enjoy your last meal, Sheggy?" Huritt asked under cover of stamping footfalls.

I gave no indication I'd heard him. My "last meal" rolled like a stone in my gut.

The 33rd Aerospace Training Wing consisted of twelve flights divided into three squadrons. Two hundred thirty-two cadets now, due to a few medical departures like Nayati, stood in orderly ranks of about twenty people. The cadet corps filled the whole parade ground.

I glanced right and left as Juno Flight cut a right face before the reviewing stand and halted with a crisp stomp. I spotted taut faces in Indigo and Kalor Flights on either side of us, as well as in Juno Flight. Reflections of my own nerves.

Commander's Call began with the dismissals. A senior spacer with jowls like an old hound's took the podium. "The following cadets will report to the orderly room for transfers to Ground Forces Basic." His voice yowled like a hound's, too.

The blustery wind died as if holding its breath. Whirling snowflakes stilled.

"From Alta Flight…"

Every flight had at least one washout. Some had two. At my periphery, a girl in Indigo Flight visibly stiffened when the man called her name. Blinking fast, she made a sharp about-face and marched out of formation, her spine still straight.

"From Juno Flight…" said the senior spacer.

I fixed my vision on the back of Lista's cap and gritted my teeth.

* * * * *

Chapter Twenty

I kept my face neutral and my hands clenched at my trouser seams. My heart thudded against my ribs.

"Kosumi, Nayati," the spacer called. "Medical deferment for six months."

Relief enveloped me. *He didn't die. He'll be all right. What you showed me was a lie, Machitew.*

"Hevovitas, Sewati."

Blockhead gave a sharp intake of breath from my left, and his mouth gaped like a landed fish.

Not surprising.

"And…"

I braced myself. Would he call me Mess-you too?

"Domonk, Jaspreet. Moving on to Kalor Flight…"

"Give the dirt dogs a kick for me," Huritt said under his breath as Blockhead lurched an about-face to follow Domonk off the parade ground. I detected satisfaction in Huritt's smirk and remembered what Kota had said about his determination to beat his cousins along with everyone else.

Huritt must've sensed my observation, because he shifted his smug attention to me. "There's always next phase, Sheggy."

His voice came through a fog. My mind gripped one fact as tenaciously as an eagle's talons on its prey. *I survived. At least for this phase, I survived.*

On the march to the barracks afterward, my boots barely grazed the wet tarmac.

Russom dismissed us, but shouted, "Mess-you."

I stopped short. "Sir."

"You're moving in with Rinn Stormun across the hall," he said. "If you two want lunch, you will do it quickly."

"Yes, sir."

My mood sank. *Burn. The cadet who crunches numbers and never smiles.*

Unlike Silva and Borbala, Rinn helped me move. While I arranged my belongings in the drawers according to regs, Rinn hung my uniforms. He squared each one on its hanger and checked the buttons and zippers. Studying the locker through a squint, he set the hangers precisely one thumb-width apart on the rod.

I didn't know whether to laugh or groan. *This is way beyond a normal Tidy Tavo.*

"Now your bed." Rinn grasped my wadded sheet and flung it over my mattress with a crisp snap. "Like this."

"Thanks." I fought an urge to snort at his solemn demeanor. *Like those stuffy manservants in old Soli mystery vids.*

I folded corners and tugged worn sheets so tightly under Rinn's analytical eye that I feared they'd rip.

"Where did you learn to do all this?" I asked. "Did you go to a military school?"

"Yes." Rinn straightened. His throaty accent riddled his second-language stiffness. "I attended the Preparatory Institute at Impelnor. You learn much faster than Sewati. He is the one who allowed the silvertails to come inside."

I smirked. "I don't drool, either."

Rinn gave a hearty chuckle that lit his eyes and tightened his scar, the first real display of humor I think I'd seen from him. "I did not think you did."

Encouraged, I dared to ask, "Is Golmolor anywhere near Caerden on Ardonar? I met someone from Caerden a few phases ago." *Already feels like a year ago.*

The light in his eyes snuffed out, and his jaw hardened. He leveled a hard hazel gaze on me. "Five decades before Ardonar achieved space travel, a king was assassinated. A great war began because of it." He growled the words. "Golmolor had alliances with one side, and Caerden with the other. More than five million people were killed in all the nations that fought.

"After seven years, Caerden's side was victorious. Peace was made, but there is still distrust between us."

"Oh," I said. "Sorry I brought it up." *Better not mention Derry.*

Rinn shrugged. "To answer you, Caerden is farther north and surrounded by the Polar Sea. Golmolor is landlocked and walled with mountains. We are mostly farmers."

Movement outside our door caught my eye. "Room, atten-*shun!*" I said, and we stiffened to attention.

I glimpsed a vicious glint in Russom's eye as he stepped inside. He started by scrutinizing my bunk. "Hmph."

He swung my locker open and arched an eyebrow. Jerked out its three drawers one at a time. Each shrieked at a different pitch, like kosas in agony. "Oil these," he ordered and reached into the top one. I winced, waiting for him to toss its contents on the floor.

"Five demerits for debris in your drawer, Mess-you," he said. "Clean it up. Your flight is waiting."

"Yes, sir." *What debris?* When he left the room, I broke attention and sprang for the offending drawer.

Russom had made a kosa's nest of it. I scooped out a tangle of gray PT shirts and shorts, and a small object fell from the folds to *clink* on the drawer's bottom. Derry's pendant.

I stared at it for three or four heartbeats. *Why did Russom give it back? Has he bugged it?*

I'll worry about it later.

I jammed the pendant into my front trouser pocket, dumped my scrambled PT clothes on my bunk, and began to fold them with fumbling hands.

"Like this," Rinn said. He folded one of my crewshirts with a few quick motions.

"Thanks." I watched in amazement and grinned. "Are you sure you're not an automaton? How do you do that?"

He chuckled once more. "I have had a lot of practice. Only my right eye is a machine."

"Your right eye?" I stared at his face, wondering if he was tugging my braid. Except for being slightly lower than the left, I couldn't discern any difference between them.

"I received it at the same time as this." He indicated his scar. "It can see the complete light spectrum. I will not need night-vision lenses." A hint of amusement colored his tone.

"How——?" I started, then stopped myself. *He probably gets asked all the time. He'd probably rather forget.*

Rinn didn't seem perturbed. He said in a matter-of-fact manner, "There was an accident while I was training a kaluç. He kicked me in the face."

I gaped, a crewshirt dangling from my hands. "What's a ka-*loosh?*"

"They are large riding animals," Rinn said, "like horses on So-lienne and some other worlds. Except they are omnivores, like bears on Satha. They have tails like dogs, but they do not wag." He glanced up from briskly folding another of my shirts, and his features grew stern. "We must hurry, Ku."

"Sorry." I shut up and got to work.

Between surviving the first dismissal and gaining Rinn as my roommate, I smiled like a well-fed ghost cat all afternoon. Still, dread swelled when we turned in for the night. *Will Machitew haunt me again?*

After Rinn fell asleep, I dug my link from my drawer and entered the hall, silent on bare feet. The tiles' iciness bit at my soles.

Please let there be something from Gram.

I slid to the floor against the wall, its rough surface grating my skin through my crewshirt, and opened my vidmail.

Two vids waited in the queue, one from Kimama, one from Gram. I let out my breath in a rush and switched from sound to subtitles to watch Kimama's vid.

She rambled about her pet tavo and held him up to show me how much he'd grown. "I call him Ku," she said, "because I miss you."

I chuckled, but her wistful features sent a pang through my heart. I whispered, "Miss you too, Butterfly."

Gram appeared somber in her vid. "Stay strong, Akuleh. Machitew always torments those he wants. Say the Warding Chant before you sleep, and learn to look up. Keep your courage. These experiences are important for you."

Learn to look up? I scrunched my forehead and thumbed glowing keys. "What do you mean about looking up, Gram?"

I returned to my room with another phrase twining through my mind. *Machitew always torments those he wants.*

* * *

I had Rinn pinned to the floor in a chokehold before my eyes opened. His spluttering and tearing at my arm with both large hands woke me fully. His eyes, startlingly close to mine, bulged like a sniper lizard's, and he gulped.

Releasing him at once, I said, "Combatives reflexes. Sorry. Don't ever poke me again, just call my name." I noted the wall chrono, its digits glowing red, and asked, "Why'd you wake me early? There's five more minutes before *On Your Feet.*"

Rinn rose, scowling, and brushed floor dust off himself. "Five minutes to put on our shoes and use the latrine so we are ready. You must never be late to the formation, because you are a probat."

"Right." Feeling sheepish, I said again, "Sorry about tackling you." I hung up the heavy field jacket I'd slept in and snagged my shoes from my locker. "You could've told me about getting up early when you said we should sleep in our PT clothes."

"I apologize." Brows still lowered so deeply he resembled Huritt, Rinn sounded more annoyed than apologetic.

We arrived at the exit to find four girls already there, hunched in their PT jackets. Ga'olani greeted us with her modest smile, but Lista persisted in ignoring me.

"'Morning." I ventured a cautious smile.

"Hmph," she said.

What's going on with her?

The first brassy notes of *On Your Feet* blasted the morning quiet to shards. We charged outside, squinting against icy blasts in our faces, and dashed to our places. With Kota and Guns on my heels, the rest of the flight thundered out behind.

Losing three people had shifted our places in formation, like a game in which players scramble among safe spots. Huritt, his expression surly, remained at my right, but Ga'olani had moved into Blockhead's place between Kota and me.

Four stragglers pelted from the building as the final note faded like our breaths on the wind, and Russom shouted, "Ten demerits, you loafers."

With everyone at attention, he said, "Uniform of the day is service blues. You are beginning your academic training today." His vision rested on me. "Although it will be wasted on some of you."

After PT and breakfast, we marched to the viditorium in a tight square of dark blue. Wind slapped our service dress overcoats around our legs and snatched at our flight caps.

Before each flight paced a cadet carrying its little flag, or guidon. Guns, who'd been appointed Juno Flight's guidon bearer because of his height, needed both hands to keep our maroon banner upright in the gusts.

My starched shirt itched across my shoulder blades and under my arms. My service-dress trousers pinched, uncomfortably snug where the utility trousers had been loose. I set my teeth and tried to ignore how they chafed with each step.

Old snow, dry and dirty, crunched under our polished shoes, threatening us with slips and falls. More than once we reached out to catch or steady each other.

The viditorium's faded blue walls enclosed several hundred wood-and-metal chairs, each row long enough to seat two flights. We filed in, swept off our caps, tugged off our gloves, and stamped snow off our shoes with an echoing clatter. We shucked our overcoats and draped them on the scratched seatbacks, but we remained standing, shifting around, blowing into our hands, or tucking them in our armpits to thaw them while we waited.

The viditorium warmed gradually. Vents along the baseboards spewed the same burned smell as the crawlers' heaters and more swirling dust than heat.

Voices rose cautiously around me, humming with curiosity like bees at a hive. The murmurs increased to chattering once our training officers withdrew to the rear of the hall.

Beside Kota and me, Ga'olani drew a small image plate from her blouse pocket and admired it. Her features, soft at first, firmed with resolve. When she noticed us watching, she angled the plate so we could see.

A uniformed Bird man smiled out of it as if through a window. He said something in their language that colored Ga'olani's cheeks and pressed his palms together.

"My betrothed, Yobo M'oke Malasa'o," she said, her face still pink.

Kota leaned in. "He's really good-looking."

Ga'olani's blush resurged. "Yes. We will marry when I, um, *graduate*? I keep by my heart for, you know, courage."

I fished Derry's pendant from my shirt pocket and pondered it. Though it had no video chip, I could hear her lilting words of goodbye in my mind and see the earnestness in her eyes. I remembered her hands gripping mine and the warm pressure of her lips near my mouth. I imagined her murmuring encouragement and allowed myself a full breath.

"… betrothed?" Ga'olani's voice cut through my reverie.

My eyes met hers. Kota appeared amused.

"No, we're not," I said. *But I'd sure like to be.*

"You are, um, fond of her?"

"Yes, I am." My face heated under Kota's regard, and I returned the pendant to my pocket.

"Ah." Ga'olani gazed toward her roommate, farther along the row. "Lista, um, liked you very much until she learned you have, you know, girlfriend."

"So now she doesn't like me?" I kidded. "Is that why she's been glaring and won't talk to me?"

"She, um, thought? believed? you liked her," Ga'olani said, "because you let her, um, fondle your hair, and you helped her climb the, um, obstacle course."

My expression must've revealed my surprise, because Kota struggled not to chuckle. I elbowed him in the ribs.

"I would've helped anybody on the obstacle course, Go," I teased, "even you."

She giggled like Kimama in a tickling match, something I hadn't expected from her, then grew serious. "She thought it because boys are not, um, good? not kind? to her."

That startled me, but before I could ask, Ga'olani went on. "She thinks you were, you know, playing with her because you didn't say you, um, have a girl."

I gaped. "I'm not in a serious relationship, but Lista came on to me. What was I supposed to do, tell her to go away?"

Kota rolled his eyes, but Ga'olani nibbled her lower lip in apparent consternation, in a manner reminiscent of Derry.

A shout of "Room, atten-*shun!*" from the front silenced all the banter, and everyone snapped to attention. A tall black man wearing service-dress blues strolled onto the viditorium's platform and said, "Take a seat."

He waited for the wooden creaks and clacking of our chairs to subside before he inquired, "Did all of you eat a good breakfast this morning?"

"Yes, *sir!*" we shouted in unison.

"Are all of you content and comfortable?"

"Yes, *sir.*"

"Very good." He flashed a smile as broad and white as a half-moon on a starless night. "I am Journeyman Xavier. Before I begin, I need to warn you, there are two things guaranteed to earn a cadet demerits during my lessons. Number one—" he raised his forefinger "—is falling asleep. That is five demerits. Number two—" he put up a second finger "—is allowing the person sitting beside you to fall asleep. That is ten demerits."

He smiled once more, and I didn't miss the glimmer in his eyes. "In light of that, I expect all of you to apply your elbows to one another's ribs as frequently and forcefully as necessary to ensure wakefulness. Do you understand?"

"Yes, *sir!*" we shouted again.

My "sir" came out as an "Oof." Something pointed had slammed into my right side with the violence of a spearhead.

I glared at Huritt.

"Stay awake, Sheggy." He sneered.

I didn't reply. I surveyed him, sitting with his arm tucked protectively to his side. *Sooner or later, you'll drop your guard, Hevo. You'll never see the counterstrike coming.*

* * * * *

Chapter Twenty-One

Journeyman Xavier paced across the viditorium platform. Behind him, a tri-D display tank stretched from one wall to the other and from floor to ceiling. Swirling light filled it like sunlit fog, mesmerizing and mysterious.

"How many of you," Journeyman Xavier asked, "know why the Soliennese Resistance Pact was formed, what the Supremacy is, and why we have declared war upon it? Show me your hands."

Most cadets put them up. Huritt started to raise his arm nearest me but abruptly lowered it to his side and thrust up the other one when he caught me watching him.

That's right, Hevo. I controlled a smile as I raised my hand on Ga'olani's side. The snug sleeve restricted the movement and increased the itch. *Who needs somebody's elbow? This itching is enough to keep me awake.*

I didn't know many details about the war, but I remembered what Chavat and Macawi had said about a religious crazy storming his way up the galaxy and killing people who wouldn't convert.

Huritt arched his eyebrows and snorted. "What does a smelly shegherd know about the war?"

"What does a spoiled kosa know?" I returned.

Huritt gave a superior-sounding "Huh."

"The leadership of the Soliennese Commonwealth considers it vital," Xavier said in his mellifluous voice, "for each of you to understand the cause for which you have been conscripted. I am about to provide you a background briefing. At its conclusion, I will answer your questions."

He gave us another wide grin. "This is the only briefing after which I will answer questions. In future, *you* will answer questions on what is presented, and each incorrect answer will earn two demerits. I advise all who wish to graduate to develop a habit of taking notes."

Ga'olani had already retrieved her link from her pocket. I readied mine, too. The viditorium's lights dimmed, Xavier stepped from the platform, and the haziness in the display tank cleared.

An immense head materialized within it, like a giant punching through the floor. A few cadets in the front rows jumped or swore.

The face surprised me. From what Chavat had said, I'd expected a bitter man in his fifties or sixties, with hard eyes glowering from a sagging face. A man like the crims on Tempest.

Safa appeared about thirty, I guessed. Medium-brown hair curled at his ears and collar and fell carelessly across his tanned forehead. His solid jaw and straight nose resembled the too-handsome digital heroes of drama vids. Only his impenetrable eyes, like fires of darkness, revealed the demon inside.

"He is young to be, um, tyrant," Ga'olani said.

The image withdrew to show Safa standing on a large rock, rallying a crowd. A tall man with a muscular chest and arms, he wore a belted tunic that hung halfway to his knees and baggy trousers pushed into the tops of calf-high boots.

The familiarity of his clothing startled me, too. Like my work clothes back home. If he had black hair and brown skin, he could pass for a Chalca farmer.

Safa spoke with obvious energy, waving an arm in short slashes. The people surrounding him pumped their fists in the air, their mouths shaping a soundless chant.

"Osaga Safa is a mysterious figure, even among his own people," Xavier said. "The exact date and place of his birth are unknown, but analysts link him to the vagabond tribes roaming the Younosso region of his homeworld, Kanek."

A tri-D map of mountains replaced Safa in the display. Dots marking towns and villages sprinkled craggy peaks and passes. Our view zoomed in on a particular dot and continued to tighten until I could see individual logs in the timber houses.

"Safa was discovered as a toddler," Xavier continued, "wandering about the village of Županja, through which a vagabond tribe had recently passed. Abandonment of young children is still practiced by tribes too poor to provide for them.

"He was adopted by the *kadar*, or village priest, who named him." A new image appeared, of an elderly man wearing a high, nubbly hat.

Where the name 'lumpies' came from, I guessed.

A small child wearing only an oversized shirt and a pout clung to the old man's baggy trouser leg. Xavier said, "'Osaga Safa' means 'Voice of God' in the local dialect."

In the tri-D tank, the image of the man and child dissolved into a grainy portrait of Safa as a youth, about our own age, his eyes concentrated and mouth set in a grim line.

"When he was nineteen, Županja came under attack by a rival tribe. Safa's adopted father was killed, and his head taken."

"That's uncivilized," somebody behind me murmured.

"Slaying an enemy's *kadar* is common among the tribes of the Younosso," Xavier went on. "Not only does it deprive the enemy of his conduit to his deity, but it also proves the superiority of one's own god.

"Upon finding his father's body, Safa withdrew into the mountains. He returned a month later, declaring that Županja's goddess, Velika, had come to him while he mourned in a cave. She demanded revenge for her murdered *kadar* and ordered him to prove her the most powerful of all deities. When Safa vowed to do so, she promised to guide his conquest."

I puckered my forehead. *Does this Velika really exist, or is she just another old tale? Did Safa really have a vision, or did he make up the whole thing?*

Images flicked through the tri-D display, showing Safa surrounded by increasingly animated crowds, usually outdoors. At later gatherings, he stood before a crimson banner, fifty spans high and thirty wide, bearing the image of a pale woman. Golden hair coiled about her head to form a helmet, flames rose from her eyes, and her snarling mouth revealed wolfish fangs.

She wore a tunic and loose trousers much like Safa's, except of midnight-blue, belted with a string of silver-bladed knives of various sizes and shapes. Four white, clawed hands brandished knives as well. She had no shield.

"Safa is a compelling and charismatic man," the briefer said. "Worshipers of Velika joined him from every tribe in the Younosso. He quickly established himself as the Supreme Leader, from which his followers derived their name."

In one image, Safa gripped a bloodied knife with a blade shorter than his thumb in his left hand. With his other hand, he held aloft a severed head. A man's body lay crumpled at his feet, trussed like an animal for slaughter.

Beside me, Ga'olani wrenched away from the display, her face twisted in a grimace, and gave a suppressed "Unh."

"Within a year," Xavier said, "Safa had begun to, in his own words, 'cleanse the false gods from Velika's realm.' Two years ago, the Supreme Forces of Velika toppled Kanek's world government."

A view across a plaza before a pillared building revealed bodies laid on the flagstones in orderly rows, like a makeshift morgue after a natural disaster. Except these bodies hadn't been drowned or burned or crushed by collapsing buildings. All had bound hands, and their heads had been placed in the center of their chests.

Like most of the cadets around me, I stiffened in my chair. Some, mostly girls, recoiled or gasped or clamped hands to their mouths.

"Slaying government leaders is consistent with the Younossi practice of killing rival *kadar*," Xavier said. He added, as the view panned along a row of corpses, "You will find no women among the dead. Female officials and wives of the deceased are taken for breeding stock, to produce new subjects to Velika, according to Supremacy general Melchor Arkadic."

Revulsion twisted my insides. *Filthy kosas.*

"Within phases of Safa's coup, Kanek's universities were razed to the ground, and all able-bodied males aged fifteen to thirty-five were pressed into military service."

Huritt leered. "Maybe you should join the lumpies, Sheggy. You're legal age for them."

"Maybe you should," I said. "They didn't mention any requirements for intelligence."

Huritt's dark eyes sparked like flint striking steel.

I glanced up the row past him and warned under my breath, "Watch it, Russom's looking this way."

Huritt fleetingly shifted to check, and I faced forward with an expression of concentrated attention.

"... exercised the same brutality on Gimel," Xavier was saying. "With each conquest, Safa's confidence increases. He considers his successes proof of a divine mandate, and he is determined to force our worlds to their knees before Velika."

New images flowed one after another through the tank, images of firebombed cities and smoldering bodies.

"This is why we fight," Xavier concluded, "to protect our worlds from Safa's terror and oppression."

The display tank darkened, dimming the viditorium, too, and Xavier returned to the narrow platform. "Do any of you have questions?" His voice rang across an intense silence.

Ga'olani sprang to her feet before his voice had fully faded. "Sir, Cadet Ga'olani M'oke Keatii from Fuago Mono." Her features intensified. "What makes Velika, um, different from the other gods?"

"Good question, Cadet." Xavier paced the platform, his features thoughtful. "Each of the gods rose from a different tribe, according to their needs as a people. Herdsmen, for example, or woodcutters. Velika, as you might expect, emerged from the tribe most frequently attacked or harassed by their neighbors. Not that they are innocent victims. They are fierce raiders who strip villages of everything they can carry.

"When you begin to deploy to combat zones, it is vital to remember two things about Velikers. First, all of them carry hidden knives, and all know how to use them, including small children. Second, they are also notorious for duplicity in their dealings with others."

"Much thank you, sir." Ga'olani sat, the crease of a frown forming between her fine brows.

To my own surprise, I rose next. Every face shifted from Ga'olani to me as if drawn by a common thread, but the question that had crossed my mind earlier demanded an answer. "Sir, Cadet Akuleh, clan Masou, from Tempest. Do you believe there really *is* a Velika, and Safa received orders from her, or do you think he made up the whole tale?"

At the rear of the viditorium, Russom stood watching me. I felt his hot-coal stare burning into my back. In the seat beside me, Huritt ducked his face into his palm in clear embarrassment.

Journeyman Xavier stopped strolling and wheeled to face me. "Excellent question, Cadet." He passed a serious gaze across the hall. "Whether Safa's goddess actually exists, whether he truly had a vision or fabricated the entire account, does not matter at this point. What does matter is, his people believe it.

"Always remember this." He raised a hand for emphasis. "There is nothing so persuasive for moving people to action, either for good or for evil, as their belief in the commands of their god."

"Yes, sir." I pondered that as I sank into my seat.

In an instant, a fleeting vision filled my mind, as distinct as the rope tearing loose from the log when Nayati grasped it. Except this time, Osaga Safa lunged at me from beside a burning brazier in a huge, darkened room. He roared, giving voice to a shock that widened his eyes and rage that hardened his jaw as he shifted a curved blade in his left hand.

Everything under my ribs seemed to stop.

* * * * *

Chapter Twenty-Two

The briefings took a nosedive after the one about Osaga Safa. The next day, we marched from lunch to the viditorium to sit through a four-hour lecture entitled "The Organization and Obligations of the Soliennese Resistance Pact."

Besides having just eaten, we found the viditorium too warm when we arrived. Hot air brushed our legs as we filed past the vents, and the burning-dust odor made several cadets sneeze.

I scanned the hall. Full stomachs, a warm room with the lights dimmed, and the most boring topic in the known universe. *This place is going to look like the aftermath of a gas attack before it's half over.*

"Why did they schedule this right after lunch?" I asked my friends while we waited for the call to attention. "We'll be poking each other all afternoon."

Rinn slid a wise smile in my direction. "They schedule it this way with intention. They want to see if we have enough discipline to stay awake. They did this at my school."

I shrugged. "Makes as much sense as anything else here."

I found one positive point in it. *At least nobody's in danger from Machitew in here, unless somebody falls asleep and cracks their head on the seat in front of them. Or Huritt and I break each other's ribs with our elbows and puncture a lung. Or the heating system catches fire.*

Don't give Machitew any ideas, Ku.

An instructor like Journeyman Xavier, whose speech rolled as musically as an early-summer river, might have kept us awake, but Preparatory Commander Gebim gave the lecture. His pasty complexion, like a crim's on Tempest, and his weedy physique and stiff uniform creases, led us to suspect he'd spent his entire career behind a desk.

His monotone voice, like a single extended low note on a ceremonial flute, soon made me wonder if he had fallen asleep where he stood, and only his death-grip on the podium's edges kept him upright.

"The original signers," Gebim said, "on the fourth day of the seventh month, Commonwealth Year 238, comprised Solienne's four Commonwealth worlds of Satha, Obolli, Tempest, and Solienne, along with the additional worlds Ardonar, Eis Ell, and Nichi."

He droned so slowly, I could have keyed his whole lecture into my link word for word. Until my eyes slid out of focus. When my head lolled, elbows skewered me from both sides.

I winced at Huritt's jab on the previous day's bruise and fumbled my link. It clattered to the floor and skated under the seat in front of me. I resisted peeking along the aisle where Russom lurked. *If he saw it, I'll hear about it. No use convicting myself.*

"Can you—?" I whispered instead to the cadet occupying the chair in question.

She bent to retrieve my link and returned it, her green eyes exuding drowsy commiseration.

"I missed the date for Fuago Mono," I told Ga'olani under my breath.

When she started, I knew she'd dozed off, too. She peered critically at her link, said, "I will tell you not here," and resumed tapping as if she'd never faltered.

"Aw, missing your naptime, Baby Cheeks?" Huritt cooed from my other side.

I flicked a glance toward the aisle. *Hope Russom's not watching. When Hevo dozes off…*

A short time later, Huritt's thumbs slowed, and the clicking on his link's keypad ceased. I watched his head sag, eyes closed. Only his chin planted on his chest kept his mouth from falling open. Fixing my attention on Gebim, I shoved my elbow into Huritt's ribs.

"Gah!" He lurched and flailed. His link spiraled into the air, and he stared about himself as if under attack.

I caught his link and shook my head in mock sympathy while he blinked. "Sorry to interrupt your nice dream."

"Masou and Hevovitas," Russom growled from the end of the row. "Against the wall, both of you."

Huritt snatched his link from me, gave me the *get snipped* hand gesture, and we sidled to the aisle, trying to avoid treading on our flight mates' polished shoes. A few cadets twisted in their seats to stare, obviously amused.

"You there, and you there." Russom pointed us to spots about a dozen spans apart and planted himself between us. "Ten demerits for both of you."

I pressed my shoulder blades to the scratchy wallcovering to prop myself on my feet and tried to focus bleary eyes on my link's display. *Ten more demerits. Why am I bothering to take notes? They'll call my name for sure at the next dismissal.*

By the time the lecture trailed to a conclusion, and we formed up to march to supper, the northern winter's early dark had closed in. New snow had fallen, too, giving the camp a pale glow and filling the air with icy glitter. We tramped through it, our crunching bootfalls marking our passage with straight lines of prints. The biting chill pinching our cheeks and noses roused us from our torpor.

Spicy aromas met us at the chow hall door, but the gleaming auto-servers filled our plates with leafy vegetables boiled to a bilious pulp and a mound of tubular noodles in red sauce.

Hungry or not, I gagged. *Looks like shegrul innards and what's inside them. All it needs is the stench.*

I opted for thick seafood chowder and black bread laced with bitter seeds instead and kept my attention on my tray. I couldn't watch my tablemates slurp those noodles.

Things got worse after supper. Rinn and I arrived for the nightly study session to be greeted by a ripple of chuckles around the dayroom. The only difference from our sleeping rooms was a close circle of metal chairs instead of bunks and lockers, and faded yellow paint instead of gray.

"Ah, Stormun," Borbala asked, "how do you keep getting the roommates most likely to wash out?"

"Especially when you have the fewest demerits of us all," Zoreba said. "What's your total now, fifty-two in four phases?"

Rinn didn't join in the mirth. Neither did Kota. Knowing the flights would lose more cadets at the next Commander's Call, Kota appeared uneasy, too.

Lista appeared to have changed tactics when the girls came in. Beaming all the way, she crossed the circle directly to Huritt and planted herself in the empty chair beside him as if claiming territory.

He regarded her with surprise for a split second before aiming a gloating grin at me.

"Bad luck, Ku-man," Ogundo murmured.

After a momentary jab in the gut, I felt an odd relief. "Maybe Huritt will give her the attention she wants."

As the cadet in charge of the impromptu study group, Rinn launched questions at one person after another in his guttural Standard. Several of the answers prompted discussions livelier than Gebim's lecture while we argued and consulted our notes.

Huritt and Lista didn't seem concerned. She freed his hair from its binding and slid her fingers through it as she had mine between glancing at me as if for my reaction. Huritt, with a soppy smile and his eyes half closed, appeared ready to purr.

"Gag," Kota said in my ear, and I chuckled.

Silva's loud question abruptly returned us to academics. "Since Tobe came in a day later, is it considered a founding member of the Pact or not?"

* * *

We debated it a few times during the next two phases' study sessions, but no one ever found out. Even Ga'olani had no success wheedling the answer from Gebim.

Huritt and Lista made it a point to sit where I couldn't avoid seeing them. Kota began referring to them as "the octopus," and Ga'olani leveled disapproving glowers on her roommate.

The night before the exam, as everyone dispersed from the dayroom, Kota and I found the doorway blocked by Huritt and Lista engaged in an extended good-night kiss. When they parted and Lista started toward the stairwell, Huritt cast a smug smile at me over his shoulder.

My innards twinged, but with it came realization. I waited until Lista moved out of hearing range to offer a quiet warning. "Careful, Hevo. She chose you to get back at me, you know."

Huritt snorted. "She chose me because she was tired of only holding hands."

Something in my midsection tensed, but I kept my jaw from tightening along with it. I nudged Kota instead, and as we started away, I said, "I'm probably going to dream about Gebim lecturing all night."

On entering our room, I took the oval pendant from my pocket and set it where I could see it while I studied. I considered Derry's eyes and inviting smile. Imagined her warm lips pressing my mouth instead of my cheek, her hands running through my loose hair to slide down my back, and my arms drawing her close. *Derry doesn't play games like Lista.*

I lay awake after Rinn slept. Rolled in my blankets on the chilly floor, I propped myself on my elbows to read.

Sometime around 0200, organization charts and descriptions of Supremacy warships on my link melded into dreams of dreadnoughts sundering through briefing scripts. Words flared and crumbled to ash before I could read them.

I woke with a gasp at a beeping in my ear and my link's corner digging into my cheekbone. Its display still glowed. I scrambled to my feet, my heart slamming into high gear as if shot full of adrenaline. *I never did learn whether Tobe is a Resistance Pact founder.*

Having never taken written exams before, I had no idea what to expect. As an apprentice chanter, I'd demonstrated each new skill, from mixing herbs for a cough remedy to performing chants or flute melodies or drum rhythms for ceremonies. I'd learned by watching and doing. Gram had taught my siblings and me to read and write Standard, but even my piloting exam had been verbal.

Filing into the viditorium, we exchanged our links for digital touch plates. "Don't activate them until you're told to do so," said the spacer who issued them.

Training officers directed us to every other seat in every other row. I couldn't help noticing, as I slid into mine, the tri-D display tank looming dark and empty at the hall's front.

No help there today.

I bounced my blank touch plate on my knees.

"I don't know why you're testing, Sheggy," Huritt said from two seats away. "Everybody knows you're already finished."

His words whipped my anxiety into unexpected anger.

With it, a cold breath tickled my left ear. "We have the power to silence him. We only have to hurl our touch plate and strike his throat."

I shuddered and tore my vision away from Huritt. Wiped my clammy palms on my trousers. *Get out of here, Machitew.*

The exam's first section included one hundred true-or-false and multiple-choice questions.

1. The Soliennese Resistance Pact began with:

A. Seven worlds

B. Eight worlds

C. Ten worlds

The correct answer would be seven or eight, depending on whether Tobe was a founding member. I set my jaw and touched B.

Many questions omitted or twisted crucial points. I strained my memory for details and debated which seemed right. My head ached by the time I answered all of them.

I enjoyed the second section, worth fifty points. We had to visually identify and list features of several ships, enemy and friendly. They appeared in the plate one at a time and rotated to display structure, propulsion systems, and weapons loads.

Only a few cadets remained in the dim hall, all appearing tense as hunted tavos, by the time I slid out of my row of seats and handed in my touch plate. Ga'olani, Huritt, Rinn, and Kota had left some time earlier.

"Good job, Cadet," said the spacer to whom I gave my plate. "Only six wrong answers on the questions, and you got all fifty right on the visual ID. You only needed 85 percent overall to pass."

"Thanks." I relaxed and accepted my link.

Relief about the exam didn't quell the stress about my demerits, though. I'd stopped keeping track two phases ago.

In the viditorium's high-ceilinged lobby, my classmates milled like shegrul's, and murmured together, or sagged wearily against the walls.

Lista and Huritt eyed me from a corner. "Packing tonight, Sheggy?" Huritt asked.

"Your gear," I said. "Except I don't think your swollen head will fit in your trunk."

I savored Huritt's furious expression as I weaved through the crowd toward Kota, Rinn, and Guns, but I had no hunger for supper. The chow hall served a chicken-and-maize stew I really liked, but dread weighted my heart and stomach like rocks under my ribs, and my head still ached.

* * *

After lights out, I touched Gram's call code on my link while I silently paced a small circle in the hallway outside our room. To my immense relief, she appeared in my display at once.

Before I could speak, she asked, "Are you ill, Akuleh?"

"No." I kept my voice quiet, but couldn't conceal my distress. "I think I'm going to be dismissed at Commander's Call tomorrow. Do you know anybody who needs an apprentice? I'll take anything."

"Akuleh." Gram's tone held both firmness and reassurance. She reached a hand toward me as if to cup my face. "The Ancients have set your Path. Trust them."

"If they even exist." I rolled my eyes. "Why should I trust them?"

"I know they exist." Calm conviction radiated from Gram's aged face.

"Then why is Machitew the only one who talks to me? I hate it. I'm... I'm..." I managed not to say *scared*.

"Akuleh," Gram said again. Her voice and eyes took on an edge of command.

I fell silent and waited.

"You will hear the Ancients," she said, "when you learn to listen for them. They don't speak as loudly as Machitew."

I opened my mouth to protest, but Gram raised her hand in the dove's wing sign of peace. "Do you say the Warding Chant before you sleep?"

Embarrassment lowered my gaze. "No."

"It's important for you to do it. Remember why I called you Akuleh. Learn to look up again."

Indignation swelled, mating with impatience. I struggled to keep my voice low. "That's all you ever tell me, Gram. 'Remember why I called you Akuleh.'"

"When was the last time you truly looked up?"

I snorted. Startled by its loudness, I whirled to check Russom's office door. No light flicked on beneath it.

"Do you trust me?" Gram asked.

I hesitated. "You know I do."

"Then trust me about the Ancient Ones until you come to know them yourself. Will you do that?"

I stopped pacing. "I trust *you*."

"Then start there. Live by what I call you. Say the Warding Chant before you sleep tonight." Gram's stern features softened. Her comforting tone returned, backed by certainty. "No matter what happens tomorrow, it will be all right."

I nodded, though I doubted it.

"I love you, Akuleh." A twinkle lit her eyes. "So do the Ancient Ones, whether you think so or not."

"Ya, Gram. Love you, too."

Grumbling under my breath, I returned to my floorbed. The Warding Chant. *Won't do any good, but I promised Gram.*

I began to recite it in a whisper so I wouldn't wake Rinn. "Shield me from the spirits of the Dark, O Sower of the Stars. Shield my mind against them that I may know your wisdom. Shield my heart against them…"

Sleep swallowed me before I finished.

I woke still feeling exhausted when *On Your Feet* blared across camp. I accomplished PT, showered, dressed, marched, and ate without thinking, a mere automaton. At different times, Rinn, Kota, and Ga'olani each asked me what was wrong. I said, "I'm fine," but I knew by their crimped brows or pursed mouths they didn't believe me.

As it had before the first Commander's Call, marching to the parade ground felt like marching to my execution. Huritt's gleeful sniggers scorched my ears the whole way.

I gritted my teeth and caged my eyes when the hound-faced senior spacer began to call names from Juno Flight. "Sajjad, Kelei... Eusebio, Mishal... Borbala, Adrian... Zanini, Obaid." I swayed in the bitter wind, listening to his rumbling voice and bracing myself.

"From Kalor Flight..."

Ga'olani's full exhalation from my left prompted me to slip her a glance. I caught the shaky smile she gave me.

Huritt didn't say anything until we entered the chow hall. Placing his tray on our table, he demanded, "Who paid off Russom to keep you in, Sheggy?"

Giddiness had begun to cut through my half-stunned mental repetitions of *I'm still here, I'm still here, I'm still here.* I leveled a calm gaze on Huritt and said in my most caustic tone, "It sure wasn't any of my shegrul-herding clan from the desert. They're all too poor and ignorant."

Recalling Kota's talk of Hevovitas family rivalries, I added, "Must've been one of your rich cousins who'd like to see you out of the running for chief of the Great Council."

I didn't expect Huritt's reaction. He paled and stiffened as if I'd shoved a hunting knife into his chest and twisted it.

* * * * *

Chapter Twenty-Three

Our last few days of Basic passed in a high-tempo blur of graduation practices, marching to the orderly room to register for pilot training, and scrubbing the barracks for its final inspection.

"It would be a shame," Russom said, pacing around us on the drill pad, "if, after making it this far, you snot noses fail to graduate because of dust on a doorframe or lint under a bunk. Failure on a single point will fail the entire inspection, so you would be unwise to sabotage one another's efforts." He paused to nail Huritt and me with warning stares.

Rinn ran through the checklist the night before the scrub-down. "It is best if everyone volunteers for tasks."

With only thirteen cadets left in Juno Flight, most of us would have to take two or three.

"I'll mop and polish all the floors," I offered, "upstairs and down."

Everyone agreed. Nobody's floors had failed when I'd mopped them the day the barracks was ransacked.

Guns flashed a smile and raised a hand. "I've got the high-altitude stuff, like the windows, doorframes, ceiling lights, and tops of the lockers."

"Good." Rinn tapped our names into his roster.

The others leaned in to eye the checklist. Huritt sat slouched and scowling, arms folded on his chest and fingers drumming his biceps like a driller bird on a cactus.

Finally Rinn said, "There is only the men's latrine. It will require three or four people. Hevovitas, you have not volunteered for a task, so I will assign it to you."

Huritt's brows lowered. For a second I thought he'd refuse, but Lista raised her hand. "I'll help in the latrines. Somebody else can help Go wash windows."

As everyone left the dayroom minutes later, Huritt leveled a murderous glare at Rinn and me.

* * *

I began upstairs on my hands and knees, scrubbing black shoe marks off the floors before I mopped and buffed every room and the hallway.

By the time I finished the downstairs hallway and lugged my mop and bucket to the men's latrine, my kneecaps bore achy smudges of bruises. Scraping scuff marks had worn my fingers raw enough to make them smart. Late afternoon darkness had settled by then, and the wind's wails heralded the coming night's cold.

I found all my flight mates in the latrine. Wielding smelly rags and brushes as stiff as kosa quills, and wearing gloves and masks to shield against cleanser fumes, they polished the fixtures and mirrors. I waited outside, stretching my cramped hands and back, and scrutinizing the drying hallway tiles for missed spots until everybody left.

Starting in the long shower room at the rear, I mopped my way, with swinging back-and-forth strokes across the greenish tiles, toward the arched doorway into the front area.

As I passed the third shower stall, which still reeked of some potent cleaner, the outer door banged shut. The doorstop gave way on a regular basis, so I didn't think anything about it. Not until a scuff like a boot sole on tile followed the door's *thunk*. I stopped, peered around, and listened.

No other sounds reached me, but the same prickling rose at the nape of my neck that I'd felt on entering Eyebrows' lair.

Somebody just came in. Somebody who thinks he's being stealthy. Only one flight mate angry enough for that.

"Angry ones are the most dangerous," my combatives trainer had once said. "Anger makes people unpredictable."

I balanced the mop handle in my hands. Wooden and splintery from heavy use, not a flimsy plastic tube, it would be sturdy enough for an expedient weapon if I needed one. I resumed mopping with all my senses on high alert.

A shadow shifted on the wall outside the shower room's entrance. I watched it. *Getting impatient, Huritt?*

On edging into the front area, with urinals and commode stalls along one wall and polished washbasins on the other, I found him waiting, arms loose at his sides, and his visage imitating a thunderhead. *What's new?*

Keeping a close eye on him, I asked, "What're you doing in here, Hevo? I'm not finished yet."

His face darkened still more. "You and Stormun left the latrine for last to make sure I got stuck with it."

I did a double-take. *This isn't about Lista or some rival cousin? Just a chore?* I said, "That's your problem. You could've volunteered for anything."

"Nobody gets away with humiliating a Hevovitas." Huritt's hands clenched and unclenched beside his thighs.

Mounting irritation stopped my mop in mid-swish. I leaned on it to face him. "Since when is doing your share of the work a form of humiliation?" I couldn't help wondering what he'd done all through Basic. Had he coerced his roommate into doing the chores?

My question clearly poked a raw spot. Huritt charged me like an askuk about to swallow a stray shegrul.

"Let him fall on the wet tiles," a chilling voice urged at my left ear. Through the spectral eyeholes of Machitew's mask, I saw Huritt slip. Saw his boots fly off the floor as clearly as I had seen the rope bracket pull loose.

"We won't be blamed when he hits his head and dies," said the phantom at my ear. "He must die. He is our mortal enemy."

"Get out of here." I snarled it aloud, at Machitew, and sidestepped Huritt's lunge.

His boot struck a wet spot. It skidded out from under him with a damp squeak, throwing him backward exactly as I'd just seen it. I had only a split second to seize his arm.

He hit the puddled floor on his backside with a soggy smack rather than striking his head, and gasped. "My tailbone!"

"You did it to yourself," I said. "You could've cracked your idjit skull."

"Masou's right, Hevovitas."

I jerked about.

Light from the front area silhouetted Russom in the shower room's broad doorway. It appeared the whole flight had crowded in after him, everyone gaping like landed fish.

"Leave the room, Hevovitas," Russom ordered. He didn't shout. He didn't have to.

Huritt gained his feet, hunching and with his face twisted in pain, and Russom said, "Stand up straight."

Huritt pushed through the other cadets to the latrine's outer door, shuffling like a centenarian, but with his eyes blazing.

Russom leveled his full attention on me. "Masou?"

I'd straightened into a brace, mop tucked to my side like the guidon staff. I swallowed. "Just finishing, sir. As soon as I scrape these new boot marks off the floor."

Russom gave a resigned shake of his head and rolled his eyes. "Carry on." He wheeled away, but not before I glimpsed a sly curl at one corner of his mouth.

When Machitew appeared after lights out and encased my head in his mask, I saw Huritt through its eyeholes again, sprawled on the shower room floor with brain tissue oozing from his split skull and blood winding like an eel toward the drain.

The apparition lunged at me, mouth wide as an askuk's on the attack. Its breath iced my blood. "It should have ended like this. He was ours. He delivered himself into our hands. We must eliminate him before he becomes our greatest threat."

I sat awake for several moon positions afterward, shaking violently, but not from the cold.

* * *

The audience at our graduation appeared to consist mostly of Soli cadets' guests. Interstellar travel cost too much for most families. They would come when we graduated from Primary Pilot Training.

We strode into the viditorium, accompanied by a martial anthem full of crisp drum cadences and blaring horns. As each flight mounted the platform in stiff single-file, its training officer stood at the wing commander's side to present his or her charges one by one.

When my turn came, I noticed how Russom forced a neutral expression when he announced my name. "Akuleh of clan Masou, from Tempest."

I snapped to attention in front of Wing Commander Lodesson and saluted as we'd been instructed to do.

"Congratulations, Cadet Masou," Lodesson said when he presented my certificate and shook my hand.

"Thank you, sir." I accepted the document, stepped back, and saluted once more. My vision flicked irresistibly to touch my training officer's, and I didn't suppress my victory smile. *Made it in spite of you, Russom.*

I didn't miss the glint in his coal-black eyes when I pivoted to leave the platform. I only let it puzzle me for about a second. *Who cares? I made it. I'm done. I'll never see him again.*

The Training Wing provided refreshments in the viditorium's lobby after the ceremony. Long tables draped with white cloths bore silver trays stacked with meats, cheeses, breads, and fruits and vegetables cut into intricate shapes. Their aromas prompted an eager rumble from my stomach, a ghost cat on the prowl.

I'd just loaded my plate with sliced venison, dark bread, and a scoop of fire radish for making a sandwich when somebody bumped my elbow. I steadied my plate to spin about, expecting to see Huritt.

"Sorry," Kota said. He puckered his brows, jerked a thumb toward the lobby's far corner, and said under his breath, "I wonder how much tax money it cost for that contingent to come."

I peered in the direction he pointed.

I'd only seen images of Great Council members in newsfeeds, but I had no trouble recognizing Huritt's mother. The second's silver-and-turquoise neck-chain of office gleamed on her ample bosom. She surveyed the room through imperious eyes, a hawk searching for prey, and thrust her chin at the people with whom she spoke.

She hadn't come from Tempest alone. A regal man, obviously Huritt's father with his square jaw, and three elders wearing the stone-and-silver neck-chains of other Council officials, clustered about her.

Huritt stumped around stiffly, still favoring his bruised tailbone. When he spotted me watching him, he leaned in to speak to his mother and pointed at me with his jutted jaw.

The chief's second turned toward me with great gravitas, her lips pursed tight as a drawstring bag. I didn't flinch, but drew myself up when she locked her obsidian gaze on mine. *She's assessing me.* She said nothing while I held her stare, but the volume of my heartbeat in my ears dampened all other sound.

At last she shifted her attention to Commander Lodesson, and Kota nudged my shoulder. "If stares were energy bursts, Ku," he muttered, "you'd be a smoking hole in the floor by now."

I shrugged it off. In my mind, I could already see myself mounting the cockpit of a Rohrspachen-55 fighter. "We might not even be in the same flight with Huritt during Primary Piloting," I said. "I'm not worried about it."

Still, the continuing conversation between Huritt and his mother, unheard from across the lobby, and their shifty glances in my direction, warned me that I should be.

* * * * *

Chapter Twenty-Four

"Onto the crawler, you wastes of skin!" Russom shouted. "You're going to have a short night as it is. Don't make me shorten it for you anymore."

As if he could, now we've graduated. I chuckled and sprang aboard the snaky vehicle. Hugging my lumpy rucksack to my chest in the narrow space, I worked my way along the aisle to the rear and sank onto the first vacant seat.

Kota dropped into the seat facing mine. Securing his rucksack on his knees, he asked, "What's so funny?"

"The expression on Russom's face when Lodesson presented my certificate," I said, "like he couldn't believe I made it."

Kota grinned. "C'mon, Ku, you know you'll miss him bellowing your name across camp eighteen times a day."

"About as much as I miss my stepmother," I said.

Rinn took the seat next to mine. His bunched brows and firm mouth revealed satisfaction, but their concentration said he'd already shifted his focus to our next effort.

Ogundo plopped beside Kota, his broad smile gleaming. "All of you ready for this?" he asked in his easy drawl.

"More than," I said.

When our classmates all found seats, the crawler's doors hissed shut like steam from a covered pot. It lurched into motion, heading for the pilot-training side of Belsken Field.

I couldn't stop smiling as it trundled around the base's perimeter, under shaggy conifers, and along a craggy coastline that dropped a hundred or so spans to ice-laden breakers. Their rhythmic crashes reached us in a distant roar. Like a steel caterpillar, the crawler chugged its way through a mid-winter flurry of crystalline snow.

It squealed to a stop in the student pilots' housing area sometime after 2200. I'd expected another row of blocky barracks, but these structures resembled small Chalca enclaves, minus the enclosing domes.

The vehicle disgorged us in an oval courtyard, into sound-muffling snow that reached our knees. Its shape reminded me of the ceremonial plaza in the center of an enclave, except between two facing semi-circular buildings.

Everybody stood in silence and stared with undisguised wonder.

Four levels and brand new, each half-circle dorm housed three flights, one on all but the ground floor, where we found a laundry and lounge area flanking the lobby. Together, the paired buildings sheltered all six flights of the newly formed 56th Training Squadron.

We stumped inside, boots clomping on shiny floors, brushing snow off our shoulders, and throwing our parka hoods back. The place smelled of newness, and I drew a deep breath. Strongest came the fresh scent of lumber, followed by the chemical odor of paint and the metallic smell of electronics.

"I like this," Kota said, but his brow furrowed at once. "Where's the chow hall?"

All of us crowded around the illuminated notice board in one lobby. Anticipation heightened most faces, while apprehension tightened a few others. The flights to which we'd belonged during Basic had been disbanded, and new ones formed, "to create new combinations of personalities and abilities," the notice stated.

We still had assigned roommates, though. On checking the roster, Rinn and I discovered we'd been paired as roommates again, in Chally Flight on the dorm's top floor. Even better, we shared an apartment with Kota and Ogundo. We all exchanged grins of relief.

"Killer!" Kota said.

We found Ga'olani and Lista in Chally Flight, too, but both of them had new roommates. Names I'd occasionally heard during Basic, but to which I hadn't attached faces, had replaced some familiar ones.

Two names at the bottom of Chally Flight's roster snagged my attention like barbs on cactus spines. Huritt and his ax-faced cousin, Enyeto.

"See who's at the end of the hall." With my chin, I pointed out their names, burning black-on-white in the roster.

Kota scrunched his nose. "Vermin in here already?"

The message crawling across the bottom of the digital notice board prompted a collective groan. Classes started at 0500. If we wanted breakfast, we'd have to get up no later than 0400.

On entering our unit, Rinn and I found a study area and separate sleeping rooms, each large enough for only a narrow bunk and a wooden clothing cabinet. We shared our bathroom with Kota and Guns in the adjoining unit.

"Good," I said. "Less competition for showers."

Knowing we'd left behind room inspections, we didn't spend much time organizing our quarters. At least I didn't. I noticed Rinn, however, resolutely folding his PT clothes into eight thumb-length squares when I withdrew to my sleeping space.

I flung myself into my bunk, exhausted, but excited for the next day. Until grumbling muffled by a wooden mask penetrated the gusts rattling my window.

* * *

The Soliennese Commonwealth's Defense Forces only accepted licensed pilots into military training, but licenses wouldn't reduce our class time. Our squadron commander, a balding but solidly built preparatory commander named Carsen Grell, explained why when we assembled in the cavern of a viditorium for the first time.

"We fly most of our missions in low-planetary and intra-solar-system space," he said, standing straight but relaxed before us, "but we fly trans-atmospheric fighters, so you've got to be well-grounded in the basics of atmospheric flight.

"We rarely engage the enemy in deep space," he continued, though his grim tone implied he had, "but it'll be essential for you to learn deep-space astrogation and maneuvering, as well."

Several of us had struggled not to doze off during the introductory speeches, so I appreciated the opportunity to stretch when our flights separated to our classrooms.

Primary Piloting squadrons consisted of fewer flights, but larger ones than those in Basic. Twenty-six of us took seats, two at each console table, in curved rows surrounding the instructor's podium like a drummers' circle.

Huritt and Enyeto sauntered in last, and Huritt swept the room with a superior gaze.

Only one console table remained vacant. The one next to mine and Kota's. Of course. The Hevos crossed to it, Huritt with his brows lowered. I watched him ease himself gingerly onto his chair.

"You should bring a pillow for your tailbone," I suggested.

Huritt glared at me, sniffed noisily, and wrinkled his nose in a theatrical manner. "Stinks of probat in here," he said, loud enough for half the class to hear. Quizzical expressions shadowed some cadets' faces, and he said, "I thought all *those* washed out in Basic." He said 'those' the way one would speak of dog droppings.

"Like Sewati and your other cousin, the wiry one?" I asked. "Does this mean you two are going to walk around in missing man formation now?"

Huritt sputtered. Enyeto's eyebrows drew together into a single thick line of black hair, like a kosa sneaking across his forehead. Our classmates sniggered.

"Room, atten-*shun!*" Ga'olani called from her seat by the door.

We leaped up as our first instructor strode into the room. Huritt, his face twisted into a grimace, wrenched into such an exaggerated brace, I half expected his flight suit's slide closure to pop. Kota and I traded glances and bit our tongues to keep from snickering, but not before Huritt spotted us. His eyes smoldered a silent threat.

* * *

We spent the first phase reviewing the fundamentals of atmospheric flight, like aerodynamics and lift, air pressure and altimeter readings, fuel-air mix at different altitudes, and visual and instrument flight regulations. Basic stuff. I chewed my stylus's point a lot to keep my mind from wandering.

Before our instructor arrived every morning, the safety officer subjected us to a stand-up quiz on emergency procedures. I blinked and stared the first time he entered the classroom.

He didn't wear a Commonwealth uniform, but unlike those of Ardonar and Fuago Mono, I recognized his flight suit's brown-and-tan-streaked camouflage pattern at once. *He's from Tempest. He's Qaletaqa!*

The name Qaletaqa meant Guardian of the People. Because the majority of Tempest's colonists had come from the Commonwealth's most notorious prisons long before my people had arrived, our leaders had created a territorial militia. They knew every encounter would be a matter of life or death.

Over time, the Qaletaqa had earned a reputation as the most effective special operations force in our galactic quadrant. They'd become famous decades before Osaga Safa started the current war. Hanuk and I had shared a dream of entering their ranks from the time we could pronounce the name.

Like a child recognizing a famous torgus player, I couldn't tear my gaze away from him. *Why didn't I know there are pilots in the Qaletaqa?*

The patch on his left pocket bore the name Noshi, sewn in both a blocky Chalca glyph and Commonwealth Standard letters. On his right pocket, he wore another patch displaying the glyph for his rank, a raptor's foot with five talons extended. Five-talon was the Chalca equivalent of Solienne's preparatory commander.

His hair, streaked silver and black as a river in winter, lay down his back in a tight braid rather than a regulation horsetail. Its leather binding didn't carry an enclave totem. Instead, he wore a small eagle shaped from amber, its wings protectively outstretched.

His face bore the deep wrinkles of a cactus fruit left to dry in the sun, giving him a permanent squint, but his flint-black eyes constantly swept his surroundings. When they rested briefly on me, I bore the weight of their appraisal.

Noshi trod the circle before our console tables, his boots soundless on the pourstone floor, his gaze flicking from one cadet to another as he described the emergency scenario of the day. At last he stopped, pointed at someone with a jut of his jaw, and asked, "What do you do?"

We never knew what to expect. A fuel leak one day, a stuck control flap the next. Noshi paced as he listened. If the first cadet couldn't give the whole answer, he pointed out a second, his grave expression never wavering.

Cadets who couldn't give a complete response got a negative notation in their training record.

On the fifth morning of our first phase, Noshi said, "Here's your situation, Chally Flight. You're flying a four-seat quad-jet atmospheric aircraft. You begin your descent to the airfield, but you're still thirty ranges out when a large bird is sucked into one engine." He touched each of us with a penetrating gaze. "What do you do?"

I stiffened. *That's what happened to me in the Darter.*

Noshi spun on his boot heel. "Cadet Brassone."

Hopping to her feet, she recited the mandatory opening for every emergency procedures, or EP, response. "First, I would maintain control of the aircraft. Then I would analyze the situation, take appropriate action, and land as soon as I could."

I nailed my gaze to the console surface before me, my mouth pressed tight as she began her detailed answer. I winced while I listened. *You can't do that with a quad. Use the rudder pedal. You've got to counter the drag from the dead engine with the opposite rudder.* My leg muscles burned at the memory.

Brassone got five sentences into her answer and went blank. I had never lifted my head, so I saw Noshi's desert-brown boots stop before my console only through my peripheral vision. "Cadet Masou."

I sprang to my feet into a brace. "Sir," I said, and repeated the mandatory opening.

By then, every detail of the landing had risen in my mind, starting with the loss of my first engine and my call to Awénasa Control. Once again, the second engine with its faltering power thrummed in my ears, and the altimeter spun down too quickly in my mind's eye. Once more I struggled to adjust the thrust as I rotated the remaining engines to set it down. I remembered the aching cramp in my leg and sweat rolling down my spine.

A few sentences into my recitation, my pulse and breathing accelerated. I started saying "I did" instead of "I would." Images flitted across my vision like wisps of cloud, smoke thickening in the cockpit, the sky tilting beyond it, and Kimama's wide eyes. My hands clenched so tightly, my fingers ached, and sweat oozed around my nose and mouth. I'd grown shaky by the time I finished.

Pounding silence brought my eyes into focus. Noshi stopped pacing. His face remained inscrutable, studying me with those piercing eyes, but I knew nobody had tipped him off. I'd never told anybody about it.

Everybody else in the room stared. Kota seemed dumbstruck, and Huritt sat scowling, drumming his fingers on his thigh.

"How long ago did it happen, Cadet?" Noshi asked.

"A few days before I left Tempest for Basic, sir." *Feels more like a year ago.*

Noshi gave a stiff nod. "Good."

After he left the room, Huritt leaned in on me, his lip curled. "You think you're the top man here, Sheggy? Good show, but the Distinguished Grad medal's already got my name on it."

* * * * *

Chapter Twenty-Five

By the second phase, we discovered the ten-hour days we'd complained about during Basic had been light duty. Here, we faced twelve hours of class time six days per moon phase, with the other twelve hours split between study, PT, sleep, and meals. To our relief, the flight kitchen always remained open.

We were required to get at least six hours of sleep a night, because tired flyers make potentially fatal mistakes. During the first few phases, I often collapsed on my bed fully clothed and didn't stir until my alarm sounded, long before a bleak dawn.

Nobody called short-notice inspections after wrecking our rooms, subjected us to extra push-ups on a drill pad, or made us march in formation. Instead, the emphasis on "attention to detail" increased, adding pressure like weights to a barbell.

"In combat," every instructor told us the first day, "a single detail can mean the difference between life and death."

Our instructors, all combat veterans, came from every world in the Resistance Pact. Each had an area of expertise, something they knew that they could teach from experience. I understood very well why a Chalca pilot taught meteorology and flying safely in adverse atmospheric conditions.

I struggled with astrogation, to my dismay, because surface navigation had always been easy for me.

We had to memorize reference points like prominent stars or constellations for nine solar systems. I did it by visualizing them with some reminder image while I recited their names.

We also had to learn new formulas for plotting courses. Unlike navigation within the limits of a planet's atmosphere, astrogation was three-dimensional. Whether we operated in a single star system or traveled from one system to another, the formulas didn't change. Only the reference points did.

I knew I had the formulas solid. I'd already passed the test on them. When I worked practice problems during study block, however, half ended with "Unknown Location" flashing neon across my console, accompanied by a deep tweet like an overfed songbird.

After my display lit for the sixth time, Huritt leaned in on me. "Deep-space yourself again, Sheggy?"

"Better deep-spaced than cooped in here with Hevo vermin." I copied my work to my link, pocketed it, and logged off my console with a frustrated sigh. "Going to the gym," I told Kota.

There goes my piloting reputation.

"I'll meet you later," he said without shifting his vision from his own display. Its light gave his face a ghostly hue.

The pilot-training side of Belsken Field had been designed for practicality. The school, Wing Operations, and six squadron buildings all bordered the two-range flightline.

Pushing out through the school's front doors, I faced the cluster of dorms. The usual wind whistled and chased itself among them, whipping up plumes of icy powder. The dorms' thermal coatings glowed golden under the lamps mounted on their sloped roofs. In mid-winter darkness, the lamps' brilliance simulated daylight.

The dorms surrounded the chow hall like youngsters crowding their six-sided mother. Each of the six squadrons had its own wedge-shaped dining area, the walls of which bore its unit crest and other memorabilia.

Vapor coiling from ports on the chow hall's steep roof exuded aromas hinting at supper. I inhaled deeply, and my mouth watered. *Smells like something meaty. Good.*

I flipped my parka's hood up and skirted the chow hall to avoid the shoving wind. Lowering my head into its bullying gusts, I tasted bitter sea brine as I passed the 58th Squadron's dorm, the 52nd's, and the 54th's.

Grounds crews cleared walkways of snow and ice each day. Still, hunched in my parka and squinting against the smart of ice flecks in my face, I picked my steps with care.

Like the dorms and chow hall, the Training Wing's gym had been built so recently, we avoided touching the walls in case the bright red and yellow wall coatings hadn't yet dried. I smelled sawdust along with the chemical bite of floor varnish. As the doors shushed closed behind me, I paused to draw another long breath, to savor the woody scent while I scraped my boots across the rasping doormat.

The facility housed a competition-size swimming pool and saunas in its steamy underground level, a three-story room of climbing walls, and a track with a rubbery surface encircling two full-size jumpball courts. Shouts and the thunder and squeak of shoes on gleaming wood rang from one court. I paused briefly to watch a three-on-three game underway.

The gym even had a half-size micro-grav torgus tank on its top level. I strolled around it to check it out and ran a hand along the tank's smooth surface as I circled it. Peering through its transparent shell, I imagined hurling head-size ovoid balls into its slender goal well.

From the locker area, I headed for the weight room. Nothing on Solienne cleared my head like pressing weights until sweat soaked my crewshirt to my skin. The rhythmic clacks and whines of several weight machines in use hit my ears as I entered the room. I spotted cadets from classes ahead of mine occupying most of them.

Searching the room for an open machine, I recognized Five-Talon Noshi working on a seated leg-curl bench near the rear wall. He greeted me with a terse nod, his mouth pressed tight with exertion.

"Sir." I returned the nod and tried to maintain a neutral façade while all the tales I'd heard about the Qaletaqa surfaced in my mind. Was it true a four-man team had once tracked a couple crims to a desert stronghold and eliminated eighty of them at once? Or that Qaletaqa rode askuks across the Awénasa Territory to keep from being detected?

I shook my head. *I'm here to work out, not ogle him like a child.*

The only free machine stood halfway along one side of the room. I started on it and advanced from one machine to another as they became available.

I'd accomplished half my usual workout circuit when Noshi finished his. I expected he'd just nod my way again as he left, but he mopped sweat from his face, tossed his towel onto his shoulder, and approached me.

I stopped at once, easing the weights down the rail to the start position with a series of sharp clicks.

"No, finish the set, Cadet," he said.

He stood there, watching me and shaking out arms as thick as python tree limbs, while I completed the last four reps. Physical effort wasn't the only thing heating my face.

"Do you know how to spot for free weights, Cadet?" Noshi asked when I finished.

"Yes, sir." I reached for my towel and rose. A few strands of hair had pulled from my cord binding and clung to my face like itchy tendrils of some vine. I swept them off.

"Start braiding your hair," Noshi said. "It's safer around machinery, including aircraft."

"Yes, sir." I retied my hair in the regulation horsetail before drinking from my water bottle.

I spent the next several minutes spotting for him. I'd never seen anybody, even on Solienne with lower gravity than Tempest's, who could bench-press five hundred pounds.

"What's your max, Cadet?" Noshi asked when he'd stood and wiped his sweat-rivered face.

"Nowhere near yours, sir." I shook my head.

I'd achieved two hundred ninety pounds the previous phase, more than I'd ever pressed at home on Tempest, but I couldn't break three hundred. Noshi studied my technique while he spotted my first press.

"It's your elbows," he said. He showed me what I was doing wrong and how to correct it. "Do you trust me, Cadet Masou?"

"Yes, sir." What else could I say? Trusting one's teammates was core to the Qaletaqa.

Noshi slid another five-pound weight onto each end of the bar. "Once more," he said. "Watch your elbows now."

Clacks and whirrs from machines around us unexpectedly fell silent. Every other cadet in the room stopped to watch as I drew a full breath, adjusted my grip on the bar, gritted my teeth, and pushed.

Noshi stabilized the barbell with a light touch when it wobbled. "Elbow," he said.

As I straightened my arms, and my elbows locked, scattered clapping and a couple shrill whistles rose from the onlookers. Somebody yelled, "Nice job, bud!"

Noshi said, "Good. Bring it down and rest your arms for a minute. When you're ready, do it again."

In another fifteen minutes, under Noshi's coaching, I pressed three hundred forty. Lowering the bar into its rack, I released my breath with a laugh. Sweat streamed off my face, salty on my tongue and smarting in my eyes, but I didn't care.

"Good." Noshi gave a curt nod. "You'll catch up to me in time, Cadet." His deep eyes glinted. "But don't neglect your pilot training to do it."

"I won't, sir." I sat up, quivering. *Exertion or excitement?* It didn't matter. "Thank you, sir."

My vision settled on his wrist braces as he released them, and I swallowed. I steeled myself for an effort more intimidating than the weights.

"Sir." *I know I'm going to blurt this out like a child. What if he laughs at me in front of everybody?* I looked him in the face and said, as steadily as I could, "I want to enter the Qaletaqa."

Noshi glanced up from his wrist brace and met my eyes with his laser-bore intensity. I held his stare for what seemed an hour, until one corner of his mouth gave a barely perceptible quirk.

"You seem like the type," he said. "You'll have questions; I've got answers. My office door is open, Cadet."

His face grew hard and grim, an unvoiced warning as he peeled off the wrist brace with a sharp rip. "Whether you achieve it will depend entirely on how much you want it. How much pain are you willing to endure to earn it?"

"All of it," I whispered as he strode away.

* * * * *

Chapter Twenty-Six

I didn't hear the dry crunch of old snow under my boots on my way to the dorm, but it seemed to glow in the broad circles cast by the light poles. My conversation with Noshi replayed in my mind, and I couldn't stop smiling. *He didn't laugh at me. He encouraged me to ask questions.*

Only when I stepped into our apartment and my gaze fell on my cluttered study console did my elation evaporate. *Burn. I still have to figure out how I'm messing up those astrogation calculations.*

A scan of our rooms confirmed Rinn wasn't in. I plopped before my console and fished my link from the chest pocket of my flight suit where I kept the portrait of Derry. I drew out the small oval along with my link, warm and smooth as a brooding hen's egg in my fingers.

I might never see her again, but that didn't stop me from day-dreaming. I lingered on memories of her encouraging words, melodious in my ears, and her brief kiss near my mouth when I told her good-bye. Her faint smile in the miniature painting seemed to say, *Yew can do this, Kew.*

I'd made a habit of setting the pendant on my console while I studied. Rinn had spotted it the first time and asked with a smile, "She is your charm for good luck?"

"Sort of." I'd tried to be nonchalant, but I kept my vision on my display, hoping its illumination wouldn't betray my heating ears.

I checked my link before plugging it into my console. A line of blue text glowed from the display.

TWO MESSAGES IN QUEUE

Good. Really need these right now.

I opened Kimama's vid first. Her round face, her eyes as bright as a bird's, beamed at me. "Ai, Ku! How is your pilot training? Is it still winter there? Why don't you vid me? I miss you lots."

She chattered about her pet tavo and the healing skills Gram was teaching her, and her features grew earnest. "I can make poultices for bruises and wounds now. You have to use different herbs for different hurts, and…" She barely took a breath.

I slouched in my hard chair and chuckled as I watched her. *Nothing like a vid from Kimmie to untie my innards.*

It had been a while since I'd sent one to her. Guilt pinged my soul. So I made a vid-tour of our quarters with my link, including a view from the window to show her how the dorms resembled an enclave.

"Now I need to study," I said at last. "Be good, Butterfly. Learn everything you can from Gram. I'll make you another vid when I can."

Gram's message began with her usual queries—How was I doing and was I getting enough to eat?—before she relayed the family news Uncle Kwahu had brought from Red Wash when he'd come to the city to trade for supplies.

Two of their shegruls had partitioned the same day, Gram told me. Aunt Lemana and my cousin Chenoa, Hanuk's younger sister, had gotten bruised ribs while helping the lunging creatures tug themselves in two. On the positive side, they expected large crops of cotton and maize this year.

The prospect of good crops prompted me to inhale. I savored remembered scents of moist soil and new plants, but I winced at the news of Chenoa with bruised ribs. Hanuk and I had often let her join our adventures when we were small.

Never have made contact with Huk. I need to try again.

Gram's voice broke my reverie. "Coming of Wanikiya Ceremony is next moon. I hope you have chanters there and can take time out of your training for it. I really hope you'll participate, Akuleh." Her eyes and tone implored me.

I snorted at the idea of requesting three days off from classes for an annual religious observance. *That'd be about as successful as asking the wind to stop blowing.*

To be truthful, I wouldn't have attended the ceremony even if I could have. I couldn't rouse much sense of obligation to deities who'd robbed me of my parents and marked me to become the incarnation of Machitew.

The prophetic Coming of Wanikiya Ceremony occurred at the mid-point of Tempest's sixteen-moon year. My ancestors had brought Coming of Wanikiya, along with the other ceremonies and traditions of the Ancients, when they'd fled Solienne.

During three nights of pageantry, dancers in wooden masks and feathered regalia, representing wolves and eagles, acted out the sacred tales foretelling the coming of the seventh shaman. They told how Wanikiya would rise during a dangerous time for the Chalca. He and his wife, Anataqa, would strengthen and lead their people as the world grew dark around them.

The battle between the eagle dancers of Wanikiya and the gray wolf dancers of Machitew took place on the third night, with flaring torches, thundering drums, and flashing swords and clubs. My favorite part when I was small.

I creased my forehead, considering an incongruous detail. Whose idea was it to use swords in the ceremony? Chalca warriors in the old times used knives and spears and clubs, not swords.

I hadn't participated in Coming of Wanikiya or any other annual ceremony since my father's death. Gram knew that, so her earnestness puzzled me.

"Kimama and I will start the ceremonial cooking in a couple of moon phases," she said. "We'll send a package to you."

Foods for religious ceremonies had symbolic meanings and were prepared to the accompaniment of prayer-chants. I imagined Gram and Kimama singing together as they worked and felt a pang of longing. My aversion to annual ceremonies didn't extend to the feast foods accompanying them.

Gram's messages always ended the same way, too. "Be safe, Akuleh. Do your best. May you always walk the Path of peace and beauty."

I had just sent a reply to her when Kota burst into our quarters through the connecting bathroom, brushing snowflakes off his shoulders with one hand, and sliding a dented box out of his parka with the other. "I stopped at the mailroom and found this." He held out the box. "Homemade shegrul sausage. Here, take some."

He'd already removed a couple, longer and fatter than our fingers, but the sausages were packed so tightly, it took some prying to get one out. It came free with a squelchy sound.

"Thanks," I said. The spicy scent roused my salivary glands. "Did I miss supper? What time is it?" I twisted to check the wall chrono. Nearly 2000. "Burn. I haven't started working the astrogation problems yet." I jacked my link into my console with a sharp *click*.

"Ma says she'll send more with her package for Coming of Wanikiya," Kota said. "There's a chanter in the chaplain's office. Do you think they'll let us take three days off for it?"

My gut lurched. First Gram, now Kota.

With my mouth full of sausage, I shook my head. Once I'd swallowed, I said, "I doubt it. Not on this training schedule. We'll be flying by then."

Kota appeared disappointed. His smile faded, but I held up the half-eaten sausage and grinned. "These are really good. If your mother sends more, and Gram sends awanatas, we'll get to feast even if we can't attend the ceremony."

Kota brightened a bit. He drew the chair out from Rinn's meticulously organized console and straddled it. "I had an idea about your astrogation problem. Were you using the right reference stars? Some sound really similar, like Campesia and Kannesia. I did that with a few of my problems."

I stared at him. "That's got to be it. I knew I'd done the formulas right."

"Attention to detail, Cadet," Kota said with a wry smile, and set another sausage on my desk before he rose.

"Thanks."

He headed to his apartment, and I scrolled through my notes, searching for reference points by solar system. Labeled tri-D star maps lit my monitor, one after another, diagrammed in different colors. *My way to tell them apart. I've got serious memorizing to do.*

Rinn found me asleep, my head on my console, when he returned a couple hours later. "Mess-*you*!" he shouted, in an unnervingly good imitation of Russom.

I jerked upright, groggy and blinking in the darkness.

"Asleep in the harness like a hard-driven kaluç!" Rinn chuckled. "You will not learn it by osmosis, Ku. Go to bed."

Still feeling bleary, I entered the classroom last the next morning. I'd eaten the second hot-sweet sausage while I reviewed reference points one last time. I knew I had most of them, but a few constellations kept slipping around in my mind.

I missed five of the fifty exam problems. I passed, but only by one question. Six wrong and I would've had to retest on my own time.

It didn't trouble me as much as something else. My low score just shot big a hole in my chances for Distinguished Grad. The thought knotted my stomach. *My reputation's on the line.*

My taut stomach wrenched when Huritt and Enyeto swaggered past me in the hallway during break, their faces smug. "So, Sheggy, have you passed any exams yet?" Huritt asked.

"Why do you want to know?" I questioned. "Feeling lonely at the bottom of the class?"

Huritt flung his head back and chortled. "Ya, you know all about it, don't you?"

My innards clenched still more when Kota caught up to Guns, Rinn, and me on the way to the chow hall. "I thought you should know, Ku," he said. "If you're worried about the DG medal, Huritt isn't your biggest threat."

Kota paused, his face serious. "I overheard Instructor Taseer telling Commander Grell that Huritt only missed two this time, but the one you're really up against is Go. She got another perfect score."

* * * * *

Chapter Twenty-Seven

I didn't put astrogation fully from my mind as we entered our third phase, though we had new topics to cover before we started training in simulators. Names of reference stars echoed in my ears, and illuminated constellations burned inside my eyelids all night.

The morning after the exam, Lieutenant Commander Hunun, another petite woman from Fuago Mono, began her lectures on maneuvering in space with directional thrusters. A tri-D tank lit up in the wall behind her shoulder, capturing our attention with a cut-away diagram of a swivel-capable thruster jet.

In a nasal voice thick with singsong inflections, she explained the physics of why thrusters were necessary in space and how they worked. We watched computer-generated thruster nozzles flare from specific points on a blocky spaceship model to nudge it about like a reluctant shegrul.

"Unlike altering control surfaces," she said, "which causes an immediate change of direction in atmospheric flight, there is typically a delay of point-three seconds for thrusters to make the same course correction in space. You must take that into account and learn to anticipate when to fire your thrusters."

I swept my vision around the room and noted Ga'olani leaning forward on her table, her full attention on our instructor, her oval eyes intent and lips set in a determined line.

Go's got to know she's leading the class since the astrogation test. Is she feeling pressure to stay there?

Rinn sat at my right, tablemates with a young man named Corwyn Waterstone. Also from Ardonar, he'd been in Kalor Flight during Basic. Rinn wore the same intense expression as Go, his dark-blond eyebrows knitted and his jaw taut.

If Go's being pressured by anybody, it'll be Rinn. He killed the astrogation test, too, and he's good with numbers. I can't beat either of them at academics. I'll have to outfly them for Distinguished Grad.

I slid a glance left at Huritt. He slouched, arms crossed on his chest as usual, scowling so deeply he wouldn't have needed a carved mask to perform a storm dance. When his gaze touched Rinn, Go, or me, lightning flashed in his eyes.

Sighing, I returned my attention to Commander Hunun, who switched off her tri-D tank and said, "I can teach you when to apply short bursts or long burns, but simulators will teach you awareness of space around your ship and how to anticipate and compensate for thruster delays."

"Sheggy has to compensate for being a probat," Huritt said half-aloud to the cadets seated at his other side.

They peered around him at me and chuckled, their eyes glittering with mirth. I returned their gazes with a glower.

"Some simulator sorties will take you through virtual debris fields and laser fire," Hunun said, her tones twanging like a strange musical instrument. "You will receive simulated damage if you are not sufficiently alert. Please complete the exercises I am sending to you now. They are mandatory prior to starting in simulators tomorrow. When you return your exercises to me, you may take your lunch break."

She sent a package of ten scenarios to our consoles. The first only involved changing course twice to avoid a weather satellite and a slow-moving freighter, but the number and speed of the obstacles increased in each vid.

Eight years of flying in Tempest's weather, anticipating and countering up- and down-drafts, and dodging wind-whipped debris at several thousand spans of altitude gave me an advantage. I finished the ten exercises in less than fifteen minutes.

When I'd touched the Send pad and collected my flight cap, I scanned the dim classroom. My classmates' concentrating faces glowed bluish in the reflected light of their displays, many of them with mouths pursed and brows crimped. Someone was nervously tapping a boot on the pourstone floor.

"Giving up already, Sheggy?" Huritt asked when I stood.

"Done," I said with a smug smile, and addressed Kota. "See you in the chow hall."

He nodded in reply.

I stepped outside into brilliant sunlight. Not a cloud, not even a wisp in the stone-blue sky. For the first time since our arrival on Solienne two moons ago, the tops of snow-buried pines had broken through gleaming drifts on the Hamskjold Mountains like a day's growth of beard from pale skin.

Frigid air turned my breath into vapor and crackled frozen tree branches when a breeze stirred them. I knew the early sunset would douse the bright daylight in another hour, but I felt a surge of excitement. *Perfect flying weather.*

I drew in a long breath as I entered the chow hall and tried to guess what might be waiting for lunch. Whatever it was, the aromas brought moisture to my mouth.

Cadets from other flights sat scattered around the 56th Squadron's well-lit hall. I exchanged greetings with them as I crossed to the food line, especially those I knew from Juno Flight during Basic. Tray loaded, I chose a table near the wall-sized front windows from which I could watch for Kota and drew out my link to review my notes while I ate.

Huritt and Enyeto approached the chow hall a couple minutes later. I watched them march up the walkway together, heads tilted toward each other inside their parka hoods, and hands shoved into their pockets. Vapor from their mouths carried off what appeared to be an intense conversation.

Huritt's voice came in a muted growl as they strode into the entry. "… reported my astrogation score." His features darkened as if he'd passed into a shadow. "Mother said I should be ashamed that a girl from Fuago Mono scored better than the great chief's son."

My brow puckered. Great chief? She had been the second when she came for graduation. What happened?

Enyeto seemed aware of the transition. "Great timing by the Ancients, giving old Mochni a ruptured appendix just when he was about to call a vote on—"

Huritt snorted and dropped his voice to a barely audible mutter. "It wasn't really a ruptured appendix, and the Ancients had nothing to do with it."

My hand fisted around my utensil, but I managed to resist the reflex to jerk my head up, despite my shock.

"Mother's in position now to establish herself as chief for life and choose her successor." Distress weighted Huritt's tone. "If I don't get the DG medal, she'll take me off her list of contenders."

Enyeto's response carried through the harsh scrubbing of their boots on the doormat. "Who else is there, Lead? She'll never let another clan have the chieftainship."

My heart rate quickened. *If Huritt thinks I overheard any of that, he'll kill me.*

I shoveled in a mouthful of savory pot roast, bent lower over my link, and tightened my vision on its display.

"She won't have to, Three." Huritt's tone as they entered bore no trace of his usual arrogance. "I have plenty of cousins on the maternal line, including you."

I stopped chewing. *Does he really think his own mother would take him out? Makes my stepmother seem nice.*

His petulance shut off abruptly, as if somebody had flipped a switch. As if somebody had switched him off. I knew he stood petrified in the doorway by the sensation of his stare boring into my ducked head. I kept my attention riveted on my link and scooped up another mouthful as nonchalantly as I could.

"Sheggy." Ice laced Huritt's voice.

I didn't have to feign a start. My head snapped up. "Sorry, Hevos, table's saved," I said around my food.

Huritt held my gaze for several heartbeats before he pushed Enyeto toward the serving line, but his last sentence lingered after him like the odor of rotting flesh.

I'd barely returned to my lunch when Kota arrived. "Go's still working on it," he said, setting his tray down opposite mine. "She looked ready to spit fire out of frustration when I left. How'd you get through it so fast?"

"Lots of practical experience," I said.

Kota grinned. "There's your edge for DG."

"Maybe. Speaking of which…" I scanned the hall, found Huritt and Enyeto seated against the far wall, and leaned toward Kota across the table. "How long ago did Chief Mochni die?"

His typically cheerful features tensed. "*What?*"

I told him what I'd heard.

"So, according to law," Kota said, "as his second, she's assumed his position." He blew out a forceful breath and lowered his focused gaze as if trying to stare through his plate. "That justifies the fears that have been flying around Awénasa City ever since the election.

"That's only the top of the anthill though. There's been some other stuff going on that—" He cut himself off and stared at me. "Does Huritt know you overheard him?"

A chill slid down my spine like a handful of melting snow. "Don't know. I kept my head down and kept eating."

Kota's features grew serious. "Remember what I told you about Huritt not issuing a challenge, but a warning?"

"Ya."

"He's another spine on the Hevovitas cactus, Ku. If he thinks you could beat him for the DG medal and embarrass him in front of his mother again, I don't think he'd hesitate to toss another log on the sudden-deaths woodpile."

* * * * *

Chapter Twenty-Eight

Simulator training took place in a high-ceilinged bay behind the school building. Its observation deck, framed by ceiling support beams, loomed above eight well-worn pods hunkering on the pourstone floor like eagle's eggs in a stone aerie. The whole chamber rang with clangs and clatters and voices blaring through speakers.

Seven classmates and I, the first eight to complete Prep Commander Hunun's classroom exercises, swapped dubious glances. I didn't know the fifth young man at all, or any of the three girls very well, but Huritt and Enyeto scowled, and Kota arched an eyebrow upon seeing the battered simulators.

"What you can't see from here," said Master Spacer Farkas, our instructor, "are the fifty-span hydraulic lifts these units are perched on, or the gyros underneath to make them respond to your directional input.

"This belt—" he pointed at a grease-blackened band circling the nearest pod "—allows it to do rolls as accurate as anything you'll experience in a real cockpit, so be careful with the thruster controls until you get used to them."

We filed through the equipment room, where spacers issued our helmets and checked their communications links. I answered "Copy" when the technician asked if I could hear his voice rattling through the earphones.

From there, we each climbed into the simulator to which we were directed. Mine had SHIP 1 stenciled in block characters on its nosecone. Another pair of spacers stood by to help me strap in. "The way your ground crew will with your real fighter," one of them said.

They locked my simulator's hatch, and smells of stale sweat and gym socks in need of washing closed in on me like an odorous fog. My nose involuntarily scrunched. *Wish we had oxygen masks in these things.*

The seat's shabby cover crunched when I shifted on it. I couldn't move much more than that without bumping the enclosing hull, as cramped as a chick about to hatch. *Hope real cockpits aren't this tight.*

Once everyone had reported "Ready," Farkas addressed us through our helmet speakers, his voice riding an electronic hiss. *"Today, you'll do a basic orientation flight. The objective is to become familiar with handling the Rohrspachen-55 multi-role fighter in low-planetary space.*

"Your simulator's computers will record your responses for evaluation, but there are instructors observing on the deck above, too. If you have questions or need assistance, use the callsign 'Control' to address us."

With the hatch secured, I couldn't see the bay. A tri-D projection filled the cockpit canopy, simulating a launch-tube aboard a space-ship or orbital station.

I studied every detail of the cockpit, the various colored toggles and displays. I ran my hand lightly across touchscreens and keypads until Farkas said, *"You won't practice takeoffs and landings today. You'll do those later. Flip the ignition switch to enter your program. It'll run for fifty-seven minutes. Everybody copy?"*

"Control, Ship One, I copy," I answered, and the others echoed my call in turn.

Something bumped under the hard seat when I flipped the ignition, followed by a steady hum and a sensation like a rising lift tube. *Must be the hydraulic lift extending.*

Glittering space, appearing to be several ranges above the massed lights of a densely populated planet, replaced the launch tube in my canopy's projection. I checked my instruments to orient myself and studied the flight profile.

I was to travel from Alta Base to Serra Base, skirting Folkstone and Nevus Bases, before orbiting Rondo Base. I had to change altitudes and headings a few times, staying alert for ship traffic en route to my objective.

Two seconds out, a ship erupted from emptiness, flashing like a red beacon on my traffic scope. One hundred seventy-five degrees low, relative to my heading, it charged straight for me as if pursued by every demon in the Great Dark.

My heart leaped. I nailed the thruster switches. Half a lifetime's heartbeats seemed to hammer in my ears during the half-second lag before my fighter rolled clear. The racing vessel passed like a flaming meteorite, so close it triggered my proximity alarm.

My pulse hadn't fully slowed before a cry rang through my helmet speakers. *"Control, Ship Six, I-I'm tumbling. It won't respond."*

I heard snatches of calls between an instructor and Ship Six, but I kept my attention on my own program. I'd entered an inbound traffic lane as dense as bees streaming to their hive. Ships of all classes careened in every direction.

"Control to all ships." A new voice pierced my earphones, overriding the simulated comms. *"Terminating the program. I say again, we are terminating the program. Remain in your pods until released by your crew."*

Before the call ended, my canopy projection darkened, and my simulator sank beneath me, swiftly enough to make my stomach lurch. The pod had hardly settled, landing with a substantial bump, before the hatch squeaked open, and a spacer with tense features released my harness using quick twitches of his hands.

"What's wrong?" I asked.

"Malfunction," the spacer said. "Got to get you clear. Head for Equipment Issue. This way."

We dashed across the bay, my classmates and their crews right behind us, all of us keeping our heads low.

From the equipment room's doorway we watched the sixth simulator continue to pitch and spin at the top of its lift.

"Can't they cut the power?" asked the male cadet I didn't know. His nametape read Cziensky.

Cadet Brassone rounded on him. "What if the lift collapses? That's a fifty-span drop."

"Her first hard landing," Huritt said with a dismissive smirk.

Kota poked me with an elbow, his face taut. "Do you know any chants to earth spirits, Ku?"

A shudder coursed through me. I shook my head to clear the memories of rocks tumbling from Red Wash's fractured wall when I'd landed my Darter among the water-smoothed boulders and stones of its winter-barren channel.

"You helped Nayati when he fell," Kota said.

"I did a healing chant. It had nothing to do with earth spirits, and I—" I gulped "—had a nightmare afterward of him dying. I told you about it."

"He didn't die. You know that, Ku." Kota gripped my sleeve, his vision burning into mine. "You've got to try."

"I never learned—" I choked on the words.

My stomach churned with self-accusation. *Whose fault is it you never learned to call earth spirits?*

"You can at least try," Kota said. He sounded angry, but his face appeared pained.

Cadet Brassone echoed him. "Please do try, Ku."

"We only have to see something to make it happen," Machitew's words echoed in my mind. The suffocating darkness of his mask seemed to close over my head.

As if the mask's eyeholes penetrated the simulator's hull, I saw my classmate being flung against her harness, as limp as Kimama's yarn dolls. Her face repeatedly smashed into the instrument panel.

"No!" I wrenched away from the tumbling pod. Stomach roiling, I pushed away from the huddle in the doorway and retreated to the corner near the helmet locker. Kota, Cadet Brassone, and the third girl, Cadet Tamaki, followed.

"Please, Ku," Brassone said again.

"I don't know any." My voice shook. My mouth had gone dry.

"You're the only one who can even try." Kota's plea sounded ranges away beyond the pounding in my skull. He tightened his gaze on me.

With my breathing too ragged to speak, I sank to a squat. I pressed my palms, slick with sweat, to the cold pourstone, the closest I could come to touching soil or real stone. Closing my eyes to shut out the faces and place, I strained to remember words I'd last heard years ago. "O, Ancient One who formed the Mother Worlds, source of all life. O, Ancient One who built the Mother Worlds, source of our strength…"

Nothing more came. Because such chants were saved for more advanced apprentices, my father hadn't begun to teach me the prayers to request the aid of earth spirits before his death. I imagined his voice murmuring in my mind and visualized his concentrating face, but I couldn't distinguish the words.

The spirits of stone who dwelled in the holy mesa had raged when sky spirits hurling lightning had struck and shattered their sanctuary. In their fury, they'd swallowed my father's body, swept him down the mesa's face with a roar, and buried him. All but one bloodied hand, reaching out of gravel-laden snow.

Earth spirits, groaning their agony with grinding like gnashing teeth, hadn't prevented Red Wash's fractured stone columns from crushing and smothering my younger brother.

Anger twisted inside me. Sweat rose around my nose and mouth. I roared at the ash-gray floor, "I can't."

From the simulator bay came shouts, and the rumbles and squeals of heavy equipment. Cadets Brassone and Tamaki darted away to watch.

Kota squatted beside me. "You all right, Ku? You look like you're going to puke."

"Feel like I'm going to puke."

"They got it stopped," Brassone called from the doorway, her voice tremulous with relief. "They're lowering it now."

I gulped a breath to steady the pourstone floor that seemed to roll in waves beneath me.

In a couple more minutes, a grating shriek like a hatch ripping open reached me from the other room, along with murmurs from my classmates.

"How does she look?"

"Is she all right?"

"She's conscious, she just raised her hand."

"They're putting a neck brace on her."

I seized the locker door and hauled myself to my feet while Kota peered over the group in the doorway. "She's talking to the medics. That's good. Must not be too serious."

Huritt and Enyeto pivoted to face us when Kota and I rejoined the huddle. Huritt leered at me. "Not such a great chanter after all, Sheggy. Who doesn't know the words now?" He waggled his tongue like a demon dancer.

"Get snipped, Hevo," I growled.

Two medics bore our classmate from the simulator bay on a whirring repulsor sled, and Master Spacer Farkas crossed to us, his face somber. "Patalos got a bad whiplash," he said, "but they say she'll be fine. In the meantime, we're standing down the simulators until they're all checked out."

* * *

As I knew he would—as he always did after an incident—Machitew appeared in my room after dark, a misty shape with icy breath and mocking eyes. I hadn't gone to bed but paced up and down my compact room, waiting for him.

Being on my feet and in motion didn't prevent him from enclosing my head in his ghostly mask. When it settled, I saw Cadet Patalos thrown about in her pitching cockpit again. Her head flopped on a broken neck, bludgeoning her face beyond recognition on a blood-smeared instrument panel.

"Why do you continue to resist our role?" the unearthly voice demanded. "We have greater power than all the earth spirits combined. When we join as one, we will be powerful enough to tear down every mountain on every world."

"I don't want your power." I snarled at the translucent shape hovering in the chilly dimness. I pressed my spine to the nearest wall. My mouth had gone dry. "I don't want to tear down mountains."

The sound of my voice in the quiet startled me. I glanced about in the darkness. *My own room. No one else to wake up, to drive Machitew away.*

I contemplated trying the Warding Chant but shook it off. *Won't do any good. The Ancients have named me Machitew. How can I ward myself off? How long can I delay the inevitable?*

* * * * *

Chapter Twenty-Nine

We didn't get a break while Maintenance had the simulators on standdown. Our instructors simply rescheduled four days of lectures and classwork.

Five-Talon Noshi came in one day to brief us about safety on the flightline. "Some points differ between sorties launched from surface runways and from a spacedock's flightdeck," he said, "but awareness of activity going on around you is always essential."

During a break between lectures, I gathered my nerve. I know he'd encouraged me to ask questions that day in the gym, but this was probably a stupid one.

Still, I squared my shoulders and approached him while he sauntered along the polished hallway between classrooms. Even in flight boots, he made no sound.

"Sir?"

He stopped, turned, and smiled, crinkling his weathered face still more. "Cadet Masou. How much weight are you pressing now?"

Habit stiffened me into a brace. "Three hundred ten a couple days ago, sir, but I can't make it to the gym every day."

"Not your highest priority." His smile assured me he understood. "It shouldn't be. You have questions for me?"

"Only one, sir, right now." I resisted the urge to wipe damp palms down my flight suit. "How do I qualify for the Qaletaqa? What do I need to do to apply?"

Noshi didn't chuckle at my ignorance. "Complete your pilot training," he said. "Focus on that for now. Do your best. Then you'll need to serve a minimum of two years on active duty." He folded his arms, which emphasized his upper body's muscular bulk as well as his matter-of-fact expression. "It's important to have experience working as part of a unit.

"You'll also have to meet and maintain rigorous physical fitness standards. Your weight training is important, but you'll have to pass timed runs and climbs, too. I'll send you the regs."

"Thank you, sir." Emboldened by his offer, I relaxed enough to venture another question. "What kinds of missions do Qaletaqa pilots perform?"

"Several types." He smiled. "Infiltration and exfiltration of surface teams, rescue and evacuation of downed or injured personnel, and close air support, among others. Most missions are classified."

My pulse stepped up, thinking about it. "Thank you, sir," I said once more.

Returning to the classroom, I felt as buoyant as I had the first day I arrived on Solienne.

"I saw you, Sheggy." Huritt's curled lip added mockery to his words. "Sniffing at the Qaletaqa's boots like a shegrul."

I returned a jeer. "Maybe I've got higher aspirations than trying to impress the right elders back home."

Huritt stiffened and stared at me as if I'd punched him in the face.

* * *

On the simulator standdown's third day, Wing Commander Lodesson ordered all training squadrons to the viditorium for a current intelligence briefing. "I feel it's important," he said, "for all of you to stay abreast of what's taking place on the battlefront."

Like our dorm buildings, the viditorium formed a semi-circle, surrounding the platform on which briefers stood. Its seats rose as steeply as those of an amphitheater or sports arena.

We trekked up a side aisle to the section designated for our squadron, and I scanned the mass of figures in gray flight suits. The sight prompted some quick calculations. Twenty-six cadets in each flight, six flights in each squadron, and six squadrons in the 33rd Training Wing. Approximately four hundred thirty pilot cadets in various stages of training.

Something else occurred to me. *Huk's got to be in here somewhere.*

On reaching our seats, I remained standing to survey the half-circle hall, searching every bronze Chalca face among the black, white, and olive-complexioned ones. I didn't find Hanuk, but I smiled at noting the high percentage of Chalca in the ranks.

Though they appeared to be well-padded, the viditorium's seats proved to be no more comfortable than the metal-and-plastic chairs in our classroom. *No chance of catching a nap in here.*

Like the briefing we'd received during Basic, this one consisted only of unclassified information.

"You won't be granted clearances until you receive your commissions," the master officer intelligence briefer answered when somebody across the vast room raised a hand and asked her about it. "Your background investigations are being conducted as we speak. You'll be 'read in' when you arrive at your first unit."

Unlike the earlier briefing, this one concentrated on current activity rather than history.

"Colonists on Gimel," the woman began, "report construction is underway on two tracts of land recently deforested under the Supremacy occupation."

A map materialized in the tri-D display forming the rear wall of the platform, and she said, "The first tract lies fifteen ranges from Bognar, and the most recent is on the outskirts of Zsiros, Gimel's two oldest colonial townships."

Red circles marking the two cities and blue squares for the construction sites expanded as she indicated each location.

"Descriptions of the structures and their layout suggest the establishment of permanent Supremacy garrisons," she went on. "Both sites resemble pre-Supremacy military garrisons in Kanek's western hemisphere."

An obsolete aerial image appeared in the tank, gray and grainy and two-dimensional. The briefer's laser highlighted one structure, then another. "This building on Kanek houses armored personnel haulers and battle vehicles. This second one is a maintenance depot for ground equipment. The buildings under construction on Gimel are identical."

Recent tri-D images materialized in the display tank, and she pointed out the structures' similar lengths and widths, their blast-proof doors, and revetments being heaped from the tan soil plowed up around them.

"You may find these facilities on your target lists when you reach your active-duty units," she said, passing a knowing smile over us before she grew serious. "We're monitoring several indicators that suggest Osaga Safa may be planning to use Gimel as a staging area from which to advance upon Ardonar."

Stillness as dense as native Tempest cotton bolls packed the broad viditorium for several lengthy seconds. When she offered to answer questions, only Rinn rose to ask one.

"Madam, when do you estimate the Supremacy will be capable of attacking Ardonar?" His voice rang through the expansive chamber, and I realized his Golmolan accent had diminished since Basic.

"If they continue to produce weapon systems at their current rate," the intel officer said, "we believe it's possible they could do so within a year."

I didn't miss the grim set of Rinn's jaw as we descended the viditorium stairs a few minutes later. I recognized other cadets from Ardonar by their anxious scowls or surly silence.

Concern dogged my thoughts as well. *Do Derry's people in Caerden know about this? Are they prepared?*

That night, a different shadow appeared in my room, like an echo of an earlier dream. The woman had spoken the name of Osaga Safa only once, but the single mention triggered images from the briefing several phases ago.

The handsome peasant standing atop a boulder, rousing his people with a chant of war. The young man brandishing his bloody knife above a decapitated corpse and declaring it to be Velika's will. The expansive plaza on Kanek on which its executed world government officials lay in stiff rows. The crimson banner of a knife-wielding goddess.

Most clearly came the fleeting scene that had penetrated my mind during the first briefing. A chill like a warning seized me when I glimpsed once more Osaga Safa lunging at me across a huge, dark room, his face hard with fury, his left hand knotted about the hilt of a hooked blade.

* * * * *

Chapter Thirty

We raced through the next few phases like an askuk across scorching summer sands. I ignored Huritt's daily verbal jabs and the increasingly dark glances he shot my way.

Once Maintenance had replaced the damaged simulator and upgraded the others—which didn't improve the smell of their interiors—we did makeup sessions along with the current ones. Sometimes back-to-back.

"Think of this as a preview for War Phase," Master Spacer Farkas said with a roguish grin.

"What is, um, War Phase?" Go asked.

"Seven days of high-tempo flight ops," Farkas said. "Two sorties every day, with breaks only for crew rest, cold boxed meals from the flight kitchen, and quick-turn reloads to switch from surface attack to space defense missions. It's quite an event. You'll love it." I caught a glint in his eyes that said, *You youngsters have no idea.*

Kota must have missed the glint. "I can't wait!"

We also had ejection seat certification. No one mounted a real cockpit without the blue patch on their flightline badge to prove they had passed.

"Classroom table ten, Apenimon and Masou," Farkas said one afternoon as we climbed from our simulators. "Your turn for the rocket seats." He jerked a thumb toward the bay's rear corner.

In a narrow room smelling of explosives that adjoined the simulator bay, two fifty-span rocket-rails stood side-by-side. The ejection seats were locked at their bases with red-tagged steel pins. Kota and I traded tight grins.

As two spacers cinched us into the seats, the younger man briefed us on correct posture. "Heels against the seat base, tuck in your elbows, and press your shoulder blades, rear end, and helmet as hard as you can to the seatback."

Kota and I stiffened into position, a mannequin posture that would become uncomfortable if we had to maintain it very long. The seatback seemed solid as a stone wall against my shoulder blades, hips, and helmet.

The spacer checked our critical points before he removed the red-tagged pins. "Feet, spine, neck, you're both good." He pointed. "The ejection handle is the yellow ring between your knees. When I yell 'Eject, eject, eject,' grab it with your left hand and tug. You should be halfway up the rail by the time I say 'eject' the second time. Got it?"

We nodded.

"Start with your arms on the armrests," the older spacer said. "You've got to be able to find the ring by feel without having to look for it."

It's by my left knee.

"Eject, eject, eject!" the younger man yelled.

Braced in the seat, I reached—

Kota's seat screeched up the rail, but my left hand closed on nothing. I fumbled. Finally I glanced for the ring.

I thought I had shifted only my eyes, but when I tugged the handle, the explosive force jammed my chin to my chest. Tiny lights like wind-tossed snowflakes swirled in my vision as the seat clanged to a halt at the rail's top.

Once it descended, both spacers dived on me like ghost cats on a lone shegrul.

"Are you all right, Cadet?" the younger man asked, his eyes anxious.

"If that'd been the real thing," the older tech said, "it would've broken your neck. A real ejection seat literally blasts you clear of your aircraft." He squinted into my eyes. "Are you sure you're not injured?"

"I'm fine," I said. Kota eyed me, but embarrassment kept me from returning his gaze. *I'm not ending up in the hospital in a neck brace like Patalos.*

"You get one more ride today," the older spacer said, "but all of you cadets need to come practice as often as you can before you go to the flightline."

I pressed the yellow ring against my knee so I could feel it there and pushed my head firmly against the seatback for my second ride.

As the chair slammed skyward, I couldn't contain a grin. I wanted to yell with exhilaration.

"Text-vid perfect that time," the younger spacer said as he released the belts.

I left the room with the blue patch on my badge, but I waited until we reached the drinking spouts in the hall outside the simulator bay, with their mildly brine-flavored water, to rub my neck.

"It's a little stiff," I answered Kota's unvoiced query and swallowed at thinking how a real ejection could break my neck. *Hope I never have to do it.*

* * *

By the phase before our exams on Visual Flight Regulations in Low Planetary Space and Trans-atmospheric Propulsion Systems, I began to wonder how much more my brain could absorb before it exploded. Whenever I reached "critical mass," I escaped to the weight room.

Or, taking Noshi's advice, sometimes I went running or to the gym's climbing room. The idea of timed climbs had surprised me until I realized how essential that ability could be for infiltrating and exfiltrating on Qaletaqa missions.

Hanuk and I and our friends had done a lot of rock climbing in the canyon upstream from Red Wash, so I found the 65-span climbing walls in the gym less than challenging. That was, until I learned one could rearrange the modular holds to preset levels of difficulty.

Winter or not, I found running laps on an indoor track boring, so I located the jogging trails on the base. The five-range path became my favorite once I discovered about half a range of it paralleled the mesh fence enclosing the flightline. From there, I could ogle the fighters on their parking stands. The fighters that had recently returned from sorties radiated with shimmering heat, blurring the frosty air around them.

I scrutinized their massive, paired engines, capable of producing enough thrust to achieve orbital velocity. Imagining that kind of power always quickened my pulse.

If I arrived to find a four-ship taxiing to the runway, I couldn't resist pausing to watch them launch. With fingers shoved in my ears to blunt their engines' rising screams, I observed each ship's takeoff. I watched as the wingmen banked into formation, one after another, in body-crushing high-G arcs. My heart rate stepped up, and my anticipation mounted.

When I noticed Rinn marking off the days until our first flight, I began doing it, too.

On the long-awaited morning, we reported to the Operations desk in the front area of our squadron building to search for our launch times on the wall-sized flight roster. Only then would we head to our classrooms. Excitement saturated the squadron lobby like breathable adrenaline. Everybody appeared jittery but wearing broad grins.

Halfway across the lobby, Kota seized my sleeve and pointed at the Ops board. "Lucky draw, Ku! We've got the first sortie. Classroom tables one and ten, Keatii, Dois, Apenimon, and Masou. Launch time is 0600, callsign…" He twisted his face with disgust. "Baby Bird?"

"It's always Baby Bird for first flights," said the senior spacer behind the Ops desk. "You two better get moving; briefing rooms nine and ten. Your IPs are waiting." He motioned toward a pair of doors opposite each other at the far end of the narrow hallway. Images of fighters in flight, above varied landscapes or cast against the black of space, lined its length between the dozen or so doors.

"Baby birds with eagles' talons," I told Kota. My face already ached from grinning.

"See you on the flightline," Kota said, and peeled off at his briefing room's blue-painted door.

I had anticipated this moment from the first day, the first painfully early hour of pilot training. I had dreamed of it through meals missed and sleep sacrificed to study. Had longed for it through hours of drilling with my friends on endless procedures and regulations.

So my heart dropped into my boots, and my smile melted like snow off a sunlit mountainside when I entered the briefing room and stared into the face of my IP, or instructor pilot.

I knew his precisely trimmed mustache, his snide smile, his coal-black eyes. Recalling the odd glint in his eyes when I'd received my certificate from Basic, my gut clenched. *He already knew he was going to be my IP.*

"Nobody's washed you out yet, Mess-you?" Russom asked, and sat back in his chair to study me. "I'm surprised, given your current academic standing. It appears it's fallen upon me to do it after all."

I met his gaze and held it. *My academic standing isn't bad. You didn't succeed at washing me out of Basic, sir, and you definitely aren't going to do it now.*

He motioned me to the table as if ordering a dog to heel. "We have a mission brief to do." As I warily edged onto the seat facing him, he said, "Pay attention, Mess-you. You'll do the briefings yourself in the future. If you last long enough."

Determination stamped out my initial shock. I set my jaw.

"This is a basic orientation flight," Russom said. "On reaching a cruising altitude of twenty thousand spans, we will proceed to training sector Demi-Folkstone."

He traced with a finger the flight profile displayed on the briefing table's touchscreen and waved through the holographic projection of the training sector. "Upon arriving, you will put your ship through a series of aerobatic maneuvers *as I direct you.*" He emphasized the last phrase.

His tone rankled me. *What does he think I am, a Hevovitas?* I said only, "Yes, sir."

His steely gaze bored into mine. Drilling to throw me off, I knew. "The mission objective is twofold. First, to become familiar with handling a *real* aircraft under full power. Second, to assess your skill level at basic maneuvering. With any luck, we'll make it back alive, though in your case, Mess-you, that's the best I'm hoping for."

My indignation simmered. I never shifted my vision from his. I wasn't about to reply *Yes, sir* to the insult.

"Cadet?" Russom's black brows lowered.

"Sir," I said.

After mission objectives, he briefed standard operating procedures, or SOPs, like radio protocols and contingency plans. What to do if the engines quit and we had to punch out, for example.

With the pre-mission brief finished, Russom rose and motioned me to follow. "Life Support is in the Wing Operations building."

We strode the walkway to Wing Ops in early-morning darkness illuminated by yellowish streetlights, shielding our ears with our hands when the brief roars of engines firing on test stands repeatedly punctured the quiet. Sea-scented air, frigid with its burden of moisture, pinched our noses until I thought my breath would crystallize every time I exhaled.

"You'll start wearing a pressure suit today," Russom said between engine firings. "You'd better get comfortable in one now, because that's what you'll wear in combat. However, if we go trans-atmospheric on this flight, you've done it wrong."

The Life Support section in Wing Ops reminded me of the gym's changing room, with tiled aisles lined in benches and steel lockers, steamy heat rolling from unseen shower rooms, and the odor of sweat mingled with the metal-and-plastic smell of pressure suits.

Voices rang through the area, some business-like, some jovial, along with fragments of tale-swapping.

"This way, Cadet." A spacer assistant with a broad smile and curly hair beckoned. He appeared to be about my age. "Your locker's over here."

I made a swift scan as I followed him through the bustling maze, and the tension in my gut eased. All around me, two-man spacer teams assisted pilots. I wouldn't have to climb into my pressure suit by myself. Even older pilots didn't do it alone.

My spacer assistants hauled my suit from my locker and held it out. Like everyone else's, it glared an eye-watering shade of orange.

"Boots off, Cadet," said the curly-haired youth.

I tugged them off with excitement-quivery hands and pushed stockinged feet into the suit's insulated footgear.

"Right arm first," the second spacer said at my shoulder, and raised the heavy sleeve. I pushed my arm in, and he said, "Now the left."

The suit encased me like some gigantic insect's chitinous shell. With both arms in, I braced against pushes and tugs as my crewmen secured the suit's seals from crotch to neck ring with nimble fingers.

Remembering Noshi's advice, Kota and I had braided our hair before leaving our quarters. One crewman poked my braid inside the neck ring and said, "Good thinking, Cadet." He handed me the bubble helmet, and his teammate took my elbow.

I attempted a few scuffing steps, surprised at the pressure suit's weight and how it altered my center of gravity, making me feel clumsy and heavy. *Now I know how off-worlders feel when they first come to Tempest.*

My spacers hadn't finished. They cinched a fireproof egress harness over the pressure suit's bulk. Its flat bundle, gray like my flight suit rather than bright orange, slapped the backs of my thighs with every step.

"Good luck, Cadet," the younger spacer said.

"Thanks."

Lumbering through the outer doors behind Russom, boots thudding like the feet of some large beast, I noticed with some satisfaction that I moved more easily in my pressure suit than he did in his. *The benefits of growing up on Tempest.*

Outside, another spacer waited at the helm of a vehicle resembling two benches attached back-to-back and connected to a tow hitch. Kota and his IP had already boarded and sat balancing their helmets on their laps.

Kota stared at me when he saw Russom, his mouth gaping in sympathetic horror. I met his eyes with determined stoicism, a silent attempt to assure him I'd handle it, though my stomach lay like a rock in my midsection.

Lista, Go, and their IPs emerged after Russom and me. Go's neck ring stood up around her ears. Though smaller than mine, her pressure suit was obviously too big for her.

As the bench-cart whirred down the tarmac, Lista slid an embarrassed glance at me and ducked her head. I hadn't seen her with Huritt since we'd graduated from Basic. I hoped he hadn't taken advantage of her desire for a boyfriend. I understood loneliness.

When Lista shifted away, I touched the spot over my chest pocket where I'd stowed Derry's pendant and recalled her good-bye kiss. In my mind I heard her say, *Yew'll do fine, Kew.*

Eagerness lit the others' faces as the bench-cart stopped at each of their aircraft. They slid off one by one, all ungainly to one degree or another. Beaming like spring sunshine, Go staggered in her over-sized suit. Only her IP catching her elbow kept her from falling on her face, but that didn't diminish her smile.

I had expected to feel the same thrill. I allowed myself a sigh of resignation.

Our middle-aged crew chief saluted Russom with a hand that appeared permanently grease-stained as we dismounted in front of our fighter. "Good morning, sir. Cadet." He nodded to me. "Ready to check her out?"

The Rohrspachen-55 Spearhead resembled an attacking spider in its basic configuration, with forward-swept wings that seemed to reach out like claws from below each side of the cockpit. Its streamlined bubble canopy allowed 360 degrees of visibility, a definite benefit in combat.

A modular spacecraft designed for both deep space and atmospheric operations, it bore hard points on its fuselage for attaching extended airfoils and wheeled landing gear, which was its configuration today.

Its hybrid propulsion system, of internal ejector scramjets and high-bypass turbofan engines for atmospheric flight and low-planetary orbit operations, automatically switched to twin magneto-hydrodynamic engines for deep-space flight.

This ship, an older model, had been rebuilt into a trainer variant, with a rear cockpit and extended canopy.

Russom and I conducted our walk-around check while the ground crew cleared away the fuel lines, maintenance cart, and other equipment. The bitter scents of fuel and lubricants burned my nostrils in spite of the cold.

Russom hovered at my shoulder like the apparition of Machitew, grunting once or twice while I inspected the engines and landing gear and ran a hand along the fuselage to check for fluid leaks.

When the crew chief handed me the maintenance record plate for review and sign-off, he said, "This bird's a proud old veteran, Cadet, with more than fifteen thousand combat hours." He smiled grimly. "Try to keep her proud, won't you?"

I noticed Russom's smirk. Fresh sweat dampened my flight suit's armpits under the stifling layers of pressure suit, but I straightened to attention. "You've got my word, Chief."

* * * * *

Chapter Thirty-One

Encased in the pressure suit's bulk, I couldn't simply swing my leg into the cockpit from the ladder as if I were mounting my straddlejet. With a grunt I hoisted myself over the rail, the lip into which the canopy sealed to the silver-gray fuselage.

If it takes this much effort for me to get into the cockpit, how in Yuma's name will Go manage it? I know she won't ask for help.

I plopped onto the seat, which I found to be as unyielding as the simulator's, and thrust my boots into the foot wells to straddle the center instrument console. *It's like sliding into a pair of steel trousers. Now I know why our instructors refer to mounting up as "putting on" their fighters.*

Planting my feet on the rudder pedals, I drew in a long breath. *You know this stuff, Ku. Forget about Russom and do it.*

Strapping in followed a strict procedure, each step in the same order every time to ensure against missing anything. First came connecting the cockpit's black air hose to a pressure suit valve near my navel. During high-G maneuvers, bladders in the suit's legs and across my abs would instantly inflate to restrict my blood to my upper body and head.

Next, I secured the egress harness and pack with metal clasps at my hips and shoulders. As I tightened the web belt across my lap, I realized I'd left my nervousness behind in Life Support. My hands moved steadily through their tasks, already well-practiced from the simulator rides.

The crew chief, gray-haired and florid of face, crouched on the mounting ladder to hand my helmet to me. I settled it over my head onto the neck ring with a small *clunk* and connected the blue oxygen hose to the port in my faceplate near my mouth.

On plugging the comms line into its jack by my ear, I tested my comlink, then the flow of oxygen. The comlink carried an electronic hiss, like a warning from a snake under a rock, and the hose gave the oxygen a rubbery smell strong enough to taste. I raised two fingers to confirm both worked properly.

Only then did the crew chief and another crewman, reaching in from the cockpit's other side, lock my helmet seals. The bolts twisted tight in a series of grating squeaks.

My gloves came next. I held up my hands and spread out my fingers. The chief and crewman pushed the bulky gloves onto them, seated their seal rings, and locked them into my suit's steel cuffs. Their latches ground into place.

The gloves' linings bore the subtle stiffness of hide, a familiar sensation. I flexed my hands to try their dexterity and tested my grip on the throttles and the toggle-loaded sidestick controller.

Movement at the corner of my eye prompted a glance around my shoulder. Behind me, two more crewmen scrambled off their ladders from Russom's rear cockpit.

When the crew chief signaled all ground crew and ladders were clear, I touched the canopy switch. Its aerodynamic bubble lowered above me without a sound and sealed into the rail with a soft *chunk*, enclosing me with Russom. I activated the cockpit's pressurization with another switch.

The gray-tinted canopy, shaped from nironnium like the shielding dome of an enclave, carried familiarity. I allowed myself a smile. *This cockpit is my enclave.*

As I tapped my helmet's comms switch to address the crew chief, Russom's voice rattled through our intraship comlink, lighting its indicator on my instrument panel with amber. *"Request run-up, Cadet."*

My jaw tightened. *I was about to, if you'd given me another second.* I said only, "Yes, sir," and punched the switch again. "Ready for run-up, Chief?" My mouth's dryness had eased. My voice sounded confident and relaxed in my helmet speakers.

"Affirmative," the crew chief answered. He signaled the other crewmembers. *"Fore and aft clear, chocks in place."*

I worked briskly across the instrument console, right to left, setting all switches to Start. Then I flicked the two that ignited the engines and eased the throttles from Off to Idle.

The Spearhead's massive engines roared to life with the fury of a den of ghost cats startled from sleep. I imagined the huge, pale-coated cats stretching their muscular legs and backs and extending their claws, each as long as my hand.

The engines' contained power rumbling under my seat made my Darter on Tempest seem like a toy. I couldn't have stopped smiling if I'd wanted to. *I'm going to enjoy this in spite of you, Russom.*

I gave my full attention to bringing up the ship's systems one at a time, watched every Ready light blink on, and confirmed every point with the crew chief. *I'm becoming Rinn. Russom can't fault me for that.*

Green lights flickered as the flight computer uploaded our navigation and mission data. *"Upload complete,"* said a female voice in my earphones. I final-checked my instruments, signaled Ready to the crew chief, and watched the crewmen pull the chocks and spring clear of the ship.

I had randomly drawn the fourth position for my first flight. Ops would assign us different positions each time, to give us experience in performing its specific duties.

When at last my crew chief signaled, I eased my throttle forward, listened as my engines' roar deepened, and rolled into the lineup following Go, the last Baby Bird in the row. Taxiing to the runway heightened my pulse. The fighter reverberated about me with a power the simulator could never match.

Gauging my distance from Go with a critical eye, I called for clearance before Russom could prompt me again. "Belsken Ground Control, this is Baby Bird Four—" I cringed at the callsign "—requesting clearance to launch."

"Baby Bird Four," Ground said, *"you are cleared to training sector Demi-Folkstone. Do you copy?"*

"Affirmative, Ground."

"Baby Bird Four," Ground continued, *"you have three ships ahead of you. Wind is from zero-two-seven at twelve knots, and skies are clear."*

I said "Copy," and Ground Control ordered, *"Switch to tower frequency."*

I did, and chatter on the tower freq rattled in my helmet speakers. "Tower, this is Baby Bird Four," I said. I kept my vision locked on the heat-shivered blast furnaces of Go's exhaust nozzles and my hand firm on the throttles.

"Baby Bird Four," Tower's digitized voice said, *"you are fourth in launch sequence. Do not acknowledge until you receive clearance."*

I nodded, and instantly felt sheepish at responding to an AI. *Hope Russom didn't see it.*

He didn't say anything, so I peered farther up the runway.

The first ship began to roll. Kota had drawn the Lead slot. Even three ships behind him, the scream of his multiple engines shook my aircraft like a high-frequency ground tremor.

I watched, breath jammed in my chest with anticipation, as Kota's fighter accelerated. Afterburners flared, and flames erupted like twin volcanoes from his exhaust nozzles. My heart quickened as his ship rocketed skyward. Its roar penetrated my helmet and canopy.

Ahead of Go, Lista's ship lurched into motion. I tracked its gradually increasing speed.

"Baby Bird Four," Tower repeated in my helmet speakers, *"you have two launches ahead of you. Hold for launch time."*

When Go began to roll, I controlled my tremor of swelling excitement. I drew a deep breath, scanned my instruments one last time, and realized with surprise Russom hadn't said a word during our wait. *I guess that's a good thing.*

"Baby Bird Four," the digitized voice said at last, *"you are cleared for launch."*

"Roger that." I fought to keep eagerness out of my voice. "Baby Bird Four rolling." Feet off the brakes, I pushed the throttles to full military power and watched the engines' indicators climb.

I felt their rising scream. It prickled the hair on the back of my neck. My Spearhead leaped like a ghost cat after its prey, mashing me into my seat. As we flashed past the first runway marker, I tightened my smile and shoved the throttles to afterburner. *Like riding a shock wave.* I wanted to yell my exhilaration. *Good thing Russom can't see my face.*

Three thousand spans down the runway, we reached launch velocity. I nudged the control stick. The Spearhead sprang off the tarmac like a sun eagle from a mesa, enveloping it in a rush of wind and a flash of sunlight.

Little too steep, I realized at once, though well within safe parameters.

"This isn't an airshow, Masou," Russom said through my earphones.

"Copy, sir," I answered with the most contrition I could muster. *Airshow? He's not confusing me with the Hevos, is he?*

Climbing to our designated altitude, I checked instruments and swept the cloudless sky while radio chatter murmured in the background. I spotted my classmates' ships as faintly visible specks in the expanding distance, banking off to their training sectors.

Watch your launch angle, Ku, I counseled myself. *Don't hand Russom anything else.*

Upon reaching my training sector, blocked in white in the flight profile on my display, I called, "Sector Control, this is Baby Bird Four entering sector Demi-Folkstone." I kept my tone relaxed and matter-of-fact.

"Copy, Baby Bird Four," Sector Control said. *"You are cleared to execute your filed flight plan."*

"Roger, Control." I eyed my plotted training space and the wisps of clouds whipping past the cockpit.

Russom said, *"Hmph. All right, Masou, let's start with something even you should be able to execute without getting us killed. Straight-and-level flight at our current altitude for exactly two minutes. Then you will perform two aileron rolls to the right with a one-second pause between each.*

"If you haven't lost too much altitude after completing the second roll, you will execute a spiraling nosedive to sixteen thousand spans, level out, and perform two aileron rolls to the left with the same one-second pause between rolls."

I visualized a diagram in my mind as he spoke the flight plan, connecting the maneuvers one after the other.

"*Finally,*" Russom said, "*you will make a vertical climb at full power to thirty thousand spans, where you will perform an engine stall-out maneuver.*" He paused. "*Do you need me to repeat anything, Masou?*"

"No, sir," I said. "Initiating two-minute straight-and-level flight now." I tapped my countdown clock.

When the flight computer's impassive female voice said, "*Two minutes, mark,*" in my earphones, I eased the control stick a hairsbreadth to the right.

The Spearhead flipped upside down as effortlessly as a mud-eel in Red Wash's spring run-off. During the one-second pause, I scanned the ice-layered topography above which we hung and checked my altimeter and attitude indicators. *Both on point.*

I knew they would be, but I smiled as I began the second aileron roll and returned the *Spearhead* to its starting point.

Russom huffed in my earphones, like an audible roll of his eyes.

What was that for?

In Rohr-55T variants, the IP's rear cockpit duplicated the front one, but with override capability on throttle and control stick in case a student got in trouble. I knew Russom could see everything on his instrument panel that showed on my own.

Satisfied, sir?

"Beginning dive now, sir," I said, and nosed the aircraft into a spiral. It flattened me in my seat and sent the snow-swept ground spinning below us.

I put the Spearhead through its paces, responding precisely to Russom's directives. He rarely spoke, but he kept his snide tone when he did. It didn't take much imagination to visualize his curled lip.

Be Rinn, I told myself and said only, "Roger, sir," in response.

I never hesitated. *Don't let him think you're too cautious. Aggressive is good in a fighter pilot. But don't let him think you're reckless, either.*

After the stall-out maneuver, we did a parabolic climb and banking turns tight enough to make us grunt against high Gs. The abrupt squeeze of the G-pants around my midsection and legs took my breath, like being gripped in a giant fist, but I managed not to gasp. I also managed not to blink when the glare of sunlight played across the canopy with our banks and climbs.

I executed every order flawlessly. I *knew* I did. By the time we departed the training sector after two hours of aerobatic maneuvers, my pre-flight exhilaration had been replaced by the confident fatigue that followed a good workout.

Russom stayed silent through the flight back to base. While I taxied to our parking space, though, he popped his helmet seals and released a noisy breath behind me. "We're alive, and the bird is still flyable. I'll give you that, Masou, but we have a few things to discuss during debrief."

I noticed sweat streaking his brow as he dismounted, and my confidence shriveled like a slug in the sun. *What could he possibly find to pick at?*

He rode the bench-cart to the squadron with the other IPs, while my classmates and I made our post-flight reports to our crew chiefs. As the last one dropped off, I was also the last one picked up. The others' excited chatter rose above the bench-cart's hum while I watched it approach, but I couldn't discern their words until it slid to a halt before me.

Go, cradling her helmet on her lap, beamed at me. She had an attractive, windswept appearance with strands of her wavy, dark hair stuck across her forehead.

"Better learn to braid it," I teased and drew my braid, also damp with sweat, out of my suit's neck ring as I dropped into the empty seat next to Kota.

The cart lurched into motion once more, and Kota asked, "How did it go with Russom?"

"All right." I shrugged, and eyed several parked fighters as we passed them before I said with genuine enthusiasm, "Launch is like riding a shock wave."

"Hold this a minute." Kota handed me his helmet with his pressure suit gloves stuffed into it. He fumbled in a pocket on his egress harness, fished out a couple twisty strips of jerky, and handed me one. "Flying always makes me hungry, so I came prepared." He tore off a bite and retrieved his helmet. "If you think that's killer, wait until we start doing vertical combat launches."

Almost did, and I can guess what Russom's going to say about it.

I didn't miss the triumphant gleam in Go's eyes as I bit morosely into the smoke-flavored jerky. *Kota says she's the one I'm up against. Maybe so in academics, but how good is she in the cockpit?*

I scooped my helmet up when the bench-cart ground to a halt outside the Wing Ops building and slid off it with the others. Sweat tickled its way down my sides in spite of the chill wind whistling around us. I'd be glad to shed the pressure suit in Life Support, but concern about facing Russom in our briefing room lashed weights to my feet. My vision followed my flight mates' shuffling steps.

I motioned the girls ahead of me into Wing Ops. Kota went with them, but I paused to stare longingly in the direction of my fighter. *Russom or not, I can't wait to fly it again.*

The others had already stumped inside by the time I reached the double doors. Just as I approached them, the doors slammed open. I had one instant's glimpse of a pressure suited figure before it plowed into me.

* * * * *

Chapter Thirty-Two

All I need is another IP on my neck. I stumbled backward out of his way. "'Scuse me, sir."

He chuckled.

I would've known his laugh anywhere in the universe. I gaped at him. "Huk!"

"Ku!" Hanuk tackled me, and I returned it. Not difficult, since we stood about the same height. Hanuk's angular face and long cheekbones mimicked his father's, but as children, we'd often been mistaken for brothers by people outside our enclave.

"How in Yuma's name did you get here?" he asked, thumping my back. His grin stretched across his face and lit up his eyes.

"I sent you some vids," I said, "but you never—"

"In or out, Cadets," somebody yelled behind Hanuk. "What's the hold-up?"

We both shifted aside and stiffened to attention to let a clearly disgruntled IP exit, and said, "Excuse me, sir," in unison as he passed.

Hanuk waved me inside to an empty suiting aisle, grinning again. "When my parents told me you'd disappeared, I told them I'd keep a lookout for you." He shouted through the clamor of lockers and voices, and his humor dampened. "Mom didn't think it was funny. She was really worried."

"Gram knew where I was going," I said. "She came to see me off. Didn't she tell anybody?"

"Ya, she did, which is why Mom got worried." Hanuk's eyes resumed their usual twinkle as if emerging from an eclipse. "What class are you in? What's your grad date?"

"Oh-three-twelve," I said. "A year from now. Yours?"

"Oh-three-oh-niner, three moons ahead of you." Hanuk smiled. "We could end up assigned to the same unit. MinDef has authorized a combat wing on Shemmon Orbital Station."

"MinDef?" I crimped my forehead.

"Ministry of Defense," said a tall cadet who'd arrived at Hanuk's shoulder.

Something about his aristocratic face with its eagle-beak nose seemed familiar. Though cropped in the regulation military style, his copper-red hair fell in a thick forelock across his brow. He studied me through keen, blue eyes with an expression of mild interest as he jerked a thumb toward the door. "Our chariot awaits, Huk. Who's the underclassman?"

"Mog." Hanuk twisted awkwardly in his pressure suit. "Remember the cousin I told you about who ran away from home? Meet Akuleh. Ku, this is His Royal Highness Mogen Ilisson Reskag, second son of King Sauvar, prince of the Isles of Skjörnbörg, and—"

"Heir to absolutely nothing," Mogen cut in, rolling his eyes. "Lose the royalty blather, Huk." He grinned and stuck out a long-fingered hand.

Too refined to be a warrior's, I thought, *with no scars or calluses, but he has a strong grip.*

"Pleasure to meet you, Akuleh," Mogen said, "but unlike your cousin, I can't afford to kindle the wrath of my IP, so if you will excuse me..." He dipped his head, bumped pressure suited heels together in parody of a salute, and pivoted away.

"I need to go, too," Hanuk said. "How about supper tonight? 1900 in our chow hall? We're in the 54th Squadron."

"Your chow hall, 1900, good," I said, and watched in joyful amazement as he strode off.

Working my way out of my pressure suit's stiff weight minutes later, I doubted even Russom could depress me. Still, I assumed a serious demeanor upon entering our briefing room.

Russom sat behind the projection table, his expression surly. "You took your time, Masou." He stopped drumming impatient fingers on the table and indicated the facing chair.

"No excuse, sir," I said, and dropped onto the seat.

Rather than using the table as he had for the pre-mission brief, he activated the monitor filling most of the room's rear wall. It displayed three sets of data. One section showed my cockpit's instrument panel, and a second played my nosevid recordings. The third ran a tri-D animation of my sortie, constructed from the flight computer's metadata. A white dart represented my ship, and dotted lines on a blue field tracked my maneuvers.

Russom began the playback with my acceleration down the runway. He didn't switch on the sound, though he could've chosen to play my communications. As I'd expected, he tapped Pause on his remote when the nosevid showed my front wheels rotating too steeply off the tarmac. "What was this, Masou?"

"I pulled the stick back too quickly, sir."

He eyed me, his face inscrutable. "Yes, you did. Save it for vertical combat launches."

"Yes, sir."

He paused the playback every minute or two to ask, "What happened here?" or "Why did you do this?" or to say, "You hesitated before beginning the nosedive." His critical tone and expression never varied.

I answered every question as fully as I could, uncertain what he wanted. He never gave any indication.

"There are only two marks given for training sorties," he said. "Satisfactory or unsatisfactory. You received a 'sat' for this ride, Masou, but you're marginal. You need to become more focused to remain in the program."

"Yes, sir," I said.

I left the briefing room scowling. *That was flea-picking. He's never ridden a better first sortie, and he knows it.*

* * *

Hanuk yelled my name across the 54th Squadron's dining area when Kota, Ogundo, Rinn, and I filed in and waved his arms above his head as if signaling Search and Rescue. He and Mogen had claimed a large table in the wedge-shaped room and reserved vacant spaces with their flight caps and study stacks.

Hanuk drew out the chair next to him when I came off the food line. "How long until you turn nineteen, Ku?" he teased, loud enough for people around us to hear.

"Huk," I said in a hiss, "if you get me washed out—" With an abrupt realization, I cut myself off in mid-sentence. "Four days," I said smugly, "until I'm *twenty* and legal to be here."

He chuckled. "Happy early birthday, then. No time for a Coming-of-Age Ceremony here, but being underage won't get you washed out as long as you can handle the training." He planted his elbows on the table. "So what did you do with your straddlejet? You didn't sell it, did you?"

My heart lurched. "It got stolen."

Hanuk gaped. "Are you serious?"

Kota chortled. "Along with his last pair of clean shorts."

I jabbed Kota with my elbow.

"This sounds like quite a story." Hanuk's arched eyebrows invited me to tell it, but I'd just forked in a chunk of steak. Besides, the memory still infuriated me. I pointed at my full mouth.

Hanuk lounged in his chair and surveyed his audience. "He had this huge straddlejet. How long did it take you to save up for it, Ku? Three years of butchering shegruls?" He slipped a glance at me.

I nodded, and he continued. "Gorgeous black machine with eight in-line repulsors. Eight!" Excitement illuminated his face. "Practically a *Spearhead* without wings. And auto-compensation thrusters for steep terrain. You've never seen steep terrain if you've never been to Tempest." He shaped the mesas and cliff-walled washes of Awénasa Territory with a few hand motions. "So what's the first thing sheg-brain decides to flight-test on his shiny, new straddlejet?" He smirked at me.

A peek up from my plate revealed five pairs of eyes focused on me. "I've got some good tales about you too, Huk," I warned through another mouthful.

He didn't pause. "Ya, the compensation thrusters. Our enclave is on a ridge by this big wash, seventy spans deep when it's dry in the winter. It's also wide enough to fly a Darter through."

"Which he's done a few times," I said.

"Ya," Hanuk said, "but I never tried to fly *across* it on a strad-dlejet." He straightened. "Ku pulls way back, up by the enclave. I'm down at the bank waiting, and I hear this roar of engines. He comes screaming down the slope like some demon from the Great Dark, and I see this huge smile inside his helmet, stretched like he's doing six or seven Gs."

Hanuk had begun to talk with his hands. I'd never met a pilot who didn't, but Hanuk could perform a whole drama with his. "He goes shooting off the edge, flies fifteen or twenty arm lengths on sheer momentum, and drops like a rock.

"I'm waiting for the crash. I brace myself and peer over the edge—" he pulled a face, one eye open, one closed "—expecting to see little, bloody pieces of Ku splattered on the rocks below with little, broken pieces of his straddlejet scattered on top of them."

Everybody had gone quiet. Rinn and Guns leaned forward. Hanuk smiled and nodded to me. "And…"

Heart-rupturing adrenaline surged through me once more at re-membering the seventy-span plummet. I sat back, surveyed the oth-ers, and stretched lazily. I tried to be casual, but I couldn't stifle my smirk. "I kicked the auto-comps up to maximum thrust. They worked."

The laughter that burst out around our table, so loud other diners turned our way to see what was going on, carried unmistakable relief.

Before it subsided, I said, "You were the inspiration for that, Huk, going snowsliding off the enclave dome."

Hanuk reddened, and I said, "Our enclave's a quarter range across, with a high dome."

"Half a sphere," Hanuk said, illustrating with his hands, and picked up the tale as merrily as the one about me. "There were drifts packed higher than the fortress wall on the west side. Dome Control opened the flight panels to let men out on tethers to clear the smoke vents, and I snuck out after them with my slider." He turned to me, still jovial.

"The men didn't know he'd gotten out," I said, "until they heard this long, high-pitched squeal." I gave Hanuk a kidding grin. "By the time they figured out where it'd come from, he was only a black speck on the tundra. They had to go out with a Darter to get him."

"I was ten," Hanuk said, "and when we got back, my mother warmed me up so well I couldn't sit for a moon phase."

We told more stories on each other while the tables around us gradually emptied. Mogen brought all of us fresh mugs of grain-scented kasse from the dispenser at the end of the food line, and Hanuk kept everybody laughing.

Finally we had the chow hall to ourselves, and Hanuk grew serious. "Ya, Ku was a sheg-brain when he was younger, but never underestimate him as a pilot. When we were twelve, I flew at his wing through a storm bad enough to bury the enclave. Really violent winds and lightning and blinding snow. I don't think he'd ever flown in a storm like that before." Huk slid a glance at me for confirmation. "I know he'd never soloed in one, but he didn't really have a choice."

I knew what storm he meant. Fixing my vision on the mug in my hands, I ducked my head to conceal a hard swallow. My heartbeat stiffened against my ribs at the flashback.

It's too fierce. My heart's hammering so hard, it's making my hands shake on the yoke. I'm not strong enough for this.

Don't look at the passenger seat. Don't see the empty seat. Don't remember your father's not there. Seeing it will make it real. Seeing it will remind you he's in the cargo hold, wrapped in a blanket. Dead.

My father's dead.

The wind shoves my Darter down a thousand spans. My stomach plunges with it. I hear my father's body bump against the hull with a heavy thunk. I pull the Darter's nose level and blink to clear my eyes.

I'm shaking. My shoulders ache. I'm not strong enough.

"Be tough, Ku," says the voice in my headset. "You're doing good. I'm here at your wing. You can do this. Be tough."

My throat pinches. I'm not going to cry. I'm not! I blink again and stare out at snow slashing my canopy like claws. I see the flashing lights of a Darter at my wing. Hanuk's Darter.

Hanuk's voice comes through my headset, calm and steady. As steady as my father's voice when he let me fly this morning. "Be tough, Ku. I'm at your wing."

I gradually became aware of the silence and lifted my head.

Everybody sat staring at me, their faces somber. I had no idea what Hanuk had said or when he'd stopped speaking. I swallowed again and said, "We've been each other's wingmen ever since."

Hanuk gripped my shoulder.

The silence broke only when an automaton rolled in from the kitchen, cleaning the floor behind the food line. We glanced around at each other, and those who hadn't yet drained their half-empty mugs did so.

Rinn checked his wrist chrono, shifted in his chair, and scanned our circle. "Please excuse me," he said, and inclined his head briefly to our group. "I must go study."

Hanuk's somber features resumed their cheeriness, watching Rinn stride away. "The DG medal awaits."

We all rose moments later, fastening our flight jackets as we stepped outside. A partial moon had risen and hung like a chip broken off the mountaintop. Glittering air cast a faint ring around its crescent. Our breaths clouded, making our speech momentarily visible while we planned our next supper together.

Hanuk clapped my shoulder again before he and Mogen started away. Though less than a year older than me, his smile appeared fatherly. "Be tough, Ku," he said. His confidence in me gleamed in his eyes. "You can do this. Stay tough."

"You know I will," I said.

Minutes later, plopping at my study console, I drew Derry's portrait from my pocket and contemplated it.

Wonder what Huk would say about her? He'd probably give me some serious kidding, especially if he knew I haven't talked to her since I left Tempest. It'd be good to see her again.

* * *

In the early hours, I dreamed of racing Hanuk through a hailstorm on Tempest. I could see him beneath his Darter's canopy, guffawing and challenging me to keep up.

Fifty-pound hailstones ripped apart heaving clouds as black as Machitew's cloak, whistled past our wingtips, struck the desert, and blasted up at us like surface-to-air missiles. We rolled, banked, and corkscrewed to avoid them.

The hailstones began to explode, ice-boulders detonating like space-mines into swelling fireballs.

"Stay sharp, Ku!" Hanuk called.

One hailstone erupted in my face. Flaming debris littered the dark all about me. It hurtled past my cockpit, striking the canopy and fuselage with a clatter like heavy rain.

Hanuk's Darter had disappeared.

I woke panting and shaking, with my pulse racing.

* * * * *

Chapter Thirty-Three

Due to our conflicting schedules, I didn't see Hanuk again for a whole phase. One day I glimpsed him in Life Support when I lumbered out to catch the bench-cart, and we shouted greetings to each other across the clamorous room. By then the dream had faded. I knew Hanuk would laugh and ask what I'd been drinking if I told him about it. It gnawed at the edges of my mind for a while, but I attributed my concern to normal pilot superstitions.

Coming of Wanikiya Ceremony came and went. We would've completely forgotten about it, under our intense training schedule by then, if our families hadn't sent boxes full of feast foods.

Kimama had included several small birds she'd cut out and folded from brown, white, and gold-colored papers in Gram's box for me. I hung them above my console where I could see them while I studied, though they reminded me more of Kimama than of the figures from the sacred tales they represented.

Gram sent awanatas to Hanuk as well, and we both shared with our roommates. I made certain I sent her a vid message. "Thanks for the awanatas, Gram! Huk says thanks, too. Tell Kimmie I'll vid her as soon as I get a chance."

* * *

I only encountered Five-Talon Noshi twice during those demanding phases, once in the gym's climbing room, and once near the three-range marker on my preferred running trail.

Entering the climbing room one day, I noticed a handful of cadets from the class behind mine working their way up the intermediate section. We all started, enough for a girl in the group to briefly lose her toehold, when a familiar voice hailed me from the top of the advanced climbers' section across the room. "Cadet Masou! It's a good view from here. Come join me."

I smiled at Noshi and crossed to the gear locker against the only nonclimbing wall. "On my way, sir."

He observed me from his vantage point while I cinched myself into the web seat-sling and checked every buckle and carabiner, as new and shiny as all the equipment in the gym. "Are you familiar with rock climbing, Cadet?" he asked.

"Did a lot of sport climbing back home, sir."

"Ah. Then you prefer a clean face, too." He indicated the section upon which he stood.

Gray and grainy, the experienced climbers' surface bore no artificial holds. One had to use whatever hollows, protrusions, and cracks millennia of wind and water erosion had created. This wall simulated granite rather than the relatively soft sandstone of the Awénasa desert, so it offered fewer pocks and ridges than the canyons to which I was accustomed.

I had bested it once before, but even if I hadn't, I wasn't about to refuse a challenge from Noshi. I snapped my seat-sling to the belay line with a distinct *clink* and tested it with a couple tugs, attached a chalk pouch to my belt, and scrutinized the sheer stone while I coated my hands with dusty whiteness.

I started by shoving my toe into a slanting crevice, like a piton, as high as I could stretch my leg, then took an open hand grip on the seam's lip as far as I could reach above my foot and pushed myself to a more or less standing posture.

"Good," Noshi said from above. "You've learned to use your legs instead of your arms. Leg muscles are much stronger."

Crawling the wall sometimes required spreading my limbs like a spider's to take advantage of every available dip and bulge. More than once, as sweat dampened my hands and my gear scraped the rough face, I believed it would've been easier if I'd had a spider's eight legs.

Noshi commented occasionally. Once, I thought he'd addressed me by my Gram-given name. "Look up," he said, "and find new toeholds before you move again, Cadet."

I did a double-take. *He's never called me that before.*

"Look up," he urged once more, "and plan your route. It's safer and easier if you do." He paused before he said in a musing tone, "You'll find looking up applies to many things in life besides climbing."

I froze, finally realizing what Gram meant every time she reminded me of what she'd called me and urged me to live by it.

A handful of emotions surfaced in rapid succession. Surprise first, that Noshi had so closely if unknowingly echoed Gram's counsel, followed by irritation at the thought of someone else pressuring me about it, and finally the fleeting fear of never escaping it anywhere I went.

Noshi towered above me, beaming like some benevolent spirit risen from the stone. I gave a curt nod in response and, with the wall's sloughing grit in my teeth and on my tongue, resisted an increasing desire to spit.

When my hand grasped the lip of the artificial cliff, Noshi extended his own and gave me an assist to join him on its top. "See?" he said. "The view is worth the effort it requires."

* * *

The other time, I encountered him where the running path emerged from the forest to follow the flightline's fence, where acrid odors of fuel and lubricants smothered the crisp pine scent. It was the stretch where I always slowed to watch the training sorties launch.

"Enough warm-up, Cadet," Noshi said with his crinkly grin as he passed me. "Keep up with me."

"Ya, sir." Though already panting, I quickened my pace.

"Every time you do something," Noshi said as we ran, his words sweeping away in wispy clouds, "push yourself harder. Take it up one more notch. Always work to exceed your previous best effort."

My lungs burned with exertion in the snow-glittered air as we passed a slower runner, but I said, "Ya, sir." A stitch pierced my side, but I wasn't about to let up in front of Noshi. We crossed the five-range marker together, jogged the trail into the gym's warm-up area, and paced another range to cool down.

"Good. Keep it up, Cadet," Noshi said as we parted.

Relief rushed through me. Nothing about looking up this time.

* * *

Winter gradually yielded to an arctic spring, shortening the long nights and revealing the mountains' beards of alpine forest as the snowdrifts receded before regular light but chilly rains.

Russom never thawed, though. Once, near the end of a long-distance point-to-point flight down Osfelga's coast of black cliffs, he said, *"Turn to heading two-seven-point-two and descend to one thousand spans."*

I completed the maneuver with exactness, shifting my sight back and forth from my instruments to the landmarks below, but I failed to acknowledge his order before I executed it.

In the briefing room afterward, Russom punched the comms recording off and shouted, "Were you sleep-flying, Masou? That's as close to an unsat as you can get and still pass."

Another time, while launching at dawn, the sun's first rays glanced like lightning across my canopy as I climbed. As I would have on Tempest, I reflexively banked to evade the strike.

"What were you doing?" Russom demanded. "If we'd been in tight formation, you would've taken off your wingman's nose. Eyes outside the cockpit, Masou, or you'll kill somebody during War Phase."

"Yes, sir," I said, and clenched my teeth when Machitew's cold breath brushed the nape of my neck inside my helmet. The fact that I had banked without a visual check first shook me. *Am I getting careless?*

I didn't go to chow after debrief, despite my stomach's growling. I returned to the school, climbed the broad stairs to the floor full of instructors' offices, and hesitated outside Noshi's half-open door.

He recognized my presence without raising his attention from his monitor. "Come in, Cadet Masou."

I slipped inside and straightened to attention to properly request a meeting, but he nodded at two chairs near his desk. They stood against the wall, allowing a clear view into the hall outside the door. Qaletaqa vigilance.

"You appear troubled," Noshi said, setting aside his work. "Sit down."

I dropped onto the nearest chair and described what I'd done—or rather, not done—on the sortie. "My only unsat, sir."

"You responded instinctively," Noshi said, "with skills you developed on Tempest. Not even all Chalca are storm-flyers."

"What if I fall back on those instincts again?" I asked.

"You won't." A knowing smile touched his creased mouth and flinty eyes.

"How do you know, sir?"

"Because now you are aware of it. You will start developing new instincts."

I left a few minutes later, feeling better. I bought lunch at the flight kitchen on my way to the dorm and placed Derry's pendant on my console display.

While I ate, I visualized her sitting opposite me, a lesson plate from my study stack cradled in her hands. I imagined her asking in her lilting accent, "Right, then, Kew, how well do yew know yer flight regulations?"

We were required to recite and explain the correct regulation when any instructor asked, "Cadet, what does it say in Section Fourteen, Paragraph One-Bando?" or, "Tell me what Section Nine, Paragraph Two-point-Two Nexus says."

I had spent half my childhood memorizing chants. I'd done it by listening to and singing the words, not by reading them. *Wonder if that'd work with these?* So I sang under my breath. If I divided long words into syllables, most regulations fit into one chant melody or another.

By the time Rinn came in from his sortie, I had memorized four complete sections. *Just hope I don't start singing next time some instructor asks me to recite.*

* * *

Spring warmed to an alpine summer. Osfelga lay near enough Solienne's northern pole for sunlight to linger into the night, though not like Tempest's unbroken summer daylight. Nor did it get hot with its occasional rainstorms. Not compared to Awénasa Territory's heat, anyway.

The plans Hanuk and I made for meals together usually fell apart as my flying schedule intensified and his never let up. Only once did we arrive at the chow hall at the same time, and I joined him for lunch in his squadron's section.

My mind had already locked on my afternoon sortie.

"You're getting a permanent crease in your forehead!" Hanuk chortled between loading in food. "Not a good sign, Ku."

"We're starting tight formations today," I said, eyeing the cream-laden seafood soup in my bowl, "and I've got the Three position."

Hanuk snorted. "You won't have any trouble with it." He sat back. "Flying formation is easier here than on Tempest, even though we do it closer here. You don't have all the up- and downdrafts that make us spread out on Tempest."

I nodded, but one question plagued my mind. *Will I remember to make visual checks before I maneuver?*

With four of us on the sortie, we had a group pre-mission briefing. Corwyn Waterstone, Rinn's classroom tablemate, had drawn Lead, so he did the talking. He described our route to the training sector, his words quick and stiff, and illustrated the maneuvers we'd perform and our return route to the base with a series of complex holographic diagrams. Clearly nervous, he glanced at his IP several times as if for confirmation.

"You better not embarrass me that way when you fly Lead," Russom said as we strode to Wing Ops afterward. "You better know your briefing inside and out. I won't be as generous as Journeyman Seres about providing prompts."

"Yes, sir," I said.

"One more point." Russom fixed me with his hot-coals stare. "If you fail to make visual checks today, Masou, an unsat won't be the only outcome. It will likely result in funerals."

My mouth dehydrated. "Yes, sir." *As if I need any more pressure.*

Noshi said I won't mess up, because now I'm aware of it. Huk said I won't have trouble flying in formation here compared to Tempest. I hope they're right.

Cadet Brassone had the Two slot, and Rinn had Four. We were to launch at ten-second intervals and close into fingertip formation. That would place Cadet Brassone at Waterstone's right, me at his left, and Rinn at my left. I visualized the spacing in my mind while I listened to the radio chatter and waited for my launch time.

The way the four Hevos used to strut around together during Basic.

For some reason it no longer seemed so funny.

My heart rate stiffened as I taxied to my place in the line-up. "Kicker Three rolling," I said when Control cleared me to launch, and I opened the throttles.

As my landing gear left the tarmac, Brassone's ship, still gaining altitude ahead of me, slid into place at Waterstone's wing as smoothly as a knife into its sheath. *"Lead, Two locked in,"* she called.

Ten seconds later, I drew up on Waterstone's left. I flicked a glance across at him to check distance and position before I echoed, "Lead, Three locked in," and peered over my shoulder to watch Rinn join us.

Corwyn ahead and Rinn behind. Keep your eyes on both of them. No margin for error. My hands dampened in my gloves, leaving the linings clammy.

We performed banking maneuvers, right and left, as a four-ship unit. I kept my eyes forward for half seconds at a time as I continually monitored our positions. *Got to maintain spacing.*

At one point, Rinn and I were to roll clear of the others to fly two large circles and a barrel roll as a two-ship element before re-grouping.

"Like a good team of kaluçes pulling together," Rinn murmured through my helmet speakers.

Russom probably thought my head had gotten stuck facing left as I tracked Rinn on my wing. I tightened my jaw and my grip on the stick until my teeth and hand ached.

We landed neatly, ten seconds apart, in trail formation. I released my breath as I popped my braking flaps.

Behind me, Russom said only, "Congratulations, Masou, you didn't cause any funerals today. Now let's see if you can keep it up."

* * *

"We have an observation platform a level below Air Traffic Control," Instructor Arturo informed us three days later. "All of you would be well advised to spend your *copious* free time—" he inflected the word with sarcasm "—studying one another's flights. You can learn a great deal from observing your fellow students."

Kota and I met each other's eyes. When he mouthed "Huritt," I nodded. We had early sorties the next day, launching about forty minutes apart. Both of us would return before Huritt's sortie launched.

I hoped Russom wouldn't stretch out my debriefing. He did, of course, and finished with, "I'm relieved you will be flying solo by War Phase, Masou. I can watch you kill yourself from the observation platform rather than from your back seat."

By the time he dismissed me, I had little time to race to the flight kitchen for some cold venison sandwiches on crusty, black bread before Kota and I headed to the control tower. We jogged up four flights of clanging metal stairs to the viewing platform.

Tinted panes comprised the three sides overlooking the runways. A dozen much-used pairs of electronic binoculars hung on a rail below the panes. A huge projection display, a much larger version of those on our briefing rooms' walls, filled the rear of the platform. On it we could track aircraft once they flew beyond visual range.

I had just downed my last sandwich when Rinn, Go, and a handful of cadets from Ekan Flight arrived. The Ekan girls, apparently from several worlds, eyed us like goods in a market stall. We reciprocated.

"You'll have to come watch these three fly," Kota said, indicating Rinn, Go, and me. "They're all in the running for the DG medal. I'm the one to watch when you need comic relief."

The girls laughed, but I said, "Don't let Kota fool you. I'd fly with him any day."

"Which, um, position is Huritt flying?" Go asked when the fighters taxied onto the runway.

We snagged binoculars from the rail, and Kota answered, "He's Four."

"You know he hates being last," I said with a grin, and scrubbed smudged binoc lenses on my sleeve.

While the fighters lined up below us, their cockpit comms crackled from speakers tucked against the platform's ceiling. From our perch, we could discern helmets under cockpit canopies and the motions of gloves signaling ground crews.

"I'd hate to be his IP," Kota muttered.

"Too bad he didn't get Russom," I said. "They'd probably kill each other off."

Huritt's position made him easy to see. After being heckled about my first launch, I wondered if Huritt, with his airshow background, had done the same thing.

If he once had, he'd overcome it. His launch could've been the example for a text-vid. He locked in at Three's wingtip with an easy precision that left me gritting my teeth. *Burn. It'll be hard to beat him.*

His sortie proved the value of his airshow experience, much as I hated to admit it. Watching the display on the rear wall, I noted how he executed every roll and turn, every dive and climb as smoothly as a fish in a river, and with the split-second sharpness of several years' practice. *He could do this in his sleep. His intership comms actually sound bored.*

Scrutinizing the screen beside me, Kota shook his head. "He almost puts corners on the curves."

I agreed with a stiff nod. *Only Rinn flies with that kind of precision. I'm not letting some self-important chief's son rob me of my piloting reputation.*

* * *

With flight performance taking more weight than academics for Distinguished Graduate, I figured Go and Rinn beating Huritt with test scores in class might not matter very much after I observed some of his sorties. Go's and Rinn's scores usually beat mine by only one or two points, compared to three or four for Huritt, so I shifted my objective to out-flying him.

He seemed to realize it. Every morning on arriving in the classroom, with Enyeto hovering at his shoulder, he greeted me with a new threat.

"Your days are running out, Sheggy," he said once.

Another time he planted a fist on my desktop, lowered his heavy brows, and said, "If you're smart, Sheggy, you'll drop out of the competition for DG."

I held his glower. "Or what?"

He opened his fist and smacked my desktop with his palm, as if swatting a fly. Everybody in the room jumped and stared, and he wiped his hands together, pretending to brush off a squashed insect. "Accidents happen."

Breathing in somebody else's ear now, Machitew? I thought.

Kota witnessed the whole thing. "I think he means it, Ku," he said afterward, his expression grim.

During breakfast a phase or so later, Kota said, "Go is so short, I don't know how she reaches her rudder pedals. Her crew must put booster blocks down her ship's foot wells."

I'd just taken a swallow of kasse, and I had to clamp a hand to my mouth to keep from spraying Kota with it when I burst into a guffaw. Ogundo, thinking I'd choked, gave me a couple firm whacks on the back.

"Seriously, you're a better flyer than her," Kota said. "I've watched both of you this phase. You'll edge her out there." He paused before he said in a lowered voice, "Huritt was in the tower yesterday, too. He issued another threat." He glanced at his roommate. "You were closer, Guns. What did you hear him say?"

"Hevo says there hasn't been a casualty in Primary Piloting for five years," Ogundo said. "He thinks it's time for another, to make sure everyone remembers how things are *supposed* to be. His emphasis, not mine." Guns eyed me directly, his usually relaxed features atypically grave. "If I were you, Ku-man, I'd start keeping a really close watch on my one-eighty."

* * * * *

Chapter Thirty-Four

I studied Huritt's sorties as often as I could between flying my own. He never slipped from the precision I'd seen in the first flight.

I knew he watched my sorties as well, and I couldn't shed an odd gratification that he considered me a serious threat to his chances for Distinguished Grad. Until I remembered what I'd overheard in the chow hall. *It isn't just about DG. It goes back to the threat from his mother.*

One day as Kota and I passed his classroom table, Huritt caught the attention of the cadets at the next one and sniffed noisily. "There's probat stench," he sneered. "Mess-you is what happens when desert clans get affectionate with their shegruls."

The vulgar implication triggered fury like magma boiling to eruption. I spun about, my face throbbing, my fists knotted.

"Ku!" Kota, taller and longer-limbed than me, seized my arm to drag me away. "If you hit him," he hissed in my ear, "you'll be dropped from training like a hot rock. Don't give him what he wants."

Huritt's insult to both my deceased parents raged in my soul. I lunged against Kota's grip, snarling into the others' guffawing faces, brown, white, and black, until someone near the door shouted, "Room, atten-*shun.*"

I spent the afternoon seething under Huritt's sneers, unable to sit still, unable to concentrate, while my mind crawled through plans for revenge.

Sometime near midnight, I woke at a wintry blast through my room. Shivering, I sat up to tug the down-filled cover from the foot of my bunk and stiffened at the dim, otherworldly glow of Machitew's bodiless mask drifting a couple spans above my bunk. Probably because of my anger when I'd gone to bed, I felt little surprise, though no less creeping dread.

"Accidents happen during Primary Piloting." Machitew's chilling breath caused another shiver. "He said it himself. We will have our revenge for his insult to our parents."

When his ghostly mask encased my head, I found myself in the observation platform, watching as Huritt and his flight mates taxied to the runway under a moonless night sky.

Through a dry mouth, I demanded, "You want me to sink to his level?" My voice rasped loud enough to startle me in the room's quiet.

"It's vital." Machitew's words hissed through his mask. "If we don't eliminate him now, he'll become our greatest threat in the future."

"How?" I shook my head inside the ghost-mask's smothering cover and glimpsed myself with my loosed hair, not Machitew's mane of oily rags, lashing in a cold wind.

The apparition didn't answer my question. "We are strongest when we ally with the spirits of air." Its voice dropped to a muffled rumble. "We only need a swift gust under one wing when he lifts off."

Machitew began a chant I'd never heard before, one that didn't begin with a petition to the Ancients.

My blood iced where I sat, but I had no power to reach for the coverlet.

As if through the spectral mask's eyeholes, I could only stare at the runway as Huritt's ship reached launch velocity.

I squeezed my eyes closed, but it did no good. On rotation, as its nose-gear lifted off the surface, I saw a swell of black wind, coiling like smoke, burst across the runway. Huritt's fighter rolled violently left, as if a giant had straightened from a crouch beneath it and shoved its right wing straight up.

The fighter's left wingtip met the tarmac. Sparks plumed, white-hot, from the furrow it plowed, and the ship cartwheeled. I watched it tumble a few spans off the surface, in such slow motion it seemed to take several minutes to crash.

It struck inverted, crushing the canopy, and skidded a hundred spans along the runway on its momentum. White-hot steel shrieked on the tarmac. As if really in the observation deck, I swayed at shock waves of multiple concussions when it exploded, and billows of tarry fuel-smoke burned my nostrils through the spectral mask. It vanished from my head only when the fireball had dissipated.

"No!" I gasped in the darkness. My ribcage felt tight, as if crushed by icy fingers. In desperation, I began the Warding Chant. I panted it in constricted breaths. The chant dimmed the searing images, but didn't fully remove them.

"We are Death Bringer." Machitew's voice wafted from every corner of my room on a chilling draft. "Do you think we can banish ourselves?"

Gram. I shot from my bunk and had to pause when I swayed on unsteady legs. Putting a hand to the wall, I stumbled to the dark study area, bare feet silent on the short carpet, and fumbled across my console with shaky hands to find my link.

One finally closed on it. I dropped onto my chair. Strands of loose hair fell across my face, and I absently tucked them behind my ears before punching Gram's call code.

Kimama appeared in the display after a few trills. "Ku!" she cried, and her eyes widened. "Why haven't you vidded me for so long? What are you doing?"

My tension eased. "Sorry, Butterfly. Is Gram there?"

Kimama pouted. "Don't you want to talk to me?"

"Ya," I said, "for a minute, but then I need to talk to Gram. It's important."

"Good!" She told me about the different medicinal herbs she and Gram had planted in low trays on the flat roof. I knew each one by sight and scent, tangy and bitter and sweet. "When they dry," she said at last, "we'll make poultices and teas and other stuff out of them."

"Sounds like Gram's teaching you a lot." I relaxed as I listened, but finally I said, "I really need to talk to Gram now, Kimmie."

"Huh!" Her pout returned.

The display blanked for a second before Gram peered out of it, her brows drawn together. "What's wrong, Akuleh?"

"I'm all right." I raked back the sweat-dampened strands slipping from behind my ears and took a deep breath to counter the crushed sensation in my chest. "Machitew was here again."

"Are you saying the Warding Chant every night?"

I sighed. "You know it won't work for me, Gram. You know what my Birth Chant says about me."

She studied me, eyes keen as if questioning, appraising me. At last she said, "Ya, I do. Do *you* know what it says?"

"I've seen people's reactions to me long enough to have a good idea."

Her pursed lips and scrutinizing gaze revealed nothing. "I can't tell you what you want to know, Akuleh. It's forbidden to reveal it before your Coming-of-Age Ceremony. You know that."

"You know what it means," I said, fighting to keep urgency out of my voice. It seemed as loud in the room's stillness as if I'd shouted.

She nodded, solemn. "Ya, I do, and Machitew does, too. You must be strong, Akuleh, very strong, to resist whatever he tells you."

Strong to resist what he tells me? Puzzlement creased my forehead. *I don't want to be Death Bringer, but if I'm destined to become him, why do I need to resist him? Is it only a matter of timing?*

My throat closed, like my lungs. I couldn't speak.

Gram must have seen the despair in my face through her link's miniature display. "I'll say the Warding Chant for you," she said, her voice comforting, and stretched out her right hand as if to place it on my head.

I acquiesced with only a nod. *She genuinely believes in it. Maybe it'll work for her the way the pain chant worked for Nayati.*

The grip on my lungs loosened by the time she finished.

"Better?" she asked, eyeing me.

I nodded again, though I remained drained of strength.

"Say the Warding Chant every time you prepare to sleep." Command replaced comfort in her voice. "Promise me, Akuleh."

"I will, Gram."

"Good," she said. "I'm saying the chants for you, too."

I ended the vid call without replying. *I need to be strong to resist Machitew? What does Gram mean?*

My increased confusion gave rise to a mass of new questions spinning in my mind like a forming tornado.

* * *

In the phase after summer solstice, when the sun set for about two minutes before it rose again, our studies shifted to trans-atmospheric and flight at low-planetary orbit altitudes.

"By the time you begin War Phase," Lieutenant Commander Hunun informed us, "all of your training sorties will be flown in low-planetary orbit. You will take shuttles to Shemmon Military Orbital Station and launch from its flight decks. But you cannot begin LPO sorties until you pass takeoff-and-landing simulator training."

Takeoffs from a simulated launch tube proved to be easier than from runways, real or simulated. Only after the catapults had blasted us clear of the station could we take control of the ship with stick and throttle.

The most important part became physically conditioning our bodies to pull six Gs for several seconds. It wasn't much of an issue for us heavy-worlder Chalca.

Landing in a ramp turned out to be much more difficult. The square hatch, hemmed with approach guidance lights that changed from red to yellow to green as one lined up one's ship for entry, gaped wider than the wedge-shaped opening in an enclave's dome, and no wind buffeted my wings. I had no problem gliding inside.

However, remembering to fire braking thrusters as I entered instead of giving my ship a little more throttle countered all my prior experience. On Tempest, I'd had to maintain enough power once inside the enclave's dome to maneuver to our hangar. I had to override the drag of gravity until I actually set the Darter down.

Conversely, in LPO's microgravity, if I lined my ship up correctly, the inertia from one brief thruster burn would carry me into the ramp with no additional power. Reducing my velocity, rather than maintaining it, became critical.

The first time I attempted it, I froze. My hands clutched the controls as the virtual landing ramp's rear bulkhead swiftly advanced on me, and acting on seven years of experience, I nudged the throttle instead of the reverse thrusters.

I managed not to crash on my second simulator flight, but only because I kept my throttle hand on the reverse thruster switches all the way in. I accomplished an acceptable landing, but Russom shook his head in disgust when he reviewed the simulator results. "I'm ordering spring-reinforced arresting nets before I do a space sortie with you, Mess-you."

Huritt's ongoing disrespect of my parents didn't help. "Ai, Son-of-a-shegrul," he said with a jeer whenever we passed each other on base.

My hands always balled into fists, but Kota clamped a hand on my shoulder. I gave Huritt the *get snipped* hand gesture instead.

* * *

The night before our first sortie from Shemmon Station, Machitew materialized in my room again. I hadn't even settled on my bunk when a pronounced chill sent a shiver from my nape to my tailbone, and the faintly luminous mask took shape at eye-level before me.

"Huritt is our greatest threat," the specter said, as it had before. "It is essential for him to die. We only have to blow him one degree off course."

I countered, "There's no air out there."

"We don't need air." Machitew's eyes, my eyes, gleamed at me through the ash-blackened mask. "Space belongs to the spirits of the air. Together, we are their master."

I shook my head against the supernatural mask enclosing it, but it made no difference. I gripped my closet's frame to keep myself on my feet.

Through its eyeholes, while Machitew's frigid breaths raked my bare shoulder, I watched Huritt's ship approach the landing ramp. My teeth clenched when his fighter wobbled. His starboard wing struck the ramp's illuminated opening, where the warning lights flashed urgent crimson.

His ship didn't tumble in slow motion that time. It simply vanished in a silent blossom of orange pyrotechnics.

I staggered where I stood, gasping, sweating, heart racing. It took some time for my pulse to slow.

The following morning, Huritt and Enyeto sauntered into the classroom last, as if they owned it. Keeping one eye on the door to watch for our instructor's arrival, Huritt leaned on my table. "You can't even scream in space, Son-of-a-shegrul."

I held his gaze, my face impassive, but I couldn't stifle a shudder at the thought crossing my mind. *Maybe Machitew's right. Huritt's making it him versus me.*

* * * * *

Chapter Thirty-Five

Hanuk's class graduated in early autumn, as the days shortened once more, and crisp winds swept migrating birds out of the Hamskjold Mountains as if with twig brooms. Along with their golden pilot's wings, Hanuk and his classmates would receive their commissions as apprentice officers in Solienne's Aerospace Defense Force.

Squadron Commander Grell had informed us in the phase before that our class would be given half a day off from our studies to march in the graduation's parade and review. "Senior officials from the Commonwealth and Resistance Pact worlds will be in the stands, not to mention the graduates' families and friends."

"No pressure," Kota said. "Is this finally the reason we spent seven hours a day drilling and yelling orders at each other during Basic? We've never used it for anything since."

I shrugged. "Probably."

With Go's standing at the head of our class, nobody blinked or begrudged the choice when Grell named her the cadet squadron commander for the parade. She received the announcement with genuine amazement and a blush as deep red as ripe cactus fruit.

Several of us, though, exchanged suspicious glances when he chose Huritt as flight commander for the parade.

"I thought you or Rinn were next after Go, not him," Kota said. "I wonder what kind of pressure somebody applied for the honor?"

"And who applied it," I said.

The privilege of being Chally Flight's guidon bearer came down to a tossing of colored chits between Rinn and me. To my surprise, I won the toss.

"Congratulations, Ku," Rinn said, and pumped my hand with an atypically formal expression, even for him.

"Thanks," I replied, "but it should've been you without a toss."

After Rinn left, Kota slid me a grim glance. "You really should be in second place, Ku."

Recalling a couple of my test scores, I shook my head. "No, I shouldn't."

Kota remained undeterred. "Huritt seems to think so. He's got himself and you singled out from the whole squadron."

"He would," I said, and faked a yawn, though Huritt's stare seared like twin laser beams into my back.

* * *

Go spent the next few days of class dropping things out of nervousness. We had only one chance to practice, the evening before the graduation, on a parade ground before a grandstand the size of a torgus stadium. Everyone mingled on the parade ground until the officers arrived.

While a chilly wind snatched at our flight caps, reddened our ears, and snapped our bright pennons at the tops of their staffs, I studied the other cadet flight commanders and guidon bearers. *My competition for the DG medal.*

The choice for Folkstone Flight's parade commander startled me. The blonde Sathi girl I'd seen on the crawler when we first arrived on Solienne, surrounded by gawking male conscripts, held the position.

The wind polished her cheeks to a fresh pink. It tugged several golden tendrils of her hair from the bun at her nape and swept them about her large eyes in a decidedly beguiling manner. "Like a doe through tall grasses" wouldn't have been an accurate description, though, because does always appeared so innocent.

She must have sensed my stare, because she glanced around, then crossed to Kota and me. "I am Allandra Pellesh," she said. "And you are?"

Her breathy voice and gleaming smile swept all coherence from my brain. "I'm Ahk, uh, Ku," I stammered.

"Kota," he said. "My pa's from Satha, from Bievre Canton in Apollona."

Her blue pools of eyes widened. "Truly? I know Bievre. I am from Paliseul Canton, east of Bievre." She asked a question in a language that sounded sensuously throaty, but nasal at the same time.

Kota responded, though with hesitance, and concluded in Standard, "I'm sorry I don't speak it very well."

"We will have to practice sometime, together," she said with another blinding smile, and winked at us as she strolled away.

Kota seemed to have missed the wink. For a second, his puckered features reminded me of Rinn. "I've forgotten more Escalleau than I thought. Pa doesn't speak it at home."

I stood there, guidon in hand, staring stupidly after her retreating shapely figure. "At least you didn't forget your own name." *She probably thinks I'm a total idiot.*

Kota chuckled, but my face burned through all three dry-runs of the parade, despite the cold.

Rehearsing didn't make Go feel any better. "I know I will, um, mess up," she confided as we returned to our dorm. "I know will I do it wrong in front of, you know, my betrothed and the whole universe."

"You'll be fine, Go," Kota told her.

"You'll do it perfectly, the way you do everything else," I added.

She lifted her head, pursed her lips, and studied me intently. I didn't miss the driven light in her eyes.

Striding down the hallway to our quarters, I sighed. *I'm up against my precision-machine roommate, a girl who's expected to excel in everything, and an aerobatic performer who's lived under this kind of pressure for years.*

That's not even counting the top cadets from the other flights, including Allandra Pellesh. I've got some serious work to do to maintain my piloting reputation.

* * *

Banners rippled in a brisk sea wind at the tops of their tall poles. Deep-blue banners bearing the likeness of Thrüss snapped fiercely, as if the war god himself had descended to witness the acceptance of his newest adherents.

Mogen pointed out his father, King Sauvar Ilisson Reskag, and the royal family seated in the grandstand's banner-draped box. "Papa's feeling incredibly relieved," he said as we formed up outside the parade ground. His eyes twinkled with self-deprecating humor. "I've never before given him reason to hope I'd make anything respectable of myself."

Hanuk and I chuckled.

When the marching began, Go performed flawlessly, of course. My duty as guidon bearer consisted mostly of sharply raising and lowering Chally Flight's green-and-gold flag when Huritt shouted,

"*Pre*-sent arms!" and "Or-*der* arms!" and holding it steady against the wind's tugs.

Wing Commander Lodesson presented awards for Best Military Bearing, Top Academic, and Top Marksman before he announced, "Finally, Distinguished Graduate for Primary Piloting class oh-three-oh-niner is Hanuk of clan Masou from Red Wash Enclave, Tempest."

Huk the DG? I stood there gawking. *The same Huk who rigged a raw egg to drop on my stepmother's head when she opened the dwelling door?* I laughed out loud. *If Huk can earn the DG medal,* I *definitely can.*

I grinned until my face ached as Commander Lodesson pinned the heavy medal to my cousin's chest.

Uncle Kwahu, Aunt Lemana, and Hanuk's younger sister Chenoa had come from Tempest for the occasion. After the ceremony, according to military tradition, his parents pinned his new rank on his dress uniform, and Chenoa pinned on his wings. We rode a public crawler, with several other graduates' families, into the city of Reskagen for a celebratory lunch.

I'd never received leave to cross the fjord into the city before. The crawler crossed a major street that ran straight up the most prominent slope, from some government building at its base to a pillared temple at its crest.

All the other roads seemed to wind back and forth across the foothills, one-lane canyons walled by narrow, many-storied structures with steep roofs to shed snow. From a distance, the buildings resembled rows of pointed teeth, much like their backdrop of sheer peaks.

Hanuk had chosen Tollesson's Pub, a mountain of a place itself, built entirely of massive logs. Built on the waterfront, it exuded aromas of seared meats through its double front doors. His class, he told us, had gone there a couple phases earlier for the customary Opening of the Orders dinner.

"Tell us about your assignment, Hanuk," Aunt Lemana said as we tapped our choices into the tabletop menu. She had to lean forward and shout to make herself heard through the rollicking music and hundreds of cheerful voices.

"I'm staying here at Solienne," Hanuk yelled, "but I'm moving up. *Way* up. I'm in 1st Squadron of the new 15th Aerospace Combat Wing on Shemmon Military Orbital Station. They're creating another two squadrons, so Ku may get assigned there, too."

His parents gazed at me, and I smiled back. Anticipation had already set in, along with impatience to finish.

"I have to move tomorrow," Hanuk went on, "because two days after that, we leave for survival school." He gave a mysterious smile. "The location is so classified, even we don't know where we're going."

Hanuk's parents didn't ask about my unexpected departure. They only knew it had to do with my stepmother. They did ask how I was doing and when I'd graduate, and made vids of Hanuk and me in our dress uniforms, arms flung across each other's shoulders and smiling broadly.

Unlike Hanuk, I still had limited off-base time, so I left soon after lunch and caught the return crawler to Belsken Field. I had planned to put in a few hours of study with Rinn, but by mid-afternoon, I'd grown as restless as a caged ghost cat. I couldn't concentrate. Uncertainties rolled across my mind like crumbling ball brush in a summer wind, so I shut down my console and retrieved my gym bag.

I never made it to the gym. Go joined me as I jogged down the stairs. "I must talk to Commander Hunun, you know, my adviser, about what I must do to, um, excel," she said.

As if she needs to excel any more. Aloud I said, "Good idea." *Haven't talked to Noshi for a while.*

Flipping our flight jackets' fleece-lined collars up around our ears, we wove through the cluster of dorms and across frost-stiffened grass, which crunched underfoot, toward the school building.

A restive wind moaned among the structures, chasing loosening leaves from their branches and scattering them, whirling and jinking, on fitful bursts. The leaves' moldering scent, sweet and herbal, overwhelmed the briny bite from the nearby sea, whose waves' distant crashing swelled and subsided at the foot of the black cliffs.

As we approached one young tree, a large leaf shook free. Its brilliant amber, heightened by the golden hue of fading afternoon sunlight, caught my attention. It descended like a pendulum, swishing this way and that.

A chant to spirits of the air came to my mind, the first air chant my father always taught his apprentices, to build confidence in their nascent abilities.

"Watch this," I said to Go, and began to sing.

The leaf coiled upward on the breath I summoned, a toy for some playful spirit, and skittered to an arm's length in front of my face.

Her dark eyes widened. "What are you doing?"

I explained, and said, "Wonder if it can do aerobatics?"

It could, but only when I let go the urge to pilot the leaf itself. It spun to the faded grass a couple times, caught by the wind rushing off the mountains, before I remembered to guide it by directing the air spirits who carried it, using hand motions and inflections of the words.

I started with an aileron roll, inverting the leaf with a wisp of breeze. After two or three of those, I attempted a barrel roll. Directing the air spirits to do that took much greater concentration.

By the time we reached the school building, I'd tried a vertical launch, a hammerhead turn, a spiraling attack dive and, to Go's hilarity, made an on-the-deck pass over a red squirrel busy stuffing its cheek pouches. The squirrel scampered up a tree, flipped its tail, and gave me a scolding worthy of my stepmother.

The sighing wind, like someone murmuring a satisfied "Ah-ha," reached me as I steered the spirits to set down the leaf in a gliding landing on the schoolhouse step. I glanced about as I opened the door, but no one else occupied the grounds. Puzzled, I loped upstairs with Go, until she split off to find Lieutenant Commander Hunun.

Whenever I had seen Five-Talon Noshi in the weight or climbing rooms or at the chow hall in the past few moons, he'd asked about my course work, and we'd talked about various topics. Now, three moons from graduation, I wanted more specific advice, a plan I could follow.

Relief put me at ease when I found him in his office, skimming through incident reports for the next day's EP quiz. A familiar astringent scent drew my vision to a small raincup cactus in a painted bowl set on his window ledge.

Something from home. Haven't seen that before.

He didn't glance up when I paused at his open doorway, but before I could formally report in, he said with genuine welcome, "Cadet Masou, come in and sit." He pointed with his chin at the chairs and switched off his console display. "You are concerned about something?"

I sank onto the chair with the best view of the hallway and gathered my nerve. "Sir, what do I need to do to earn the DG medal?"

His graying eyebrows bunched.

Amazing how much people can say with their eyebrows. Gram does it, and Russom, and the crim in the alley back home with the really bushy ones.

Noshi's wrinkle-hidden eyes probed mine. "Why is the DG medal important to you, Cadet?"

The question startled me. "I have a reputation as a pilot to maintain, sir."

Noshi's eyebrows quirked. "To the airshow boy, or to your brother?"

"Hanuk's my cousin, sir." I realized aloud, "I've never had to prove anything to him."

I remembered Huritt's challenge before we left Tempest. Remembered telling Kota how my reputation as a pilot was all I had left.

Still is, unless I yield to Machitew. I suppressed a shudder.

Noshi leaned back in his chair, making it creak, and folded those thick arms on his muscular chest like a python tree coiled for winter. "The best combat pilots I've known," he said, "the quickest and smartest and most courageous ones, weren't the DGs in their piloting schools.

"There's nothing wrong with earning DG." He motioned with one hand. "Don't take me wrong, Cadet. But it's a fleeting glory. It doesn't mean anything in battle. Accomplishing the mission and getting your team back safely are what counts."

I didn't say anything; I just considered his words. *Will accomplishing the mission be good enough to maintain my piloting reputation? Good enough to evade Machitew?*

"It's natural to compete," Noshi said. "It's healthy if it drives you to improve yourself." He gave me a wise smile. "Don't compete against your classmates, Cadet Masou. Work to become the most effective warrior you can be. Remember what I said about pushing yourself harder, taking it up one more notch, and always exceeding your previous best effort."

When I nodded, he continued. "Apply it to everything you do. Your fiercest competitor should always be yourself."

"Ya, sir," I said at last and stood. "Thank you, sir."

His words replayed in my mind as I joined Go in the echoing foyer. She appeared satisfied and cheerful, unlike my lingering doubts.

Early dusk had settled since we'd entered the building, casting the base into varying shades of blue. We fastened our jackets against the deepening cold, and Go slipped her hands into her fleece-lined pockets.

Engines running up to launch screamed like eagles from the nearby flightline as we stepped outside. The sound tugged our gazes in its direction, and we paused to watch. We knew exactly where the aircraft would burst above the screen of trees and steep-roofed buildings.

Four pairs of afterburners lit the autumn evening, binary suns rising at twenty-second intervals. Their power shook us where we stood.

As each climbed in vertical combat launches directly over our heads, ground lighting illuminated their retracting landing gear and a full load of live ordnance under their wings.

Go and I exchanged stares as their roars receded into the distance, and I knew she realized it, too.

That was no training sortie.

* * * * *

Chapter Thirty-Six

Machitew didn't have to wake me that night. I was still moving around in my room when he appeared between me and my bunk. No longer the bodiless, hovering dancer's mask, he towered to the ceiling in the form of a powerfully built man, though still insubstantial as oily-black smoke.

"Come with me," he said, and stretched a hand to me.

He gave me no chance to refuse before the bucket-like mask settled over my head.

Through its eyeholes, I saw myself standing at the crest of a mountain, glassy-black as obsidian. I surveyed all of Tempest, its sparse cities hunkered under pale nironnium domes. Golden lights glowed from enclaves scattered upon deserts, tundra, and equatorial forests, and bluish ones pulsed on superstructures of ships on tossing seas.

Machitew loomed at my left shoulder and his frozen breath raked my ear. "Spirits of the air are our most powerful allies. You have proven yourself willing to call them."

I stiffened. "Leave me out of your plans."

He sighed, a resigned sound, and I remembered the sigh I'd heard outside the schoolhouse door. "You called on air spirits to entertain your non-Chalca friend. You flaunted a teaching chant in defiance of the Ancients."

333

My guts knotted. My father's solemn admonition to his apprentices, to safeguard our sacred chants, whispered across my mind, and guilt heated my face. I shrugged away from the looming presence.

Grimness replaced Machitew's patience. "Do you know why the Ancients refused to grant me birth into a body of flesh like they received for themselves?"

I lifted my head, jaw set. Glared at him through the mask's eyeholes. "Because you rebelled against Star Father."

He uttered a low chuckle. "So the tale goes. It's partly true. They denied me birth because they know my power. They fear me. When we have flesh and bone, we will wield more power than all of them, and they know it. We *must* become one."

Machitew's tone laid bare his intention. My heart rate accelerated. "No." I took a combat stance, hands poised to block an attack.

"You will resist us with the very bone and blood we need?" the apparition asked. "Open yourself to me."

"Never!" I shouted.

A sensation like ice-water spilling over my head drowned my yell. Ice seemed to pour through my skull and into my torso, a torrent through skin and muscle that flooded to my fingertips and toes.

Machitew spoke again, but his voice rose from my own throat, raw and grating. "Now," he said, "we are one."

He had always spoken with the sound of my voice when he appeared, but not through my own mouth. I clenched my teeth.

Words rose from my throat, indistinct through my gritted teeth. My arms lifted against my will, reaching to skies roiling in black and mottled gray as if for an embrace.

He'd never physically controlled me before. Even the first time he haunted me, he'd shown me a copy of myself. I hadn't felt the knife in my palm, or his hand driving mine to slash my stepmother's throat.

I did remember the sensation of hot crimson spilling over my hand and the iron smell of blood. I cringed as I had then.

My shoulders and upper body burned with my efforts to lower my arms. I couldn't so much as curl my fists.

The entity inside me flung my head back forced my mouth open. My throat and tongue shaped words. My voice cut through the rising wind. I'd never heard such a chant before, but I knew, because Machitew's mind had penetrated mine, that it summoned demons.

I closed my teeth again to stop the chant, but only succeeded in biting the insides of my cheeks. Salty blood welled from the ragged smarting.

The demon chant called clouds of tormented sky spirits to enshroud Tempest. A massive funnel rose from the largest of the southern oceans and coiled like an askuk rearing. It sucked power from white-crested waves, enough to drive a storm surge a hundred spans high onto the land. I watched a domed city and several coastal enclaves vanish under its grungy foam.

Twisting winds on the high plains snatched embers from a lightning strike, breathed glowing life into them, and spun them into dancing pillars. They roared across dry grasslands and desert, leaving a wasteland riddled with flying sparks. The conflagration devoured uncounted enclaves. Faint screams echoed inside my skull, cleaving my failing consciousness like an ax.

Machitew bellowed in triumph, using my mouth. "Air demons drive water and fire demons. Water and fire destroy the spirits of earth. Air demons are the masters. *We* are the master!"

My torn mouth throbbed. *Got to stop the chant. Got to drive him out. How? Think!*

I can still think. He's seized control of my body, but not my mind. Not yet. Concentrate.

On what? I wondered in desperation.

The Warding Chant came to my mind. *It's all I've got.*

I closed my eyes. Ignoring the thick blood taste and the rawness of my mouth, I focused on the words. *Shield me from the spirits of the Dark, O Sower of the Stars. Shield my mind against them that I may know your wisdom.*

Something twisted, convulsing under my ribs like a wounded snake.

Shield my heart against them that I may have your peace.

"You are mine. We are one," Machitew insisted through my mouth. "We are more powerful than all the Ancients together."

I didn't pause in my soundless recitation. *Shield my hands against them that I may work with skill and patience.*

Spasms wrung my arms and legs. I screamed at rending pain through muscles and joints, and landed hard on my knees. Ignoring my bruised kneecaps, I centered all my thoughts on chanting. *Shield my feet against them that I may walk your Path in safety. Shield me from the spirits of the Dark, O Sower of the Stars.*

I lay limp by the end of the chant. Clammy sweat gleamed on my chest and rivered my spine, but I started once more. *Shield me from the spirits of the Dark…*

"We are *one*!" Machitew protested, but his voice rose only inside my head, no longer from my mouth.

With my tongue freed, I began to chant aloud. "Shield my mind against them."

The icy entity inside me thrashed, contorting my limbs. Lightning lanced through my neck and spine, through one hip, and down my leg.

"Get out of me!" I shouted between gasps and kept yelling. "Let go of me! Get out of me, Machitew. Shield me from the spirits of the Dark, O Sower of the Stars!"

A crash ended the vision, but the spectral mask's darkness still partially occluded my sight.

As if from a distance, a familiar voice shouted in accented Standard, "Ku, what is happening? Ku, what is wrong?"

It took several seconds to shed the darkness still clinging to my mind. My breath came in ragged heaves. Shaking violently, I fought my way out of sweat-soaked bedcovers, entangling me like thick ropes.

"What is wrong, Ku?" Rinn asked again.

"I'm—" I gulped. My innards lurched in warning. "Move!"

Somehow, I made it to my feet and shoved past him through the doorway. I reached the bathroom barely in time.

I didn't think the heaving would ever end. I wondered if my stomach would come up, too, once it had nothing left to expel. With my sight still blurry, I sat on the cold floor, sagging against the toilet while it auto-flushed. My hands remained tremulous and tingly until I fully caught my breath.

"Yo, Ku-man," Ogundo said, sounding stunned. "What in the name of homemade sin did you eat to cause *that*?"

I lifted my head and glimpsed Guns and Kota wedged between the doorframe into their adjoining quarters, and Rinn filling the doorway to our shared study space. Muted lighting etched fear on all their faces.

"You sounded as if you were having a dream," Rinn said. "I heard you from my room. I could not understand what you said. You were thrashing on the floor when I came in."

"A dream?" Kota questioned me with his stare, then nudged his roommate. "Guns, you and Rinn go check if the flight kitchen has some kind of tea."

They left, shrugging their coats over their pajamas, and Kota came fully into the bathroom. Eyes intense, he dropped to his heels. "Like the dreams you have after performing a chant?"

I nodded, and started to speak, but gritty bile in my mouth prompted another gag. I spat into the toilet and drew a cautious breath. "Ya. Not even a prayer, just a practice chant for apprentices." I hesitated. "I summoned air spirits to fly a leaf for Go."

Kota regarded me with a sternness that reminded me of my father. Fresh guilt lowered my gaze.

"What happened in the dream?" Kota asked. "Did anybody get killed?"

"Lots of people," I said. My torn mouth throbbed, slurring my speech. "He—used me to do a demon chant. Summoned disasters. Wildfires and storm surges. Wiped out cities and enclaves."

Kota appeared shocked. "Do you think it's real?"

I spat blood and sour saliva. "Hope not."

"I didn't know your dreams were so bad," Kota said. "I'll never ask you to do a chant again."

By the time Guns and Rinn returned with a container of steaming tea, I'd dragged myself to our study area and plopped on my desk chair. Every muscle in my body ached, but my hands had stopped shaking. I accepted the covered cup with an exhausted, "Thanks."

The others left reluctantly, Kota and Guns to their own apartment, and Rinn to his room, after repeatedly asking if I'd be all right. Once the tea settled my stomach, I limped into my room, too.

I had torn the bedcovers off in my wrestle with Machitew. They lay twisted on the floor, still damp with my sweat. I peeled one heavy blanket loose, flung it about my shoulders, and seated myself in a corner as I had after the hauntings during Basic. *Got to talk to Gram.*

Wincing at the fire in my limbs, I crawled to my bedside cabinet. In the darkness, unable to see, I fumbled through the stuff I'd carelessly tossed on it. After a couple minutes of groping, scrabbling, and shuffling, I found my link. *Please be there, Gram.*

My pent-up breath released when she appeared in my display. I asked at once, "Is everything all right on Tempest? Are there any hurricanes or wildfires?"

"No." Her brow creased. "Why, Akuleh?"

Head drooping in contrition, I confessed to flying the leaf for Go. "I know I shouldn't have. I used the chant to show off, not for practice. Machitew knew it, and it left me completely unprotected from him."

I described the haunting. "He said a demon chant, and he…" I swallowed a fresh wave of nausea at the totality of his violation "—he got inside me and used my voice and hands."

A clammy cold told me I'd paled again. I squirmed before Gram in my sense of filthiness and desolation, feeling I'd lost some part of myself I could never recover. I heard my heart thudding in the weight of her silence and couldn't meet her eyes. "I *really* don't want this, Gram," I whispered.

"I'm so sorry, Akuleh." Her tone held comfort, a verbal version of wrapping me in her arms.

"Why me?" I pleaded the question.

"Because Machitew knows who you really are," she said.

Who I really am? Of course, he knows who I am. I peered at her. "You make it sound like—"

She cut me off with a shake of her head, ponderous as a mother bear. "I can't tell you anything more. You know that. Stay strong, Akuleh. Always say the Warding Chant."

"I did, Gram. I kept saying it and saying it until… until it finally drove him away."

"Good." Gram reached out as if to cup my face. "Say it whenever you need it."

Exhausted though I was, I spent the rest of the night starting awake. Every draft from the ventilation mimicked Machitew's wintry breath. Every creak of the walls or floor might have been his step. Every time something woke me, I whispered the Warding Chant.

Morning found me drained, my limbs and spine aching from their involuntary contortions, my mouth so swollen and tender, even thinking about eating hurt, and my vision still bleary. I went to class, but I must have been pale, because Kota kept glancing at me as if afraid I'd pass out, and Go asked me twice if I was ill.

Thankfully, I had an afternoon sortie, enough time for my stomach to calm so I could eat, and my hands to steady. Russom eyed me when I entered our briefing room, but he didn't ask questions. He just threatened me with an unsat for some miniscule infraction, as usual.

I responded, "Yes, sir," out of habit, but started in mild shock when I realized Russom no longer scared me. Machitew had claimed that distinction.

* * * * *

Chapter Thirty-Seven

Through the last stretch of classwork and sorties before War Phase, I never fully relaxed, especially at night. I couldn't shake my gnawing guilt for inviting Machitew's attack. Fearing he might make another attempt on me, I heeded Gram's counsel to say the Warding Chant every night before I slept.

"You are very, um, quiet lately, Ku," Go observed once while we waited for the bench-cart to our aircraft. "You always seem angry or, you know, far away."

"Sorry, Go," I said. "Pressure."

As if she's not feeling it too. I mentally kicked myself. *Mine's a different kind, though.*

Every day in class, Huritt leaned in to show his teeth and mutter something like, "Scheduled the crash trucks for today's sortie, Sheggy?" or, "They say your IP keeps his hand on the ejection ring when he flies with you," or, "What do shegrul herders do for a funeral when there's no body to bury?"

"What do swollen heads do," I snarled in return, "when they get their teeth shoved down their throats?"

Ironically, my sorties seemed to be the one time of day I had any control of my life. For two or three hours, I knew only the power of my aircraft and endless depths of sky in which to challenge it and myself. So when Commander Lodesson greeted us in the wing's viditorium one morning with, "Welcome to War Phase, class," Kota and I silently cheered to each other.

"During the next seven days," Lodesson said, "you will experience the high-tempo operations of an active combat unit. You'll fly at least two sorties every day, at all hours of the day and night."

As we watched, the expansive tri-D tank behind him rippled and illuminated, revealing an aerial battle between two Rohr-55s. One had been painted with Supremacy flashes on its fuselage and wings.

Lodesson strolled casually across the viditorium platform, silhouetted against the ongoing confrontation. All the sound, the thunder of engines and voices crackling through cockpit comms, had been muted so he didn't have to shout.

"Tomorrow," he said, "you will begin vortex sorties. Your IPs will accompany you for those, but all non-vortex sorties will be solo. Your IPs will observe from the tracking deck aboard Shemmon Station."

I rejoiced at the prospect of flying solo. *I'll perform a lot better without Russom's constant criticism from the back seat.*

"This will be exceptionally demanding," our wing commander said, "so it's crucial you take every opportunity for meals and rest. The risk of accidents increases exponentially when people are tired. We want all of you to graduate, proud of your accomplishments and prepared to enter active duty."

Lodesson stopped pacing, briefly drawing our attention away from another dogfight in the display tank. "During the last phase or two, some of you have observed aircraft launching with a full load of live missiles. As future combat pilots, you have the right to be fully informed of what's taking place."

They had made a similar statement during Basic, the day we'd had the background briefing about Osaga Safa and how the war had begun. I set my teeth and saw several classmates' features tighten.

"Some of you have asked if we're flying training sorties with live munitions," Lodesson said. "We most certainly are not. Nor have there been any attacks on Solienne. However, the threat is very real." He swept us with his grim gaze. I imagined myself in his position, viewing our intense faces.

"To pre-empt the kind of attack that captured Gimel," he said, as the tri-D tank segued into a third combat scenario, "the Ministry of Defense has ordered continuous early-warning operations. Like other aerospace bases across Solienne, we are conducting combat air and space patrols. These are the aircraft you've seen."

He resumed pacing the platform. "Because you will fly combat patrols yourselves in the coming months, we've added simulated combat patrols to the War Phase curriculum."

In spite of the dogfight vids, we exited the viditorium in subdued moods, matched by early winter skies smothering the base in bone-penetrating gray. Kota and I lowered our faces to avoid snow crystals as abrasive as Tempest sand while we strode toward the squadron building.

As we stepped inside, my link chirped with an incoming live call. Puzzled, I stopped to fish it from my jacket pocket.

Apprentice Officer Hanuk's cheerful face glowed in its display. "Ai, Ku!" he said. "What's going on?"

"On my way to a pre-mission briefing right now." To Kota I said, "It's Huk. Go ahead, I'll be there in a minute."

Kota proceeded down the corridor, and Hanuk studied me, crimping his brow. "Your first or second sortie of the day? This is War Phase, right?"

"Ya," I said. "We just left Lodesson's introductory speech. First sortie, but I have a quick turn afterward. Refuel, reload, relaunch."

Hanuk smiled. "Ya, I remember. Fun, fun. Which means you're coming up on graduation."

"Four more phases," I said. "Not soon enough."

"Wait until your final exam." Hanuk's eyes twinkled. "Three or *four* sorties a day. If you think War Phase is tough…"

"Let me get through this one first." I squinted to make out the indistinct background. "Are you on the surface or aboard Shemmon Station?"

"On the surface today."

"Good," I said. "I want to hear about survival school."

Hanuk's enthusiasm visibly dampened. "Not so fun. Are you doing vortex sorties yet?"

"Starting tomorrow. Why?"

"Since you won't come back puking tonight, want to join us for dinner?" Hanuk asked. "There's someone I want you to meet. Tollesson's at 2000?"

I scanned my schedule on my link. "Should work."

Hanuk's smile resurfaced. "Killer. See you then."

Pocketing my link, I started after Kota, though I stopped at the intel office's front desk before I entered its briefing room. A spacer technician retrieved a small box bearing my name from a steel cabinet and set it on the counter.

I unloaded my personal effects into the plastic box under her vigilant gaze. Colorful unit patches, which I peeled off my flight suit.

My military ID ring with its nanodot containing my military records, medical records, and pay account. My link, and Derry's pendant.

Anything from which an enemy could gain intelligence information or use for coercion, should we be captured on a combat mission, stayed behind. We had to sign for it when we returned. No risk of capture during training, of course, but our instructors all emphasized forming habits now that could save our lives later.

I studied the pendant briefly before placing it in the box. Derry's slight smile boosted my confidence and cheered me on. *Never did tell Huk about her. Maybe tonight.*

"Your girlfriend?" the spacer tech asked with a knowing gleam in her eye.

I simply smiled in return. *I wish.*

"The briefing starts in ten minutes," she said.

I found Kota seated in the middle of the small briefing theater, which always smelled of snack foods, and dropped into the next chair. "Huk and I are meeting at Tollesson's tonight, 2000. Want to come?"

Kota sighed. "Sorry, Ku. I'll be launching on my second sortie by then. What's the occasion?"

I shrugged. "Glad to be back from survival school, I think. He didn't say. Wants to introduce me to some friend of his."

Once the others with morning sorties had shuffled in, the briefer began. She covered developments in the War Phase exercise scenario, doing her best to make it sound real-world. Among other points, Supremacy reconnaissance craft had been sighted inside Solienne's planetary defense zone, and miners in Marroquin, a southern nation, had found a hasty weapons cache consisting of energy rifles and fragmentation grenades near a working mineshaft.

From there, we dispersed to our individual briefing rooms with our IPs. Kota and I had drawn a two-ship combat patrol sortie with me as Lead, which meant I had to do the talking.

Recalling Russom's criticism of Cadet Waterstone, I had rehearsed with Rinn in our dorm before breakfast, using my study console's display for the projection table. Rinn had purposely asked several in-depth questions, which I'd answered easily.

You know this stuff solid, Ku. Just do it.

Still, except for greeting them when we entered, I avoided glancing at Kota's IP or Russom. I began with the scenario and our mission objective. "We're flying a four-hour, low-planetary-space patrol at an altitude of four hundred ranges. Our mission is to watch for and repel any incursion into Solienne's low-planetary space by enemy ships of any kind.

"On departing Belsken Field, we'll proceed to training sector Nevus-Indigo, where we'll establish a patrol track originating here at oh-niner-two." I touched the glowing alpha symbol superimposed on the map in the projection table and drew my finger along the patrol track's glowing oval. "Unless we encounter Supremacy ships, flight time for each lap will take approximately one hour."

I endured Russom's scrutiny, the pressure of his hot-coals stare, and consciously slowed to keep my nervous tongue from tangling itself. "According to intel, during the last phase or so, Supremacy fighters have been testing Solienne's defenses."

I queued an image of a Supremacy fighter with loaded missile rails into the projection. "Some of them have penetrated the five-hundred-range space defense zone, or SDZ. So far, they've withdrawn when confronted by Soli fighters, but in the last two days, they've gotten more aggressive.

"If Supremacy ships enter our sector, we'll challenge them and escort them from the SDZ. If they refuse to comply, we'll issue a warning with a single cannon burst across their noses. If they continue to refuse compliance, we are authorized to engage and destroy."

When I glanced at Kota, he nodded. I shifted my attention to Russom. His lowered brows and pursed mouth returned my gaze to the projection table.

After verifying callsigns and freqs, for communicating with Soliennese and Pact fighters operating in neighboring sectors, I described the primary Supremacy fighter and its capabilities using new tri-D images.

"The Sevicha 9," I said, "is capable of greater speed than our Rohrs, but that's a disadvantage in a turning fight. Rohrs are more maneuverable and have a tighter turn radius, even in space. We also have longer-range weapons."

I listed our munitions load, simulated for training and painted the same blink-inducing shade of orange as our pressure suits. I described how sim-hits on the enemy or sim-damage to our own ships would appear on our instruments. I covered our contingency plans, in case of mechanical failure or simulated shootdown, and concluded with, "Any questions, gentlemen?"

When Kota said, "I've got it, Lead," I faced Russom.

He checked his wrist chrono before addressing Kota's IP. "Do you have anything for him?"

The other shook his head. "He covered the whole thing very thoroughly."

"You took a full hour, Masou," Russom said. "You better get your tail to Life Support. I'll be watching from the tracking deck."

Kota and I jogged to Wing Ops, with a crisp sea-salt breeze slapping our faces the whole way. Lodesson's kickoff briefing hadn't allowed time to battle-braid our hair before leaving our quarters, so we'd have to do it in Life Support.

Once our support crews had sealed us into our pressure suits and egress harnesses, I began braiding Kota's horsetail, using quick tugs. Nobody blinked at pilots assisting each other with their gear, but Chalca flyers braiding each other's hair often drew stares from non-Chalca cadets.

Kota was finishing mine when somebody called through the clang of lockers and scuff of pressure suit boots around us, "Look, everybody, it's beauty school day!"

Chortles echoed off the lockers and blue-speckled tiling, rising above the noise. At my shoulder, Kota reddened as if he'd been sunburned.

Huritt, I thought first, except Huritt and Enyeto had started battle-braiding each other's horsetails, too.

"What color ribbons shall we wear today, boys?" the same unseen speaker said, this time in falsetto. "Do you prefer pink, or would you rather have yellow?"

My ears burned. My jaw tightened as Kota tied off my braid. I wheeled to face the mocker.

An underclass cadet smirked from the head of our suiting aisle, a rangy youth with spiky hair. Large black triangles had been tattooed on his cheeks and forehead so their points joined on the bridge of his nose. His buddy sported tattoos as well, imitating a hollow-eyed skull.

Pahana, I knew at once. Descendants of Winéma, whose clan had separated from the Chalca when the Great Council rejected her bid for chief. The Pahana had raided and pillaged the Chalca until their War of Extermination drove our great-grandparents off Solienne to Tempest.

"Looks like Soli recruiters aren't picky about what they scrape up anymore," I said as I snatched up my helmet. I pressed my palm to my locker door's scan plate and beckoned Kota with a jerk of my head.

The Pahana cadets' lockers stood between ours and the outer doors. I strode deliberately toward them. After a year on Solienne, the buoyancy I'd experienced in our first phase had long passed. Still, even in bulky pressure suits, we Chalca moved with an ease others envied. We often glimpsed it in their eyes.

I must have appeared menacing, advancing on them, because everybody in Life Support shut up. Every eye followed me. I didn't pause. Didn't so much as break stride. I just wrinkled my nose as I passed them. "Ya, I knew I smelled something rotten in here," I said, loud enough for my voice to carry throughout Life Support. "Is that why you've got a hazardous waste symbol tattooed on your face?"

Fresh guffaws rang through the suiting room, but two pairs of dark stares burned like acid into my back.

* * * * *

Chapter Thirty-Eight

"Reeking Pahana," Kota said as we exited Life Support.

We hefted ourselves onto the bench-cart outside the double doors, along with four more cadets who were still chuckling.

"Do you know those two with the tattoos?" one asked.

"Old family friends," I said with sarcasm.

The bench-cart whirred along the flightline through a persistent wind, laden with sea mist that peppered our faces. The cart passed a number of sky-gray fighters parked on the ramps and halted before a remote shuttle bay.

Like the family hangars at Awénasa City's airfield, they resembled giant bowls with domed covers. These, though, were five or six times larger, and built of pourstone rather than adobe. We lumbered aboard the waiting shuttle, an ovoid craft with abbreviated wings, and found our IPs already seated in the passenger hold. We belted in under their assessing gazes.

The shuttle launched minutes later, shaking like a ground tremor, while G-forces pressed us into the reclined and deeply cushioned seats, like adult-size baby chairs. Though I'd ridden the shuttle several times, its acceleration always boosted my mood. With Russom in full sight opposite me, I suppressed the smile of anticipation tugging at my mouth.

Other cadets dozed through the two-hour flight to Shemmon Station, but I didn't. I ran our mission plan through my head instead and listened to our IPs muttering together.

Three decks of the space station had been designated to the 33rd Training Wing. Along with a separate flight deck, we had our own briefing rooms and crew areas for trainees and IPs, though more compact than on the surface, and framed with titanium bulkheads.

Entering the station through the docking lock reminded me of arriving on Solienne, except without the blue-fire vortex ring. In the station's lower-than-standard artificial gravity, we bounced even in pressure suits. We ambled through the passage to our launch bays. The rip, rip, rip of our heavy boots on the stick-mesh deck covering, like cloth being torn in a sequence of tugs, echoed in the curved corridor.

The launch bays smelled of fuel and lubricants. Metal replaced the stick-mesh there, so the deck clanged under our boots. Pipes of different colors, which identified what they transported, ran along the bulkheads in bunches, replacing the large hoses lying underfoot in the surface base's parking stands.

My fighter in its catapult cradle appeared impatient, as if it sensed my eager heartbeat. The wing extensions attached for atmospheric flight had been removed, as well as its wheeled landing gear. Clamps had been added to its forward-swept wings, for catching the anchor rail upon entering the null-G landing ramp.

I made my walk-around check, examined every thruster nozzle and simulation sensor, shadowed the whole time by my crew chief and Russom, who would follow the sortie from the tracking deck.

While my deck crew helped me strap in, I concentrated on preflight and launch procedures. On making the routine comms checks,

I started at the crispness of my voice through my helmet speakers, like some experienced veteran.

I lit the engines one by one. Their screams, like ghost cats in rut, shook the launch cradle, and I released the smile I'd concealed aboard the shuttle. Once more, I thought it a good thing Russom couldn't see my face.

As it had in the simulators, shooting through the catapult tube seemed tame compared to vertical launches off the runway. We pulled six Gs for about four seconds, mashed into our seats so we had to grunt for breath, but we were only along for the ride until we exploded from the tube.

Kota's ship burst into space, shimmering with heat, thirty seconds after mine. Ten seconds later, he slid into position off my right wing, as if his ship were an extension of mine, and said, *"Two locked in."*

"Copy, Two," I replied. "Eyes wide open. You know they won't let us just fly laps around the track."

"Roger that," he said, and chuckled in his voice pickup.

On approaching our training sector, an empty patch of space marked only by the coordinates in our astrogation computers, I called, "Sector Control, this is Searcher Element entering sector Nevus-Indigo, proceeding to point oh-niner-two."

Sector Control acknowledged, and Kota made a half-roll so his ship flew inverted at my wing. In low planetary orbit, where "right side up" and "upside down" were irrelevant, flying inverted to one another provided near-complete visibility of our surrounding space.

At an altitude of four hundred ranges, Solienne's sun sparkled on the North Strelna Sea and cast the mountains into relief, shadowing their western slopes in blue. Clouds blurred the ragged cliffs of the coastline, as if a clumsy finger had smeared wet paint.

From the edge of space, I scrutinized clouds of stars. I had learned Solienne's constellations, of both northern and southern hemispheres, during Astrogation. The Sitting Dog, the Giant King, the Two Ships. Supremacy fighters could appear anywhere among them, in attack formation or as lone reconnaissance probes.

We searched the dark, constantly shifting our heads inside our helmets. Our faceplates' metallic coatings sharpened images and reduced the glare of reflected light.

We spoke little, except to answer Sector Control's requests for position checks. Minimal cockpit chatter broke the distant buzz in our earphones.

As we completed the third lap of our patrol track and began the fourth, my alert level ratcheted up. *Any minute. They'll expect us to be relaxed by now. They'll try to catch us when they think we've given up paying attention.*

"Lead," Kota said, *"I've got something, two-point-three-four and two-seven-six, distance six-two-niner ranges."*

"Right on time," I said under my breath when the blip appeared in my threat scope, too. "He's all yours. I'm on your wing as Two."

That was the rule. Whoever spotted the enemy got the first shot. I dropped back, maintaining cover from the inverted wing position, and let Kota take Lead.

"Targeting active," I ordered my computer, and tracked the incoming bogey's trajectory, a bright line of blips in my threat scope. "Check energy cannon charge."

We peeled out of our patrol loop and Kota said, *"Two, I'm vectoring for lead pursuit, activating energy cannon for warning burst."*

"Copy, Lead," I answered. I glanced at my weapons display. All lights glowed solid green.

I expected the single blip to split into two, maybe four, or even six as we closed to five hundred ranges. It didn't. It simply swelled on my scope, driving fast as if late for an appointment.

Kota opened the universal radio channel. *"Incoming ship,"* he said, *"identify yourself. I repeat, incoming ship, identify yourself."* I heard tension in his clipped words.

Coarse static answered, through which I made out a faint voice. The words consisted of harsh consonants and a guttural growl, but nothing I could understand.

Now they're even simulating lump head radio chatter. Anything to make War Phase more authentic. I chuckled.

As we completed our arc to intercept the bogey and began to close on him, red pulses like the heartbeat of a machine became visible against the dark. Wingtip running lights.

"Got a visual," I told Kota. "Forty degrees and low."

"Got it, too," Kota said. He switched again to the universal frequency. *"Incoming ship, identify yourself and withdraw from Soliennese space."*

Static-garbled words rattled in my earphones. I detected a defiant tone, the only thing I could understand.

"Split now,*"* Kota ordered, and I rolled clear.

He passed above the bogey, and I shot beneath it. As I did, I got a brief but clear view of it.

For training, veteran pilots experienced with Supremacy tactics acted as hostiles. They flew old Rohr-39 Spikes painted with the Velika crest and carried orange sim-missiles in their wing racks.

This ship resembled a thick carpentry screw, minus the threads. Its blunt nose, covered with sensor pods like blisters from a burn, contrasted with its three pointed canards. Too small to be real wings, they were mounted around the exhaust nozzle like an arrow's feathers.

My breath caught. On the spacecraft recognition chart in the intel shop, it was labeled as a Kn-T18 Asp, the Supremacy's one-man reconnaissance ship. Asps were lightly armed, with a single energy cannon in the nose, but they could inflict lethal damage.

My pulse jumped. My palms dampened in my suit's leather-lined gloves. Our only weapons were electronic simulators to light up the aggressor's damage display.

As required by regulations under the circumstances, I reclaimed my role as Lead. "Two, form it up." I gulped it as adrenaline quickened my breaths.

Kota had recognized the Asp, too. He locked in at my wing with a stiff, *"Yes, sir."* He sounded as if he'd gone pale.

"Sector Control," I called, "this is Searcher Lead. We have a real-world incursion in sector Nevus-Indigo. I repeat, real-world incursion. Visual ID on a Kalor-Tanker-one-eight Asp at," I checked my display for the spy ship's position, "point oh-niner-three, heading two-seven-six. Requesting real-world backup in sector Nevus-Indigo."

"Searcher Lead, copy." Control's response crackled in my earphones. *"Maintain five-range separation from hostile at all times. Continue to track and report status changes. If hostile departs the sector, report egress coordinates, but do not pursue. We are alerting surrounding sectors."*

"Roger, sir." I scanned my traffic scope and proximity readout and swallowed. My heartrate had stepped up, throbbing against my ribs and into my throat. *Only three ranges of separation.* "Two, braking thrusters," I said, "two seconds on, three off to increase separation."

"Roger, Lead," Kota said.

Seconds later, Sector Control broke in. *"Searcher Lead, vectoring real-world combat patrol to your position, ETA eight minutes."*

"Copy, Control."

At five ranges distant, the Asp's running lights kept him visible, a taunting distance. I said, "Combat spread," and Kota slid off a hundred spans to my right, still inverted. We scanned space all around us and kept an eye on our long-range traffic scopes.

Something we'd learned in a briefing burned in my mind. Sometimes the lumpies flew reconnaissance in pairs, which meant this *Asp* could be the bait, while his wingman snuck up behind us with his cannon.

"Two," I said, "keep an eye on our one-eighty for his wingman."

"Roger, Lead," Kota said.

My hands tightened on throttles and stick. Sweat oozed down my sides, itchy under my pressure suit as if it had been invaded by ants on the march. My rapid breaths fogged the lower half of my faceplate, partially obscuring my vision.

The Asp shifted headings a few times, banking left once, dipping toward the surface minutes later. He didn't seem to be in a hurry, though he undoubtedly knew he had a tail.

We banked after him, maintaining our distance and always watching for a wingman. I passed every change of coordinates to Sector Control, my voice taut, and mulled our options.

With no real weapons aboard, all we can do is buzz out if his wingy shows. No problem getting clear. Our Rohrs are a lot faster, but... The thought of running gritted my teeth.

Could circle around, stay out of their detection range, and track both of them until backup gets here.

A female voice bursting through my earphones startled me out of my contingency planning. *"Searcher Element, this is Springer Lead, inbound from your two-eight-one. We have your spy-boy on visual."*

"Springer Lead, Searcher Lead, copy, ma'am," I said, and scanned my traffic scope for Springer Element's white blips. "Handing him off. Searcher Element returning to base."

We had been expected to return more than an hour earlier.

Another hour later, we coasted into our landing ramps on Shemmon Station. My pulse and respiration had returned to normal by then, and when the ramp had pressurized enough for me to pop my canopy, my hands had lost their adrenaline-fueled tremor. Once on the deck, I made my usual post-flight report to my crew chief.

On entering the passage, though, I found more than our IPs waiting for us. Squadron Commander Grell and several personnel from the 15th Aerospace Combat Wing's intelligence office crowded the narrow space.

Burn. Hope this doesn't take too long. I'm already late for my second sortie.

I slipped Kota a *heads up* glance when he entered the passage, too.

Preparatory Commander Livald, a stout woman with silver-gray hair, was officer in charge of the 15th's intelligence office. "What just happened out there, Cadets," she said with business-like briskness, "is going to require more than your normal post-sortie debrief."

"Ma'am, I have another sortie in—" I began.

"You've been scratched from it, Masou," Grell said. Combat veteran or not, we'd rarely seen him as grave as he appeared right then, with deep creases across his brow. "This is more important. Get out of your pressure suits, you two, and see to your needs ASAP. I'll escort you up to the active-duty intel conference room."

"Yes, sir," Kota and I said together.

"They're acting like this is something really big," Kota said as we lumbered away. Puzzlement shadowed his eyes.

I nodded. "You'd think we shot him down."

The trainees' section had its own Life Support, complete with showers. We washed quickly and tied our still-damp hair in horsetails, but had to put our sweaty flight suits on again.

We also had our own lounge, with vending machines and small round tables and chairs, all anchored to the deck in case the artificial gravity failed. Commander Grell met us there and waited while we armed ourselves with water bottles and bags of jerky from the vending machines.

He led us back to the flight deck, to a lift tucked into a corner behind a column of thick conduits. There, he leaned close to a retinal scanner beside the door and said, "Deck twelve." When the door slid open, he motioned us in ahead of him.

We stepped into a surprisingly broad, curved corridor, with images of various fighters in combat mounted on the pale gray bulkheads. Striding along in Grell's wake, I heard the *whoosh* of air handlers and muted, unhurried voices beyond our boots on the stickmesh. The scent of fresh kasse brushed my nose, rather than odors of burning oil and hot machinery.

I felt puzzled at the lack of personnel moving around or past us until I noticed door plaques reading Administration, Logistics, Personnel Support, and Chaplain beside their half-open entries. Desk pilot country.

Commander Grell repeated the retinal scan at the monitor outside the closed door marked Intelligence, and declared, "Escorting Cadets Apenimon and Masou for debriefing," when a male voice questioned him from an invisible speaker. When the vault-like door sighed open, the solemn-faced master spacer within pointed us through another door at our right and bolted the outer door.

We found everyone standing around a circular projection table in the dimmed conference room. Everybody eyed us except Russom. He glowered at me.

Prep Commander Livald said, "Please be seated, Cadets."

We sank into the nearest chairs, scoop-shaped but with rigid backs, and popped open our water bottles. Kota tore open his jerky, too. Its smoky scent taunted my nose, but the apparent seriousness in the room squelched my hunger and dried my mouth.

Livald began by projecting several holographic images of various ships. She rotated them above the tabletop and asked us to identify the craft we'd encountered.

I didn't hesitate when a Kn-T18 appeared. "That's it."

"It had the flat nose and three canards," Kota added.

Everyone exchanged glances, and several arched their brows, but no one said anything. Russom rolled his eyes.

Questions followed about the ship's markings, with more images to choose from. They asked where we'd first spotted it and played a portion of our sortie comms recordings. They questioned us about its maneuvers in response to ours, above what areas it had decreased altitude, and on and on.

None of the intel staff ever sat. While they took turns quizzing us, demanding specific details in sometimes brusque tones, they gradually edged in closer around the table. I began to understand how a prisoner of war might feel under enemy interrogation. Kota's sidelong glance revealed the same tension. He had hunkered low in his chair, like a beaten dog expecting another blow.

When they played our nosecone vids and cockpit voice recordings, I watched a young spacer hunch close to listen to the enemy pilot's garbled voice. *Linguist, probably. Wonder what he's picking out of it?*

After a full two hours, Livald swept the group with her gaze. "Do any of you have anything else for them?"

Everybody shook their heads or answered, "No, ma'am."

"I have a question, ma'am," I said. "What happened after Springer Element took over? Did they get him?"

"We'll have a more complete picture after we debrief them," she said, clearly avoiding a direct answer. "Thank you for your cooperation and patience. You two have provided us with a great deal of critical information.

"You must realize," she added in the next breath, her features stern, "that the matter of this incursion is extremely sensitive. You must not mention it to anyone, or even discuss it between yourselves outside this conference room.

"You will both sign nondisclosure statements before you leave. If anyone asks questions, tell them you witnessed an in-flight incident. It's still under investigation, and you're not at liberty to discuss it. Do you both understand?"

"Yes, ma'am," we said in unison. My stomach tightened as if hard fingers had closed around it.

"Good." She motioned to a spacer, who handed us data plates and styluses. While we read them and signed, she faced Grell. "We'll have a briefing for the 15th by tomorrow morning, Carsen."

Grell nodded and addressed Kota and me. His taut features had relaxed some, except for his eyes. "Kudos to both of you. You did everything exactly right, on the sortie and in here. You handled it like true professionals."

"Thank you, sir," I said. *Hear that, Russom?*

"Apenimon," Grell said to Kota as we stood, "you've still got your sortie this evening. Get a real meal and some rest. Masou, take the next shuttle to the surface. You'll be on the ops board first thing tomorrow."

"Yes, sir." I scooped up my empty water bottle and unopened bag of jerky.

Russom and Kota's IP stood like pillars at each side of the conference room's door. I met Russom's gaze as I approached and caught a dark glint in his eyes and a twitch at one corner of his mouth. "You attract trouble like a magnet, Masou," he said. "I'm surprised you haven't killed somebody yet."

* * * * *

Chapter Thirty-Nine

An arched bridge over Strelna Fjord and public crawlers running on a frequent schedule connected Belsken Field to the city of Reskagen. Armed with an off-base pass, I boarded a crawler displaying a placard reading Waterfront, along with several other pilot trainees.

Inside, I worked my way up the aisle, gripping one seatback after another against the vehicle's swaying, and searched the bright compartment for a seat.

A dignified elderly lady wearing a heavy coat patted the empty bench beside her. Thankful I'd had time for a real shower and change of flight suits, I accepted with a smile, though her heavy perfume probably would've masked me.

Darkness fell early in Osfelga during winter, but only at Winter Solstice did the sun not rise at all. Outside the crawler's frosted windows, fresh snowfall encased the toothy Hamskjold Range, which towered above the city's equally steep roofs.

Where the buildings ended, part way up the rugged slopes, alpine forests began, thick as a sentry dog's coat all the way to the timberline. The naked peaks towered another two thousand spans above the line, and I could imagine the wind's roar across their bare faces. *The mountains were frozen this way when I arrived on Solienne a year ago.*

Reskagen's lights lay like a lap quilt upon the foothills. On the highest hill, the stone temple to Osfelga's pantheon stood like a blocky beacon. Though always visible from Belsken Field, except during fogs, tonight it glowed white. Lights shaped like flames trimmed its pillars and high façade.

Somewhere I had learned that religious festivals always included illuminating the temple, but I couldn't remember which deity white lamps represented. I only hoped the narrow streets wouldn't be choked with parading celebrants.

Myriad twinkling lights wound about the rails and webbed support cables of the bridge, blocking the view of the rugged chasm below as the crawler huffed and rattled up the steep incline. The abyss, carved by the tide's constant battering, plunged three thousand spans. I had peered into it when I'd come with Hanuk's family after his graduation. The waves' remote crashes reached me, even through the grinding engine noise.

When the crawler had descended the slope and began to chug along the waterfront several minutes later, I noted how brightly the metal lanterns hung out by devotees lit the piers and sparkled off the rippling water beneath. I couldn't hear the gentle swish of waves rolling to shore under the crawler's clacking, but the salty scent overrode the warm smells of so many people pressed together.

The crawler hissed, then jerked to a stop directly outside Tollesson's Pub. Rising, I thanked the lady who had let me share her bench and eased my way up the tight aisle with several other passengers.

Mogen had said the pub was older than the temple, built to lodge seafarers while ashore between voyages. The massive logs framing it had been cut and hauled out of the nearby slopes long before stone quarrying began.

A carved dragon's head painted in greens, reds, and blues protruded as if from an ancient ship's prow above the outside door. The sight of a square feast-lantern swinging from its fanged lower jaw gave me a chuckle.

The aroma of seared venison, a delicacy unknown on Tempest but common in Osfelga, enveloped me. It teased a rumble from my stomach as I crossed the entry, which stood like an airlock between winter's blasts and the cavernous lodge within.

Sweeping off my flight cap and scarf, and unclasping my jacket, I strode through the inner doors into the welcoming warmth of its half-lit clamor. Lively voices rose above spirited folk music loud enough to shake the floor planks.

I searched the broad common hall, then alcoves along the sides with their half-log tables and benches. It took me only a second to find Hanuk leaning from an alcove. He waved wildly and shouted my name. I headed toward him, chuckling.

In the next heartbeat, I spotted the young woman seated beside him. My heart stopped, caught on my ribs.

She wore a winter uniform, dark blue with heavy sleeves, not the fluttery pastel blouse of my memories, but I knew her immediately. How many times had I gazed into her storm-gray eyes in the pendant and drawn encouragement from her hesitant smile? How often under the increasing pressures of training had I drawn the pendant from my pocket and imagined her touch?

Derry's eyes widened when she saw me crossing the hall, and her smile brought radiance to her whole face.

With my vision fixed on her, I didn't see the second woman who sat across the table from Derry until I arrived at the alcove. Its high partition had concealed her. Hanuk waved me to the bench beside her, and I slid in awkwardly, completely giddy.

"I hear you've already met Leftenant Derry Kerk," Hanuk said, still smiling broadly, "so I'd like to introduce Doctor Captain Erzebet Moseva from Eis Ell. Or is it Captain Doctor, ma'am?"

The woman, a few years older than Derry, had a pixie-like face. She wore her hair as short as Derry's, but the lamplight tinted it a rich brown. She rolled her eyes at Hanuk's joking introduction and said, "Call me Erzie."

"She and Derry were roommates at the university," Hanuk said. "Now she's a flight surgeon."

"Ma'am." I acknowledged Captain Moseva with a nod. She smiled warmly, and I returned my attention to Derry.

"You look like you're locked on a target, Ku." Merriment lightened Hanuk's tone.

Derry stretched across the broad table to take my hands in hers. She gripped them tightly, as she had when we'd parted on Tempest, and her smaller hands radiated warmth to my cold ones. She squeezed my fingers as if to thaw them. Her eyes, which had been downcast the day we met, held radiance. "It's *sa* good to see yew again, Kew."

"Same here," I said, and felt stupid. I couldn't think of a coherent thing to say, but my face ached with smiling.

"Did you know she speaks Chalca?" Hanuk asked when Derry finally released my hands.

"Only the bi' Kew taugh' me, Hanuk." She slipped me a self-conscious smile and touched his hand.

He enfolded hers in his own.

The meaning of his gesture took a moment to register. Then my breath left me as if Hanuk had plowed his fist into my chest. I sank back on the bench, stunned. Despite some unseen hand squeezing my throat, I said with emphasis, "What *I* taught her."

Hanuk glanced around. "Where's Kota?"

With my mind tumbling like a Darter in a maelstrom, it took me another second to realize Hanuk had spoken. "Flying," I said. His mention of Kota prompted the fresh memory of our encounter with the spy ship, but it no longer mattered, even if I could have talked about it. In that moment, nothing mattered.

My vision dropped to the polished tabletop's touchscreen menu, but my appetite had deflated like ball brush. Completely on autopilot, I jabbed the pad for my favorite venison steak and scanned my ID ring's credit chip for payment. "His second sortie today."

"This is War Phase," Hanuk told the women. "It's a really intense, high-tempo training exercise. They start flying space vortices tomorrow."

"No wonder yew seem weary, Kew." Derry reached for my hand again. The floral fragrance I remembered from Tempest brushed my nose.

I lifted my head. I resisted the impulse to take her hand, as I had so often in my daydreams, but I avoided making eye contact with Hanuk. I tried to smile, but everything inside me felt so crushed, it probably came off as a grimace.

"You all right, Ku?" Hanuk's brows drew together in an anxious expression.

You're sitting there with my girl! some bereaved creature roared within my soul. *Thinking about her has been my source of encouragement all year. And now you...*

I mastered the turmoil, at least for the moment. "Long day." I shrugged. "Had a pretty rough first sortie. You know what War Phase is like. Sorry."

When our food came, I gave my full attention to the sizzling steak, more than a thumb-width thick. Despite its tantalizing scent, it had no flavor in my mouth. My stomach seemed to have shriveled in my midsection.

Dialogue swept around me, sliding in and out at the edges of my awareness. My eyes flicked from one happy face to the other. The rest of the world had vanished in a dull fog.

"… met on Shemmon Station," Hanuk said around a mouthful. "… just got back from survival school…"

"… arrived earlier from Ardonar, Erzie and I." Derry, in her musical lilt.

"… mess hall was more crowded than… let us share their table…"

"… began to talk." A mischievous light touched Derry's smile. "We've done a grea' deal of talking ever since."

"… asked where I was from on Tempest…"

"I told him I'd journeyed there once… kind young man who helped… I never expected to see yew again, Kew."

"Never thought I'd see you again either." I mumbled it. *But I always wished.*

"… injured his leg," Derry told Hanuk.

"It was fine," I lied.

"… had to be you," Hanuk said. "… couldn't stop thinking how funny…"

I glowered at my plate. *It's not funny.*

When we finished eating, the women excused themselves. Hanuk followed Derry with his eyes as they threaded their way among crowded tables toward the ladies' room. I returned my own vision to my plate.

"What's going on, Ku?" Hanuk asked. Seriousness swallowed his usual clowning manner. "You look like you want to kill somebody."

Ya, you. I hadn't realized I was still glaring, but it didn't surprise me. "Nothing," I said.

"No, I mean it." Hanuk planted his elbows on the wooden table, straddling his metal platter of stripped ribs.

The last time he'd used that tone had been when my father died. I had sat there in my Darter on the enclave plaza, too deep in shock to stir after the women carried my father's body away. Only Hanuk could have coaxed me out of the cockpit.

You're the one person I could've talked to if it'd been Derry and anybody else. I kept my scowl fixed on my plate. *But now I can't even mention it to you.*

"So?" Hanuk's tone grew more insistent.

Come up with something.

I dragged in a breath. "These two Pahana in Life Support this morning. They humiliated Kota and me about battle-braiding each other's hair. I wanted to put a fist through their tattooed faces." I lifted my head, my hands knotted on the table.

Hanuk straightened abruptly on his bench. "Don't even consider it, Ku. Fighting is a punishable offense."

"I know that."

He leaned in and lowered his voice. Not that he needed to in the ongoing cheery ruckus reverberating through the hall. "Always remember, coming from Tempest, we're stronger and have faster reflexes than people from stan-grav worlds, even without combatives training. If you hit him in the face, you wouldn't just knock him out, you'd probably kill him. Walk away from it."

I nodded and forced myself to meet Hanuk's eyes. It took a long while to ask with feigned lightness, "How's it going with... her?" I couldn't bear to speak Derry's name. My throat tightened on it.

Hanuk relaxed against the log bench back, his grin lighting his face again. "I've never been so happy in my life. I feel like I'm flying even when I'm not."

I know. I forced a smile. "Remember what they say, Huk. 'Flea bites make you itch, but lovebugs make you stupid.'"

He laughed out loud at the old proverb. "They're not wrong. I only met her about a moon ago, and I'm already thinking of marriage."

My shriveled knot of a stomach wrenched.

"If it works out," he said more seriously, "I'd like you to be our Guardian."

A man's brother normally filled the Guardian role, but Hanuk had only his sister.

Huk's been more of a brother to me than my real ones. I dredged up another breath to ease the crushed sensation in my ribcage, but everything compressed still more. Several seconds passed before I could say, "I'd be honored to."

When the women returned after what seemed a very long time, Derry seemed strangely shy, her lower lip pinched in her teeth. She avoided my eyes, but she didn't meet Hanuk's, either. Captain Moseva, I noticed when I rose to let her slide onto the bench, fixed Derry with a stern expression.

Did they have an argument in the ladies' room?

It seemed like a good time to leave. I didn't think I could bear watching Derry and Hanuk together any longer, so I scooped up my flight cap and scarf and stood. "Need to head back," I said, fastening my jacket. "Got an early sortie tomorrow."

Derry's eyes widened. She darted a glance at her friend, swallowed, and said, "'Scuse me for a bi', will yew, Hanuk? I need a word with Kew."

Hanuk appeared as startled as I felt at the request. I said nothing, but held Derry's coat while she shrugged it on.

She took my arm to make our way across the busy common room, but she didn't speak until we stood in the entry. There she drew me aside, out of the way of patrons coming and going, and faced me directly. She gripped my hands as she had at the table, and I recalled once more how she'd done it when we'd parted a year ago on Tempest. *It didn't happen how I planned it then. Is she going to say goodbye forever this time?*

Through the lamps' flickering dimness, I read sorrow in her eyes, which puzzled me more than her asking to speak to me alone. I hoped I had concealed my pain.

"Oh, Kew, I'm sa sorry," she said. Regret burdened her voice too. "Please know, I never mean' to hurt yew." Her words spilled out as she searched my eyes. "I treasure the time we had on Tempes'. I missed yew after yew lef', and I… I grieved a' thinking I might never see yew again."

She paused, her face rose-colored in the lamplight. "And even if I'd dared to hope i', I never though' yew could fancy someone as—" she ducked her head "—as sullied as me."

I opened my mouth to protest but had no idea what to say.

She drew a shaky breath. "Yew need to know, Kew, I think verra highly of yew. If not fer yer kindness to Mum and me, and the Chalca phrases yew taugh' me—" she gave me a weak smile "—I'd never have given Hanuk a glance. Neither he nor I had any idea—"

"It's all right," I said. I sounded strangled even to myself. My soul had gone numb.

"Come here then." She let go my hands and opened her arms.

I enveloped her in mine. *I've ached to do this for so long, and now…*

I expected only a brief hug, but she clung to me, her head on my shoulder. People came and went, some eyeing us. The doors repeatedly whined opened and closed, subjecting us to brief blusters of icy pellets.

When I shifted to release her, she tightened her hold. "I dream' of us once." She whispered it as if fearful of being overheard, but urgency touched her words. "Standing at the mouth of a vortex tunnel, we were. I don' know where to, bu' I had to go, and yew had to stay. I longed for yew to come with me, and when I woke, my face was wet, and I felt sa terribly alone."

Her words stunned me as much as anything else since I'd arrived at the pub. *What's that about? What am I supposed to say?*

She let go of me at last. Gazed into my face once more. Studied me. I must have appeared to be in shock, because she asked, plainly anxious, "Will yew be a' righ', Kew?"

I could only nod. Everything I'd wanted to tell her of my feelings for her, of how my memories of her had strengthened me, jammed in my throat. At last I donned my flight cap and stepped outside into the wind.

* * * * *

Chapter Forty

Few people occupied the crawler when it arrived minutes later. I slumped onto one of the gray-plastic benches, pressed my shoulder to the ice-glazed window, and stared into the darkness beyond the reflections of the crawler's lighted interior.

Everything Derry had said whirled in my head like dust on an autumn wind. My emotions milled as well, a storm of grief, anger, humiliation, and a fleeting breath of gratitude for her honesty.

The crawler lunged into its climb onto the bridge, and I unfastened my jacket to fumble in my flight suit's chest pocket. Chill-stiffened fingers found the smooth oval and drew it out. I didn't peek at it. I couldn't.

The ache beneath my ribs swelled as I gripped the pendant in my hand. Swelled until, once more, I could scarcely draw a breath. *I'll get it over with. Now.*

Only one person shared my compartment, a middle-aged drunk with several days' growth of graying whiskers and a tattered coat. He reminded me of Demothi, except with both eyes and an odor of alcohol rather than unwashed body. He hadn't raised his head when I boarded, but sat slumped on his seat, swaying with the crawler's motion. He didn't stir when I stood.

374 | D.T. READ

I gripped the window's sash. Half a thumb length of icy glaze sealed it shut. I yanked at it two or three times to shatter the ice enough to get the window open.

The crawler paused at the bridge's peak. Without a final glance at it, I hurled the pendant with all my strength into the unseen abyss. White lights along the rail played on it for an instant as it spun, a pale glimmer like a star arcing and vanishing into the blackness. My heart seemed to vanish with it.

With a little pitch, the crawler trundled down the other side. The drunk jerked his head up and cursed loudly in Osfelg when I slammed the window shut, but soon sank again into his stupor.

I staggered getting off the crawler at the base gate. A couple huddled together there, waiting to board, and they stared at me. I recognized Huritt, but not his girlfriend, swaddled in her scarf.

"Too much night out so early, Sheggy?" Huritt jeered as I slid my off-base pass into the gate's reader.

I glowered but didn't reply.

The wind had stiffened to a ripping squall off the North Strelna Sea by then, driving the clouds like a pod of frightened shegruls. Their passage alternately revealed and concealed the stars and Solienne's two moons and their limited light. I wrapped my scarf around my head like a crim's concealing hood, flipped my jacket collar up, and shoved my hands into my pockets for the hike to the dorms.

The odor of herring stew from the flight kitchen smacked me in the face when I entered our quarters, and I swallowed to keep from gagging. Rinn peered around at me from his study console. "Is it very cold out there?"

I swallowed a sarcastic reply. *Don't take it out on him.* "Ya," I said in a monotone, and dumped my sodden flight cap and scarf on my own console as I strode past it.

"Our vortex pre-flight briefing is at 0700 in the viditorium," Rinn said.

"Thanks," I said without even pausing.

I crossed to my bedroom, said, "Off," to keep its light from automatically coming on when I stepped inside, and fell across my bed fully clothed. The shriveled sensation in my middle had spread, overlaid with a hollow ache from my throat to my navel, as if all my innards had been scooped out like seed pulp from a squash.

She treasures the memories of our time together. She missed me when I left. She thinks very highly of me.

Not highly enough to drop Huk for me, though.

Eventually, I sat up to pull off my soggy boots, in time to see the light in our study area switch off and be replaced by the one in the bathroom. Rinn moved around in there for a few minutes, turning water on and off, and opening and closing his cabinet before he entered his room. At last his light darkened, and his bed squeaked as he got in.

The wind moaned against the dorm's outer shell, its pitch swelling and flagging like a demon in the Great Dark. It wailed for hours, mournful as a funeral chant, and frigid enough to penetrate the rugged walls. It smothered the *whoosh* of the heating system coming on, but not the dry smell issuing from the vents.

All I need now is for Machitew to show up again.

Still wearing my flight jacket, I curled onto my side and hugged myself, more out of unaccustomed dejection than from cold as the temperature in the room stabilized. By the time the wind wore itself out, sighing despondently into stillness, Rinn's snores from the other bedroom had replaced its wails.

Machitew never made an appearance, but I never slept.

When my alarm chirped like some overeager bird, I punched it, sat up stiffly, and sighed. The ache centered before in my chest had concentrated into persistent throbs in my head and an emptiness in my soul. I winced and blinked when the bathroom light came on.

I fumbled my way through showering and dressing, as if my hands had lost all coordination. I had to do everything two or three times.

Guns, applying beard foam at the other sink, eyed me warily. "You all right, Ku-man? You didn't eat something nasty again, did you?"

I grunted in response. I had no desire to say anything else.

"I'll come later," I told Rinn when he paused at the apartment door and scrutinized me from beneath bunched brows. I knew he wouldn't want to wait. He couldn't stand being late. Not in a mood for company, I sighed with relief when Kota and Guns went with him.

By the time I left our quarters, I didn't have time for the flight kitchen. Not that it mattered. I had no appetite, either. Hunched in my upturned jacket collar, I squinted as I slouched through gusts of snow-laden wind to the school building.

I entered the viditorium seconds before they closed the doors, slogged up the steps to our squadron's section, and found my roomies had saved me a seat. "Thanks," I said as I dropped heavily into the chair. I forced myself not to slump.

Before they could start asking questions, the platform's full-width tri-D tank lit, the viditorium's lights dimmed, and a new instructor,

Master Officer Liborio, strode out in front of it. I wondered if he would comment on the previous day's spy-ship encounter, but he didn't.

"Today," he said without preamble, "you will fly your first vortex sorties. This requires precision piloting, much like landing aboard the space station. It can be unnerving the first few times, so you will be accompanied by your IPs."

Relief touched some faces, but I wasn't the only one who groaned. *Russom is the last person I want to deal with today.*

"Spaceborne vortices have several characteristics to distinguish them from the surface version," Liborio said. "The most obvious is, they do not have physical portals. The entry point is projected by an operator at your outbound vortex terminal."

Liborio reminded me of our first Obollan instructor in Basic. Journeyman Xavier's lecture style had been a bit too soothing, especially in a stuffy viditorium right after lunch. Liborio's rolling tones, though, did nothing to relax me.

"The entry point is not made visible in space," he said, "specifically to prevent enemy ships from entering it. For that reason, the operator must terminate the projection as soon as all of his ships have cleared the portal.

"Until you have entered it, you will not see any indication of the portal except a blue circle on your astrogation display."

An azure circle with crosshairs like a targeting reticle's appeared in the tri-D tank.

"As you enter the vortex," Liborio continued, "the circle will appear to expand from your display into a tunnel of blue light surrounding your cockpit."

The image in the tri-D tank stretched and brightened to illustrate his verbal description, until we seemed to be rocketing through a passage of blue lightning.

In a blink, the tunnel in the tank rotated to a lateral view. It appeared as a series of rings, so pale copies of the first one seemed to form a tube.

How afterburners look when you see them at night.

"This is an illusion," Liborio said. "A vortex does not stretch space, but bends it."

Bends it? I scrunched my brows.

"The tube of light surrounding your spacecraft is called the membrane. It is not physical, and you cannot crash into it. However," Liborio's voice grew grave, and he cued a simulation, "research has determined that when objects penetrate the membrane, they are disintegrated in the violence of bent space."

We watched a chillingly realistic, computer-generated fighter image crumple like paper being wadded as it pierced the cobalt skin, then shatter like a clay pot dropped on a stone floor. The shards didn't tumble and spread, but appeared to be swallowed by empty space.

"The debris is not trackable and cannot be recovered," Liborio said, and passed his serious gaze across us.

Scanning my classmates, I read tension in several faces.

"Also unlike vortices at surface terminals," Liborio went on, "passage through a spaceborne vortex is not instantaneous. It may take several minutes, even under full power. Therefore, it is vital to maintain a firm hand on your control stick at all times."

I hadn't noticed Huritt and his cousin sitting behind us in my hasty arrival. They must have come in late as well, because I knew my roommates would have avoided sitting near him.

At Liborio's last statement, Huritt prodded my shoulder with his boot toe. "How steady are your hands after last night's party, Sheggy?"

In my volatile state, I squashed hair-triggered fury only with concentrated effort. "Why?" I asked. "Are yours feeling shaky?"

Huritt's jeer buckled into a scowl.

I departed the viditorium for the squadron building as quickly as possible when the briefing ended. Only Guns had an early sortie, so he came with me. We ducked our heads into the flogging wind and didn't talk, but I didn't miss the anxious sideways glances he slid at me. I ignored them.

Russom had already arrived when I pushed open our briefing room door. He sat with his chair tipped back, its front legs off the floor, his arms crossed on his chest in Huritt's favorite posture. "You took your time getting here, Masou," he said.

"No excuse, sir."

Before I could step inside, he dropped the front legs to the floor with a solid *thunk*. I flinched and froze in the doorway.

He scrutinized me through narrowed eyes, his kasse-dark glower deepening. "You're hungover, aren't you, Masou?"

"No, sir." The accusation startled me out of my torpor. I swallowed, thinking fast. "Something I ate last night."

Russom arched his thin eyebrows. "Have you seen the flight doc about it?"

"No, sir."

"Do it. You're not going near a cockpit until you get it out of your system." He rose from behind the briefing table, his piercing stare burning into mine. "You better do it fast. If you miss your sortie tomorrow, too, it'll be an automatic washback."

"Yes, sir."

Russom came around the table. He pushed past me, where I still stood in the doorway, and paced casually up the hall.

I remained for a minute on the briefing room's threshold, glaring at his receding back. Hating every molecule of him.

Defiance surged in my soul, swelling like the breakers hurling themselves against the cliffs below Belsken Field. Striding fully into the room, I paused only to slam the door shut.

"Nobody messes with my piloting career!" I shouted at the enclosing walls. I smashed my fists onto the projection table with a bang. Half disappointed it didn't crack, I yelled, "Nobody's taking this away from me. Not you, Russom!"

My breathing quickened and deepened, the way it always had before combatives matches. My feet reflexively shifted into a combat stance. My fists stayed knotted, poised. "*Nobody's* taking it away from me!" I roared again. "Not even you, Huk."

* * * * *

Chapter Forty-One

With fury still simmering beneath a determined façade, I headed to the gym from the squadron building. I hadn't had time to lift weights for a few phases, but I knew it would exorcise my anger better than anything else.

Striding between the dorms, head down against the smarting flecks borne on the biting wind, a thought struck me. *What if Noshi's there?*

I stopped short, weighing the pros and cons in my mind. I could certainly use his words of confidence right now. Maybe I could spot for him on the free weights, and we could talk about Indoc training in the Qaletaqa.

On the other side, perceptive as he was, Noshi would likely recognize my distress. If he asked, I wouldn't get away with mumbling something about Russom's threats to wash me out. Noshi would see through it in a blink. Would he press me about it, or leave it alone? I had no desire to discuss losing Derry with anyone, even him.

I stood motionless on the walkway for a long space before pressing doggedly toward the gym.

Minutes later, I hesitated again outside the weight room's door, where the odor of fresh sweat struck my nose, and rhythmic clacks and rings alerted me of several machines in use. *You can't avoid people forever, Ku. Besides, it might not be Noshi in there.*

It was. I spotted him the instant I stepped inside, and he saw me as well. "Ya, Cadet Masou," he called. His greeting rang across the room.

"Ya, sir." I managed a wobbly smile and moved straight to the nearest available weight machine.

As always, he drew up beside me upon finishing his workout. Sweat darkened his sleeveless crewshirt and plastered it to his torso, defining his solid musculature.

Someday I'll be built like that.

Noshi mopped sweat from his face with a towel and waited until I completed my set to ask, "How are you doing, Cadet?"

"Three hundred fifty pounds on the free weights, sir." I could honestly smile about that. I snatched my own towel off its hook and swabbed my face, too.

He gave me a tight smile and asked, "Are you flying through vortices yet?"

A guilty pang jabbed my soul. *Should be doing it right now.*

I swallowed and made myself meet his eyes, but I had to force a second smile. "First thing tomorrow, sir."

He nodded. His eyes narrowed in their weathered folds while he regarded me. As on other occasions, his obsidian stare bored into my soul. This time I knew it would uncover my anger, my ache, my humiliation. *Don't ask questions, sir.*

He didn't. He clapped a hand on my shoulder and gave it a solid squeeze. "Stay focused, Cadet, and all will be well." Something in his penetrating gaze told me he wasn't referring only to vortex flying.

I drew a deep breath. "Thank you, sir."

Steadied by his counsel, I pressed three hundred fifty again before I left the gym.

* * *

Russom found me waiting for him in our briefing room the next morning. I sat with my teeth locked in a ferocity I hadn't known for several years. He studied me, and his lip curled. "Got over it, Masou?"

A dull soul-ache remained. I thought it probably would linger forever, but I refused to let it interfere with my other dreams. "Yes, sir," I said, voice clipped.

He gave a stiff nod and drew his chair out from the table. "You're starting spaceborne vortices a day late, so you'll fly two sorties today, and two more tomorrow to catch up."

No time to think about anything but flying. "Good," I said.

Russom eyed me sidelong. "We'll see if you're saying 'good' after your first sortie. Cadets with stronger stomachs than yours have tossed it the first time." His narrowed eyes grew threatening. "A word to the wise. If you puke in your pressure suit, you'll clean it out yourself."

I shrugged. I hadn't been airsick since I was four.

Russom grunted. "We have a shuttle to catch, Masou, so get on with the briefing."

"Yes, sir."

Because vortices could only be projected outbound, making pilots dependent on operators at the far end for their return leg, operators on the station plotted loops for our training flights, with the exit portals established a hundred ranges or so from the entrances.

I briefed the sortie details to Russom exactly as I had received them from the Ops desk earlier. "We'll enter the vortex at full military power and make a gradual bank to port following the projection's curve."

Tracing the flight profile's illuminated line through the holographic projection with my finger, I continued, "It'll take exactly one minute to complete the passage. On clearing the vortex, I'll contact Shemmon Control."

"Why are you going to wait until you're clear to initiate contact?" Russom asked.

"Because communications can't cross from a vortex to real space, sir. It's a communications blackout."

Russom nodded approval. "Never forget it."

I covered comms procedures, our emergency procedures, the whole slate. Meticulously. I kept my voice professionally crisp despite the squeezed sensation in my heart. *You're not taking this away from me. Sir.*

When I finished, Russom sat there and scrutinized me for a long while. I held his exploratory gaze with mine, my features firm. At last he shoved himself to his feet. "Don't waste time suiting up."

We didn't speak on the way to Wing Ops. I strode briskly, squinting ahead through the predawn dark and random gusts, my jaw hard again.

The steamy heat from Life Support's shower area as I entered from the icy outdoors would have fogged my helmet's faceplate if I'd been wearing it.

I didn't falter until I came upon Kota and Go standing at their lockers with their arms outstretched while their crews sealed them into their suits. I tried to grin as I drew up to them.

"Ku." Go, her forehead creasing, asked, "Are you well? I saw, um, DNIF by your name on the Ops board yesterday."

Duty Not to Include Flying. Russom must've put it there.

"I'm fine," I said. I crossed to my locker and swiftly scanned our suiting space. *No Pahana in here today, thank the Ancients. Not sure I could keep my fists to myself, no matter what Huk says.*

Kota stumped around, a slow-motion pivot in his bulky suit, to study me. I knew by the tightness around his eyes what he was thinking. *Another Machitew dream?*

"Ate something bad the other night," I said.

"At Tollesson's? I don't believe that." Kota's skeptical tone and features made it clear I hadn't fooled him.

I didn't answer at first, just palmed my locker open. *Let him think it was another Machitew nightmare. Less humiliating.* At last I said, "I'll braid your horsetail if you'll do mine."

On boarding the shuttle to the station minutes later, I lumbered to the far end of the passenger cabin and focused on my hands as I strapped into the reclining seat. I fumbled with the hooked latches and hoped Russom, seated opposite me, hadn't noticed.

Huk's based on Shemmon Station, kept running through my mind. *And Derry.* My stomach twisted. *What if I run into them?*

You won't, I told myself firmly. *The training decks are completely separate from the active duty sections.*

I rested my head against my suit's neck ring, closed my eyes to visualize my flight profile, and drew deliberate breaths to slow my laboring pulse. I ignored Russom as completely as I could.

Once in my ship's launch bay, I concentrated on pre-flight and launch procedures to block any stray thoughts. *Stay focused, Noshi said.*

Russom didn't comment when I carried out the comms checks, snapping my responses.

I pulled in a full breath and braced for the crush of six Gs when I threw the catapult toggle. The launch tube passed in a blur of titanium gray and a belch of red flame. My earphones blocked its explosive roar.

On reaching my designated training sector, I called in. "Shemmon Control, Ace Hand Zero-Five standing by for vortex coordinates."

"Ace Hand Zero-Five, Shemmon Control. Sending coordinates now. Acknowledge when received," Control said.

A sapphire point identified by a line of blocky digits materialized on my astrogation display. The portal lay only twenty ranges away. I confirmed receipt to Shemmon Control and swung easily toward the point with a few bursts of directional thrusters.

Seconds later, a bright ring containing crosshairs replaced the blue dot and digits in my display. We had practiced attack runs against orbital targets a few phases ago, using a variety of simulated weapons. Only its blue distinguished the vortex entry ring from a targeting reticle.

"Keep your fighter's nose aligned with the crosshairs' intersection at all times," Russom said from the rear cockpit.

"Yes, sir." Unexpected tautness in my voice betrayed the sudden tension in my muscles. I knew Russom heard it, too.

As I approached, I watched the vortex ring expand to the edges of my display. At its center hovered the dart-shaped symbol for my fighter. Hand snug but not strangling the control stick, I held the dart steady on the enlarging reticle.

The instant the laser-blue ring dilated off my display, it seemed to swallow my cockpit, encircling my ship as Liborio had shown us in the simulation. The scintillating light made judging distance difficult, but the ethereal membrane appeared to blaze no more than an arm's length beyond each wingtip.

My fighter gave a violent shudder as it pierced the vortex portal.

* * * * *

Chapter Forty-Two

For a second I thought I'd flown into a storm cell on Tempest. Blue lightning engulfed my ship. Pressure like a gale-force wind tried to shove it sideways. All my piloting instincts screamed at me to get out, to arc away, climb or dive, take some action to get clear. We *never* flew into storms, always strove to avoid them as much as possible.

I held to my course with a shift of the stick.

My heart raced like a tavo being pursued across the desert. I began to hyperventilate, and sweat soaked the back of my flight suit. Only Liborio's vid replaying in my skull, of the simulated ship being disintegrated by the violence of bent space, kept me from wrenching the stick to roll clear, kept it steady in my hand. My whole body seemed frozen in my seat. *Is this what it means to be paralyzed with fear?*

I couldn't see a passage through the ceaseless flashes of blue-white light. A muted crackle and hiss like radio static filled my earphones. I imagined faint tingles at the metallic joints of my pressure suit and the taste of ozone left by a close lightning strike in my helmet's air.

It's sensory overload. Is the tunnel there, and I'm missing it? I couldn't spare an instant to blink, to clear my vision of the continuous after-images. *It's like being swallowed by ball lightning.*

"Sir, I can't see a tunnel," I said.

"Keep your nose on the crosshairs," Russom said from behind me, his voice calm.

Never before in all my hours of flying with him had I been thankful to hear his voice in my earphones.

Lightning crackled up the nosecone, enveloped the canopy, tightened around us. Closing in. Narrowing the already invisible tunnel. The tingling in my suit joints increased to prickling, and I knew my hair would've stood on end had it been loose.

My ship swayed from side to side like an askuk winding through brush and rocks. *There's no room to maneuver. Keep the nose on the crosshairs, keep the nose on the crosshairs, keep the nose on the...*

My taut hand rode the control stick. I knew my knuckles would be white inside my pressure suit gloves. My breaths rasped in my helmet speakers, too quick and shallow.

I fixed my attention on the astrogation display, on the dart symbol wavering in the reticle as my ship rocked and slid and shimmied and wrenched. My stick hand grew cramped, holding the dart to its target, but I never shifted my vision from my instruments. I didn't want to see the sparking vortex membrane lashing at my wingtips. *Too close. It's too close.*

The curve to port appeared only in my astrogation display, a bright diagram of successive rings like a bent spring. Nothing altered in the lightning storm shattering around me. Sweat trickled down my pecs and sides as I began the bank. *Nose on the crosshairs, nose on the crosshairs...*

My fighter bucked in protest, like a Soliennese horse under a saddle for the first time. I eased back the throttle, reined it in. It shook, but plowed on.

At the half minute mark, acceleration outside the ship shoved me hard into my seat. Remembering the icy wall I'd been pushed through in the surface vortex to Solienne, I tightened my abs as we did for pulling high Gs. The impact snatched my breath. I gulped for air, and Russom did, too, a short sound in my earphones. Both of us huffed against the pressure.

Constantly watching the reticle's dart, I leaned on the stick as we finished the curve. I fought to keep it from sliding off the crosshairs as the rocking increased, like Nayati's fishing boat on an angry ocean. Lightning lanced along my fighter's skin and sent new tingles through my pressure suit's joints.

Several seconds that seemed like hours later, we burst into real space. Solienne appeared in ragged swirls of blue and brown, as if through shimmering heat waves rising off a desert. Shemmon Station's silvery ovoid rolled in the foreground.

I swear I'm going to kiss the deck when I land. I drew a couple deep breaths and released them slowly before I called, "Shemmon Control, this is Ace Hand Zero-Five clearing the vortex."

Behind me, Russom released a breath, too. "Level it out for approach."

After the vortex's blue-fire confines, the landing bay felt like a broad cavern. I eased my ship inside, locked wing clamps on the landing rail, and sagged in my seat for a minute.

The whole sortie had taken only half an hour from launch to landing, but my body shook from the strain, physical and mental, as I clambered off the mounting ladder. Even my stomach curled, atypically unsettled. I clutched the ladder's rail and stared at a bundle of colored pipes on one bulkhead until the deck stopped rocking under my boots.

Russom dismounted a few moments later and studied me through unreadable eyes. I held his cold scrutiny. At last he strode away, shaking his head.

I watched him go. *Burn. He knows how much that scared me.*

I couldn't shake Russom's assessing stare the whole time while climbing out of my pressure suit, peeling off my sweat-soggy flight suit, and showering. I set my face, imperturbable as a ceremonial dancer's wooden mask, when I entered our on-station briefing room a few minutes later.

We did the usual step-by-step playback of the complete sortie, tracked the metadata on the wall projection, and listened to the cockpit voice recordings.

I nailed my vision to the projection table when it played my call about the invisible tunnel. *I sound half panicked. I* was *half panicked.*

Russom didn't comment until we finished the replay. Finally, he leaned back in his chair, folded his arms loosely, and eyed me from beneath his ebony eyebrows. "What did you learn from this sortie, Masou?"

That's the kind of question Noshi would ask. I pondered for a minute before I said, "It reinforced the necessity of trusting my instruments and," I didn't meet his eyes, "my instructor."

He said nothing, simply waited for me to continue, so I considered some more. I remembered my desperate urge to escape the lightning. "I learned to override my instincts."

Russom nodded at my periphery, never breaking his hawklike stare. "What else?"

I couldn't come up with anything. I rubbed at the table's rounded edge with one thumb while I dredged my mind. "What to expect next time I fly through a vortex?"

Russom said, "Hmph." He reached across the projection table and punched the audio track.

The recording played, "Sir, I can't see a tunnel."

"What did you hear in your voice, Masou?" he asked. "Why was it shaking?"

I ducked my head. "Fear, sir," I mumbled. *Are you going to wash me out now?*

"You acknowledge it." Neither Russom's expression nor his tone conveyed mockery. "Good. Now you know what fear is, you only have to decide how you're going to handle it."

After another second, he said with his trademark smirk, "It's about time something scared you." He stood and stretched. "We have a two-way sortie this evening, Masou. Better use the next four hours for crew rest."

In my fatigue, his statement took its time to sink in. *Did he actually praise me for something?* Still puzzled, I headed for the crew lounge.

Need a long drink before I sleep. Sweating had left me furiously thirsty. I bought two chilled water bottles from a vending machine and plopped at the nearest table.

I had downed one and half emptied the other, ignoring the water's plastic aftertaste, when Go and a cadet from Alta Flight slogged in, both as pale as if recovering from a long illness.

"Vortex flying is hard work," Go said when she saw me. She crossed to a vending machine and returned to my solitary table with a package of candy-coated nuts. "Wait until you do, um, both ways sortie."

"Got one this evening," I said, and furrowed my brow. "I thought Liborio said vortices don't go both ways."

"You fly to Arno, you know, the far-away moon," she said, tearing open her package. "You make orbit, then the operator at, um, Bogorad Base projects vortex back. Long flight. Very hard work." She tipped several colorful ovals into her hand and pushed the package across the table to me. "Want some?"

I wasn't hungry. Hadn't been since leaving Tollesson's. "Maybe later."

She stared me in the face. "Your, um, stomach isn't your problem, Ku." Her tone reminded me of Gram. "A person's stomach doesn't make them, you know, sad."

I stiffened. Annoyance surfaced through my melancholy. Annoyance at myself for not masking it. It shaded my tone when I said, "It's personal," and downed the rest of my bitter water.

Go blushed with embarrassment. She dipped her head in a gesture of apology, whispered, "Very sorry," and gave her full attention to her candied nuts.

Guilt poked me. Hard. Softening my voice, I said, "Sorry, Go. I didn't mean to take it out on you."

Sighing, I pushed away from the table, tossed my empty water bottles into the nearest recycler, and started toward the sleeping spaces one deck up.

I didn't sleep well. Machitew didn't come haunt me, but he lurked at the fringes of my dreams, hurling globes of blue lightning at my fighter like anti-spacecraft weapons.

When I returned three hours later, I found Kota in the lounge, mulling the choices in the vending machines. "Out of jerky," he said with disappointment. "I wanted to get some for the shuttle drop to the base. I think I could destroy a whole shegrul right now. Are you finished for the day?"

"Got a second sortie at 1900," I said. "I just came off crew rest."

"Ya, don't neglect your crew rest, Sheggy," somebody said behind me.

I pivoted to face Huritt.

"Everybody's baby-faced hero these days, aren't you?" he said with derision. "Yuma only knows what might happen to the Aerospace Forces if you fell asleep at the stick in the middle of a vortex sortie."

"What was that about?" I asked Kota after Huritt and Enyeto strutted away.

Kota leaned in and lowered his voice, his face growing serious. "I think he found out about, uh, what happened on our sortie the other day. Somebody must've leaked something. He confronted me yesterday as if we'd deliberately done something to make him look bad."

"Huritt's really getting paranoid." I rolled my eyes and assessed the vending machines' brightly wrapped contents. "He doesn't have to beat me anymore. I'm pretty sure yesterday wiped me out of the running for DG."

"I think the competition for DG is only a symptom of his real issue," Kota said. "I think the pressure from his mother is increasing."

Snatches of the conversation between Huritt and Enyeto I shouldn't have overheard flitted across my memory. I fidgeted and settled for spicy sausage sticks from the vending machine, though I would've preferred jerky, too.

"Keep an eye on your one-eighty, Ku," Kota advised. He tore his sausage package open with his teeth and hesitated before he turned to leave. "I don't trust Huritt."

* * * * *

Chapter Forty-Three

I didn't think about Kota's warning through the rest of War Phase, probably because Ops never assigned Huritt and me to fly together. Keeping up with my flight schedule and preparing for the objectives to be accomplished on each mission gave me more than enough to focus on.

At least one of the sorties each day, and sometimes both, took us through vortices. Even knowing what to expect, my pulse accelerated during every passage, sometimes so fiercely I could hear it despite the white noise in my earphones.

While teaching me to fly the Darter, my father had drilled into me the importance of keeping my attention outside the cockpit, of maintaining situational awareness in the skies around me. Under normal conditions, one needed only brief glances at one's instruments.

Vortices were not normal conditions, though. I couldn't resist the impression I'd flown into a storm cell every time I entered one. Each time its crackling light enclosed me and the electric tingling set in at my pressure suit's metal joints, I had to battle the urge to roll out. Only riveting my vision on the dart symbol and blue-fire crosshairs held me steady.

By the last day of War Phase, we'd progressed to solo flights, even for vortex sorties. Squadron Commander Grell pointed out, "You won't have anybody in your back seat during combat."

We had three phases left to complete our course work, which seemed to increase the closer we got to the finish. I took breaks from studying or flying only for crew rest, and squeezed in eating when I could. I made a lot of treks to the flight kitchen during odd hours, but hunger constantly gnawed at me. At least my rumbling stomach kept me from dozing during lectures.

* * *

Our final exam, scheduled for our last phase of training, consisted of an Operational Readiness Exercise, or ORE, that ran non-stop day and night.

"This will give you a better feel for the high tempo of combat operations than War Phase did," Grell told us.

Uneasiness shadowed several of my classmates' faces, and I recalled Hanuk saying, "If you think War Phase is tough…"

Everybody flew three sorties a day, sometimes in two-ship formations, sometimes in four, and never twice in one day with the same leads or wingmen. I flew most of mine with cadets from other flights, cadets whose names or faces I recognized, but about whom I knew little else.

We always engaged "hostiles," senior pilots flying the old, repainted *Spikes* Kota and I had been expecting the day we'd encountered the Asp. Every dogfight ended with "kills," which were always cadets.

For my third sortie on the second day, I drew the Four slot as wingman to Jehan Tomaso, a lanky Soli youth with dark hair, who was in Demi Flight. A wingman's primary duty is to protect his Lead.

As Three and Four in the formation, Jehan and I had to protect our Lead and Two, both from Bando Flight. I'd only flown with each of them once before all year, but I knew our Lead this time, a young woman named Leontina, to be alert and decisive.

On entering our sector, Leontina ordered, "Combat spread with weapons free. Stay sharp, and call out your contacts." Her voice rang crisp and businesslike.

We acknowledged in turn and slid to our positions. Combat spread put us in a single front a hundred arm lengths wide, with Cadet Svendsen in the Two slot, and me at Four flying inverted. We couldn't do that in atmospheric flight, of course.

"Masher Four locked in," I said, and hit my internal comms. "Check targeting," I requested of my computer. "Check energy cannon charge and missile status."

Simulated or not, the same procedures applied. I watched my weapon lights blink green in quick succession, then dim to amber for Ready/Standby.

We hadn't been in our training sector three minutes when Svendsen said, *"Got a contact!"* Nervous excitement clipped his words as he called out distance and heading. Something about his precise statements reminded me of Rinn.

He hadn't finished before the bogey lit my scope, too, followed by a second scarlet blip. It rocketed from "below" our formation in a trajectory meant to head us off. A lead pursuit.

"Second contact," I said. "Heading oh-six-four low at two-niner-three ranges."

They'd seen us. Tracks across our scopes revealed them splitting and swinging wide in opposite directions for a pincer maneuver.

"Masher Three and Four, vector to intercept second bogey," Leontina said. *"Masher Two, follow me."*

"Roger, Lead," Jehan said, and nosed into a negative-G dive. I rolled and followed, to draw up on his wing like a cloud-gray shadow.

What had begun as a two-versus-many scenario became two one-versus-two engagements. Not a bad tactic for mutual cover and support in a limited area. However, when our bogey realized we'd spotted him, he abruptly arced away. Then he doubled back and tried to outrun us.

Jehan and I pursued like starving dogs after a tavo. Until our prey swung around once more as if to take us head on.

With my pulse heightening, I said, "Targeting active, missile one active." The missile's amber Standby light flicked green. The white reticle in my targeting scope slid and bounced for a second before locking on.

He would come for me, I knew. They always targeted the wingman first, believing him or her to be the less experienced of the pair. I had longer-reach missiles, though. If Jehan missed his shot, I'd take the bogey.

"Offensive split now!" Jehan practically yelled through my helmet speakers. *"We'll bracket him."*

I peeled away from Jehan. As expected, the bogey banked toward me, his thrusters flaring red against the black of space. I swung wider, wider to keep him in the bracket, to let Jehan close in for a rear-quarter shot. My pulse quickened still more, but a grin tugged at my mouth.

It took a moment to realize how far the bogey had drawn me away from my lead, into an ambush. When my threat scope flashed a warning, I stared around, startled.

"Sket!" I swallowed rising dread while I searched space around me and banked as tightly as a Rohr's turn radius could cut it to rejoin Jehan.

Two seconds later, a third bogey screamed out of nowhere from behind me. *"Masher Four, you're dead,"* a gravelly voice said in my earphones.

As he plowed over my right shoulder, a faint *pop* sounded in my helmet speakers. Every display on my instrument panel flared crimson for an instant before all my power shut off, leaving me in a dark cockpit.

Rigged for simulation, our ships stayed powered down for two full minutes after a "kill," leaving one temporarily adrift and occasionally tumbling like a dead hulk until everything rebooted. My ship didn't tumble, but continued unhindered on its last set trajectory while every blank scope and display on my instrument panel seemed to stare at me with accusing eyes.

An hour or so later, I stiffened to a brace as the briefing room's door closed behind me. I caged my vision to the opposite wall, unable to meet Russom's coal-black eyes. He neither spoke nor shifted in his chair for several endless seconds. He simply studied me through a smirk. At last he said, "Congratulations on getting yourself killed, Masou."

"Sir," I said. I didn't break attention.

"That is, without doubt, the most idiotic thing I've ever seen you do," Russom said. "Before we replay it, tell me what you did wrong. And at ease, for Gbadu's sake."

My jaw tightened. *You're enjoying this, aren't you?* I relaxed from the brace but didn't sit.

I'd had plenty of time to rerun the dogfight in my head while I circled on the border of our training sector and waited for the others to finish the battle. I had visualized my threat scope, the red and blue ship-darts arcing and twisting in it, and recognized where I'd gone wrong, what I'd missed.

Before Leontina and Jehan had formed up for the return flight, Svendsen had joined me in the "dead zone," but it hadn't lessened my exasperation with myself.

"Lost my element Lead," I said. *My most serious mistake.* "When the bogey tried to avoid our bracket, I stretched it to keep him in." I reenacted the bogey's direction and my ever-widening circle with my hands. "I was concentrating on him and lost my situational aware-ness. I didn't see the third ship until two seconds before he hit me."

"How do you feel about it?" Russom asked.

"Stupid, sir," I said. *As half a shegrul.*

"You should. Anything else?"

I thought about it. *Humbled? Ya. Why did it happen? Was it fatigue? Did I get careless and let my guard down?*

Oddly, the idea I'd "died" didn't rattle me any more than losing a game would have. Disappointment motivated me to learn from my mistake, but I'd never really had a sense of danger. Not as I'd had while wrestling my bird-stricken Darter to a landing, or tracking the Asp, or flying through vortices. I creased my forehead.

Russom leaned back. "Everybody gets killed two or three times during these exercises," he said. "Try to stay alive a little longer next time, will you?"

* * *

We gathered in the viditorium at 0500 every morning for a Lessons Learned session and situation report. By the final day, my classmates all appeared as bleary-eyed as I felt. New snow had fallen in the night, calf-deep powder that would sparkle like diamonds once the sun rose.

The walkways hadn't been cleared yet, so we shuffled to the school, hands stuffed into our fleece-lined jacket pockets. None of us wasted energy with talk, but our breaths left puffy contrails adrift on the frozen air.

Stamping snow off my boots at the main doorway, I searched the vaulted room for empty seats. When I spotted several in the middle of the upper row of our squadron's section, I beckoned to my room-ies. We fell in with the other cadets slouching up the aisle and sighed with relief in the artificial warmth.

Kota unexpectedly swore and seized my sleeve. I wrenched around, questioning him with raised eyebrows.

"Look at your second sortie today," he said, and pointed with his chin.

Floor-to-ceiling projection screens, uncovered for the exercise, flanked the tri-D tank. Throughout this phase, one had served as the squadron Ops board, displaying each day's mission schedule. Each sortie listed the pilots' names and positions, launch times, callsigns, and weapons loads in black characters set on luminous white.

My stomach tumbled like a rock off a mesa. "Wingman to Huritt?"

It seemed inevitable, since we hadn't drawn one sortie together all year. Huritt's muttered threats during class and him telling Kota and Ogundo it had been too long since the last training accident materialized in my mind. My gut tightened.

Rinn had the Three slot for the sortie, and Allandra Pellesh had been slated to fly Four.

Rinn furrowed his brow. "Who is Cadet Pellesh?"

"The tall, gorgeous blonde in Folkstone Flight," I said.

"From Apollona, Satha," Kota said. "Parade-and-review practice for Huk's graduation, remember?"

"Ah, yes." Rinn gave a decidedly wolfish grin.

I followed Guns and Rinn to the empty seats. "She was parade commander for her flight."

Kota scrunched his face. "Four DG contenders on—"

"Not me." I sank into my seat.

"—the same sortie," Kota finished. "What're the odds on that? Who's working in Ops Scheduling this phase?"

"Why does it matter?" I asked.

Kota surveyed the area and lowered his voice. "Huritt's got a serious grudge against you, Ku. I don't think he's kidding with his threats. Maybe we should talk to somebody in Ops and see if you can get a different sortie."

I hesitated before I asked, "You want me to walk into Ops and say, 'I think Huritt's planning to kill me, so would you put me on a different sortie?'"

Kota subsided, but his features grew atypically grim. "Just make sure you stay really alert."

* * *

With the sortie scheduled for early afternoon, I stopped at the flight kitchen before going to the squadron. Thinking of flying with Huritt unsettled my stomach, but I knew I'd need all my energy.

I spotted Noshi entering the chow line as I headed toward the exit, a warm meal box cradled in my hands. The aroma of a thick chowder wafting from it moistened my mouth, but it had been phases since I'd last talked with Noshi. When his gaze met mine, and he nodded a greeting, I waited for him.

Stepping outside minutes later, he didn't comment on not having seen me at the gym for a while. Instead, he fixed me with a serious stare and asked, "What is the most important thing you have learned in the last moon, Cadet Masou?"

I considered. New weapons systems? Combat tactics? Vortex flying? No, none of those. "To face my fear, sir."

He studied me, eyebrows lifting. "Very good. What have you learned about facing your fear?"

I didn't have to think that time. "To press through it, sir. You can't let it stop you."

"Very good, Cadet," he repeated. A shadow deepened on his weathered face. "Soon, you will learn to face death."

* * * * *

Chapter Forty-Four

Noshi didn't mean simulated deaths in our training sorties, I knew. My innards tightened as if something had squeezed them in a scaly fist. As I strode to the squadron building, his words mingled with Kota's warning from earlier. I didn't hear the dry crunch of the previous day's snow under the new layer or feel the frigid wind burning my nose and ears.

On reaching the squadron's break area, I found an empty table, but had to force myself to eat. The chowder didn't taste as good as I'd expected, and it clumped in my throat. Only knowing I'd need the strength for flying a challenging sortie spurred me to finish.

I repeated the Warding Chant in my mind as I headed for the briefing room. *Shield me from the spirits of the Dark, O Sower of the Stars.*

Our IPs hadn't flown with us since War Phase, nor would they this time, but all four attended the pre-mission briefing. They stood against the walls, where they could see the projection table, while Huritt spoke.

"We have an interdiction mission," he said. He pawed the table's touchscreen to open a map of a mist-swirled surface. "According to intel, the lumpies have a staging area on Tobe. The garrison is here, outside Dalvik." He tapped an icon designating a scientific outpost set among a cluster of volcanoes, pimples swelling on the young planet's surface.

The intelligence office had invented the scenario with fictional civilian colonies and enemy garrisons, but we all knew Supremacy staging areas on Tobe, a barely habitable Commonwealth possession, could easily become a reality.

"Today," Huritt said, "the lumpies are transferring weapon systems to Godafoss." He pointed at a green dot, symbolizing a community of two- to five-thousand people on an empty plain some distance across the map from Dalvik. "Godafoss is a major city by Tobe standards, so it has one of the three vortex terminals on the whole planet."

He frowned at Rinn, Allandra, and me. "Intel says when the lumpies enter the vortex, it will be to attack Solienne."

We nodded acknowledgment, and Huritt went on. "The lumpies are using a convoy of heavy haulers. We have to destroy the convoy en route to prevent collateral damage to the civilian colonies.

"There's only one surface route from Dalvik to Godafoss. Most of it is a sixty-range bridge across an active geyser basin, here." He drew his finger along the black line of the fictional bridge across the vapor-obscured plain. "It starts in a canyon here, outside Dalvik." He traced the track's line through a tri-D gorge. "The bridge and canyon would both make good kill boxes.

"But it won't be as easy as it sounds." Huritt lifted his face again to scan the rest of us. By the twist of his features, one would've thought he had something extremely bitter stuck in his teeth. "For one, reconnaissance drones have identified surface defense systems along the route. For another, intel thinks the lumpies have mounted portable anti-spacecraft weapons on their haulers."

"We will have a busy day," Rinn said.

Being Rinn's roommate for so long had accustomed me to his gift for understatement and his dry sense of humor, but Huritt glowered across the table as if Rinn had belittled him. I exchanged glances with Rinn, rubbing my nose to hide my grin.

We discussed ingress routes, attack runs, and how to evade surface defense weapons, both the ones intel expected, and any others. "Hits" from simulated anti-spacecraft artillery or surface-to-space missiles would light up damage diagrams in our cockpits. Those could "kill" us, too.

Every time I made a comment, Huritt grunted dismissively or ignored it. My irritation simmered, but I kept my mouth shut. *Stay professional, Ku. Russom's watching.*

Finally, Huritt's IP stepped forward. "Masou had a good idea about the kill box here, Hevovitas. You might want to give it more serious consideration."

Huritt uttered a low, "Yes, sir," in a grumble, and I riveted my attention to the tabletop display.

This proved more challenging than expected with Allandra leaning on the projection table. Unlike Go's, her flight suit fit a little too snugly in all the right places, and its slide closure never made it all the way up to her collar. She also managed to smell of some spicy fragrance after two sorties instead of stale sweat like the rest of us.

When she responded to comments in her breathy voice and favored us with her bottomless blue gaze, even Rinn, with all his discipline, lost his line of thought. Huritt pinned his vision to the table's surface after he went blank in mid-sentence the second time.

In Life Support after the briefing, standing with our arms outstretched while our crews sealed us into our pressure suits, Huritt eyed me. "Today we'll find out how well a shegrul herder completes a strike mission." He said it with a smile and in the kidding tone often heard between competing buddies, but I didn't miss the curl of his lip or black venom in his eyes.

I'd only seen that kind of dark fire in anyone's eyes once before, during our first briefing about Osaga Safa. I countered the prickly sensation at the nape of my neck with a deliberately relaxed smile and said, "I'll do fine."

Huritt sat silent through the shuttle flight to Shemmon Station. I thought it unusual, with Allandra among us. Huritt never lost an opportunity to strut for the women, even with our IPs present.

We dispersed to our launch bays from the shuttle dock, made our pre-flight checks, mounted up, and strapped in. Huritt and I spoke only to accomplish our routine comms checks. He sounded curt and dispassionate in my earphones. Being in separate launch bays, I couldn't see his face, but I could imagine his perpetual scowl.

As I brought my engines online one after another, and their impatient roars shook the launch cradle with increasing power, I reached to touch the small oval that always lay in my flight suit pocket under my pressure suit.

Not there. I threw it away.

I couldn't afford to think about it. I had to stay focused for the mission.

Seconds after blasting clear of our launch tubes, the blue point of light and string of coordinates identifying the vortex portal illuminated our astrogation displays. Two minutes later, we began our three-minute transit to Tobe.

I'd flown fourteen or fifteen vortex sorties in the phases since my orientation flight with Russom, but every muscle in my body still tensed whenever I entered a portal. Following standard operating procedures, we made the passage in loose trail formation due to the lightning tunnel's narrowness.

Apprehensions or not, three phases of flying vortex sorties had toughened us. We no longer burst into real space feeling as if we'd flown through a tornado. The portal spewed us into low-planetary space, so Tobe filled most of the starfield before us. The planet's wispy cloud cover, whipped by high-altitude winds, gave it the appearance of being wrapped in medical gauze.

Huritt, his voice terse, ordered us to combat spread as soon as Allandra, in the Four position, cleared the exit portal. I activated my threat scope after sliding into the inverted Two position.

At Huritt's word, we dove for the surface. When our ships' sensors registered atmospheric elements, our propulsion systems auto-switched to the high-bypass turbofan engines. An alerting chime and a faint *whoosh* through my omnidirectional speakers seemed to come from the rear inside my helmet.

We skimmed wind-tattered clouds to cloak our ingress. Intel hadn't mentioned enemy fighters, but clouds could conceal them as easily as us. My vision constantly flicked from my threat scope to our surrounding space. *Not going to repeat any mistake that got me "killed" before.*

Tempest had few geothermal areas, so the abundance of them on Tobe stirred my curiosity. Upon piercing the shifting cloud-veil, I recoiled.

Weak sunlight revealed a bone-white expanse, bleached by a thin layer of steaming water laden with numerous minerals. Under the constant flow, the pale flats could have been diseased and bloodless flesh, pocked with boils and cankers that oozed bright yellow and rust-orange fluids, or burbled up muddy pus.

Tufts of shriveled vegetation, probably grasses or mosses, clung to protruding rocks like remnants of mange-riddled fur, and vapor coiled and swept and drifted across the entire plain.

"Do people live here?" Rinn asked. His revulsion carried through my helmet speakers.

"Only at the research stations, I think," Allandra said. *"In one of Satha's mythologies, 'Tobe' is the world of condemned souls. They say the air smells of sulfur."*

"It looks like a place for condemned souls," Rinn said.

The mission profile uploaded to our flight computers included a string of coordinates and a green overlay on the digital map to mark our ingress route.

Intel couldn't tell us where along the track we might find the convoy, or what specific weapons the haulers might carry, but they'd told us what types of anti-spacecraft weapons the lumpies had concealed along the route. Those had been set in cracks and under canyon ledges to make them difficult to find and destroy.

The first coordinates scrolled onto our nav screens as we entered our training zone. One hundred ranges from the point they marked, Huritt ordered us from combat spread into echelon. Now in two pairs of ships, one following the other, we descended in radio silence on the festering lava cones sheltering Dalvik.

By ten ranges out, we had descended to one thousand spans. Two volcanos towered before us, craggy shadows in the smoky near distance. We activated targeting, charged energy cannons, and checked the status of our defensive systems and ordnance loads.

I recognized the mouth of the pass from two ranges away, a ragged fracture like a mountain torn in two. Cruising at five hundred spans, a sharp *beep* seized my attention, and a yellow symbol flashed on my threat scope.

Low-altitude artillery. We've been detected.

* * * *

Chapter Forty-Five

"**L**ead, Two," I called. "Alta Tanker four-six at three-five-eight." Its symbol throbbed, flame-colored in my threat scope.

"I see it," Huritt said. His irritated tone implied he already knew. *"Jammers active. Three and Four, close it up."*

You can't jam AT-46 search scanners. I remembered the class lecture on enemy detection systems. The vid replayed as vividly in my mind as if from a digital chip. They're passive motion detectors, sensitive enough to pick up a sparrow, but easily confused by multiple targets and movements. We should spread out and start evasive maneuvers.

"Negative on jammers, not effective," I said. "Need to spread out and start jinking."

Only in the following dense silence did I realize I had contradicted my Lead, and my Lead happened to be Huritt. The venom in his eyes seared through my recent memory.

Abrupt anger clenched my teeth. *What am I supposed to do, let him kill us with his incompetence?*

It's an exercise, I reminded myself. It's only a training sortie. Nobody's really going to get killed. His IP will rip him apart for it during debrief.

"Activate jammers," Huritt said again. *"Three and Four, tight echelon."* He didn't address me, but his tone clearly said, *Don't* any *of you ever question me.*

The flashing warning symbol switched to steady orange when we entered the pass, a steep-walled gorge of stone as dark as a moonless sky made solid. It seemed to have been created by some violent upheaval.

"Lead, it's locked on," I said. I kept my voice neutral, but frustration had stiffened my pulse. It pounded in my temples and against my ribs. My hands knotted around the control stick and throttles instead of into fists.

Seconds later, Allandra's cry rang in my earphones. *"Lead, Four, I am hit! My starboard engine is lost. I am losing power."*

I bit off a groan. I could see that coming.

For training purposes, our crews had applied sensors to key areas on our aircraft. When a simulated weapon hit a sensor, the system it represented shut down enough to replicate the handling limitations and characteristics of such damage. We could learn to fly a crippled fighter under controlled conditions before we had to do it in real-world combat.

We tripped seven more AT-46 nests during the next two minutes. Under Huritt's lead, we lanced through volleys of red-and-white tracers. My traffic scope showed Allandra's fighter falling behind due to its decreased power.

A minute or two later, I saw Rinn's ship rock from a hit. *"Lead, Three,"* he said, *"my port wing is damaged, and my landing gear—"*

I didn't hear the rest. My own ship lurched at a strike from my right. My hands reflexively tightened on the controls, steadying it as I spared a glance for my damage display. A scarlet flash, digital blood in electronic water, warned I'd lost my starboard torpedo rack and its munitions load.

Sweat glued my flight suit to my chest and coursed down my spine, but my mouth dried up. *If those munitions had been real, the hit would've vaporized my ship.*

Ten ranges farther, we engaged heat-tracking missiles.

"Launch flares," Huritt said.

At least that makes sense. I launched two and watched their sparking plumes cut white arcs across the darkness to draw off the missiles.

Seconds later, a dozen square objects in a crooked line became visible on the track's green overlay. The bulky forms lit our threat scopes like stars in a rare alignment. The Supremacy hauler convoy.

"Three and Four, hold off for the second pass," Huritt said as we closed on our targets. *"Two, you're with me."*

"Roger, Lead," I said, and made my final weapons check. The tension tasted like bile on my tongue.

My ordnance load had consisted of eight tracker torpedoes, four under each wing. The port rack's icon glowed amber for Standby, but the starboard one flashed red for Non-operational. *Nonexistent now.*

"Ordnance launch to Ready," I said.

The port rack's icon blinked green.

"Energy cannon to Ready."

More green lights popped up in a rapid sequence like young plants in a tight row.

"Lead is in hot," Huritt announced, and rolled into his attack run.

My chronometer counted twenty seconds, square digits flipping over at a crawl in their miniature window. My pulse rate quickened with each one.

"Two is in hot," I said at last, and dove after him.

The line of glowing boxes expanded in my targeting reticle. I squeezed the launch toggle and held it down.

Intel had been right about the lumpies arming the haulers. Energy bursts from more anti-spacecraft artillery blazed in crimson streamers around my cockpit and peppered my fuselage.

We egressed the gorge in a vertical climb, rocketing out of reach of the surface-to-space missiles mounted along its rim. My threat scope flashed eight or nine missile icons from positions planted like stray teeth on each side of the canyon's black maw.

As I banked into an oval patrol track half a range up, Rinn called, *"Three is in hot."*

Allandra echoed seconds later, *"Four is in hot."*

I tracked their attack runs against the convoy. Simulated hits on the blocky targets produced pink flares far below. As they shot clear, one after the other, green text scooted across my target scope.

Battle Damage Assessment:

67 Percent Destruction of All Targets

I huffed a frustrated breath. It briefly fogged my lower faceplate and rattled in my helmet speakers. *Mission incomplete. Probably due to pre-strike damage.*

Allandra's fighter banked sluggishly, climbing out of the gorge. Only one afterburner flared against the starry darkness, a desperate beacon punching the smoggy air.

"Black Blade Flight, report status," Huritt said.

I scanned my display. "Lead, Two. Heavy damage. Starboard engine at 30 percent power, starboard ordnance rack destroyed."

Rinn and Allandra reported in turn, both reciting extensive lists of battle damage.

I fumed. *Completely unnecessary. Huritt's stubborn as well as stupid. If this was real, Allandra might not get home, and I'd already be dead.*

Our sim-damaged systems returned to normal on leaving our training sector. Once we crossed the boundary, damage diagrams shut down, engines returned to full power, and instruments came back online. I heard Allandra's shaky exhalation through my helmet speakers.

Our engines auto-switched to the quiet pulse of magneto-hydrodynamic drives upon reaching low-planetary space. Minutes later, Huritt relayed the vortex coordinates for our return passage.

Except for acknowledging with a stiff, "Copy, Lead," I didn't speak through the flight. I sat with my teeth locked to keep from muttering in exasperation.

When the guidance reticle appeared in our astrogation displays, we slid into loose trail formation and entered the portal's blue-fire ring at regulation twenty-second intervals. I pushed aside my disgust to give the transit my full attention.

In multi-ship passages, the blue reticle's crosshairs and our proximity monitors were vital for maintaining safe spacing in trail formation. The vortex tunnel's strobing light, enough to induce a headache, distorted one's depth perception and ability to gauge distances.

I kept my usual firm grip on my control stick. The twisting light and static hiss in my earphones seemed to exaggerate my fighter's shimmying and rocking. The by-now familiar tingles began at my wrists, crackling like static electricity, and gradually reached my fingertips.

Despite my concentration, images of Rinn's ship rocking from the hit to his wing and Allandra's ship barely clearing the gorge's rim played across my mind's eye. *Get snipped, Huritt, you arrogant idiot.*

My chronometer's flipping digits counted the seconds until emergence into real space. *Not fast enough. It's never fast enough.*

I'd never known how long a second really lasted until I began flying vortices.

Thirty-five seconds from piercing the "wall" at the tunnel's midpoint, scarlet bursts caught my peripheral vision, wrenching it away from the blue crosshairs. The split-second flares came from Huritt's braking thrusters, I realized with my next heartbeat. *What in the——? Is something wrong?*

"Lead," I called, "are you all right?"

"Two, back off, back off!" Huritt's voice shook in my earphones.

Is he angry, or scared? I couldn't tell.

"You're too close!" he shouted, and his braking thrusters plumed again.

I had no time for puzzlement or shock. No time to glance at my proximity monitor. I knew I was too close.

If I plow into Huritt, the fireball will kill all four of us. If I brake, too, I'll endanger Rinn and Allandra the way Huritt's endangering me.

The realization struck like a blindside blow to my temple. My whole body seemed to ice over. My heartbeat shook my frame so my hands trembled on stick and throttle.

My proximity scope flashed red. Its warning horn blasted like a call to wake the dead, jarring me from my shock.

COLLISION IMMINENT

I had only one course of action. Pitching my nose up would shoot me clear of Huritt's fighter, buy Rinn and Allandra a few more seconds to increase their separation, and send me through the vortex membrane.

* * * * *

Chapter Forty-Six

I shifted my hold on the control stick with a steady hand. *I'm going to die. You lost, Machitew.*

Half roll—now.

The words in my mind, firm but calm, came more clearly than a voice in my earphones. I twitched the stick.

My ship inverted with a shriek of ripping metal, a shiver felt through its frame rather than heard. Blue-white fire showered off my starboard wingtip as if from a crazed welder's torch. I couldn't see Huritt's fighter, but my proximity monitor flared like a pulsar, and its bleat punched me repeatedly between the ears.

"Two!" Rinn's voice, atypically shaken, cut across the pulses. *"Two, are you all right?"*

I gulped a breath. Sweat beaded my face, and nausea rippled in my midsection. I'd just hit the "wall."

A new light flashed red on my instrument panel, out of synch with the proximity scope, but equally persistent and demanding. *I've got damage. Real damage this time.*

My stomach barrel rolled. I sucked another breath and swallowed. *I'm not going to puke, I'm not going to puke, I'm not going to puke.*

"Two, are you all right?" Rinn shouted again.

"Affirmative," I said. *Why won't the reeking beeper shut up?* I scanned my traffic scope and the coiling lightning storm outside my cockpit. *Can't even see Huritt.*

"*... status, Two?*" Rinn asked.

"Three, I've got damage," I said between panting. "Lost a—a wingtip." *And my rotting prox alarm won't stop. Is it damaged, too?*

"*Hold your position, Two,*" Rinn said with an urgency I'd never heard from him before. "*Stay steady, stay steady. Thirty seconds to portal.*"

My ship wavered in the strobing turbulence. My proximity and damage lights blinked an erratic contrast. I gripped the stick with a sweaty hand and locked my gaze on the blue crosshairs. A different kind of tingling replaced the static sensation in my fingers.

"*Hold your position,*" Rinn repeated. "*Ten seconds.*"

Hours later, it seemed, I burst into real space, gasping for breath and with my proximity alarm still squalling.

I didn't understand the reason until Huritt said, "*Shemmon Control, Black Blade Lead clearing the vortex.*" His terse voice in my omnidirectional helmet speakers came from directly beneath me.

I froze. An image of his fighter a hair's breadth from mine seared across my mind.

It took me a few heartbeats to report, "Shemmon Control, Black Blade Two clearing the vortex," without a tremor in my voice.

Pitch up before you complete the aileron roll.

Like the order to half-roll, the one to pitch up came as distinctly to my mind as a ground controller's instruction.

A quick burst of steering thrusters nosed my ship clear of Huritt's. Solienne and the station briefly careened out of my sight, and the proximity alarm silenced at last, though it still echoed in my skull.

I completed the roll to align my ship for approach. My stomach lagged as I maneuvered into formation, but I waited until Rinn and

Allandra had cleared the vortex to report my damaged starboard wing.

"Black Blade Two to landing ramp Golo," Control said with a voice as dispassionate as my flight computer's. *"Emergency crew standing by."*

Golo ramp. Emergency crew. It's my Darter after the bird strike all over again.

I remembered the crash foam and flashing lights. The same embarrassment surged, but this time, I said only, "Roger, Control."

Fire-shielded bulkheads, gray and carbon-scored, separated Golo ramp from the other flight decks. Twice the size of normal bays to accommodate compromised landings, it contained equipment for every kind of emergency.

The ramp's approach guidance lights flashed green. My entry alignment was good. My hands still tingled, but no longer shook on the controls.

I extended the anchor clamps. The one formerly mounted on the starboard wingtip was gone. I couldn't see the damage from the cockpit, but a blood-colored overlay on my damage display marked its absence, same as for my missing forward steering thruster. *This could get tricky.*

"Control, Black Blade Two," I said, and started at the routine tone of my voice, "starboard landing clamp is gone."

"Copy, Black Blade Two," Control said. *"Break off your approach for another go-round. Deploying arresting nets in Golo ramp."*

I acknowledged and nudged the stick. Had to use my port thrusters to make a wide circle. I applied the braking thrusters as I approached once more.

Amber lights glared in warning around the ramp opening. I'd lost my entry alignment.

I eased the stick down and to port with my hand clammy in my glove and slippery on the control stick. Sweat trickled from my scalp and smarted in my eyes. I blinked it away and shook my head. Salty droplets spattered the inside of my faceplate.

When the AG lights switched from amber to green, I fired the braking thrusters again and released my breath. Momentum would carry me the rest of the way.

My ship struck the arresting net like an insect hitting a spider web at high speed. It lurched and rebounded, wrenching me in my crash harness, briefly blurring my vision before partial gravity slammed it to the deck in a controlled crash. My fighter bounced once and settled.

The bay door sealed with a soundless slam, and a pressure-suited deck crewman on a walkway above me hand-signaled Good and Shut Down. My gloved hands, awkward in their shakiness, fumbled across the instrument console, shutting off all systems as swiftly as I could. All the while, I kept breathing deeply.

The Pressurization Complete beacon lit high on the bulkhead, and I loosened my helmet's toggles with tingling hands, shoved the helmet off, and popped the canopy. I knew I'd be fine once the bay's flow of chilly air hit my face. A few full breaths steadied my stomach, despite the odor of burned rubber.

Then my gaze tripped on my starboard wing. The outermost two arm lengths, including my landing strobe and second steering thruster nozzle, had been shredded off as raggedly as if a ghost cat had used it for a scratching tree.

It shook me more than I expected, though I already knew I'd lost part of my wing. I wobbled my way down the mounting ladder and stood still, grasping its rail. *Did Huritt seriously try to* kill *me?*

Kota's repeated warnings snaked through my mind.

"Masou!" Russom shouted behind me.

Startled, I wheeled ponderously to face him as he crossed the bay. The rigidity of his long strides ringing on the deck plates animated his outrage. I'd never seen him so livid. His normally kasse-dark complexion bordered on ebony, and his eyebrows had bunched so tightly they resembled a pair of black caterpillars above his flinty eyes. I braced to attention when he stopped face-to-face with me.

"What in the name of Gbadu were you doing?" he shouted, leaning so close his breath's heat brushed my face. "Yes, we witnessed the whole thing. That's what tracking decks are for. Do you want to explain to me now, or in front of a court-martial?"

Anger overrode my receding shock. I locked my vision on his. "In-flight emergency. *Sir*."

Russom snorted. "Get out of your pressure suit and up to the briefing room. You have ten minutes, Masou."

"Yes, sir." I started across the bay. My legs didn't threaten to buckle, but they remained quivery with adrenaline.

Between my bootfalls clunking across the deck plates, I overheard Russom addressing my crew chief. "Pull it all, Gowda. Ship-to-ship comms, nosevid, the whole sensor array, and shoot it to briefing room two ASAP."

Even after a hasty shower and a side trip to the crew lounge for a bottle of water, I arrived before Russom. The adrenaline hadn't fully subsided, and I couldn't sit still. I kept pacing the compact briefing room, taking restless pulls from the water bottle.

I didn't stop until Russom entered, his eyes still smoldering. He clutched a remote's tab in one hand. Shutting the heavy door with a *thunk* loud enough to make me jump, he said, "Where did this in-flight emergency occur, Masou? We'll start there. We might not even bother with the rest of the sortie."

"During the return vortex, sir." To my relief, my voice stayed even and matter-of-fact as when I'd reported my damage to Control.

Neither of us sat. I stood before the projection table, my hands curled tightly to control the vestiges of their trembling. Under Russom's glare, I described what happened.

"Hevovitas gave no explanation for firing his braking thrusters?" Russom asked. "He stated no intention to do so?"

"No, sir. Play our intership comms."

He did.

"Hmph," Russom said. He aimed the remote at the projection screen on the rear bulkhead, much larger than the one in the tabletop.

The projection rippled and split. Half of it played my nosevid recording. The other half ran a tri-D animation of four fighters, white shapes on a cobalt field synthesized from my ship's external sensor data, along with the flight computer's metadata.

Russom said, "Return vortex, thirty seconds in, all data layers, slow to 50 percent."

We watched the recording straight through the first time. At half-speed, my nosevid revealed the braking bursts pluming from Huritt's ship like twin geysers on Tobe. Twice.

I watched my nosecone begin to pitch up an instant before the forward view blurred into the half-roll. My stomach rolled with it. I swayed on my feet and steadied myself against the projection table.

"There's the trash bin," Russom said without glancing at me, and nodded at the metal can in the corner.

I controlled the urge. "No need, sir."

In the dorsal view of the white-on-blue animation, only Huritt's nosecone remained visible, protruding two or three arm lengths ahead of mine.

"Lateral view," Russom said.

The white-and-blue projection flipped. Seen from the side, my ship and Huritt's flew belly-to-belly like mud eels mating in a spring flashflood. I noted the nosecone of Rinn's ship spaced precisely twenty seconds behind my aft stabilators.

No wonder the proximity alarm kept blaring. At that speed, one miniscule twitch…

Russom swore under his breath in some Obollan language.

I must have paled, because he said, "If you puke on my briefing table, Masou…" but the flinty edge had left his eyes and voice.

"I'm fine, sir."

On the second play, Russom paused the recording as my fighter began its roll. The view beyond the cockpit froze in an indiscernible spiral of bright light.

"Why did you do this?" he asked.

"To avoid a collision with Hevovitas, sir. The idea to roll just… came to me." My voice quivered slightly. The source of the directive puzzled me. *Definitely not Machitew.* "It wasn't what I'd planned to do."

"What *did* you plan to do?"

"Pitch up, sir." I tasted gorge in the back of my throat, thinking about it. It burned, and I swallowed. "So I wouldn't endanger Stormun and Pellesh."

"Do you realize, Masou, what would have happened if you had carried through on the pitch?" Russom's voice had gone deadly quiet. His stare bored into mine.

I swallowed again. "Yes, sir." No tremor that time. My hands curled tightly enough at my trouser seams to make my fingers ache.

Russom's scowling stare continued to drill me, second after second, his mouth taut beneath his fine line of a mustache like a statue of an angry Obollan god.

We both jumped at a rap on the briefing room door. When Russom snapped, "Yes?" it opened a couple thumb widths.

Rinn's IP, an older man, peered inside, his face grave. "Roos, I need a word."

Russom stepped outside. The two IPs moved off a few arm lengths, their backs toward me, unaware the door hadn't fully closed. Though my pulse still throbbed in my ears, fragments of their conversation drifted in to me.

"… Stormun's nosevid," said Rinn's IP. "… believes it was intentional."

"… Hevovitas say?" Russom questioned, his voice curt.

"… lost power… ran diagnostics…"

My jaw hardened. I hadn't thought my fists could tighten any more, but they did. *The Hevo vermin* did *try to kill me.*

I shoved clear of the table in a resurgence of adrenaline and reflexively dropped into a combat stance.

Russom returned a few minutes later with his brows lowered in their usual glower. He hesitated in the doorway on seeing my posture, and I immediately relaxed. He kept an eye on me as he reentered the room and asked, "Masou, do you have any reason to believe Cadet Hevovitas might have intended to do you harm?"

What I had replied to Kota that morning reverberated in my mind. *You want me to walk into Ops and say, 'I think Huritt's planning to kill me?'* I never did take either Kota or Huritt seriously.

I met Russom's grim gaze. "Yes, sir."

He studied me. Assessing me. Finally, he said, "Your friend Stormun and his IP believe so as well, after watching Stormun's nosevid recording. They've already informed Squadron Commander Grell. He's initiating an investigation."

Russom never broke eye contact. "Hevovitas claimed in his debriefing that his engines lost power, and you closed up on him." He folded his arms, his fingers gripping his biceps. "His crew chief ran diagnostics on his engines and found nothing wrong. When they analyzed his flight computer data, it proved he had manually fired his braking thrusters."

"Huritt's an idiot," I said. "How did he think he could get away with it?" Fury consumed my shock at last. "Did he say why, sir?"

"I hoped you could tell me."

"Me?" I shook my head. "We're competing for the DG medal. We've been riding each other since Basic, but—"

"I'm aware of that." One corner of Russom's mouth curled in a scant smile. "That's hardly motivation for a murder. What else?"

"No idea, sir. My friend Kota—uh, Cadet Apenimon—says he's under pressure from his mother. Something about politics back home."

I recalled Huritt's conversation with his cousin in the chow hall moons ago, but I quashed it. *I'd believe it of the Hevos, but it's only hearsay.* I said instead, "I don't know what any of it has to do with me."

Russom scrutinized me for a while longer. Finally he said, brow still furrowed, "Tell me if anything else occurs to you."

"Yes, sir." I knew I'd been dismissed.

Starting for the crew lounge, the roar of voices reached me. A lot more of them than usual, and heightened as if with apprehension. Still, I didn't expect to see half our class sitting there when I entered.

I needed a minute to locate Rinn and Allandra in the crowd. I spotted them sitting with Kota, Guns, and Go at a table near one bulkhead. Rinn's features bore solemnity beyond his normal stoicism, and Allandra appeared pale. I quickly made my way to them around the other tables, ignoring the curious and somewhat anxious stares of their occupants.

"Are you two all right?" I asked as I drew up.

Allandra sprang to her feet, her eyes welling, and flung both arms tightly about me. "I have never before been so frightened during flight."

"It's over now, Allandra." I returned a comforting hug.

Rinn stood, too, towering above me. "We are fine," he said when I released Allandra. "Thank you, Ku." He said nothing else, but I read full comprehension in his eyes.

"You would've done the same thing, Rinn," I said, "if our positions had been reversed."

Still uneasy under the questioning gazes of everybody else in the lounge, and noticing how they all leaned closer to hear, I lowered my voice to address my circle of friends. "What's going on? Why is everybody just sitting here?"

"When our shuttle docked," Kota said, "Security Forces sent us here and told us our sorties were on indefinite delay while they investigated an in-flight incident." He favored me with an I-told-you-so expression.

"We saw, um, Security Forces taking Huritt away wearing, you know, handclasps," Go said.

"Handcuffs," Kota corrected. He shook his head and narrowed his gaze on me. "I don't think this is finished, Ku."

* * * * *

Chapter Forty-Seven

The crawler swayed and shushed to a halt at Tollesson's Pub, and my heart clenched inside my ribcage. I hadn't been here in the moon since the dinner with Hanuk and Derry. I blew out a breath in a small cloud, which hovered for a second, and pushed the memory away with it. *They won't be here tonight.*

Squinting in the cold of the star-sprinkled night, I noted the Osfelg temple on the hill, aglow with its normal lighting. I jammed my hands into the warmth of my jacket pockets and watched my classmates bound off the crawler. *Nobody celebrating tonight but us. About time we found out where we're going after graduation.*

"Where's Guns?" I asked Kota when Ogundo didn't emerge from the crawler.

"He's coming later," Kota said. "He had some last-minute stuff to do at the orderly room. I said we'd save him a place."

We crunched to the pub's broad entrance on nubbly ice, refrozen after the day's thawing to slush. The painted dragon above the lintel appeared more ferocious without a feast lantern dangling from its teeth. *Nowhere near as huge and dangerous as an askuk, though.*

Radiant warmth and the scents of grilling and spit-roasted venison beckoned us inside. The staff had arranged five or six of the trestle tables into a single long one up the middle of the timber hall.

Some cadets' friends, including Go's fiancé in his dress uniform, had joined us on the crawler at Belsken Field. Others would meet us at the pub. I had debated whether to invite Hanuk, knowing he probably wouldn't come alone. Could I deal with seeing him and Derry hand-in-hand again?

When I'd decided I *would* deal with it and contacted him, he said, "Rot, I knew this would happen. I'm on combat space patrol that night. Send me vids of it, will you?"

Knowing Hanuk's penchant for surprises, however, I surveyed the hall. I half expected him to pop out of some crowded alcove, beaming and saying, "Did you really think I'd miss this?" The other half of me wavered in uncomfortable relief at his absence.

Kota dropped his flight cap on the chair beside his to save it for Ogundo, and we tapped our orders into the tabletop menus. Encouraged by the aromas wafting all around us, my salivary glands kicked in.

Laughter and joking roared along the table like spring water through a desert wash, until Squadron Commander Grell arrived. Then we shut up and leaped to our feet as one. The scrape and rumble of our heavy chairs on the lumber floor echoed through the great hall, momentarily dampening the jovial talk of people in surrounding alcoves.

Our classroom instructors had come, too, and with a swell of gratitude, I noticed Five-Talon Noshi among them. He slid me a half-smile as the officers took their seats at the table's head.

Grell scanned us from beneath lowered brows for a few tense seconds. I wondered if we were about to receive a reprimand for conduct in a public place unbecoming of fledgling officers. Then the scowl burst into a broad smile, and he shouted, "Carry on!"

The celebratory ruckus resumed at once, with a swell of hilarity and revelry.

Ogundo slipped in, shedding his scarf and cap, about the time the barrel-shaped automaton servers came to deliver our platters. Dodging one of them to slide onto his chair, he leaned toward me and said, with uncharacteristic grimness, "Ku-man, I just overheard something in the orderly room I think you need to know."

A sensation like ice water spilled down my spine. "What's going on, Guns?"

Though we spoke quietly, my question caught Kota's ear and Rinn's and Go's attention across the table. They hunched in to listen, their features tense.

Ogundo glanced toward the table's head, at the officers conversing together over their dinner, and lowered his voice further. "They've released Huritt from custody. There's not even going to be a hearing, let alone a court-martial."

Go gasped. "Why?"

"Political pressure, far's I can tell," Ogundo said.

"Figures." Kota snarled it. "His mother is chief of the Great Council of All Clans. They're the governing body that negotiates Commonwealth agreements for all Chalca, including things like military conscription." His expression darkened, a rising thunderhead more typical of Huritt. "I knew there'd be something like this."

"Yeah, and it gets worse." Guns sat forward. "They're letting him back into pilot training, in the class after ours."

"What?" Kota sounded shocked.

"The folks in the orderly room are saying Lodesson fought it," Ogundo said, "but he got overruled by MinDef. Huritt's mother must have some serious pull." He met my stunned stare. "Sorry about that, Ku-man."

For the second time in a moon, I had a juicy-rare venison steak sizzling on a platter under my nose, and I didn't have an appetite.

Commander Grell waited until most of us finished eating to announce assignments. He issued them one at a time, throwing in some ribbing along the way.

Some of our classmates had orders to the 11th Aerospace Combat Wing at Bogorad Base on Solienne's distant moon, Arno. I groaned on learning Ogundo had been assigned there, but Kota seemed as stricken as if Grell had announced a death in his family.

Ogundo responded to Grell with his normal unruffled grin and, "All good, sir," but I read disappointment in his eyes, too.

Several more classmates, Allandra Pellesh among them, received assignments to the 15th Aerospace Combat Wing in 2nd Squadron.

"Masou, Akuleh!" Grell called eventually.

I leaped to attention to face him, the expected procedure, as cheers for the previous cadet subsided.

"Where do you want to go, Masou?" Grell shouted down the table, as he'd done to each classmate before.

"Anywhere I can fight lumpies, sir," I yelled back. That seemed to be the standard answer for the evening.

"How does 15th Aerospace Combat Wing, 1st Squadron sound to you?"

"Outstanding, sir!" I answered.

Amid fresh cheers as I returned to my seat, Kota asked, "Isn't that Hanuk's unit?"

"Ya, it is."

Kota shook his head. "You've got too much luck, Ku."

He, Go, and Rinn all received their assignments to 1st Squadron, too. I gloated about it until Rinn asked, with a joking gleam in his eye, "Does this mean we will have to be roommates *again*?"

I pitched a crusty roll across the table at him. "Yi! I'm not that bad of a slob."

My mind wandered afterward. Three moons ago, I couldn't have imagined a better assignment than being in the same unit with Hanuk. A brand-new unit, full of opportunities to set standards, and establish its reputation, and prove ourselves. It would be the same as it had been all our lives, I had naively believed. Now, though, doing stuff with Hanuk would mean including Derry as well.

Adding any girl to our twosome would've changed things, I supposed. I could have accepted it if the girl had been anyone but Derry.

My ribs seemed to tighten with crushing force around my heart. *Burn you, Huk. Glad I've got Kota and Rinn for company.*

Still, I couldn't resist calling him when we boarded the crawler for the clamorous ride back to the base. When his face materialized in my link's display he said, "Great timing, Ku. Mog and I just got in. So where are you going?"

"You only get one guess," I shouted through the riotous voices around me, "so you'd better make it good!"

"15th and 1st?" Hanuk asked, his eyes widening hopefully.

I chuckled. "Got it!"

Hanuk's whoop, rising from my link like an emergency siren, startled several other nearby cadets. "Outstanding!" he said. "Back to the good times. We'll see you at your graduation."

My elation wilted. I knew "we" didn't mean Huk and Mogen.

* * * * *

Chapter Forty-Eight

I waited until we returned to the dorm to call Gram. "Can you and Kimmie come for my graduation?" I asked. I fought to keep a plea like a whiney child out of my voice.

She sighed. "I'm sorry, Akuleh. Vortex travel is beyond my means." She studied me and added with her gentle smile, "I'm very proud of you, you know."

"I'm proud, too!" Kimmie beamed at me in turn through my link's display. "Send me some vids."

A mid-winter blizzard, the worst all season, moved our graduation indoors to the viditorium. It meant no parade-and-review, but I supposed only the top military officers and Commonwealth government officials seated in the blue-draped upper balconies would miss it.

The odors of damp winter coats, reminiscent of wet dogs, permeated even the viditorium's vastness when our class marched in through its lower-level doors. I kept my vision forward as we filed into the front rows of seats. Didn't glance about the half-circle amphitheater, where several hundred families and friends, who had arrived before the storm forced the local vortex terminal to close, stood to watch us arrive.

Huk and Derry are out there somewhere. I wasn't sure how I felt about it.

Maybe to make up for the lack of a parade, the speeches ran longer than I remembered them being for Hanuk's graduation. I don't know what provoked my restless impatience, but the seat below me seemed harder than it ever had before, and I couldn't keep from shifting around. Kota couldn't sit still either, and even Rinn wore an *Is this ever going to end?* expression.

When Lodesson began to present awards, I straightened in my seat, but only out of curiosity. Rinn received the certificate for Best Military Bearing, and Go for Top Academic. Having expected as much, I cheered heartily for them. Several other awards went to cadets in other flights.

At last Lodesson said, "And now, the Distinguished Graduate for Primary Piloting Class oh-three-twelve is… Allandra Pellesh from Apollona, Satha!"

Everyone in Folkstone Flight sprang to their feet as if launched by ejection seats, clapping and whistling. Allandra rose to march forward, blushing to the roots of her honey-blonde hair, but flashing her stunning smile.

I stared about myself in shock. Next to me, only Rinn's half-hearted applause betrayed his disappointment. Farther along the row, Go appeared as dazed as if she'd just been clubbed in the head.

"They've got to be joking." Kota groaned it in my ear as Lodesson made the medal presentation.

I shook my head. "I was sure it'd be Rinn or Go."

Allandra returned to her seat, her whole face as bright pink as her lip-color, and Lodesson cleared his throat.

The applause promptly subsided, and he said with gravitas, "We have one more medal to present today, one normally awarded only to active-duty combat pilots. Presenting this recognition to a cadet had to be approved at the Ministry of Defense level."

Complete silence fell in the viditorium as abruptly as if somebody had hit a mute button. The whole audience seemed to be holding its collective breath. I leaned forward in my seat, suddenly interested, and riveted my attention on our wing commander.

Lodesson peered from the platform as if searching the amphitheater. "Akuleh of clan Masou from Red Wash Enclave, Tempest, please come forward."

I went limp in the hard seat.

Rinn and Kota, both appearing startled but pleased, shoved at my back. I got awkwardly to my feet, clumsy with surprise, and trod on a few polished boot toes as I made my way to the aisle. "Sorry," I muttered again and again without glancing at anyone. My face burned. *I must be as red as Allandra.*

On reaching the platform, I snapped to attention facing Commander Lodesson. At his cue, we pivoted to face the audience. One glimpse of several hundred faces staring at me made me quite certain my own would combust from its heat.

In the split second before I caged my eyes, I spotted Huritt in the audience, flanked by his new classmates, the Pahana cadets with the tattoos. Huritt's gaze caught mine. He whispered to the Pahana with the triangles like a hazardous waste symbol on his face, and they both sneered.

Now Huritt's got allies. They'll graduate in another three moons. My hands, tight at the seams of my uniform trousers, knotted into fists.

"Attention to orders!" called the spacer at the podium.

A ripple and rustle flowed across the viditorium like long grass in a stray wind as the audience rose to its feet.

The spacer's voice rang across the huge hollow. "Citation to accompany the award of the Valorous Flying medal to Akuleh of clan Masou."

A near-tangible silence, heavy with suspense, left me listening to taut pulsebeats in my ears until he began to read.

"Cadet Akuleh of clan Masou distinguished himself in the performance of piloting duties while flying a four-ship vortex training sortie on the twenty-ninth day of the eleventh month of year 239 Commonwealth Standard Calendar.

"When the actions of another trainee forced his ship into a potentially lethal situation, Cadet Masou's quick thinking under extreme pressure, and his consummate piloting skill, preserved the lives of his three fellow cadets, while accepting the ultimate risk to his own."

I couldn't help wondering at Huritt's reaction, but I didn't spare a peek at him. I caged my vision to the rear wall instead, my face throbbing with the beats of my heart. *Anybody would think I'd died doing it.*

If Huritt had had his way, I would have.

"The heroic actions of Cadet Masou," the spacer concluded, "reflect profound credit upon himself and the Aerospace Defense Forces of the Soliennese Commonwealth."

I pivoted to face Lodesson once more. He pinned a weighty sunburst of gold-colored metal to my service jacket and said, as we exchanged handshakes and salutes, "Well done, Cadet."

"Thank you, sir." My mouth felt as if I'd inhaled a throat full of desert dust, making it difficult to speak.

Our IPs sat in a row at the rear of the platform, behind Lodesson, like so many birds perched on the top of a wall. As I passed them to return to my seat, I glimpsed Russom through the corner of my eye. His face remained completely inscrutable.

I clambered to my place as ineptly as I'd left it and sank as deeply into my seat as I could squeeze myself. Kota, Rinn, and everybody else within reach seemed determined to beat me to death with congratulatory thumps on my back and shoulders, while thunderous applause reverberated throughout the vaulted space.

The swearing in, with both arms raised above our heads and palms open in petition to Thrüss, and the march across the platform to receive our certificates and pilot's wings passed in a blur after that. When Lodesson finally shouted, "Primary Piloting class oh-three-twelve, *dis*-missed!" we all lunged for the aisles.

My classmates and their well-wishers scattered throughout the lobby and hallways for private rank-pinning ceremonies. Hanuk and I had planned to meet in a corridor painted with a mural of Soli fighters flying over the Awénasa desert, a popular location for new Chalca pilots' pinnings. The same spot where Hanuk's family had pinned him.

As I started toward it, Noshi emerged from another set of viditorium doors and intercepted me. His eyes glinted with satisfaction. "Congratulations, Apprentice Officer Masou."

"Thank you, sir." I tapped my medal. "And thank you very much for this. I didn't—"

"I'm not the one to thank for your medal, Apprentice." He favored me with his enigmatic smile. "You must talk to your IP." He indicated the building's second level with a jut of his chin.

I stared at him. *Russom? The tyrant who spent every sortie searching for an excuse to wash me out?*

Noshi's smile widened a bit, as if he'd read my dumbfounded thoughts, but his crinkle-wreathed eyes grew stern. "I expect to see your application for the Qaletaqa in two years."

"You will, sir."

"Good." Noshi nodded, excused himself, and strode toward the corridor with the Tempest mural.

I hesitated, still stunned, before I about-faced and headed for the staircase to the second level.

I spotted Russom across its lobby, talking cordially with a new Obollan pilot and her family. I stood clear to wait, but he noticed me around their heads. When they left, he faced me directly.

Habit born of a year of duress stiffened me into the usual brace. "Sir," I said, my mouth desert dry as usual. A torrent of questions flooded my mind. I didn't know which to ask first.

Russom smiled. Not the sneering smile with which he'd goaded me every day since our first meeting at the old barracks, but one of genuine satisfaction. "Congratulations, Masou." He extended his hand.

I accepted it, still wary.

He gripped mine firmly. "We had to be sure you wanted your wings badly enough to fight for them. We can take only the most determined for combat."

"Yes, sir." In an instant, like a tri-D tank shimmering on, all the pressure and harassment made sense. "Thank you, sir." After several dazed seconds, I indicated the Valorous Flying medal pinned to my chest. "Five-Talon Noshi said…" I trailed off.

Russom quirked another smile. "You deserve it. I'll see you on the flight deck, Apprentice."

"Yes, sir."

I stood frozen for a moment before I retraced my steps down the staircase. By then, I had to weave my way among milling knots of new pilots and their families to reach the Tempest corridor.

Just inside its double doors, Kota's mother beckoned. "Ku, come join Kota in some vids and tell us about your medal."

Kota and I struck a few hero poses for his family before I politely extricated myself and pressed on along the hallway.

My innards wrenched when I spotted Derry waiting with Hanuk at the far end. Hanuk's smile, so broad I thought his face must hurt, always had been contagious, and I caught it. Derry in her Caerdish service dress uniform, midnight blue with silver braid on the sleeves, fairly glowed.

"Kuruk sent this. He says congrats," Hanuk said without preamble, and drew a flat package from his pocket. His eyes twinkled. "Another cousin," he told Derry.

I unwrapped the package and chuckled at its contents. White Standard characters glared a warning from a red adhesive strip as wide as my hand and two spans long.

TEMPEST'S ON YOUR TAIL

"It goes on your cockpit rail below your name," Hanuk said with a chortle. "Hold it up and let Derry vid it." He handed her his link.

She did, then made vids of Hanuk and me stretching to point at a pair of Rohr-55s soaring above russet mesas in the mural.

"You didn't make DG, Ku," Hanuk said in mock reproof, his eyes lit with their usual mischievous glitter, "but this sort of makes up for it." He bounced my medal in his hand, still clipped to my chest. "Wearing this must be like bench-pressing three hundred."

"I'm up to three-fifty," I said, and immediately cringed. *Who are you trying to impress, Ku?*

Hanuk grew serious. "We learned about the vortex incident on the active-duty side, but they didn't give names. It became the subject of a flight-safety briefing. They even showed your nosevids." He shook his head and eyed me like a concerned father. "The Ancients must have a really serious Path for you."

My stomach tightened. *Don't think so.*

Derry broke the silence. "Righ'. Per'aps we should ge' on with pinning him, then."

"Oh. Ya." Hanuk fished a pair of apprentice officer rank pins from his uniform pocket. "It's tradition to pass on your first rank, so these are the ones my parents pinned on me."

Hanuk attached them to my collar, and we exchanged salutes while Derry recorded the whole thing with my link. *Gram and Kimmie will appreciate this. I'll send it to them tonight.*

"Why don't you pin on his wings, Derry?" Hanuk suggested. He took my link from her and handed her the golden pin.

I tried not to notice her wildflower fragrance enveloping me. Tried to ignore her hands lightly touching my chest and the tingle they sent coursing through my body.

"Congratulations, Kew," she said. She hesitated, and with a faint smile reminiscent of the one in the miniature portrait, she leaned in to press a quick kiss to my cheek. Very close to my mouth.

Startled and with my face heating, I glanced at Hanuk as she stepped away.

He appeared surprised, too, his eyes as large as hen's eggs.

Something inside me relished it, but I didn't dare look at Derry when she said, with a touch of embarrassment, "It's a Caerdish tradition, yew know. A kiss for luck."

"Thank you," I said solemnly, and moved off from her while the beast coiling in my soul groaned, *I'd rather have you kiss me for love.*

The blizzard had ended when we strode outside a few minutes later, but the low and darkened sky warned of another incoming storm.

# # # # #

About the Author

According to her mother, Diann "DT" Read began writing as soon as she could pick up a pencil, though her first "stories" were mostly drawings of horses. By age 10 she'd appropriated her father's old college typewriter and learned to type, with two fingers, because it was faster than pushing a pencil. At age 14, with the encouragement of a schoolteacher aunt, she entered the Utah League of Writers Contest for Young Writers and won 1st place in the Junior High Division. She started her first novel, a fantasy based on the Arthurian legends, in high school, but got sidetracked into science fiction in college and never finished that book.

Her first military science fiction trilogy, The Sergey Chronicles, was published by Tor in the late 1990s. Now available for Kindle, Nook, and Kobo, the Sergey trilogy continues to earn royalties after all these years. She also has a handful of published short stories.

Diann took a hiatus from fiction writing when she was mobilized to active duty in the wake of 9/11. She served for 23 years in the U.S. Air Force, and retired as a lieutenant colonel in 2009 to return to writing. Diann learned her craft from such mentors as Orson Scott Card, Elizabeth Moon, and David Farland, and worked for David as an editorial assistant for several years. She is married to Jon Read and they live in Texas.

Connect with Diann at www.facebook.com/d.t.read.author, www.patreon.com/DTRead, and her website https://d-t-read-author.com.

* * * * *

The following is an

Excerpt from Book One of the Lunar Free State:

The Moon and Beyond

John E. Siers

Available from Theogony Books

eBook, Audio, and Paperback

Excerpt from "The Moon and Beyond:"

"So, what have we got?" The chief had no patience for inter-agency squabbles.

The FBI man turned to him with a scowl. "We've got some abandoned buildings, a lot of abandoned stuff—none of which has anything to do with spaceships—and about a hundred and sixty scientists, maintenance people, and dependents left behind, all of whom claim they knew nothing at all about what was really going on until today. Oh, yeah, and we have some stripped computer hardware with all memory and processor sections removed. I mean physically taken out, not a chip left, nothing for the techies to work with. And not a scrap of paper around that will give us any more information...at least, not that we've found so far. My people are still looking."

"What about that underground complex on the other side of the hill?"

"That place is wiped out. It looks like somebody set off a *nuke* in there. The concrete walls are partly fused! The floor is still too hot to walk on. Our people say they aren't sure how you could even *do* something like that. They're working on it, but I doubt they're going to find anything."

"What about our man inside, the guy who set up the computer tap?"

"Not a trace, chief," one of the NSA men said. "Either he managed to keep his cover and stayed with them, or they're holding him prisoner, or else..." The agent shrugged.

"You think they terminated him?" The chief lifted an eyebrow. "A bunch of rocket scientists?"

"Wouldn't put it past them. Look at what Homeland Security ran into. Those motion-sensing chain guns are *nasty*, and the area between the inner and outer perimeter fence is mined! Of course, they posted warning signs, even marked the fire zones for the guns. Nobody would have gotten hurt if the troops had taken the signs seriously."

The Homeland Security colonel favored the NSA man with an icy look. "That's bullshit. How did we know they weren't bluffing? You'd feel pretty stupid if we'd played it safe and then found out there were no defenses, just a bunch of signs!"

"Forget it!" snarled the chief. "Their whole purpose was to delay us, and it worked. What about the Air Force?"

"It might as well have been a UFO sighting as far as they're concerned. Two of their F-25s went after that spaceship, or whatever it was we saw leaving. The damned thing went straight up, over eighty thousand meters per minute, they say. That's nearly Mach Two, in a *vertical climb*. No aircraft in *anybody's* arsenal can sustain a climb like that. Thirty seconds after they picked it up, it was well above their service ceiling and still accelerating. Ordinary ground radar couldn't find it, but NORAD *thinks* they might have caught a short glimpse with one of their satellite-watch systems, a hundred miles up and still going."

"So where did they go?"

"Well, chief, if we believe what those leftover scientists are telling us, I guess they went to the Moon."

* * * * *

Get "The Moon and Beyond" here:
https://www.amazon.com/dp/B097QMN7PJ.

Find out more about John E. Siers at:
https://chriskennedypublishing.com.

* * * * *

The following is an

Excerpt from Book One of The Combined Service:

The Magnetar

Jo Boone

Available from Theogony Books

eBook and Paperback

Excerpt from "The Magnetar:"

Chalk felt the inertial shift even through his suit. Every warning the *Magnetar* possessed went red, bright terrible red, on every display. They had minutes, maybe less, before the ship's structural integrity began to fail from the damaged areas outward, possibly in ways they could not stop. On the tactical display, Sasskiek's analysts had added acceleration arcs that showed when the scout ships would be able to engage their gravitic drives and another arc that showed the *Magnetar's* own projected course and location. Underneath that was the faint gray line that no spacer ever crossed, showing where the minimum safe distance would be for the *Magnetar* when the two scout ships engaged their drives.

They might make it.

If the remaining reactors held. If the *Magnetar* didn't go to pieces first.

If Gabbro didn't miss.

"How close?" Chalk said. Too far, and the scout ships could easily evade or counter the *Magnetar's* offensive barrage. Too close, and they risked doing themselves more harm—but that might be better than letting the scout ships engage their drives.

"Adjusting firing solutions now," Gabbro replied, battle-calm.

"Five more ships approaching," Sasskiek reported. The ships appeared as uncertain yellow diamonds on the tactical display. "Lead ship is Terran configuration, gaseous atmosphere, two-four-zero rotation two-one-zero, four hundred million kilometers. Four trailing ships have octopod configurations, seawater atmosphere, pursuit course."

Friend or foe? Chalk wondered, but he could not address it now. Two minutes from now, it might not matter anyway.

The *Magnetar* and the scout ships were closing on each other rapidly.

"Three hundred thousand kilometers," Sasskiek reported. "Two hundred fifty thousand kilometers."

He counted it down slowly, while Lieutenant Rose at the helm and St. Clair in engineering pushed the ship for all it could give; pushed for that green curve that represented safety—at least, from one of the hazards they faced.

Chalk sat on the edge of his chair. The orders were given. Nothing he could say now would change the outcome.

Was it enough?

He hated the helplessness; it came with a wave of despair, a preemptive surge of grief for the failure that had not yet come.

He would not be able to mourn afterward.

But he did not dare give in to it now.

His hands clenched around the arms of his chair.

"One hundred thousand kilometers," Sasskiek reported. Maximum effective weapons distance. "Fifty thousand. They're firing."

* * * * *

Get "The Magnetar" now at:
https://www.amazon.com/dp/B09QC78PLJ/.

Find out more about Jo Boone at:
https://chriskennedypublishing.com.

* * * * *

The following is an
Excerpt from Book One of This Fine Crew:

The Signal Out of Space

Mike Jack Stoumbos

Now Available from Theogony Books

eBook and Paperback

Excerpt from "The Signal Out of Space:"

Day 4 of Training, Olympus Mons Academy

I want to make something clear from square one: we were winning.

More importantly, *I* was winning. Sure, the whole thing was meant to be a "team effort," and I'd never say this to an academy instructor, but the fact of the matter is this: it was a race and I was in the driver's seat. Like hell I was going to let any other team beat us, experimental squad or not.

At our velocity, even the low planetary grav didn't temper the impact of each ice mogul on the glistening red terrain. We rocketed up, plummeted down, and cut new trails in the geo-formations, spraying orange ice and surface rust in our wake. So much of the red planet was still like a fresh sheet of snow, and I was eager to carve every inch of it.

Checking on the rest of the crew, I thought our tactical cadet was going to lose her lunch. I had no idea how the rest of the group was managing, different species being what they are.

Of our complement of five souls, sans AI-assist or anything else that cadets should learn to live without, Shin and I were the only Humans. The communications cadet was a Teek—all exoskeleton and antennae, but the closest to familiar. He sat in the copilot seat, ready to take the controls if I had to tap out. His two primary arms were busy with the scanning equipment, but one of his secondary hands hovered over the E-brake, which made me more anxious than assured.

I could hear the reptile humming in the seat behind me, in what I registered as "thrill," each time I overcame a terrain obstacle with even greater speed, rather than erring on the side of caution.

Rushing along the ice hills of Mars on six beautifully balanced wheels was a giant step up from the simulator. The design of the Red Terrain Vehicle was pristine, but academy-contrived obstacles mixed with natural formations bumped up the challenge factor. The dummy fire sounds from our sensors and our mounted cannon only added to the sense of adventure. The whole thing was like fulfilling a fantasy, greater than my first jet around good ol' Luna. If the camera evidence had survived, I bet I would have been grinning like an idiot right up until the Teek got the bogey signal.

"Cadet Lidstrom," the Teek said, fast but formal through his clicking mandibles, "unidentified signal fifteen degrees right of heading." His large eyes pulsed with green luminescence, bright enough for me to see in the corner of my vision. It was an eerie way to express emotion, which I imagined would make them terrible at poker.

I hardly had a chance to look at the data while maintaining breakneck KPH, but in the distance, it appeared to be one of our surface vehicles, all six wheels turned up to the stars.

The lizard hummed a different note and spoke in strongly accented English, "Do we have time to check?"

The big furry one at the rear gruffed in reply, but not in any language I could understand.

"Maybe it's part of the test," I suggested. "Like a bonus. Paul, was it hard to find?"

The Teek, who went by Paul, clicked to himself and considered the question. His exoskeletal fingers worked furiously for maybe a second before he informed us, "It is obscured by interference."

"Sounds like a bonus to me," Shin said. Then she asked me just the right question: "Lidstrom, can you get us close without losing our lead?"

The Arteevee would have answered for me if it could, casting an arc of red debris as I swerved. I admit, I did not run any mental calculations, but a quick glance at my rear sensors assured me. "Hell yeah! I got this."

In the mirror, I saw our large, hairy squadmate, the P'rukktah, transitioning to the grappler interface, in case we needed to pick something up when we got there. Shin, on tactical, laid down some cannon fire behind us—tiny, non-lethal silicon scattershot—to kick up enough dust that even the closest pursuer would lose our visual heading for a few seconds at least. I did not get a chance to find out what the reptile was doing as we neared the overturned vehicle.

I had maybe another half-k to go when Paul's eyes suddenly shifted to shallow blue and his jaw clicked wildly. He only managed one English word: "Peculiar!"

Before I could ask, I was overcome with a sound, a voice, a shrill screech. I shut my eyes for an instant, then opened them to see where I was driving and the rest of my squad, but everything was awash in some kind of blue light. If I thought it would do any good, I might have tried to plug my ears.

Paul didn't have the luxury of closing his compound eyes, but his primary arms tried to block them. His hands instinctively guarded his antennae.

Shin half fell from the pivoting cannon rig, both palms cupping her ears, which told me the sound wasn't just in my head.

The reptile bared teeth in a manner too predatory to be a smile and a rattling hum escaped her throat, dissonant to the sound.

Only the P'rukktah weathered this unexpected cacophony with grace. She stretched out clearly muscled arms and grabbed anchor points on either side of the vehicle. In blocky computer-generated words, her translator pulsed out, "What—Is—That?"

Facing forward again, I was able to see the signs of wreckage ahead and of distressed ground. I think I was about to ask if I should turn away when the choice was taken from me.

An explosion beneath our vehicle heaved us upward, nose first. Though nearly bucked out of my seat, I was prepared to recover our heading or even to stop and assess what had felt like a bomb.

A second blast, larger than the first, pushed us from behind, probably just off my right rear wheel, spraying more particulates and lifting us again.

One screech was replaced with another. Where the first had been almost organic, this new one was clearly the sound of tearing metal.

The safety belt caught my collarbone hard as my body tried to torque out of the seat. Keeping my eyes open, I saw one of our tires—maybe two thirds of a tire—whip off into the distance on a strange trajectory, made even stranger by the fact that the horizon was spinning.

The red planet came at the windshield and the vehicle was wrenched enough to break a seal. I barely noticed the sudden escape of air; I was too busy trying, futilely, to drive the now upside-down craft...

* * * * *

Get "The Signal Out of Space" now at:
https://www.amazon.com/dp/B09N8VHGFP.

Find out more about Mike Jack Stoumbos and "The Signal Out of Space" at: https://chriskennedypublishing.com.

* * * * *

Made in the USA
Las Vegas, NV
16 October 2022

57417699R00256